November 14, 2015

For Katie, Shane and the
expected bundle of joy,

With best wishes,

Dead to Rights
by Robert L. Gold

Printed in the United States of America.
Published by Marcinson Press, Jacksonville, Florida

For bulk purchases or to carry this book in your library, school, or bookstore, please contact the publisher at marcinsonpress.com.

ISBN 978-0-9893732-7-2

Published by
Marcinson Press
10950-60 San Jose Blvd., Suite 136
Jacksonville, FL 32223 USA
http://www.marcinsonpress.com

Dead to Rights

Robert L. Gold

In memory of

my remarkable brother,

Michael,

and his loving sons,

Daniel, Joseph and Steven

ACKNOWLEDGEMENTS

First and foremost, I want to acknowledge my brother, Michael, for the seemingly endless help he gave me in the writing of *Dead to Rights*. No one else gave so much time and effort to the editing and completion of the novel as well as the two other mysteries in the series. Perhaps, more important, he believed in the validity of a Colonial City Mystery Series and was a constant source of encouragement. Unfortunately, Mike died in August 2014, before he could see *Dead to Rights* in print and read my tribute to him.

David Conrad, my old friend and history colleague, also contributed to the editing of the book. He was always available as a knowledgeable source when I needed information about the outdoor world of horses, snakes and sailing.

I am also indebted to Mike Siegel and Kathy Clower for editing the first draft of the book and for Kristi West's help evaluating the novel's historical themes.

I am also appreciative of Kat LaMons' assistance. Her literary knowledge and expertise in English were critical resources I gratefully used during the editing.

The artistic appearance of the entire book, including the striking cover, the setup, interior design and organization, is the work of Trish Diggins. Her extraordinary talent as a graphic artist has made *Dead to Rights* a book that stands out on any bookshelf or bookstore counter.

Last and certainly not least of all, I want to acknowledge the critical help of my wife, LaDonna, who was by my side with advice and suggestions throughout the entire writing process. She was also an eagle-eyed reader whose help as a proofreader involved scrutinizing every single word in the book.

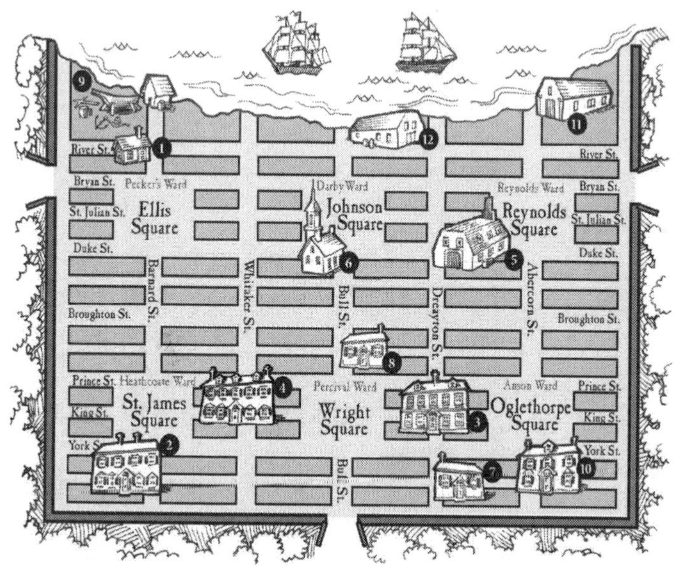

Savannah & Environs

1. Morgan's House
2. Thomas Sterling's House
3. Claudia Barclay's House
4. Governor James Wright's House
5. Courthouse
6. Christ Church
7. Doctor Nunes Ribeiro's House
8. George Chapman's House
9. The Parkers' Boatyard
10. Archibald Willington's House
11. Sterling Shipping Company
12. Douglas Shipping Company

N
Savannah River
Morgan's Creek
SAVANNAH
Augustine Creek
Hidden Lake

PROLOGUE

ST. AUGUSTINE, FLORIDA – APRIL 24, 1763

The squad of Spanish soldiers reached the ruins at dusk. It took the squad three hours to march from St. Augustine to the small Indian village north of the presidio. The setting sun cast rays of light over the tired soldiers as they stood looking at the blackened logs of the house. The stench of burnt flesh made them cover their noses with handkerchiefs. No one moved, knowing what had to be done. They knew what remained of the bodies would have to be picked out of the charred debris and buried.

"Vamos," ordered the lieutenant, annoyed at the squad's inactivity. "Sergeant, get these men moving – it'll be dark soon." The officer dismounted effortlessly with the reins in his hand.

"Sí, Señor." The sergeant pointed his forefinger at six of the blue-uniformed soldiers and sent them off toward the destroyed house. He gestured to the other men to begin digging graves near a wheelless wagon that lay overturned in the dirt.

"You heard the lieutenant. Let's get it done before dark," the sergeant barked as the men moved away.

"Do we know anything about the raiding party, Sergeant?" The lieutenant frowned as he watched the soldiers walk reluctantly toward the ruins.

"The Indians from the nearby houses said there were six of them. They spoke English, but were not uniformed soldiers. They wore colonists' clothes and must have come down from one of the English colonies. Who knows which one?"

"Probably Savannah since it's closer than Charles Towne." The lieutenant gently stroked the side of the horse's face.

"That would be my guess, sir, if they're colonists. They also might be English outlaws looking to loot the presidio. There's that outlaw village near the Altamaha River – I forget what it's called." The sergeant, a short, stout man, shifted the rolled sheet of patched canvas he carried from under one arm to the other.

"It's called New Hanover and may well be the home of those bastardos. They've raided our lands and robbed travelers on the roads for years. I wouldn't be at all surprised to hear they are the asesinos who slaughtered this poor family." The lieutenant returned the sergeant's salute and watched him walk toward the smoldering ruins. He saw the sergeant unfurl the canvas sheet that would be used to carry the corpses to their graves.

"What brutes, these English are. How many in the family?" The lieutenant spoke to an obese Franciscan who stood beside him. His brown cloak was food stained and wet from sweat.

"There were six." The friar counted on his plump fingers. "The Mestizo Juan Vargas, his Indian wife and four children. The youngest was a ten-week-old baby boy, recently baptized, and the oldest, a girl of fifteen. There were two other boys, one eight and the other fourteen. I recall the older boy was confirmed a year or so ago at Nombre de Dios. His name was Fernando." The friar held a yellow stained handkerchief in his hand and used it repeatedly to wipe the sweat from his tonsured head. "Dios mío, it's already devilishly hot," he sighed wearily, "and the intolerable Florida summer is only weeks away."

"It is and the damned mosquitoes have come out with the heat." The lieutenant swiped at a buzzing insect at the back of his neck. He scowled, seeing the sun beginning its descent into the western woods. "It looks like you'll have to pray for the dead in the dark."

"Sí, lastíma." The friar shook his head and exhaled loudly. He turned to see the gravediggers taking turns with a shovel.

"We're fortunate the other families escaped the raid." The lieutenant wiped his face with a white handkerchief. "If any more had been killed, we would have been out here digging graves for hours." He sighed. "I can't understand why the English, whether colonists or outlaws, would come all the way down here to attack these poor defenseless Indians. They had little or nothing of value. What could they have possibly hoped to get from these three miserable houses?"

"Three hogs and a cow." The friar snorted.

"It makes no sense since they will soon get all of this land." The lieutenant moved away from the Franciscan, trying to escape his body odor. "By treaty, the British bastardos will get all of La Florida this summer. They have only a few months to wait. So, why would they send their raiders here to kill these Indians? Of course, they haven't the cojones to attack St. Augustine and face our Spanish troops."

"Quién sabe. Who can know the blasphemous hearts of these Protestant heretics? They are the devil's servants." The Franciscan nodded knowingly.

Several minutes later, the sergeant left the ruins and

walked over to the lieutenant. "We found five bodies, Señor, los dos padres y tres niños. There also was a dead dog."

"All the children?" The lieutenant shook his head. "How could they kill the little ones? What fiends they are!"

"One might have survived, sir." The sergeant turned his eyes to the friar. "I heard you say there were four children in the family, so I sent one of the men to search around the house and in the woods. The frightened child may be hiding."

"Bueno, let me know what he finds." The lieutenant looked at the monk. "Let's hope at least one child escaped the slaughter."

"Si Dios quiere (God willing)." The monk made the sign of the cross.

The sergeant shook his head when he returned a half hour later. "No one escaped, Señor. We found the other child's body under some burnt logs – near the back window of the house."

"Damn these English!" the lieutenant shouted. "Have they no souls?"

"They do not, they're Protestants!" The Franciscan shook his fist. "A pox on them!"

Surrounded by the Indian villagers, the soldiers finished burying the last body by the light of a lantern. An owl screeched in the nearby woods as the monk mumbled the rite of committal. All the men crossed themselves and bowed their heads in prayer.

The lieutenant and friar were the last to leave the gravesite as the infantry squad formed for the long march back to St. Augustine. They walked slowly to the Franciscan's horse-drawn wagon. The young officer took short steps so the fat man could keep up with him. Handkerchief in hand, the friar repeatedly wiped his brow and cheeks as he waddled along.

"Six dead – the whole family. Los diablos ingléses!" The

lieutenant sighed. "Fortunately, the other two families survived. How many escaped into the woods?"

"Fifteen. One child is missing – a twelve-year-old boy, but I expect the Indians will find him in the morning. God willing." Two soldiers helped the monk climb into the wagon, which creaked under his weight.

"The boy is probably frightened and hiding nearby." The lieutenant pointed to the dark woods as he mounted his stallion.

"That would be my belief." The friar sighed wearily as he settled his bulk on a wooden bench in the wagon. One of the soldiers took the horse's reins and urged him ahead of the squad of marching men.

A cool breeze came out of the west as the little column set out on the road to town. The lieutenant led the way, lit that night by a nearly full moon.

CHAPTER ONE

SAVANNAH: MONDAY, MAY 4 – SUNDAY, MAY 17, 1766

Choosing their steps carefully, they went slowly down the steep hill to the lake. The fat man in the purple suit led the way, though he had never been there before. There was no path to follow and he tripped now and then as his shoes struck protruding rocks and tree roots. The effort to maintain his balance soon tired him and his legs trembled from the exertion. Halfway to the bottom, he was exhausted, but struggled on determined to stay upright.

The sudden steepness of the hill forced them to rush downward and they lurched between trees, running into branches, palmetto fronds and prickly bushes along the way. They moved too fast to look for snakes among the rocks and roots. With hands raised to fend off entangling vines and spider webs, they careened down the last few yards to the bottom of the hill. They both were panting by that time and relieved to be standing on level ground.

The fat man stood leaning against a large water oak. He

was sweating profusely, his face beaded and bright red. He stood unsteadily, his chest heaving, panting for breath. A town man, he had not walked much beyond his office and nearby home in many years. In an effort to cool himself, he took off his tricorn hat and weakly waved it in front of his face. His trembling hand could barely hold the hat aloft. He did not have the strength to swat the mosquitoes that buzzed about his ears.

The tree limb struck him on the head as he turned to speak. He saw the limb for only a second before he felt the blow. He made no sound and fell face forward into the soft soil at the edge of the lake. Stunned, he lost consciousness for several minutes and was unaware of being rolled over on his back and dragged by his feet.

When the man awoke, he struggled to get up, but found he could not move or speak. His head, aching from the blow, was held down by a wide cloth band that ran across his forehead; a second band circled his neck. His midsection was secured by another band and his outstretched arms and legs were tied down as well. From the corners of his eyes, he could see the bands that held his wrists had been tied to wooden stakes in the ground. A balled piece of cloth had been stuffed into his mouth and also held in place by a band. The gag kept him from saying anything intelligible. He tried to shout out for help, but the attempt made him retch.

"You'll choke to death if you keep that up," a voice said somewhere to his right. "Even if you could cry out, no one would hear you. Not many in town know of this place. That's why we came here."

The man's heart raced. He turned his eyes to the right and saw the face of his attacker. Bound tightly on his back, he could see nothing else except the motionless pine boughs above the face. Again, he tried to speak, but could do little more than mumble incoherently.

"There's no purpose in trying to speak. What you would say is of no interest to me." The voice was calm, but the black eyes seemed to stare into his soul.

He frowned, not knowing what else to do. He felt something, probably an insect, on his left foot. He was now aware that his shoes and stockings had been removed.

He struggled and with all his strength tried to break his bonds. His face turned red with exertion as he put every bit of his energy into the effort to break his arms and legs free. "If only I could just pull one arm loose," he thought, "I could break myself free." He concentrated all his strength on his right arm, but the stakes remained firmly planted in the ground.

"You won't break loose; the stakes are buried two feet deep." A gloved hand appeared above his eyes showing him a wooden stake and the carpenter's hammer that had pounded the stakes into the hard ground. "These were here waiting for us to arrive. The other things I carried with me. They were in the woven bag you offered to carry for me."

A cold chill suddenly swept down his spine. The fat man shivered. He realized now that everything had been carefully planned so there would be no escape. Tears filled his eyes as he was overcome with fear, dreading what was to come. Somehow he had to plead for mercy. He knitted his brow to show his bewilderment.

"Why? I will tell you why in good time." The face moved out of his line of sight and he sensed he was alone.

He again tried to loosen the band on his arm, this time on his left side. He had no better luck straining his arm and suddenly knew he would die. He shivered uncontrollably as the cold he had felt before spread through his body. A sharp pinch on his big toe distracted him from his fear for a moment and he shook his foot to get rid of whatever had bitten him.

The face reappeared with a long knife in hand. The knife

was poised above him and he shut his eyes and tensed his body, expecting to feel the blade plunge into his heart. Instead, he felt the edge of the blade graze his skin as his clothes were stripped from his body. He exhaled slowly in relief. Maybe, he would not be killed after all. In seconds, he lay completely naked, his cut up clothes lying in a little pile only a few feet away. Astonished, he looked up into the face, but, before he could signal with his eyes, the face left his line of sight again. The fat man felt another pinch on his left foot below his big toe. Again, he shook his foot.

A hand now appeared with a brush that looked to be soaked with a thick amber-colored substance. He thought it might be honey or molasses and sensed it was sticky. The hand began to brush what he now knew from the fragrance was honey all over his body. A line was applied to both legs and feet, from toes to thighs, and on his outstretched arms, from hands to shoulders. The hand worked meticulously and missed nothing. It brushed another line from under his chin down the center of his chest to his genitals, which were thoroughly covered. The brush tickled and he tried to shift his groin to avoid the sensation. He noted every facet of the expressionless face above him as the brush spread the honey over his bald head. The hand coated his face last, dabbing honey into his nostrils, the openings of his ears and his eyelids when he closed his eyes. He could taste the honey as the brush briefly painted his lips and he licked it with his tongue.

Opening his eyes cautiously, the man sensed himself alone again, but he knew he had not been deserted. And seconds later he heard scraping sounds at his feet. "What was happening?" he wondered. "Why in God's name had he been covered in…?" He knew the answer instantly. The honey would attract ants – fire ants! That was what he had felt on his foot before and now he felt them biting the bottoms of both feet. His eyes widened in horror; he tried desperately to shout, but gagged on the ball of cloth in his mouth.

"Now, I will tell you why." The face appeared over him again. In seconds, he heard it all, though distracted by the biting ants. The cold black eyes stared down at him and, seeing the comprehension in his eyes, moved out of sight. "Now, we will wait a bit," were the last words spoken to him. He heard them only vaguely, his mind concentrated on prayers for salvation.

Tears fell from the fat man's eyes as he felt the ants running up his legs. He clenched his teeth as the pain from the stinging bites increased beyond tolerance. He looked up into the sky and watched a wayward cloud before closing his eyes. The man recalled another similar day as a boy lying on his back making clouds into ships; he saw it all as if it were yesterday. He lay in his father's pasture when a golden eagle suddenly flew into view. It glided effortlessly on the wind and wrecked all the beautiful ships he had built.

The saddled but riderless horse reached town that evening, though no one noticed it until morning. By that time, the missing assemblyman, Thomas Sterling, was the talk of Savannah. His wife, Abigail, alarmed that her husband had not come home for supper or sleep that night, awakened her neighbors to search for him. The Justice of the Peace, Major James Morgan, was also awakened at midnight. Morgan glared at the man in the doorway and told him the search would begin in the damned morning when he could see something. He then went back to sleep.

Morgan was a former army officer who had served in the French and Indian War and lost his left arm during the British military campaign in Canada. The wounded man returned home to Georgia, where his father, Matthew Morgan, had a rice plantation. The elder Morgan had been one of the first settlers to come to the colony with James Oglethorpe, the founder of Savannah.

Bitter and moody, the one-armed veteran did little more than drink and gamble during the first three years of his return to civilian life. Finally, in the summer of 1762, with the influence of his father, Morgan was appointed the community's justice of the peace. Still a heavy drinker, he carried out his duties with all too evident indifference and disdain. Most of his work involved disciplining disorderly drunks and penalizing petty thieves. Scornful of those he arrested, the justice typically treated them harshly, if not with cruelty.

Morgan was known to be brusque and unmannerly with almost everyone he met in town. Outside his office, the justice appeared less unpleasant, but could never be considered a friendly man. Only a drunken or foolish man would dare approach him for an uninvited meeting or talk. Morgan was a man of few words and most of them tended to be sarcastic. Most people avoided him with the exception of two other former officers and an old Jewish physician who served as the colony's medical examiner. Morgan drank and gambled at faro with the officers and spent an evening or two playing chess with the physician. Once a week, he visited his sixty-five-year-old father, whose painful rheumatism kept him from traveling much beyond his home south of town. Local gossips also knew that the younger Morgan made all too many nightly visits to a widow's home in Anson Ward. He was seen arriving at dinnertime and leaving at the break of day. The large elegant house was owned by a wealthy Spanish woman named Claudia Barclay, whose late husband, a silk merchant, had lost his life at sea.

Morgan owed his tenure in office to the continuing peace and quiet in the community and lack of serious crime, achievements his more likable predecessor, Captain Conrad, had not been able to claim. Without such success, he would have been removed from office by the attorney general who supervised his office. Over the years, Morgan had been reprimanded several times for his surly remarks to Savannah residents and, on one occasion, he had almost been discharged for striking a wealthy cattle trader. Morgan had knocked the man down when he saw him beating an old horse with a whip. Attorney General Oliver Palmer, like almost everyone else in Savannah, found Morgan abrasive and only reluctantly retained him in office. Palmer would have happily replaced him at once if another able man had applied for the position.

By 1766, it appeared that even with his reputation for keeping the peace and maintaining law and order, he had made too many enemies and would not survive in office. In the last year of a second two-year term, few if anyone in town expected that the bad tempered officer would be reappointed by the governor of the colony. Morgan himself doubted he would be retained.

The justice of the peace arrived at the Sterling house the following morning at first light. A thin man almost six feet tall, he looked almost skeletal in the frayed officer's uniform he still wore everyday. Morgan looked older than his forty years with a deeply lined face and gray hair. He refused to powder his hair or wear the wigs commonly worn by army officers and gentlemen in town, and ignored the dress customs expected in society. Morgan's disdain for local customs and good manners made him even more unpopular in Savannah, which had pretensions of being more sophisticated than an ordinary planters' colony.

Bleary-eyed and crabby from too much rum and too little sleep, Morgan arrived in a bad mood, scowling every step of the way to Sterling's house. One tavern regular, who had been beaten and jailed when seen urinating in the street, said the scowl seemed fixed on the justice's face like a witch's wart. Morgan, in a foolish effort to walk off his lingering headache, left his horse at home and walked the short distance to the assemblyman's house. The usual ten-minute walk from his house off of Bernard Street to the Sterling mansion on St. James Square took him twenty-two minutes. It was seven o'clock when the justice finally reached the house and he felt the first rays of the sun on his back as he knocked on the door. Morgan hated the summer heat and, anxious to get out of the sunlight, he used his walking stick to knock as loudly as possible.

Thomas Sterling's costly three-story clapboard house built in 1763 stood surrounded by four massive live oaks that the owner boasted to be four hundred years old. Except for the front entrance, the entire structure was shaded by the enormous limbs and leaves of the trees. Sterling claimed the natural canopy kept his spacious home warmer in the winter and cooler in summer than the other houses on the street. Unaware of the owner's claims, Morgan was pleased when he found the interior not only cooler than the outside street, but also much cooler than his own stuffy house. The small dilapidated building he owned stood on an almost treeless lot exposed all day to the sun.

A white-haired houseman opened the door and welcomed him inside with a bow. "Good morning, sir," he said with a lisp.

Morgan nodded to the man and followed him into the spacious hallway. He noted that the stoop-shouldered slave walked with a limp and suspected he had once worked for his master, a wealthy shipper, on the docks.

Sterling's house was expensively furnished with gilded mirrors, large mahogany chests and tables, and crystal glass ornaments. As Morgan entered, he could see glass chandeliers in three of the downstairs rooms that opened into the entrance hall, the most ornate chandelier with five tiers of candles hanging above a long dining room table. He saw freshly picked flowers in what he assumed were crystal vases in all the rooms he passed.

Abigail Sterling, a short squat woman with prominent blue eyes and luxurious black hair, politely welcomed him into the sitting room. Morgan thought she must have been a pretty girl in her youth. Her three grown children, two portly young men and a plump woman, all in their twenties, sat in the room with their mother. Morgan knew all three by sight, but did not know their names until Abigail Sterling introduced them. The sons were named Luke and Mark, the daughter Margaret.

During Mrs. Sterling's introductions, Morgan did little more than nod perfunctorily in the direction of the children. He held his faded hat in his hand and, instead of offering each a polite greeting; he said nothing and coldly looked them over. It was a well-known mannerism of the justice that most townsmen found insulting. "It's as if you're no more than a slave for sale," one indignant merchant told the attorney general.

In tears throughout his visit, Abigail Sterling dabbed her eyes with a lace handkerchief as she answered his questions. She sat in a stiff-backed maple chair, while her children sat together on a green and gold stuffed sofa. Morgan was guided to a matching green and gold stuffed chair across from Mrs. Sterling. He had refused her offer to take his hat and kept it in his lap.

"Has your husband stayed out all night before, Madam?" Morgan questioned the woman without any effort to make polite or preliminary conversation. He crossed his long legs and saw Margaret make a face when she saw the mud he had tracked onto the woven green rug at his feet.

"Of course not," the tearful woman replied wringing her hands. "Why on earth would you ever think such a thing?"

"It doesn't matter what I think, Madam." Morgan spoke

bluntly. "I need to know your husband's ways, especially his comings and goings."

"Hold on, can't you be more civil to my mother?" Mark spoke up angrily and pointed his finger at the justice.

"I'm not here to be civil, young man." Morgan glared at him, a blond youth with a florid face. "I'm here to learn all I can to find your father… and your interference is not helping me. I would be obliged if you would speak when spoken to. Is that understood?"

"Yes, sir." Mark looked down at his hands held in his lap and said nothing more.

"Thomas is a man who lives by schedules." Abigail Sterling answered quickly to protect her son from the justice's well-known temper. "He is never tardy. He certainly never misses his supper – he loves my cooking. Nor does he miss sleeping in our bed." Mrs. Sterling broke down and sobbed, hiding her face in her hands.

"There, there, Mother." Margaret quickly got up and put her arm around her mother's shoulders. "I'm sure Major Morgan will find Father." Tenderly holding her mother, she looked over at the justice of the peace. "In all my years at home, I have never known Father to be gone from the house at night without notifying Mother. Of course, he goes to community meetings in the assembly house, but Mother always knows about them. Once he leaves the office after it's closed, he comes home and seldom goes out. After dinner, Father usually works at his desk for an hour or so and then reads before going up to bed."

"What time does he usually come home at night…?" Morgan paused unable to recall her name. His mind still dulled from drink, he had instantly forgotten it after the introductions. He held his bloodshot eyes on her, thinking she was quite comely even if a bit too plump for his taste. Morgan was about to turn his eyes back to her mother when she spoke.

"My name is Margaret."

"I remember your name," he lied. "I lost my arm, not my memory." The justice frowned and exhaled his breath loudly to show his irritation.

Margaret's face reddened, but she made no retort. "Father comes home promptly at 6:30. Luke and Mark come home with him." She looked over at her brothers.

"Not last night." Mark shook his head. "Yesterday afternoon after lunch, I think it was one o'clock or so, Father told us he had an appointment and would be back before closing time."

"Did he mention with whom he had the appointment?"

"No, sir." Mark shook his head and looked over at his brother, who also shook his head from side to side.

"Did you see him leave?" Morgan moved his eyes from one boy to the other.

"I saw him, sir." Luke spoke up and looked at the justice. Already balding, he had thin brown hair; his mother's protruding eyes and looked to be the older brother. "He took his horse and rode off toward Johnson Square."

"Did he say he was going to Johnson Square?" Morgan crossed his legs again and more mud fell from his boots.

"No, sir." Luke shook his head.

"Then why do you think he was going to Johnson Square?" Morgan sighed again.

"Some afternoons he goes there to talk to the pastor at Christ's Church."

"I see. On those occasions, does he usually return to the office before closing time?"

"Yes, sir, always!" Luke bobbed his head up and down.

"We saw him leave, but didn't watch him riding away," added Mark hesitantly, fearful he had spoken out of turn. "All we know is that he was heading into town and… that's the last we saw of him."

"What way does he go to Christ's Church?" Morgan

stroked the stubble on his chin. "I know the Sterling Shipping Company is on the river north of Reynolds Square."

"Yes, sir." Mark nodded, anxious to be helpful. "He usually rides along Abercorn Street and then takes Bryan Street over to Johnson Square. I've gone to the church with him a time or two and that's his usual route."

"Did you notice if he took Abercorn Street when he left?"

"Yes, sir, I did." Luke spoke up before Mark could answer. "I was looking out the office window. Father told Moses – he's our oldest slave, some sixty years old – to saddle his horse. I saw Father mount his horse and Moses hand the reins to him. Then, then he rode off."

"We waited for him until well after 6:30 last night." Mark looked at his brother. "When he didn't return, we went home without him." He shrugged his rounded shoulders. "We kept looking back as we walked to see if he was behind us."

"Has that happened before?" Morgan stared into the young man's eyes.

"No, sir – not recently at least." Mark quickly turned to his older brother looking for his support. "Isn't that right?"

Luke nodded. "I can't recall the last time he wasn't in the office at closing time."

"Oh, where can he be?" Mrs. Sterling moaned and swayed in her chair. Her face lost all color. Margaret, fearing her mother might faint, hurried to her side. Luke kneeled on the floor to steady his mother in the chair, while Mark ran into the kitchen to get her a glass of water. After a few sips of the water, she seemed to recover her composure and color returned to her face.

"Forgive me for my outburst, Major. I'm feeling fine for now." She looked at Morgan through reddened eyes. "We can continue the interview."

"Are you certain, Mother?" Margaret stood behind her mother, her hands massaging the older woman's shoulders.

"There's no need, Mrs. Sterling." Morgan stood and bowed to her. He had been moved by her tears and near collapse. "You have told me all you know. Be assured, I'll do everything possible to find your husband. However, should he return home in the meantime, do let me know. Good day, Mrs. Sterling." He bowed again and walked out of the room.

Morgan made a face when he felt the heat outside. Not a leaf on the live oaks stirred as he walked into the street. He knew he would be drenched in sweat by the time he got home to feed his horse and eat his breakfast. The streets would be steaming when he set out for the courthouse and it would be an effort to get even a breath of air. "How I hate the summer," he said aloud.

As he started out into the square, a well-dressed man leading a saddled horse approached him. Holding a hand over his eyes, Morgan squinted to identify the man. When they met in the middle of the cobblestone road, the man saw his arm and immediately recognized him. "You're Major Morgan, are you not?"

"I am and who are you?" Morgan had the vague memory of meeting or seeing the man somewhere once before.

"My name is James Johnson. I'm Thomas Sterling's nearest neighbor." He pointed to a large white house across the square. "I'm the publisher of the *Georgia Gazette*."

"I see." Morgan now recalled meeting Johnson in his bookshop on Broughton Street. He had bought a copy of *Gulliver's Travels* from the man as well as some stationery and ink for his office and one of the first printed editions of the *Gazette*.

"We have met before, Major, but that's not important now. I'm sure this horse belongs to Sterling – I've seen the assemblyman riding him any number of times. I found him nibbling on my wife's flowers at the back of my house. I know the man's missing and, finding his horse wandering about with his reins dragging on the ground, makes me worry about him. I was on the way to his home to return him to the family."

Morgan nodded. "When did you find the horse?" He noted that the big chestnut stallion was a good-looking thoroughbred. He guessed him to be about fifteen hands high.

"About a half hour ago. My wife saw him in the garden. She was looking out an upstairs window." Johnson rubbed his hand over the horse's head. "He's a good natured fellow."

Morgan gestured for Johnson to lead the horse over to a shaded spot under an overhanging tree limb. Out of the sun, he looked the stallion over, examining his flanks and legs. He then got down on his knees to look at his chest and belly. Standing, Morgan ran his hand over the horse's withers and lightly patted his head. "Good boy," he said, noting that the stallion had not shivered nor shown any sign of concern during his close examination. Morgan reached into the pocket of his red army jacket and, bringing up a brown sugar cube, offered it on his palm to the horse.

"There doesn't appear to be anything unusual on the horse." Morgan brushed a fly from the stallion's back. "The saddle is on straight so it doesn't look like he fell or was shot out of it. It looks like Sterling got off the horse and either poorly tethered him or let him roam free."

"That would be my assumption, too." Johnson held the stallion's reins in his hand. "He looks fine and does not appear to have been ridden hard."

Morgan nodded. "I would say he walked or trotted here. I doubt he ran hard and I don't think he has been here in town all the time since yesterday." He pointed to the horse's hooves. "The red clay shows he was somewhere outside the walls – perhaps as far as the western woods."

The justice's assistant, Sergeant Richard Stockwell, met

him outside his office when he arrived at the courthouse an hour later. Stockwell, an English commoner from Cornwall, fought under Major Morgan in the final Canadian campaign of the French and Indian War. The veteran soldier had served as the cavalry officer's aide and had been wounded in the same battle that cost Morgan his left arm. They fell on August 27, 1758, as the English forces took Fort Frontenac, a fort situated at the east side of Lake Ontario where it connects to the St. Lawrence River. During the first assault, the French defenders directed a withering barrage of musket fire on the cavalry and mowed down the horsemen as they charged the walls. Morgan was among the first to fall. A musket ball struck him in his upper left arm and another hit his horse in the neck. Stockwell, running to help the major, also was shot. The ball grazed the sergeant's right side, but, when he paused to recover, another cavalryman's horse fell on him and broke his left leg in three places.

After the battle, Major Morgan lay close to death for two weeks. His arm was so severely damaged that the army surgeon had no choice but to amputate the entire arm below the shoulder. As usual following battlefield amputations, the accompanying shock and fever almost killed him. Fortunately for Morgan, the fever eventually abated and he luckily escaped the typical infections to his wound. Still, his life remained in doubt for a time and he might not have survived without the constant attention of his sergeant.

Unlike Morgan, Stockwell mended quickly and, within a week, managed to drag himself around with splints on his leg. When the splints were removed, he used a cane to walk, although with a limp. By that time, his severe pain was gone and he devoted himself to the care of his sick superior. Even when the sergeant could have escaped the damp, foul smelling and insect infested infirmary, he remained at the major's bedside doing whatever was needed for his recovery.

Stockwell changed his bloody bandages, bathed him with

cool water when his fever raged and sat for hours beside him brushing away the hovering flies. Later, he brought the major hot food and fed him when he was finally able to eat. He even carried away the fetid contents of his chamber pot. The sergeant also built a one-foot-high wooden platform for Morgan's straw pallet so the wounded man's bed would stand above the damp stone floor, where ants and cockroaches scurried about. When the major was well enough to sit up, stand and then walk, it was Stockwell who helped him make his first painful movements off the makeshift bed.

By early October, Morgan had moved out of the infirmary and into a tent he shared with Stockwell outside the fort. Though still thin and weak, he felt strong enough to walk two miles a day and share meal preparation with the sergeant. He also was learning how to care for himself with one arm and one hand. Morgan found dressing himself to be the most difficult daily task he faced, even harder than mounting a horse. At the end of the month, when the first snow fell and the major no longer needed the sergeant's willing help, he knew it was time to go home.

Morgan discussed his plans with Stockwell one day before their evening meal. They were sitting across a cooking fire the major had made. He asked Stockwell if he wanted to join him on his trip to Savannah. Morgan told Stockwell he would either find him well-paying work in town or on his father's rice plantation. The major pointed to his bad leg and promised he would make sure that the work would not require standing or walking for any length of time. The sergeant's ability to read and write, he said, would assure him of some kind of supervisory post wherever he worked. Stockwell spent only seconds considering the offer and then, with a wide smile, nodded in agreement. The nine-year veteran knew his limp left him without a future in the army and few, if any other options outside the king's service. They shook hands and shared a dram of Jamaican rum to bind their agreement. While the officer went to fetch firewood, Stockwell brushed away tears, knowing he had been given a second chance in life; he would never forget the gift, or the man who gave it to him. When Morgan returned with the wood, they ate a pair of pheasants the sergeant had shot in the woods and drank into the night until they emptied the quart bottle.

The major made his official request for a release from army service on the last day of the month. Citing his weakened state after being wounded in battle, Morgan asked his commanding officer to assign the sergeant to accompany him on his long journey south to Georgia. He made no request for a financial settlement from the army. The aristocratic British colonel, a pragmatic man, could see no further use for a crippled cavalry officer and his lame aide and readily agreed to Morgan's written petition. Within two days of the major's appearance before him, he sent the two men on their way with signed and sealed retirement papers in hand as well as military letters of transit allowing them to travel freely through all the colonies to Georgia.

The helpful colonel also permitted the major to buy two army horses for three times their worth and similarly sold him saddles and riding gear for twice their purchase price. Morgan said nothing about the obvious exploitation, but he knew the cavalry commander intended to pocket the extra profit for himself. Out of earshot of the colonel after handing over the money, Morgan muttered to the sergeant that the greedy bastard was a typical British aristocrat, only interested in what he could possibly take home from the colonies. Stockwell nodded in agreement.

They left Fort Frontenac on the third of November at dawn. A driving rain pelted their tent the night before they left and they had to pack up and saddle their horses in sodden sleet that turned to snow by the end of their first day on the road. The two men rode bundled up in woolen blankets that soon became soaked and all but useless against the slashing wind. They made little time in the snow and it took them two weeks to leave Canada and another five weeks to cross the Appalachian Mountains. A heavy snow covered the mountains and, for a week, they huddled in a cave with little to eat. It was not until three days after Christmas that the exhausted horsemen finally reached the first outlying farms of Philadelphia. By that time, they both were wracked with fever, constantly coughing and too weak to go on. They recuperated for ten days in an old inn south of the city and lay in bed through much of the first week of the new year.

A welcome week-long winter thaw in late January warmed them as they reached Virginia and camped overnight outside of Norfolk. The horsemen proceeded southward along the ocean and rode past miles of empty fields where tobacco would be planted in the spring. Arriving on the Carolina coast in late February, they stopped over in Charles Towne for new horseshoes and a rest before the last part of the trip. They stayed four days in a tiny three-bedroom inn, where a cheerful Scottish family welcomed them with plates of home cooked food, spirited conversation and a warm room with a fireplace. Virtually emaciated from the harrowing journey, the hungry men gorged themselves on pork and rabbit stews and hot baked bread at midday and custards, gingerbread cake and sassafras tea at night. They also bathed and slept in beds for the first time in seven weeks.

With regrets, the men left the hospitable Scots and rode south along the sea. They finally entered Georgia in early March. On one of the first warm sunny days in the middle of the month, the two bearded and ragged-looking horsemen rode through the city gates into Savannah. They waited while posted guards looked over their papers before allowing them entry into the colony. Still at war with France and

Spain, the English soldiers stood guard night and day all along the western walls to defend the colonists against a land attack.

Their first three months in Savannah, they stayed with Morgan's father in a rented house in town. The elder Morgan moved there during the war. But, at the end of May, he ignored the advice of the army commander of the province, General Jonathan Abernathy, and returned to his plantation home south of Savannah. The general warned him that the war was not yet over even if French Canada had been taken. He reminded the planter that the Indians remained unreliable and the Spaniards in St. Augustine still posed a serious threat to the colony. Morgan disregarded the general's warnings and left town saying he had waited long enough.

The sixty-three-year-old man was anxious to resume control of his plantation after three years of periodic visits because of the war and worries of Spanish attacks. Morgan owned 5,000 acres of fertile lowland five miles south of town and he reluctantly left the rice production in the hands of Abraham Cabot, a supervisor who had worked twenty years for him. He trusted Cabot, but longed to be back in his house again and in charge of all aspects of plantation life, including the 102 slaves who planted and cultivated the rice crop.

His son and Stockwell remained in the town house together over that summer. Then, in the fall, Morgan got the Englishman a job supervising dockworkers for a shipping company and Stockwell moved to a small rental house near the Savannah River. Morgan paid the sergeant's rent despite his objections. He was not a man who would ever forget the devotion Stockwell had shown him when he lay near death in Canada. Then, when Morgan received his appointment as justice of the peace, he made Stockwell his assistant and paid him a salary out of his own pocket. The sergeant was unaware of the source of his earnings and thought the money came out of the colony's operating funds. An unkempt man with unruly black hair, a tangled beard and wrinkled clothing, Stockwell was no more appreciated in town than the surly justice.

Though seemingly jovial in manner, the sergeant's lop-sided grin gave most townspeople the impression that he doubted everything they said to him. His imposing size also made them wary. A burly man with wide shoulders and thick arms, Stockwell, even with his limp, looked too strong to be challenged physically by other men. The burly sergeant was not a bully, but no one got seated or served before him in a tavern and most townspeople went out of their way to be polite to him.

On the lookout for Morgan that morning, Stockwell met him in the corridor outside his office. The big Englishman seemed to fill the hallway where he stood and had to press himself against the wall to let people pass him. When Morgan reached him, Stockwell waited until the busy corridor had emptied before speaking.

"His nibs upstairs wants to see you." Stockwell raised one of his long muscular arms and pointed his finger at the ceiling above them. "He sent that little twit Thackery down here twice to bring you up to his office. The last time, the poor lil' lad ran and was all out of breath when he got here. Palmer must be in a snit."

"I'm not surprised." Morgan grimaced and shook his head from side to side. "Well, let's see what he has to complain about now." He started to walk away, but abruptly turned back to face Stockwell. "Have you heard about the missing man?"

"Yes, sir. It's the talk of the town this morning. They say he disappeared yesterday."

Morgan nodded. "What have you heard about Sterling?"

"Not much at all. It's said that he rode out of town yesterday afternoon and hasn't been seen by nobody since. Of course, that's more than a bit hard to believe about the man. He's much too fat to be missed." Stockwell grinned, amused at his own remark.

"He is at that. What I meant was have you heard anything about him in the past?"

Stockwell pursed his lips. "Can't say I've heard much about him. I don't recall hearing any talk about the man. Never seen him in the taverns or with the wenches. One of those good church-going men, I suppose."

Morgan nodded.

Stockwell raised a finger. "Wait a bit. I do recall it said he came into a lot of money all of a sudden. It happened some years ago at the end of the war. It was said his shipping business was in trouble and then, all of a sudden, the man had enough money to buy a new dock. Not long afterwards, he had that big house of his built."

"I see. Well, the man may very well turn up sometime today." Morgan again turned to leave, but paused to look at Stockwell. "Sergeant, are you aware of any red-clay road or path a horse might have taken from the western woods to town?"

"Not offhand, sir." Stockwell scratched his head. "But, I'll think about it."

Morgan nodded and then turned to walk toward the stairway that led up to the next floor and the attorney general's office. He walked leisurely, in no hurry to listen to a tirade from the ever-critical and pompous Oliver Palmer. As he climbed the stairway, Morgan wondered if he really wanted another term as justice of the peace. He was sick and tired of dealing with drunks and officious Englishmen.

"But it's better than supervising the plantation with my father," he said to himself.

The attorney general's office, located at the top of the stairs on the right, was the smallest of the three offices on the second floor. The other two more elegant offices had been furnished by the provincial governor, James Wright, and his lieutenant governor, John Graham, but neither official spent much time at the courthouse. Even though Savannah had been made the capital of Georgia, Wright refused to use his office and conducted most of the province's business from his large mansion on St. James Square.

The courthouse was only two years old. Called the Filature, it had been built in 1764 as a silk factory and once contained some 15,000 pounds of cocoons. But, with the unexpected collapse of the silk industry in Savannah, the assembly bought the Filature in a bankruptcy sale and converted it into a meeting hall and courthouse. The assembly hall took up most of the first floor with only enough space left to construct seven small offices held by minor officials like the justice of peace. Morgan remarked that his room was slightly larger than a jail cell. Except for the specially built offices set aside for the governors on the second floor, the former factory had no distinguishing architectural or decorative features. It served only as a practical meeting place and center for the governor's few colonial officials.

Oliver Palmer's office looked much like the rest of the Filature. It had only one window and was small and cramped. Palmer had improved the office as best as he could, though limited by space. He threw out all the previous attorney general's furniture and replaced it with costly oak chairs and desks and a floor-to-ceiling bookcase. His massive desk, situated in front of the window, took up almost the entire end of the room, while another much smaller desk bought for an assistant was situated near the door. His wife, Esther, bought maroon drapes for the window and a blue and maroon Persian rug for the plank floor. She also had a portrait of King George III hung on the side wall opposite the bookcase. Esther made certain her houseman had given the walls two coats of whitewash and had stained and polished the floorboards before she permitted the new furnishings to be moved into the office.

Palmer, appointed attorney general by the governor, was the most powerful official in the courthouse. He carried out the governor's orders and executed the laws of the colony passed by the assembly. He also selected all the officials who served in the province, including Justice of the Peace James Morgan. The position of attorney general had come into being when Georgia became a royal colony in 1752 and Oliver Palmer was only the third man to hold the office. He came to Savannah with Governor Wright, who had been the attorney general of South Carolina.

Palmer, the son of a small landowner in England, had been educated in law and came to America to make his fortune. On the advice of a cousin already in Richmond, Virginia he sailed to Charles Towne, a bustling port-city with few educated men. Beginning as a petty clerk in the office of Sir James Wright, in only three years Palmer's devoted service led him to the position of assistant and trusted advisor to the attorney general. The ambitious lawyer also married well. His wife was a wealthy tobacco planter's only daughter and her sizeable dowry assured him of all the money he would ever need. In Charles Towne, Palmer lived with Esther and their three children in the richest section of the city, enjoying every pleasure his wealth and society could offer. He enjoyed a similar lifestyle in Savannah.

Before Morgan could knock, the door was thrust open by Edward Thackery, the attorney general's assistant. "Well, there you are – at last." The small thin man clucked his tongue. He squinted through his spectacles and gave the justice a disapproving look.

Morgan glared at Thackery and made him jump quickly aside as he strode into the room. His sword, which he wore on his left side, brushed against the little man's vest as he walked by. In the office, the justice stood in front of the attorney general's desk. Oliver Palmer, seated in a high-backed cushioned chair, looked up with affected indifference as Morgan scowled down at him. Palmer held a cup of tea in one hand and, with a careless flip of the other, he motioned the justice to a wooden chair facing him.

The five-foot-long oak desk, polished to a high gloss, held only two piles of neatly stacked papers along with two quills and a small pot of black ink. The two silver candlesticks that usually adorned the desk had been placed on a sideboard along with a silver teapot and three more cups and saucers on a platter. Palmer's costly creamware was made in Leeds, England from Cornish white clay. There were also five baked biscuits, a pot of orange marmalade and a silver spoon on a creamware plate. Everything was within easy reach of the attorney general's chair and he held a half-eaten biscuit in his hand. He ate the last of it as Morgan sat down.

"Well, Major, so you finally deigned to appear." The heavy-jowled man leaned back in his chair and looked at the justice with half closed eyes. He rested the cup of tea on his ample stomach and took occasional sips as they talked.

"I've been looking into the disappearance of Thomas Sterling." Morgan crossed his legs and intentionally scraped mud from his boots onto Palmer's Persian rug. The attorney general did not see the mess he made, but Thackery, whose desk stood near the door, saw the muddied rug and clucked his tongue.

"Have you indeed? I assume you are referring to Assemblyman Thomas Sterling. And what have you done about it, Major?" Careful to steady the cup on his stomach, he leaned over to the sideboard, spread marmalade on a biscuit and, in two bites, devoured it. Palmer drank his tea and ate two more biscuits without offering anything to the man sitting across from him.

Morgan ignored Palmer's correction. "I've interviewed the Sterling family and looked over the horse he rode yesterday."

"I see." Palmer nodded his head, leaving white powder from his wig on the cloth back of the chair. "And, ah, what is your notion of what has happened to Assemblyman Sterling?"

"I'm not certain yet. However, it appears he went out of town yesterday and obviously hasn't returned. The reappearance of his horse without him is an ominous sign."

"I should say so." Palmer leaned forward and placed his teacup in its saucer on the desk. "Ah, so Major, tell me what you intend to do next?" He raised his hand to his assistant, who sat silently at his small desk facing his superior. "The tea is lukewarm, Thackery, do take care of it. Freshly steeped! You know I cannot abide reheated tea."

"Yes, sir." Thackery hurried over and took the teapot away.

Morgan frowned and looked out the one window in the room. From where the justice sat, he could see a few of the upper limbs of a live oak. It infuriated him to see Palmer's humiliating treatment of Thackery and, avoiding the sight of the pathetic man scampering out of the room, he watched a pair of sparrows flying to and from a nest of twigs they were building. Morgan was fascinated by the careful way the birds built the nest.

"I asked you what you intend to do." Palmer frowned and raised his voice. He did not like having to repeat himself to inferiors.

"A search will need to be started as soon as possible, of course." Morgan turned his gaze to the attorney general. "With a signed order, I'll get the militiamen to help with the search. I'll begin as soon as I leave here."

"Yes, that's what you need to do. And do make sure you keep me advised of everything you discover. I'll have Thackery bring you the order shortly." Palmer again leaned back in his chair and stared at the justice as he stood to leave. "One more thing, Major." Palmer paused to brush crumbs from his gold-laced vest.

Morgan sighed and placed his hand on his hip. "What now?" he thought. "What will the pompous fool say now?"

Finished brushing his vest, Palmer looked up at the justice. "Do keep in mind, Major, that Mr. Thomas Sterling is a colonial assemblyman and no rock should be left unturned in the search for him. Is that understood?" He sighed wearily as if he had been forced to give instructions to a recalcitrant child.

"It is." Morgan immediately turned and walked away.

At midday, Morgan, Stockwell, twenty militiamen and a Creek Indian guide rode out of Savannah and started their search for the missing assemblyman. It was a hot sunny afternoon and everyone was sweating within minutes. They spent the first two hours looking for ground made of red clay. Stockwell found a narrow strip just beyond the town walls and a militiaman named Caleb Wells found another at the edge of the woods. Neither, however, showed any signs of horses' hooves or human footprints. The Indian, Apaktouchi, carefully studied the ground and searched the western woods, but saw nothing except a lone fox slinking through the tall grass.

Morgan then spread out the men at fifteen-foot intervals and sent them searching on foot all along the southern edge of the western woods. He urged them to walk slowly and look from side to side as well as forward as they scanned the ground. The searchers used their swords like machetes, cutting away underbrush as they looked for any sign of the missing man, a piece of his clothing or something he carried. Many, if not most of the men, expected to find his body. When they found nothing, Morgan had them repeat the search in the center and then the northern edge of the woods until the exhausted militiamen had thoroughly examined a forty-foot section of the land all around the city. They searched throughout the afternoon and at dusk they gathered at the northern gate to talk about what they had seen.

There were reports of several snakes including a six-foot rattlesnake, a number of rabbits, raccoons, and field rats, but not one sighting or sign of Thomas Sterling. They found a number of items townsmen had lost in the woods, among them an Indian arrow, a rusted knife, a couple of broken cups and even one George II silver shilling, but nothing that might have belonged to the assemblyman. The tired men were noisy and talkative as they described their finds and animal encounters, but they had little to say once Morgan inquired about the missing man. By that time, the searchers could barely see each other in the dark and the justice sent them home.

The search continued the following morning even as torrential thundershowers pelted the militiamen, now numbering forty, throughout most of the day. With little possibility of finding any tracks of the missing man or his horse after the rain, fewer men showed up to assist Morgan and Stockwell the next two days. Only five worn-out men appeared at the courthouse on Friday morning. By Saturday, Morgan knew any further searches would be futile. He told the attorney general that if and when Sterling was found, it would be because of some unforeseen event. To his surprise, Palmer agreed and told him to call off the search.

The body of the missing assemblyman was found eight days later. Two men from town, defying the provincial laws prohibiting hunting on the Sabbath, found what remained of the man while hunting in the woods. They found Sterling as they searched for a wounded wild boar one of the hunters had shot earlier in the day. The hunters chased after the wounded animal, but lost him as he disappeared among the trees and foliage of the forest. A trail of blood told them the boar would not live long and, when they saw vultures circling a stand of pines in a ravine below them, they assumed he had died there among the trees. The two men scrambled down the hill, looking forward to the boar meat they would carve up and carry home. They hoped to reach the carcass before the vultures could pick it apart.

When the hunters finally reached the bottom of the hill and ran to the pines, they saw the vultures as well as a dense cloud of flies. There were more than a dozen vultures covering the carrion with their flapping wings. Anxious to save whatever they could of the meat, the hunters rushed toward the birds shouting and waving their arms. As the vultures scattered and flew off, they stopped abruptly in unison. There, in front of their eyes, they were horrified to see the grisly skull and picked-over bones of a man staked to the ground.

CHAPTER TWO

SAVANNAH: MONDAY, MAY 18 – TUESDAY, MAY 19, 1766

"I'll never be forgetting that awful sight. Never! I expect I'll see it in my mind's eye the rest of my days," said Samuel Canfield, a round and pink-cheeked man. He ran a freckled hand through his thatch of thick blond hair. "I vomited up my lunch soon as I seen it. So did Henry." Canfield looked at his companion who sat across from him.

"It's true." Henry Colby, a balding man with small brown eyes, shook his head. "I still can taste the bile in my mouth every time it comes to mind." Colby shuddered, remembering the eyeless skull with strips of bloody flesh and hair sticking out of it. "God, it was awful!"

"Did you know it was Assemblyman Sterling?" Morgan had instructed Stockwell to bring the hunters to his office the morning after the body was found. Stockwell roused them from bed at dawn and brought them to Morgan before anyone else had arrived at the courthouse. The two sleepy men sat in hard wooden chairs in front of the justice's desk. They were given tea to drink.

"Yes, sir." Canfield again looked at Colby for confirmation. The two men were friends and spent hours together hunting and fishing. The forty-year-old Canfield worked as a carpenter for the army and his slightly older friend owned one of the four shoemaking shops in Savannah.

"We guessed it was him." Colby yawned loudly. "He was gone missing the whole week before and everybody was looking for him."

"We also knew when we seen his fine clothes piled up on the ground, even though they was in pieces" added Canfield. "I seen him a time or two in that suit." He nodded, recalling the sight of the fat man walking in the street with his purple coat and breeches and white stockings. "I don't think anyone else in town has a fine suit like it with all them gold buttons."

"What about his wig? Did you see it in the pile of clothes?" Morgan leaned forward on his elbow, his hand balled into a fist under his chin.

"No, sir. I didn't see no wig." Canfield turned to Colby, who was sipping his tea.

"No, sir." Colby nodded. "There weren't no wig there I seen."

"Did you go through his clothes?" Morgan narrowed his eyes and glared at them.

"No, sir," they said in unison.

"We only looked and then left as quick as we could." Canfield exhaled his breath.

"What did you do after you found the body?"

"Nothing, sir. We didn't never go near it." Canfield shook his head vigorously from side to side . "Never mind the look of it, the stench alone would keep anybody from going near it."

"How close would you say you were to it?" Morgan looked at Colby.

Colby bit his lip. "I'd say near six feet. Isn't that right, Sam?"

"If that close." Canfield shivered, recalling it vividly. "Once we seen it, all we wanted to do was get out of there – fast as possible."

"What did you do next?" Morgan moved his eyes back and forth looking at both men.

"We ran back the same way we come." Canfield looked at Colby. "We bumped into each other as we ran and Henry almost fell in the lake."

"I stepped in it and got my shoe full of water." Colby nodded. "It almost fell off when I run up the hill to the horses."

"Where did you tie the horses?" Morgan looked at Canfield.

"They was at least a half mile away under a tree where we first seen the boar."

"I'd say they was more than a good mile away." Colby frowned at Canfield. "We was out of breath an sweating like slaves when we got there."

"What did you do next?"

"We jumped on the horses and rode right to town. We never even went back to look for the boar." Canfield made a face. "Lost a lot of good eating."

"That's what you get for hunting against the law." The justice scowled. "You should be put in stocks for a couple of days and that's exactly what will happen to you both if you don't tell me everything that happened."

"We're telling you everything that happened there, sir." Colby's face reddened. "We left nothin' out, Major Morgan. Nothin'!"

"There's nothin' else to tell, sir, believe me." Canfield feared they would be beaten. He had heard about Morgan's harsh treatment of men who broke the law in Savannah.

"What about the horses' hooves? Was there red clay on

them?" Morgan again looked at Canfield, knowing he was the more observant of the two men.

"No, sir, but there was red clay on my shoes."

"That's right and the wife yelled at me for tracking it into the house." Colby nodded his head up and down, remembering the scolding he got from her.

"Where did you step in the clay?"

Canfield and Colby looked at each other not knowing what to say.

"Try to remember where you stepped in the red clay." Morgan lowered his voice. "Was it near the body?"

"I don't think so." Canfield shook his head from side to side. "There was clay down by the lake, but it wasn't red. I'm pretty sure of that."

"So am I. We must have stepped in red clay somewhere up the hill on the way to the horses." Colby shrugged his shoulders.

Morgan saw Stockwell standing in the open doorway. He raised his eyes and the justice nodded, knowing the attorney general wanted to talk to him in his office.

"That's enough for now. I'll let you know if and when I want to talk to you again. For now, you'll be spared the stocks, but keep in mind that I'll be watching both of you. Follow the Sabbath laws or you'll pay the consequences."

"Yes, sir," they again said in unison. They stood and put their cups on Morgan's desk.

"Before you go home, I want you to ride out to the woods with Sergeant Stockwell. You will show him where you tethered your horses yesterday and the paths you took to and from the body. Is that understood?" Morgan gave them a severe look.

Both men nodded, but looked glum.

"That's the price you pay for breaking the law." Morgan scowled at them as they stood.

At first light, the colony's medical examiner, Dr. Samuel Nunes Ribeiro, rode out to the murder site in the woods. It was a cool morning for mid-May and the physician wore his coat. He was accompanied by a militiaman named John Martin who took the old doctor to the woods in a horse-drawn coach.

The medical examiner had been informed of the dead body the night before, but decided against examining it in the limited light of a lantern. It was Stockwell who came to tell him the news. The doctor heard him ride up to his house and opened the door as he dismounted.

"Come in, Sergeant, have glass of wine." Doctor Nunes Ribeiro was a small bearded man with large black eyes and thick white hair.

"Thank you, sir, but I'll take you up on it another time." Stockwell stood in the doorway as he told the doctor about the body the hunters had found in the woods. He spared no detail in his description of the gruesome condition of the corpse. After seeing so many broken bodies in battle, Stockwell had not been shocked at the sight of the skeletal remains of Thomas Sterling.

"My God, we've never seen anything like that here before."

"No, sir. Doctor Nunes, I need to get back and tell the major when you will be looking at the corpse." From the doorway, Stockwell saw the doctor's young housekeeper, María Adela, in the kitchen. She stood at the table cutting up vegetables. He wanted to speak to her, but her back was turned while he talked to the medical examiner.

"Tell the major that I'll examine it first thing in the morning. I want to see it in the light of day. It's near dusk now and it would be too dark by the time I rode out there. Tell the major I'll be on my way at first light."

Stockwell nodded. "The major said to tell you the corpse is covered and a man will stay and guard it overnight. He's worried the scavengers will take what's left of it. There'll be a man to pick you up in the morning. It's a good ways out there and he'll take you by wagon."

"Good. That will be soon enough. The corpse is unlikely to show any significant change overnight. How far away is it?" Bent over from age, the old doctor grimaced as he looked up at the tall sergeant.

"I'd say it's about four or maybe five miles from town. It's an easy ride out to the woods, but it's hard getting down the steep hill to the lake. It's treacherous. If you're not careful, the slippery leaves and pine needles will make you lose your footing. I fell on my face when I tried to run down the first time. The lake is there at the foot of the hill and the body is a little way to one side to the left of the lake. I'll leave a marker for you to follow."

"Thank you, I'm sure I'll find it." The doctor saw Stockwell's weariness as he leaned against the door frame. "How many times have you ridden back and forth to the woods?"

"A few, sir." The sergeant straightened up. "But I'm fine and this will be my last trip out there tonight. After I report to the major, we'll both be returning to town."

"One more question before you leave, Sergeant. Does Major Morgan have any idea who murdered the assemblyman?" The doctor felt a sudden draft of cold air on his ankles and knew he would use his fireplace that night.

"No, sir, but he said whoever did it is clever and cruel. He said if he believed in the devil, this murderer is one of his demons."

"I see. That's quite a statement coming from him." He shared a smile with Stockwell.

"That it is." The sergeant inhaled deeply. "Well, I better be on me way. Be sure, sir, to bring something to fend off ants. There's fire ants in the rocks there and the fierce lil' buggers will give you bites you will never forget. The mosquitos are also already out now, too." He turned to walk to his horse tied in front of the house.

"Wait a moment, Sergeant." The doctor went inside and Stockwell saw him take a bottle of wine from the table and fill a cup to the top. María Adela turned around as he poured the wine and smiled shyly when Stockwell waved to her.

"You're looking lovely as usual." He returned her smile as Doctor Nunes arrived with the wine. María Adela blushed and turned back to her work.

The doctor's hand trembled as he held the wine glass out to Stockwell. "Drink this down for your good health and the long ride out to the woods."

Paul Miller, the twenty-year-old militiaman who had the bad luck to draw the short straw, got the assignment to stand guard all night beside the body. He was ordered to stay awake and keep the vultures and other scavengers away from the covered corpse. Sickened by the stench and frightened by the many strange sounds in the dark woods, the young man, a cabinetmaker's apprentice, had wanted to run away any number of times that night. Miller tended a fire a few feet from the body, but the damp seemed to seep into his clothing, making him shiver even when standing close to the flames. The sounds of what he imagined were unseen beasts moving about also frightened him. At dawn, his teeth chattering, Miller could hardly wait for his replacement and was ready to sprint up the hill when, at last, he heard men thrashing through the trees above him. When they reached him, he made a brief report to the morning guard, John

Martin, and then, without another word, fled up the path to his horse.

The old doctor came down the hill walking closely behind Martin. He steadied himself by holding one hand on the young man's back. For additional support, he kept his other hand free to grasp whatever branches or vines he passed. When he felt in danger of falling, the doctor grabbed Martin's belt or clung to his arms. He slipped once on wet leaves, but the younger man managed to catch him before he fell to the ground. At the bottom of the hill, the physician stood unmoving for several minutes regaining his breath. He was exhausted and his back ached from the exertion of the descent. He put his hands on his hips to straighten himself up.

The doctor looked at the lake while he rested. Shaded by the trees, the lake looked green except at the very center. There the water was blue and sparkled in the sunlight that penetrated the canopy of trees. He assumed an underground spring fed the lake since the water looked clear from where he stood. He saw a trout swimming near the shore and wished he had the strength to return by himself and spend an afternoon fishing.

Martin waited patiently for the doctor to catch his breath and then he took his arm as they walked along the lake's edge. In his other hand, he carried the doctor's heavy bag. Stockwell's marker, three sticks forming an arrow, pointed them to the left and they went that way in silence. Everything seemed still at that time of day. There was not one ripple on the lake's surface or a sound in the surrounding woods, not even the squawk of a bird. Seconds later, they reached the clearing and the doctor sighed as he looked down at the covered remains of Thomas Sterling.

Dr. Nunes Ribeiro, well into his sixties, had arrived in Savannah in July 1733, only seven months after its settlement. The physician and forty-one other Jewish refugees from Portugal and Spain immigrated to the colony from England, where they fled the Inquisition. Before escaping to England, the doctor himself had been imprisoned by the Inquisition in Portugal. His crime had been his outspoken resistance to the conversion of Jews to Catholicism.

In Georgia, the founder of the colony, James Oglethorpe, welcomed the Jews courteously, but was especially pleased to receive the Jewish physician. At the time, the settlement suffered from the fevers that had killed twenty people including their only physician. No sooner had the Portuguese doctor arrived in the colony than he began to treat the sick community. He treated the colonists with cold baths and cool drinks and in a short time most of them were well enough to resume work on the new settlement. Oglethorpe praised the Jewish physician for saving the colony, and despite opposition from some of the colonists and trustees, he granted property rights to the Jews in Savannah. Lawyers in nearby Charles Towne told Oglethorpe that King George's charter for Georgia only prohibited Catholics and slaves from residing in the colony.

The Jewish immigrants remained in Savannah and, for the next three decades, Dr. Nunes Ribeiro served the colonists as their trusted physician. A good-humored and gentle man, he soon learned English and became a respected member of the colony. The doctor also served Savannah as medical examiner, an appointment given to him every year after his arrival.

It was not until the physician reached sixty-three that the aging man reduced his practice to include only the families of the colonial officials and a few old patients whom he had treated for years. By that time, four much younger physicians had established medical practices in town and, though they sometimes consulted him for advice, they tended most of the sick in the colony. Alone after his wife's death in 1765, the doctor maintained his medical practice to keep himself occupied. Dr. Nunes Ribeiro still served as Savannah's medical examiner at the time of Thomas Sterling's death, although he had decided to resign the position at the end of the year. The frail man did not feel well and knew he did not have long to live.

At the clearing, the doctor kneeled beside the body and motioned Martin to move back a few steps. He looked up at the young man. "I expect this will be disgusting for you to see and I don't recommend you look at it. But if you must see it, I suggest you take a quick look when I remove the cover. If you feel ill, turn your eyes away from it. Do you understand, Martin?"

"Yes, sir. I won't look at all. The smell alone is enough to make me sick."

"Bom. (Good.)" The doctor bent over and, taking one edge of the cover, he pulled it off the body. He glanced at the militiaman and saw that the young man had moved farther away and was looking toward the lake. "Don't look, Martin! It's much worse than I expected."

The doctor opened the leather bag the militiaman had carried for him and withdrew two large ceramic jars which he set upon the ground. They were tightly stoppered and it took a few seconds to pry them open. He then picked up one of the jars and, holding the heavy jar against his chest, he dipped his fingers inside and began sprinkling a liquid over the corpse.

"I'm sprinkling alcohol on the body," he spoke to Martin's back. "It should reduce the smell somewhat and hopefully repel the insects. There are a lot of them still on the body."

"I can smell it. It smells much better than before."

"The alcohol is working – the insects are leaving." He watched as a horde of ants, beetles and cockroaches scurried away into the leaves."I'll now begin my examination, but it will take a while. I suggest you take a walk around the lake and wait for me to call you when I'm done. It shouldn't take too long." He patted Martin's arm.

"Yes, sir. I'll do that, but call me if you need a bit a help."

"I will." The doctor watched the militiaman walk away and then he turned his attention to the corpse on the ground. He sprinkled the remainder of the alcohol around the site, making sure everything was wet, even the wooden stakes. Both jars were empty when he finished. He leaned over what was left of the body and noted that the ants and other insects had disappeared. Knowing they would return as the alcohol dried, he hurried to make his examination. At most, he had two hours before they returned in numbers.

The doctor spent the next hour and a half studying the body and the clearing where it had been staked to the ground. He initially looked down at the corpse from a number of positions – first from the head, then the feet, the sides and even from several feet away in all directions. He then got down on his knees and scrutinized the body as it lay face up, moving a magnifying glass from the top of the skull down to the tips of the toes. The old man grimaced as he crawled about on the hard ground and swore in Portuguese when a wayward fire ant bit the tip of his finger.

The doctor examined every exposed surface that remained of the body including the arms and legs. He next looked at the bindings and stakes that had held Sterling to the ground. At the ankles, he carefully avoided the first ants returning to the corpse. Untying the bindings, one by one, he turned what remained of the body over. Without internal organs and most of the flesh, it was easily moved. The back of the body looked better than the front side. There was more flesh on that side, though pitted with tiny holes he suspected had been made by ants and cockroaches. The doctor used his magnifying glass to study the back, crawling on his knees around the body. He grimaced when his left knee struck a sharp rock.

When his examination was finished, he leaned back on his haunches and put his hands on his thighs. With his eyes closed, the doctor rested a few minutes and then reached over to grasp the canvas cover. Still on his knees, he spread it over the body and called for the militiaman.

Feeling pain in his legs, the doctor groaned when he tried to get up from the ground. He bent over on his hands and knees and tried to use his arms to push himself up. As he strained to stand, the militiaman arrived and rushed over to help. Martin squatted down, put his arms around the doctor and lifted him to his feet. He heard the creaking of the man's bones as he stood.

"Thank you, Martin. I don't know if I would have made it without you." The doctor patted the young man on the back. "Now, let's look at Sterling's clothing." He walked over to the neatly folded pile that lay to the side of the body.

Before he could bend down for them, the militiaman picked up everything except the dead man's shoes. He brushed off the pine needles and leaves and held the clothing out to him. The physician smiled up at the taller man and patted him on the arm.

"Keep that up, Martin, and I'll ask Justice Morgan to permanently assign you to help me around my office."

"It would be my pleasure."

"Be careful, Martin, I may hold you to that." The doctor smiled at him and then began to look through the clothing. Martin held the pile while the elderly man went through the garments one by one. He noted that everything had been slashed except the victim's wig, cravat and white stockings. His tricorn hat and shoes had not been touched either.

"What do yo think happened? Why are some things cut and others not?"

"I'm not certain, but I suspect Sterling was tied down first and then his clothes were cut – it was probably done in that order so he couldn't put up a fight. I wonder why he was stripped."

"Doctor, I want to show you something I found in the bushes." Martin walked to a patch of bramble bushes at the edge of the clearing, bent down and returned with a broken pot in his hand. He held it out to the medical examiner.

The doctor took the pot and felt the sticky inside with his fingers. He smelled his fingers and gasped. "Meu Deus! It's a honey pot. The fiend spread honey over Sterling's body!"

Martin nodded. "That's what I thought when I found it."

"Once he was naked, the honey was spread over his body so the ants would be attracted to him. I'm sure you've seen how fast ants can find leftover food or sweets in the house."

Martin nodded. Many a morning he had awaken to see a trail of ants on the kitchen floor. Following the trail, he would find them moving to and from a morsel of food or sticky area. He shuddered, thinking of the hundreds of ants that had run over Sterling's body biting him.

"I'm finished now." The doctor handed the pile of clothes to Martin. "Take them to the justice when you go to town. The pot also must be taken to him. Que coisa! (What a thing!) I assume you will stay here until they bring out the death wagon to pick up the body."

"Yes, sir. I 'spect they'll be here any time now."

"Martin, before I leave please dig up one of the stakes. I want to see what the end looks like." He stood and stretched trying to relieve the backache he felt from leaning so long over the body.

"Yes, sir." The militiaman drew his sword and dug out a stake. It took him longer than he had expected and he grunted with the effort. "It was down deep, maybe two feet." He handed the stake to the doctor. "You can see from the smashed top it was hammered into the ground."

"Yes, I see." The doctor ran his finger over the end of the stake. "It's been brought to an almost perfect point."

"It was needed. The ground is full of rocks and brick

hard." Martin pointed to the hole.

"So I see. Take the stake along with the clothing to Major Morgan." The physician again patted Martin on the arm. "Now, I would appreciate your help climbing the hill to the wagon. I can surely handle the reins well enough to get myself back to town."

"Yes, sir." The militiaman was willing to do almost anything for the elderly doctor. He had treated Martin's ailing mother for years without charging her and had comforted her at home the last painful night of her life. When assigned to take him to the murder site, Martin had been more than willing to leave his blacksmith's stall and spend the morning with him.

The old physician smiled at Martin, a twinkle in his brown eyes. "You see what's ahead of you, John? Weakness and dependence! That's what long life gives you."

"Yes, sir. But it seems to me you're doing fine. I doubt I'll do near as well at your age. Even now you surely do things I can never do." Martin held out his hand to help him up the hill.

"I'll accept your flattery, but I don't believe a word of it." The doctor smiled again and grasped the young man by his forearm. "What can I possibly do that you cannot?"

"Well, sir, for one thing, I couldn't never get that close to any dead body – 'specially one with that stink. Worse than a skunk." Martin pointed to the covered corpse behind them.

"Yes, you could if you had all my years of practice. It's like shoeing a horse amid piles of manure. An experienced blacksmith becomes accustomed to the smell and never notices it."

While the medical examiner was in the western woods

that morning, Morgan met with the attorney general in his office. As usual, the justice sat in the chair facing the Englishman's desk. This time Palmer ate his breakfast of eggs and sausage while talking to Morgan.

"Ah, so Major Morgan, what have you to report to me about, ah… the terrible killing of Assemblyman Sterling?" The attorney general paused in the middle of his question to chew a piece of sausage. "I assume you saw the body of the poor man," he mumbled, bits of sausage showing in his mouth.

"I saw what remained of the man late yesterday afternoon. As you undoubtedly know, Sterling was staked to the ground and…"

"You do mean Assemblyman Sterling, don't you?" Palmer smiled over his cup of tea.

"Assemblyman Sterling was stripped naked, covered in honey and staked to the ground near a fire-ant nest – those little black ants whose bites are so painful. The honey attracted the ants to the assemblyman's naked body, and, since they are also drawn to fatty meat, which he possessed in abundance, his death was inevitable. By the time the unfortunate man was found, most of his bodily flesh had been consumed by scavengers and all his bones were exposed. His eyes had been plucked out by birds and…"

"That's quite enough. Can't you see I'm eating my breakfast? I'm all too well aware of the cruel manner of his death. What I want to know is your progress in finding his murderer."

Morgan could not suppress a smile, knowing the pompous Englishman would be upset by his description. "It's too early to report anything; we're just beginning to gather information."

"I damn well know that." Palmer glared at the justice. He had seen Morgan's smile and knew the gruesome description had been delivered to annoy him. "What I want to know now is what you are doing to find the murderer."

"I've already interviewed the men who found the body and sent Dr. Nunes Ribeiro to the site to examine the few remains of the dead man. Sergeant Stockwell has also been sent into the woods to find the route Sterling's horse took to town."

"Is that old Jew competent enough to find anything of importance? He must be seventy years old by now." Palmer knew Morgan and the doctor were friends. "I doubt Governor Wright will appoint him again as medical examiner." He ate the last of his eggs and dropped his silver fork noisily on the plate.

"The doctor is in his early sixties and still *quite* competent as both medical examiner and physician." Morgan now glared at Palmer. "And unless I'm mistaken, Mrs. Palmer will see no other physician in the colony nor will she take *your* children to anyone else."

"That has nothing to do with the Jew's competence as a medical examiner." Red-faced, the attorney general slapped his hand on the desk spilling his tea. "Clean it later," he shouted at Thackery, as the little man stood and started over to wipe up the spill.

Suppressing a smile again, Morgan spoke softly in contrast to the attorney general's raised voice. "There's no question about the doctor's competence as medical examiner. He continues to be informative, extremely thorough and insightful and I expect him to be of critical help in this murder investigation."

"I certainly hope so." Palmer had resumed his calm demeanor and he leaned back in his chair looking at Morgan with half-closed eyes. "I expect a written report on his efforts and any significant findings he makes."

Morgan nodded. "I'll talk to him later today when he returns from examining Sterling's corpse – that is what's left of it."

Palmer pointed his finger at the justice. "You need to show more respect for the remains of the distinguished assemblyman."

Morgan frowned in thought. "What is that Shakespeare wrote? 'Imperious Caesar, dead, and turn'd to clay, might stop a hole to keep the wind away.'"

Palmer sneered. "Oh, you've read Shakespeare, have you, Major? Then, what about his words, 'I read as much from the rattling tongue of saucy and audacious eloquence.' Ah, yes, Major, it seems evident you should use your attempts at wit on your colonial companions rather than attempt to be clever with better educated English gentlemen."

Morgan clenched his teeth, seeing Palmer's smug smile. He desperately wanted to reply with another literary insult, but knew it would further enrage the attorney general.

"Shall we go on?" Palmer continued to smile. "As you well know, Major, what happens to the old Jewish physician will be decided by Governor Wright – with my recommendations."

"The governor told Dr. Nunes Ribeiro that he would hold the office as long as he chose to do so." Morgan stared at Palmer, thinking how he hated the pompous Englishman. He saw him as a fat spider sucking the moisture out of a fly. He was like all the Englishmen who came to the colonies, making their fortunes and then returning home to live in luxury with colonial wealth.

"That may be as long as he's competent – in my judgment!" Palmer drank the last of his tea and beckoned Thackery to take the dirty dishes away. "Major, why is Stockwell looking for the route the horse followed to town?"

"It's our thinking the murderer rode the assemblyman's horse close to town, let him loose and then walked in through one of the gates."

"Why do you think that?" Oliver Palmer wiped his mouth with the white linen napkin. A tiny bit of egg remained in the corner of his mouth.

"The assemblyman's thoroughbred stallion is well known in town and the murderer faced the possibility of being seen if he rode the horse through the city gates."

"I see. Then how did his horse get into town without a rider?"

Morgan frowned. "We don't know that yet."

"I assume you will now speak to the guards at the gates to find out who might have come and gone the day Assemblyman Sterling rode out of town."

"That's correct. The problem is that Sterling left town two weeks ago and more than five hundred people have come and gone through the gates since then. We now can only hope the murderer made a memorable impression on one of the guards as he passed through the gates. It's unlikely, but we might get a bit of good fortune."

Palmer nodded. "I will expect your reports at least every other day unless something of significance is discovered. Then, of course, I will want to know it immediately. The assembly and the governor expect quick results. This is not the murder of some commoner in town after all. The governor himself visited the widow to offer his condolences."

"Do you want written reports as well?' Morgan stood, knowing the meeting had ended.

"Of course, Major, but do use Johnson's dictionary to correct your spelling. It has been appalling of late." Palmer smiled broadly as Morgan scowled and then abruptly turned and left the office.

After lunch, the justice walked to Christ Church. Halfway there, he was caught in a rain storm that pummeled

Savannah. Trying to avoid a soaking, Morgan took refuge under a large live oak until the downpour subsided to a drizzle. He hurried the rest of the way and only his hat and the shoulders of his military jacket were wet when he reached Johnson Square. The pouring rain returned as Morgan crossed the square and he ran to the church. A bolt of lightning flashed overhead as he opened the door. Inside, he shook the water from his hat and removed his sodden jacket. There was nothing he could do with his white stockings which had been soaked when he had splashed through a puddle in front of the church. Morgan moved to the side of the partition that separated the vestibule from the church interior and, wearing only his shirt and breeches, he strode unconcerned down the aisle. His shoes squeaked and left wet prints on the stone floor.

Reverend Percy Bartholomew stood talking to two elderly men at the altar. They turned to watch the justice as he approached. The men held stained towels in their hands.

Bartholomew gasped in mock surprise when he saw Morgan. "As I live and breathe, can it be that James Morgan has come to pray in the house of God?" Bartholomew's booming voice reverberated off the walls of the empty church.

Morgan smiled as he reached the pastor and received a hearty pat on his good shoulder. "You know better, Reverend. I continue to be the same unrepentant sinner."

"Ah, that's too bad, but I still have hope." Bartholomew, a mountain of a man well over six feet tall and weighing some 300 pounds, loomed over him. "Ah, James, with the exception of our occasional meetings in the street, I haven't seen you in the church since…"

"Since my mother died one year ago." Morgan nodded and held up one finger.

"I'm sorry, my son, I certainly did not intend to bring up sad memories." The minister spoke softly. He handed Morgan a clean white towel to dry himself.

"I know. The memories come whether provoked or not. But that's not why I'm here." Morgan dried his face on the towel and, after rubbing it over his hair, he hung it around his neck.

"I thought not." Bartholomew gave him a knowing look. "Do you know Mordecai Clay and Jason Wilson? They're here patiently putting up with my incessant suggestions on how to polish the church's altar pieces and communion plate. You can see how the silver chalice shines beautifully already. It's our monthly cleaning which these two good men have expertly done for forty-some-years."

"Fifty-eight years and three months, that is, including today's cleaning!" Jason Wilson glared at Bartholomew. The reverend smiled and nodded in agreement. "Please forgive me, Jason, I'm reaching that time in life when I too often forget things – important things"

"Yes, we know each other by sight." Morgan nodded at the men and, returning his silent greeting, they went back to work.

"Well, James, how may I be of help? I doubt you are here to talk about resuming your place in the church." Bartholomew stood with his arms crossed over his chest.

Morgan nodded. "We need to speak in private." The justice looked at the men cleaning the silver, but they did not turn their heads toward him.

"I see." The minister put his hand on Morgan's shoulder and guided him toward a bench at the back of the church. "We'll be out of earshot there." He pointed to the last row of benches before the vestibule.

Reverend Bartholomew had arrived in Savannah eight years earlier when the provincial assembly adopted the Church of England as its official religion. The articulate Anglican pastor, who soon became well known for his inspiring sermons, attracted a large following from all over the colony. Membership in Christ Church reached its highest level while he served in Savannah and even the front-row pews were packed on the Sundays he preached. Georgia colonists from settlements as far away as Darien and even Midway left home well before first light to reach the church in time for his sermons. Confident of his religious meaning in the colony, Bartholomew refused to make membership in the Anglican Church compulsory. All other local Protestants as well as Catholics and Jews were free to practice their faiths in Savannah. The nonconformists, however, were required to pay taxes to support Church salaries throughout the province.

Bartholomew gestured Morgan to a back bench on the main aisle, while he found a single chair which he moved into the aisle to face him. He sat close enough to reach over and touch the man across from him on the knee when he wanted to make a point. Morgan sat down and again wiped his face and hair with the towel.

"I assume you are here to talk about the terrible death of Thomas Sterling." Bartholomew sat heavily in the squeaking chair.

"Yes, Reverend, I've come to talk about the assemblyman." Morgan crossed his legs and several drops of water fell from his shoe to the floor. He spoke softly to make sure the men at the altar could not hear his words. "Tell me what you know of the man."

"I see you got soaked in the shower. Well, James, what I can say about Thomas Sterling is that he was a good Christian man – a fine father, a good husband and a caring member of this church and community. I sincerely mean what I am saying. I knew of no vices in the man and whatever flaws he may have had, he certainly never revealed them to me. Nor did I ever hear any other parishioners speak ill of him. In my opinion, Thomas Sterling was one of the best men in this town. He will be sorely missed."

Morgan shook his head. "Forgive me for saying so,

Reverend, but not many men receive such praise even at their funerals."

Bartholomew solemnly nodded in agreement. "It's true and I will repeat much of what I have said to you at his funeral this Friday. The man deserves praise and not the brutal treatment his body received from the fiend who murdered him. From what I've heard about the manner of his death, we will have to conduct a closed-casket service for the poor soul."

Morgan nodded. "Reverend, I would appreciate anything else you can tell me about the man. Was he a strong member of the church?" The justice ran his hand through his hair.

"Yes, absolutely. Thomas Sterling attended church regularly with his family and always was willing to donate his time, industry and money to the church's many projects and repairs. I never knew the man to be stingy – quite the opposite! He gave generously to whatever cause our church asked of him. He was, in fact, next on the list to be appointed to the vestry. Sterling was truly a good, good man." Bartholomew had tears in his eyes. "We will miss him very much," he murmured hoarsely, clearing his throat.

"Would you know of any enemies he might have had?"

"I would not. As far as I know, he was well liked and highly respected in town. I would assume he had some business competitors who might have resented his success and wealth, but I don't know who they would be." Bartholomew shook his head.

"I have only one more question. Sterling's sons told me he came to the church now and then in the afternoon. Would it be possible for you to tell me what he did while here with you? If it concerns his confession, I know you cannot…"

Bartholomew knew what Morgan intended to say and interrupted him. "He did not come to see me or confess. He came to meet the junior warden, Archibald Willington. It seems they had been friends for awhile and the assemblyman would meet him here every so often."

"Ah." Morgan nodded, wondering why Bartholomew had emphasized the word seems. "I understand Willington only recently became the junior warden of the vestry."

"That's correct. Willington had served for three years as a vestryman and, at the meeting in March, he was unanimously elected junior warden."

Morgan raised his eyebrows. "Isn't that a short time of service to become a warden?"

"Yes, it is given his very limited knowledge of church doctrine and obvious lack of vestry experience." Bartholomew frowned. "There are at least ten other more knowledgeable and much wiser vestrymen who might have been selected for that important post."

"Then, why was he elected?"

"I'm not certain since I was not invited to attend that meeting. Apparently, I made the mistake of telling the senior warden what I thought of the man before the meeting of the vestry." Bartholomew shook his head from side to side. "I would guess Willington was elected because of the *copious* financial contributions he has made to the church in the last few years. With only three exceptions, he has given the most generous contributions in that time."

Morgan smiled and leaned back and folded his arms across his chest. "Surely that's not surprising to you, Reverend. Doesn't money always decide such decisions? My father has said it well, 'money makes any man smell good, even if it's well known he never bathes.' There must be something else about Willington you don't like."

"We both know your father is as cynical as you. You are truly birds of a feather." The reverend's face reddened and he raised his voice. "No, a man's wealth is not always why he is made a vestryman or warden of Christ Church. We have several men on the vestry who are of humble means. But, of course, with the upcoming costs of refurbishing the church interior and repairing the old leaking roof, money is needed and the vestry does look for large contributions from its members. Surely even you can understand our financial needs." Bartholomew saw the men at the altar looking at him and lowered his voice. "Well, we were talking about Willington," he said, sighing in an effort to calm himself.

Morgan nodded. "I asked you what was it about the man…"

"I know what you asked me," interrupted Bartholomew, still irritated. "I assume what I say will not be repeated, James." He stared into Morgan's eyes.

Morgan nodded. "After all these years, you know me well enough, Reverend. I'm not a gossip and I don't talk out of turn." He saw doubt in the minister's eyes. "Nor do I reveal secrets when I drink, if that's what you are thinking."

"That's not what I was thinking." Bartholomew saw Morgan's narrowed eyes and tight-lipped mouth and knew he was angry.

"What then?" He leaned forward. "Do you think I talk in my sleep to Claudia Barclay?"

"Please, James. I'm not worried about what you might say. It's that I don't usually talk about our vestrymen – that is, speak critically about them. But *that man* worries me."

"I see." Morgan sat back in his seat again and stretched his legs out in the aisle.

"I think I can sum up my concern about the man by quoting Shakespeare. Caesar's view of the villain, Cassius, is quite the same as mine about Willington. 'Let me have men about me that are fat, sleek-headed men such as sleep o' nights. Yond Cassius has a lean and hungry look; he thinks too much; such men are dangerous.'"

Morgan hid his smile. It amused him to think Shakespeare had been used three times as an insult, once by himself. "So, you don't know why Sterling and Willington met?"

"No. I never understood why Thomas Sterling would

have a friendship with Willington. It may be that the junior warden invested or loaned some of his considerable wealth to Sterling's shipping business." Bartholomew grimaced when he referred to Willington as the junior warden. "The Sterling Shipping Company was in dire straits before Willington arrived in town. At the time, Thomas himself told me he feared losing everything. It seems he lacked the dock space to handle the new ships and larger shipments sent to and from England. His competitors who built longer docks along the river came to control most of the commerce and Sterling lost most of his customers. Then, he had his own wharf extended and everything changed for the better. Where Thomas got the necessary money to pay for the costly extension, I don't know." Bartholomew frowned. "It was at the same time that Willington arrived in Savannah and that's why I suspect some of his money was put into the Sterling Shipping Company."

"I think that's a reasonable assumption." Morgan stroked his chin. "Well, we'll know soon, when Sterling's sons take ownership of the shipping company. If Willington has claims, I'm certain there will be lawyers involved in the settlement of Sterling's estate. They're like flies on a carcass in such a case."

"Yes, indeed. If Willington has money in the company, you can be sure he will hire the most ruthless lawyer in town to pursue his interests."

Morgan nodded. "When did Willington arrive in Savannah?"

"Three or four years ago. I'm not sure exactly when he arrived. He was not a member of the church initially." Bartholomew rubbed a hand over his forehead.

"Do you know where Willington came from?"

"He told everyone he was born and lived in Virginia, but I seriously doubt it. He said he made his fortune in tobacco and then sold his land and slaves to move here."

Bartholomew shook his head. "I had my first church in Williamsburg and lived there eight years before coming here. But, in all those years, I never head of a tobacco planter named Archibald Willington; in fact, I never heard of him at all. Keep in mind, Williamsburg is where the Legislature meets and most of the planters congregate there when it's in session. Even the small planters come to town then, though as you would expect the large planters dominate the Legislature. It's the same in all the colonies, isn't it? Anyway, since the planters come to Williamsburg time and time again, they're well known to the townsfolk."

"So, in all your time in Williamsburg no one named Willington ever came to town."

"No, not that I recall."

"I see. Well, whether or not Willington came by his wealth in Virginia, we'll soon see if he put any of it into Sterling's company. If so, that would certainly explain their friendship and the frequency of their meetings." As Morgan stood to leave, it occurred to him that a financial arrangement between them might also have had something to do with Sterling's murder.

Bartholomew nodded and stood facing Morgan. "Well, James, I sincerely hope to see you here in church someday soon." Bartholomew's eyes twinkled as he smiled. "It would also be a blessing if your father accompanied you."

Morgan handed him the wet towel.

A cold wind unexpectedly blew through Savannah early that evening and, by six o'clock, everyone in town had their fireplaces going and previously stored blankets returned to their beds.

The wind came out of the northwest and followed the

afternoon rains that left almost impassable puddles on the streets. After an exceptionally warm spring and even warmer early summer, the townspeople were stunned to find themselves shivering in late May. They huddled around their fireplaces at home before bedtime and wore winter nightclothes to bed, hoping the cold would be gone the next day. Following sunset, they stayed inside behind tightly closed doors and, except for hasty trips to outhouses, rarely ventured outside. Most of those who did leave the warmth of their homes left only to run to woodpiles for armloads of logs. The many who had used up all their wood in the winter were forced to wrap themselves in blankets.

Morgan was one of very few men in town who rode his horse after dark. He left home at eight o'clock when the wind finally slackened. Dressed in his woolen army coat, he ignored the cold and rode his stallion through the empty streets to the house of Claudia Barclay. Bent low in the saddle looking for potholes, Morgan guided the horse around deep puddles and past gapping holes and gullies. A full moon helped him find his way, but buffeted on and off by the wind, it took him forty minutes to reach the big white house on the square.

Morgan rode to the stable at the back of the two-story building and, dismounting, he threw open the heavy door and led his black stallion inside. He walked the horse into the second of the three stalls and left him to eat the pile of hay that had been set out on the floor. Morgan entered the house through the unlocked side door and walked through the kitchen, dining room and into the sitting room. He found Claudia Barclay standing in front of the stone fireplace, flaming logs lighting the chimney behind her. Morgan stopped for a second, struck by the sight of her smiling face haloed by the light of the fire. He then strode across the room and put his arm around her.

Claudia, a small slender woman with hair and eyes as

dark as night, sighed as he bent to kiss her. Morgan threw his coat on the floor and nestled his head in her hair. He smelled the flower fragrance she always wore and hugged her to him. Continuing to embrace her, Morgan closed his eyes thankful she loved him.

Claudia Barclay was a thirty-three-year-old widow from Spanish St. Augustine. She met her deceased husband, Ruben Barclay, twelve years earlier when he sailed south to Florida to sell a shipment of silk. Her father, Miguel López Moreno, purchased several rolls of fabric from the English merchant the first day he arrived in port. The Spaniard bought the silk for his wife and four daughters and, while his wife selected the colors and patterns she wanted, the Englishman visited his home and met his family. Barclay was immediately enchanted by Claudia and, three days before his ship sailed, he asked her father for her hand in marriage. López Moreno agreed, though with some reluctance. He would have preferred his eighteen-year-old daughter marry a Spaniard, but with few worthwhile suitors in St. Augustine, he accepted Barclay's proposal.

He told his wife, "The Englishman will give Claudia a good home and many comforts, even if he is a Protestant. She will get much more with him than with any of the arrogant and useless officers in this presidio. Besides, Claudia seems to like him well enough." Her father's only condition for the marriage was Barclay's promise to permit Claudia to remain a practicing Catholic in Savannah. Ruben Barclay agreed to the Spaniard's condition and, six months later when he brought Claudia home to Georgia, she became one of a small group of Catholics in the Protestant community. Despite the many years she had lived in Savannah, Claudia Barclay still spoke English with a distinct accent and used Spanish words and phrases.

"You look much chilled to the bones." Claudia looked up at him and stroked his face with her hands. "Sit yourself and

I bring to you a glass of vino rojo."

Morgan sat in a stuffed chair near the fireplace, looking into the flames. He felt at peace for the first time that day. It always seemed that way when he entered her house and was in her arms. Claudia made him feel warm and secure and wanted for himself. It was a feeling he had not found with any other woman since his return to Savannah with one arm. The three women he courted before Claudia had said his missing arm was unimportant to them, but he never believed them. He feared they saw him as the future heir of his father's prosperous rice plantation and a rich prospect for marriage. Morgan felt no such worries about Claudia. She had no need of his wealth. Her deceased husband had left her a handsome annual allowance as well as the house in Savannah and sugar lands in Jamaica.

Morgan also felt confident that his lost arm was of little concern to her. She treated him as if he had few if any bodily limitations and could do almost all the things other men could do, though somewhat slower. The things he could not do with one hand, like lifting a heavy pot, she helped him handle as if they were everyday tasks requiring two people's hands. The more time Morgan spent with her, the less he worried about what she thought about his missing arm. After seven months in Claudia's company, he did not even flinch when she touched his left shoulder or accidentally brushed her fingers over the stump. Claudia saw the changes in him and, though he never spoke of his feelings, she sensed his comfort with her. By that time, she even took the risk to tease him about the time it took for him to undress her before they made love.

As Morgan sat waiting for her return, he smiled, thinking about the last time she teased him before they nakedly came together in her soft feather bed. Claudia saw him smiling when she returned with a bottle of wine and two glasses.

"What is funny to you?" She looked into his eyes.

"Nothing. I was smiling, thinking of you." Morgan grinned at her.

"Ah, mentiroso (liar)!" Claudia handed him a glass of wine and carefully eased herself into his lap, a glass in her hand. She touched the edge of her glass against his and toasted him in Spanish. "Salud, amor y pesetas y el tiempo para gustarlos."

"You know I like that one." Morgan sighed contentedly. "Health, love and money and the time to enjoy them. There's really nothing else in life, is there?"

"No, mi amor, nada más." Claudia kissed his forehead.

Morgan smiled as she leaned back and snuggled against him. The warmth of her body immediately spread over him and, in seconds, the chill he felt from outside disappeared.

"I forget almost to tell you, mi amor, Precioso returns at last. Pobrecito! He suffers a torn ear. He fights the gray cat from the house of the Simpsons."

Morgan wondered how the Simpsons' cat had fared after a fight with Precioso. Claudia's orange cat looked to be as big as a bobcat and his head was as broad as the palm of his hand. "If he fought with their cat, I'm sure you'll hear about it, that is, if he's still alive."

"Sí – yes. Señora Simpson only talk to me, how you say it, when to complain." Claudia sighed weary of her neighbors' disapproving looks. Even their children turned their backs to her when they saw her in the yard She knew it all stemmed from Morgan's nighttime visits.

Morgan grimaced. "I'm sorry, I know it's because of me." He drank the last of his wine and, holding the empty glass by the stem, rolled it around.

"No importa." Claudia stuck out her chin in defiance, but her eyes were moist. "I have no worry what they think. Only mi familia makes me worry." She sighed and reached over for the wine bottle.

"I know." Morgan sighed. He knew her family would condemn her if they learned of her love affair with him. Without marriage she would be regarded as a whore and Claudia lived with dread that they would hear of her life with him. He saw a tear appear in the corner of her eye. "Your family is too far away to know about me, mi amor and no one in Havana has talked of visiting. So, how would they find out?" Morgan kissed her cheek as she refilled his glass.

Claudia's entire family now lived in Cuba and no one had visited her in Savannah since the death of Ruben Barclay in the summer of 1765. Two of her sisters and their husbands had sailed from Havana as soon as they received her letter. They stayed with Claudia for six weeks, helping settle her husband's financial affairs. Her father had refused to join them on the voyage. He hated anything English after England had taken Spanish Florida following the Seven Years War.

López Moreno and his family sailed from St. Augustine along with 3,000 other Floridians as English soldiers arrived in St. Augustine. The Spaniards completely emptied the two hundred-year-old colony at the urging of their king, Charles III. He warned the Floridians of the Protestant heresy that would come with English rule. Within days of the king's message, preparations were begun for the abandonment of the colony. In the end, the entire Spanish population left Florida, except for seven people, one a spy. They boarded ships sailing to Havana and Vera Cruz and some of the recent dead were even taken to be buried in Spanish soil.

López Moreno and his family were aboard the first ship to leave. He wanted nothing to do with the arriving English bastardos. The family sailed to Havana and purchased a home in an older residential district of the city.

"Sí, mi amor. But who knows what happens in time. It is said escándalo (scandal) flies everywhere on the wind. If my father hears, it kills him. He would lose his honor. Without honor, he dies." Claudia choked as she spoke and tears fell down her cheeks.

"That won't happen. He won't find out." Morgan tried to calm Claudia, but he knew her father could indeed learn of their love affair. A merchant carrying goods to or from Cuba might spread a story about them that would reach López Moreno's ears. It could happen at any time.

"I hope no, mi amor. Que Dios no lo permita. (Hopefully, God won't let it happen.)" Claudia dabbed her wet eyes with the linen napkin she had placed on the table. She sighed.

"How is Carolina today?" Morgan changed the subject. "Has her fever gone down yet?"

Carolina Braga Furtado was a forty-year-old Portuguese widow who lived with Claudia. She and her retarded son, Felipe, moved into the house seven weeks after Ruben Barclay died. Claudia invited them at the suggestion of Doctor Nunes Ribeiro. The doctor thought the widows would be less lonely living together. They were both Catholic and had become acquainted at the home of the family, where Mass was performed twice a month. An itinerant priest from Charles Towne rode to Savannah during the first and last weeks of each month. Carolina and Felipe had two rooms upstairs on one side of the house and Claudia occupied a suite of four rooms on the other side. The women shared the downstairs rooms and took turns cleaning them weekly. They ate most of their meals together even when Morgan spent the night.

"It leaves. Carolina is better, but lastíma (sadly) Felipe suffers now the high fever. He no can sleep and cries all the night. Pobrecito!" Claudia drank the last of her wine and rose to refill their glasses.

"No more, tonight. I've already drunk too much and have a headache. Let's go to bed."

"Sí, mi amor."

Morgan saw the sadness in Claudia's face as she turned to him with outstretched arms. He had failed to assuage her anxiety and knew she still worried her father would find out about them. There was nothing he could say or do to dispel her fear of discovery. All he could do that cold night was to hold her close and caress her to sleep.

That night, another resident of Savannah also feared discovery – the discovery of who had killed Thomas Sterling. It seemed unlikely that anyone would find out and yet it was hard not to worry. Everything had gone precisely as planned, but a mistake might have been made and overlooked at the time. "If so, what could it be? Surely, no one had seen them together."

They left town separately and Sterling rode to the lake alone. They met at the top of the hill and no one had seen them there or down by the lake. Except for the little noise Sterling made stumbling down the hill, there were few other unnatural sounds. Once he was bound and gagged, the muffled sounds of his moaning could not be heard much beyond where he lay on the ground. What followed was quiet as well. The dense woods seemed as serene as if nothing had happened. Afterward, the departure from the lake had gone as expected. With the exception of three grazing deer, no one saw the climb up the hill. Sterling's stallion stood at the top where he had been tied and no one saw him or his hooded rider moving slowly through the woods. Nor had anyone seen the horse set free outside the city or the nonchalant walk out of the woods and through the busy southern gate into Savannah.

It was probably foolish to worry about being discovered. No one had seen anything that could lead to suspicions or arrest. Yet, the fears remained even after a solitary walk in the chilly night air and a hot cup of tea at home. A restless sleep had followed with nightmares of the dead man covered with ants rising from the ground.

CHAPTER THREE

SAVANNAH: THURSDAY, MAY 28 – TUESDAY, JUNE 3, 1766

Morgan and Stockwell spent all Thursday morning looking over the murder site a second time. They found nothing new. The heavy rains earlier in the week had washed away all signs of human presence at the lake. Even the shoe prints of the men who carted off the corpse were gone. With the stakes removed, the place where Sterling had been bound was now covered with pinecones and needles. The entire site looked much like it did before the murder.

"It looks like nature has restored the woods with one rainstorm," observed Morgan.

"It does and even that awful stench is gone," Stockwell nodded. "It's good we looked the place over before the rain. I don't think anything would be different if I came out here yesterday either. I wouldn't have seen anything else, I'd wager." On Wednesday, Morgan told Stockwell to take a last look at the site, but a cracked horseshoe kept him in town at the blacksmith's stall.

"You're probably right. It would've been too muddy out here." Morgan sighed. "Except for the wooden stakes and bindings, the murderer left nothing behind to find."

"What about the honey pot?"

"It's much too common to be useful. There must be hundreds of them in town – one exactly like it is in every house and tavern."

Stockwell sneezed, took a wrinkled handkerchief from his pocket and blew his nose. "I get the catarrh every year this time. It makes my eyes itchy and my nose runs all the time."

"You ought to ask the doctor about it." Morgan waited as Stockwell sneezed again.

"It don't last long." He blew his nose again. "You know, he did make one mistake, the murderer. He let the horse go with the red clay on his legs."

"True. But that only let us know that he had ridden over red clay on the path through the woods. It doesn't tell us anything about the rider."

"It told us he lives in town and how he got back there."

"Yes, and wasn't that clever? He rides Sterling's horse along the path to a spot near the southern gate where he can easily walk into town. He walks casually into town without anyone noticing him. Why? Because he looks like everyone else." Morgan smiled crookedly. "Oh yes, this murderer's quite clever. It's obvious he planned the murder well ahead of time."

"Do you think it's worth looking the path over again to see if he dropped anything along the way? Those two fools was with me when I rode that way before." Stockwell made a face. "I might have missed something with them babbling behind me."

"I doubt it, but I suppose to be thorough you should look the route over again. But walk it this time. Didn't you tell me that Canfield and Colby walked behind your horse? I assume they didn't see anything or you would have told me."

"They was there all right, but I wouldn't believe anything they said they saw. They didn't want to be there to begin with and was too busy blaming each other for losing the boar to look at anything. I told them to shut up and look along the path, but that did me little good. I should go look now I'm here. Maybe I'll see something I missed." Stockwell saluted the major and led his horse toward the path.

Morgan stood alongside his horse and watched Stockwell disappear into the woods. He could feel the sun's heat on his shoulders and knew it was near noon. The brief cold period had ended and, when the winds subsided, the heat and humidity returned with a vengeance.

"They came back like cockroaches in the night," thought Morgan, recalling the old saying his mother had often used. He wiped the sweat from his brow with his fingers and smeared it on the empty sleeve of his jacket. "Damned heat! It's already too damned hot and there're at least a hundred days of summer yet to go." He hit a mosquito that landed on his neck.

Mounting his horse, it occurred to Morgan that once the summer arrived he felt less pain in the shoulder where his arm had been amputated. Some summer days, in fact, he felt no pain at all. Doctor Ribeiro told him to expect those times in the summer. The doctor said he would feel more pain in the cold and damp and less in the heat and as usual the wise old man was right.

"I suppose I should stop complaining and look at the brighter side of life," thought Morgan as he urged his horse to a trot toward town. His father used the same words when he complained or cried as a boy. He remembered one such incident when his father refused to give him a horse until he was big enough to saddle him. He had a vivid recollection of his father facing him in the stable, shaking his head from side to side as he begged and whined. He had stomped out of the stable as his father repeated the words.

Morgan had to admit that he liked living in Savannah despite the long hot summers. As he approached the southern gate, he thought of how striking the area around town looked in late spring and early summer. With blossoms and new green leaves on the trees, everything seemed fresh and lush. There was even a sweet smell in the air. He inhaled deeply, wondering what tree had flowered to produce such a fragrance. He looked around, but could see no blossoming tree he recognized.

Arriving at the gate, Morgan found himself in a long line of ten horsemen and six wagons waiting to enter Savannah. He waited an hour when the rear axle on a merchant's wagon broke and the heavily laden carriage collapsed and blocked the entrance. The merchant had reached the head of the line before the accident and it took the two guards and nine other men to unpack the wagon and push it out of the way. The merchant, a bent-over old man from Charles Towne, could do nothing but watch the men straining to move the heavy carriage. While other horsemen dismounted to push the wagon out of the way, Morgan remained seated on his stallion, knowing he would be of little help. Afterward, at Morgan's insistence, the merchant gave each of the men who helped him a shilling. The old man wanted to refuse when told to pay them, but Morgan's commanding voice changed his mind. He made a sour face and reluctantly handed the coins out one by one to the men.

Morgan held his horse to a walk when he finally entered Savannah. Glancing around, he thought the colony looked especially good in spring. Flowers were in bloom all around town and house gardens flourished with the blossoms and buds of the first vegetables already in sight. A number of the older houses had been freshly whitewashed and most of the streets had been swept clean. Everything seemed bright and spotless in the sunlight, though Morgan knew a closer look at the buildings would reveal cracked paint, broken planks and rotted roofs. Still, the old town's sparkling appearance that sunny day made him smile with pleasure as he rode through the streets.

After thirty-two years of both good and bad times, Savannah finally had begun to display signs of a sustained prosperity. The province's cotton, rice and tobacco production were steadily increasing every year and the Savannah River at the eastern edge of the settlement had become a major trade route to and from England. The known success of local farming and river commerce had produced a new movement of immigration and settlers and traders from the other American colonies as well as abroad arrived in town every time a ship docked at the pier. With the influx of new residents, house building seemed to be in progress on every piece of empty land in town. Morgan thought that at one time he knew or at least recognized everyone in the colony and now he saw strangers walking the streets every day of the week.

In the last fifteen years, the population had grown from 2,000 to more than 3,000 people, including slaves. The founder of Savannah, James Oglethorpe, had strictly forbidden the use or residence of slaves in the settlement, but by 1749, only a few years after he left America for the last time, the local planters had been granted the right to use slave labor in the colony. Matthew Morgan had been one of the most vociferous advocates of slavery and his son had been equally vociferous denouncing the planters' demands for slaves.

Morgan, then twenty-three years old, spoke out publicly and called the planters *Currency Christians*. He denounced them at a town council meeting, where the planters gathered to make their demands. Red-faced with anger, he stood and accused them of hypocrisy. "You're greedy hypocrites!" he shouted. "You praise the founder for his foresight and astute planning and then you seek to reject his prohibition of slavery. A firm prohibition, I might add. You make grand sounding speeches and talk of the need for Christian morality among the people in Savannah and then you want to buy other people as chattel and use them as slaves on your plantations. Tell me, what kind of Christians are you? Greedy Christians, that's who you are! It's all because slaves will cost only a few morsels of food and free men must be paid for their work."

An outburst of angry replies followed and young Morgan was shouted down. His father said nothing at the town meeting, but later told him his remarks had been foolishly idealistic and naïve. They quarreled bitterly and did not talk to each other for months. Morgan moved to town when the first slaves arrived at the plantation and thereafter visited his parents only on Sundays. He smiled recalling the incident. "I was naïve," he said aloud. "I was too young to realize then that greed is always present in men's affairs. And, I expect when the Sterling killing is settled, greed will somehow be involved."

At two o'clock that afternoon, Morgan rode over to the house of Doctor Nunes Ribeiro. Returning to the courthouse, he found a note on the office door inviting him to a mid-day meal. Morgan usually visited the physician in the evening on Monday and Friday and, on those nights, they played chess and talked late into the night. The two men became friends after the wounded soldier returned from the war. Morgan went to see the physician about a nagging infection in his shoulder and, during visits for treatment, they found their time together enjoyable and decided to meet for an evening of chess. That first evening led to many more over the last five years.

Before Morgan visited the doctor, he rode to the town cemetery and, from far behind the many gathered mourners, he watched the final moments of Thomas Sterling's funeral. He then rode home to clean up after the dusty ride. The major washed his face, neck and chest and put on a clean but badly wrinkled shirt. By the time he left, his house was already hot from the mid-afternoon sun and his shirt stuck to his back as he closed the door. Trying to stay out of the sun, Morgan rode beneath the sprawling tree limbs as he rode to the Portuguese section of town.

Built under a huge live oak with widely outstretched limbs, the small four-room house was spared much of the daily sun and remained relatively cool during most of the summer. "At least until July," the doctor told the patients who came to his house for treatment. In May and June, his little house was cooled by a light breeze that blew through the rooms in the morning and the late afternoon. The *welcome wind* as the physician called it, seemed to emerge from the base of the live oak at the back of the house. It came in through the bedroom windows and flowed out the windows in the front room. When the wind ceased at mid-day, he closed all the windows to keep flies and mosquitoes from entering the house. "It's all very mysterious," he told Morgan. "I have no idea where the wind comes from or why it visits twice a day. I can only think that it's a gift from the live oak for leaving it intact when I had the house built."

The morning breeze had ended by the time Morgan arrived, but the house still felt cool as he sat down to eat with his host. María Adela served the meal to the men and then joined them at the table. No one ate until she prayed aloud, thanking God for the food. Her prayers at meals had become a daily ritual in the doctor's house despite his indifference to religion. María Adela had come to his home as a girl to nurse his dying wife and, over the past few years, she had taken charge of all the household affairs. Appreciative of her devoted care of his wife and her help later in his surgery, the doctor readily agreed to her request for prayers before meals. He looked down at his hands as María Adela closed her eyes and prayed.

The physician had been religious in his youth, but lost his fervor over the years. "I was steeped in Jewish scripture as a young man," he had told Morgan. "In fact it was my obstinate resistance to conversion that ultimately led me to interrogation by the Portuguese Inquisition."

They ate braised deer meat seared in the fireplace, pickled beets and baked bread. With the meal, they drank a bottle of Spanish red wine a patient had given the physician. The major finished most of the bottle, while the doctor, who drank little more than a medicinal tumbler at bedtime, nursed a half glass of wine. María Adela did not drink since wine made her sick. The doctor opened another bottle, a deep red port, after their meal. He always kept a full bottle in the house for Morgan. He carried it along with their glasses to the low table that stood between the two cushioned wooden chairs in the front of the house.

The front or main room served as a kitchen and sitting room. It was sparsely furnished with a table and four chairs at the rear of the room and the two cushioned chairs along with a low table in front. The table stood between the chairs. A built-in wall bookcase filled with medical books and the doctor's large collection of leather-bound literature, mostly written in Spanish and Portuguese, took up one side of the room and the fireplace the other side. The doctor's surgery was in a separate room connected to the living quarters by a door, built into the bookcase. The surgery had its own outside entrance.

"Well, mi amigo, how do you feel this week?" The doctor looked at Morgan as he filled a glass of port for him.

"Actually, I feel pretty good. Almost no pain, except in the morning when I first get up."

He noticed the doctor's trembling fingers as he handed him the glass of wine. Morgan had not seen any trembling the last time they were together and it worried him. "That was no more than a week ago," he thought.

"Bom. Now that it's warmer you should feel better each coming day."

"How about you? How are you feeling?" Morgan tried not to stare at the older man as he questioned him. He noted that his face looked drawn and pale and his hair and beard seemed somehow whiter than usual. Morgan made a mental note to talk to María Adela alone and ask her about the doctor's health.

"Oh, I'm fine, James. Of course, I'm getting older and I feel it every day." He snickered. "I could give you a lengthy list of complaints and minor pains, but let's not talk about the rusting of this old wagon. I would much rather talk about the murder of Thomas Sterling..." He paused, seeing María Adela at the door.

"I'm going to the market. Is there anything you want from there?"

"No, but please stop at the Douglas Shipping Company and see if any of the medicines I ordered have come in from London. If so, tell them to put the charges on my account."

María Adela nodded. "Adiós." She smiled shyly at Morgan.

"Até logo," the doctor replied as María Adela quietly closed the door. "That girl is a gift from God I worry I will lose one of these days. I don't know what I would do without her." He sighed. "She's as good to me as any daughter could be. But one day I know she will marry and be gone. I hope I'm dead and buried by that time."

"Is anyone courting her?" Morgan sipped his port.

"Any number of men, some with very good prospects, have tried to court her, but she has rejected all of their advances. Your man Stockwell has been one of them, although he has been quite subtle in his approach." The doctor smiled. "He does little more than say hello to her."

"I'm not at all surprised. His mere presence makes most men stammer, but with women he's the one who can't find a word to say."

"I've seen that when he's here with María Adela. Well, I think we should talk about the murder of Thomas Sterling. There's a lot to discuss."

Morgan nodded. "There is."

"His murder certainly was vicious. That's a physician's understatement, of course. I've never seen anything like it all my years as medical examiner."

"It was incredibly cruel! It's obvious the murderer hated Sterling and carefully planned his death to be as painful as possible."

"That would be my assumption. Everything was set up before he and his victim arrived at the lake. The spot was cleared of broken branches and tree debris; the stakes I suspect already were there as well as the hammer and honey pot. I would think they were hidden in the bushes or under leaves. They would have been much too heavy and bulky to carry there at the time of the murder and, if seen, of course, would have raised suspicion." The doctor paused to take a white handkerchief from his pocket and wipe the moisture from the corners of his mouth.

"I agree. I also suspect the murderer tested the ground sometime earlier to see how deep the stakes would have to be driven to hold the man down."

"I'm sure you're right. Those stakes were hammered as many as twenty inches into the ground. Sterling had no chance to free himself."

"None! He could barely move, if at all. I don't know anyone, including Stockwell, who could pull up the stakes from a supine position. He tried when we returned to the murder site this morning and had trouble even standing over them. The stakes varied a bit in length, but none was shorter than twenty-four inches; so, four inches stood above the ground. Whoever killed Sterling had to work hard to pound them twenty inches into the hard ground. He had to be very strong of arm. The stakes were an inch and a quarter square and made of yellow pine."

"What do you think they were made from? They are too thick to be barrel staves." The doctor reached over and filled Morgan's wine glass again.

"I think they might be slats used to make cages for animals. Maybe for hogs or hunting dogs. I've seen cages with similar slats, some on wagons."

"Ah, yes. That makes sense. Lógico." The doctor nodded.

"I've sent Stockwell to talk to the town carpenters, but, as yet, none of them has recalled anyone asking recently for similar slats or slatted cages. So far, he has talked to about half the carpenters in town."

"You are assuming the man lives in town, are you not?"

"I am. The fact that he rode Sterling's horse through the woods so he would be near the southern gates tells me he lives here. The cloth bands used to bind him are also from some local man's corduroy breeches. They are old faded brown breeches and probably were discarded here in town. There was also a corduroy-cloth gag in Sterling's mouth. You didn't see it – I took it when I first saw the body."

"I noticed some threads in his teeth and intended to tell you about them."

"The honey pot is also from town – made in Isaiah Thorpe's ceramic shop over there on Broughton Street. His initials are cut into the bottom of the pot as well as all the others in town. You probably have one like it in your house."

"I do. In fact, we broke ours and bought a new one a couple of weeks ago. María Adela brought it to me this morning for my tea. By the way, it was the blacksmith, young John Martin, who found the honey pot." The doctor sipped his port. "I've known him since he was a baby – actually I helped bring him into this world. He had a twisted umbilical cord."

"Is that so? He gave me the impression that you found the honey pot."

The doctor smiled. "Martin is a fine young man – quite intelligent as well as modest. He knew at once the murderer had spread honey on Sterling to hasten the ants to his body."

Morgan nodded. "That's another sign of the murderer's careful planning. He's a clever one! He knew those black ants would be attracted to a sweet substance like honey. He also was aware of their nest in the rock pile so far from town."

The doctor nodded. "He is shrewd, quite shrewd! He's a man who knows a lot and thinks ahead. Do you have anyone in mind as the murderer?"

"No, not yet, though I think he's a white man. Of course, there will be those who will see the use of ants in the killing as the act of an Indian. The honey is likely to add to that impression. We must make sure the honey is not mentioned in town. I don't want some drunken fool to hear about it and accuse the Indians of killing Sterling. That could lead to an angry mob and a bloody war with them. They have been restive lately as it is."

"Quite so. This isn't a murder that can be blamed on the Indians."

"No. That's why I told both Stockwell and the blacksmith to say nothing to anyone about the discovery of the honey pot. Nothing but trouble can come of it."

"A wise decision. The Indians might well have used that method to kill an enemy, but they would not have used the white man's materials to do it. They would have used cords made from animal hides to bind the man, not manufactured cloth made in England. Nor would they tie him to stakes made by an English carpenter. They would have cut and shaped tree branches for that purpose."

"That's my thinking." Morgan sipped his wine. "I also can't imagine an Indian carrying honey to the site in one of Isaiah Thorpe's honey pots."

The doctor chuckled. "There's one more element to the murder that rules them out."

"What's that?"

"It's the way the bindings were tied." The doctor reached into his pocket and pulled out a piece of the cloth binding he had taken from one of the stakes. "They were tied with knots only a white man would make." He reached across the table and showed Morgan the knot. "See how the binding was crossed twice before being tied; that's to make certain the knot won't slip loose. The double crossed knot is commonly used by seamen, as well as physicians doing surgery. I use it when sewing up wounds to make sure the stitches stay in place. I assume other white men use the knot, too – fishermen, for example."

Morgan raised his eyebrows. "Very interesting. I don't tie a knot that way, but I can see how it would be more secure. It's another example of the cleverness of this murderer."

"It is indeed." The doctor again wiped the moisture from the corners of his mouth.

"You know, one of the questions that troubles me is how the murderer managed to get out to the woods without being seen. I know he didn't ride out with Sterling. Stockwell spoke to the soldiers who stood at the gates that afternoon and, although Sterling was observed, none of them saw anyone with him. Two of them recalled seeing Sterling leaving town through the southern gate. That purple suit was hard to miss. He was also seen by a squad of cavalry troops on the west road. The lieutenant who led them said he was riding alone."

"That means the murderer either rode out separately or went there in a carriage or wagon. Of course, he could have walked, but it would have taken even a strong man a couple of hours to get to the lake. I would think it's about five miles from the southern gates."

Morgan nodded. "It is and I can't imagine the murderer putting himself through such an ordeal, never mind wasting that much time. He's too shrewd for that."

"So what other possibilities are there? Of course, he could have ridden his own horse and pulled Sterling's horse behind him on the way back to town." The doctor grimaced as he crossed his legs. "Arthritis," he explained.

"I considered that possibility, but I see it as too risky. A single man on a horse would be much less likely to be noticed than a man leading a second horse, especially Sterling's stallion. I think this murderer is too clever to take such a risk."

"You're right. He also could have ridden part of the distance and left his horse secreted somewhere along the way."

Morgan sighed and drank the rest of the wine. "That's possible, but I think there would be too many hazards to that scheme as well. There would be the possibility of someone finding the horse or seeing him leaving or returning to the hiding place. He would also have to find a way to return to the horse without being seen."

The doctor nodded. "So, that leaves a carriage or wagon as his only reasonable means to reach the lake. However, I saw no wheel lines or flattened grass when I arrived except for those made by Martin's wagon. I also carefully looked over the ground again as I left. Of course, the death wagon arrived after I left and I assume its wheel marks were there as well."

"There were none when I returned there. The rains obliterated all signs of the murder as well as any tracks the wagons made." Morgan grimaced. "So, for now, we are left without an explanation of how the murderer reached the lake; that means he might have walked."

"But you don't think he walked, do you?"

"No." Morgan shook his head. "No one saw a man walking north that day. Stockwell talked to two men who went fishing for trout near the lake. They fished in a stream no more than a half-mile away. They saw Sterling ride by on their way to the stream. They said he seemed in a hurry. But they saw no one else on the road, riding or walking."

The doctor stroked his beard. "Not that many people walk out of town anyway. Why would they and where would they go? In the spring, many people go out to the woods to pick mushrooms and, in the summer, wild blackberries and black walnuts, but I know of no one who would walk all the way there and back."

"That leaves someone's coach or wagon as his way to the lake. I suppose he could have ridden most of the way and walked the remaining distance. There's a point on the road only two miles from the lake. I looked at a map of the colony including its roads and found a place easily accessible on foot. It's where the last storm blew down those pines. Do you know the place?"

"I do. Horace Reynolds has a farm near there. He and his family are patients of mine."

Morgan nodded. "So, the murderer could have walked that short distance in less than an hour. His only problem would be walking through swampy land. But by taking that route, he would not have been seen by the fishermen."

"Riding in a coach or wagon would also let him take Sterling's horse after he killed him. His only risk would be the possibility of being identified by the man or men who rode with him. I assume you spoke to someone at the coach company. I can't think of the company's name."

"It's *Charles Johnson and Sons*. I spoke to both drivers who take passengers to Charles Towne; one goes at first light in the morning and the other at noontime. I asked them about the fourth of May – the day of Sterling's disappearance. Neither of them remembered dropping off passengers en route to Charles Towne, though they picked up a couple along the way. The only passengers boarding the coaches on the return to Savannah did so in Charles Towne."

"What about traders? The murderer might well have ridden in one of their wagons. At least a hundred leave Savannah everyday, with most traveling on to Charles Towne."

"That's the problem. There are simply too many traders to interview and, even if I could talk to them all in Savannah, I would miss those who go north to towns beyond Charles Towne."

The doctor sighed. "Well, for now, I guess the murderer's way to the lake remains unknown."

"So it seems. Tell me what you learned from looking at Sterling's corpse." He watched the doctor stroke his beard and was again aware of his pallid face.

"First, let's talk about how the murder took place. I don't think Sterling walked to where he was killed; I think he was dragged there. I saw a wide line in the earth that extended from the bottom of the hill to the clearing some fifteen feet away. The line was the width of a big man's shoulders, which of course suggests that the murderer dragged Sterling by his feet to the clearing. It would be the easiest way to move a man of his bulk. Where the line began I found a thick limb stripped of leaves. It was about two inches in diameter and had a trace of blood on one end. So, it seems the attacker struck Sterling at the bottom of the hill. He then dragged the senseless man to the clearing where he tied him to the stakes. I think most, if not all the stakes were already in the ground. Given the hardness of the ground, he would not have wasted time hammering them into place. He had one intention in mind – the excruciatingly painful death of Thomas Sterling."

"Well done," said Morgan, looking at the doctor with admiration.

"The murderer then spread the honey on Sterling and let the ants and scavengers do the rest. There's not much else to say about his corpse you don't already know. Vultures probably consumed most of the unfortunate man, but his missing left foot and right-hand fingers suggest another animal took away some of him as well. The ants and other insects began the process of flesh removal since they are usually first to find the dead. They take little pieces, but in a short time they can strip the flesh from a body. Ants are especially voracious including the fire ants of this area. The tiny ants are not only ferocious, they are seemingly insatiable especially when they number in the many thousands, as that nest in the rocks must contain. You saw what was left of him – a few strips of flesh on his head and upper arms on the front side and the flesh on his backside. In another two days or so, little more than his skeleton would have remained to be found."

Morgan exhaled audibly. "What a way to die!"

"Indeed, a hideous way to die and I think the murderer watched Thomas Sterling die."

"No!" Morgan threw his hand up as if to ward off the doctor's words. "What makes you say that?" He reached for his glass of wine.

"There's a large rock in the clearing, only five feet from where the man was staked. It's relatively flat on top where it faces the clearing."

"I saw it. Are you suggesting he sat there and watched the ants attack Sterling?"

"Yes, I am. There's soft dirt at the base of the rock and I saw two discernible shoe marks, which, I suspect, were made by the murderer's shoes. I think he sat on the rock and watched much of Sterling's suffering as he went to his death. It's my guess the unfortunate man actually died of a heart attack, before the animals stripped the flesh from his body. The intense and incessant pain would have produced it."

"I'm not surprised. But, tell me, why do you think it was the murderer, whose shoes left the indentations, and not one of the other men who was there at the clearing?"

"There's no account of anyone else sitting on the rock. Who would want to sit so close to the sight and stench? Did you or Stockwell?"

Morgan paused to think. "No, we stood the entire time studying the site. Stockwell held the lantern. What about the hunters who found the body or the militiaman who guarded it?"

"The hunters took one look at the body and ran to their horses. The guard, Peter Miller, told me he leaned against a pine tree most of the night. Miller had a clear view of the body from the tree, which was about ten or so feet from it. He would walk to the edge of the clearing every so often to make sure nothing disturbed the body. Miller admitted that the stench of death and his fear of the fire ants kept him at a distance. Therefore, he never went near the rock."

Morgan shook his head. "My God, this man is more of a monster than I ever imagined."

The doctor nodded. "Yes, he seems to be the dark demon of our nightmares."

All day, Captain George Chapman looked forward to the secret voyage he had planned for the afternoon. It was on his mind when he awoke at four o'clock that morning, with him as he ate breakfast with his wife, Martha, and still on his mind as he rode to the shipyard. He continued to think about it as he stood in the sun supervising the crew's work on his ship, the sleek schooner, *Brazen.* This was their sixth and hopefully their last day scraping barnacles off the hull.

At noon, anxious to get on his way, Chapman turned the work detail over to his first mate and left hurriedly in his horse cart. He rode over to the dock where he had tied his skiff, *Beacon,* and, stopping only long enough to leave his horse with the watchman, he set sail southeast on the Savannah River. Chapman had mounted a single sail in the skiff and built a small cargo hold in the stern. The flat-bottomed boat had been built at the same time as the *Brazen* and it was used to ferry his crew to and from the schooner and carry cargo into shallow water ports.

The captain pushed off with an oar and, turning about from the dock, the sailboat caught a strong wind blowing toward the ocean. The wind never slackened and, in only two hours, he reached the buoy marking the tidal inlet where Augustine Creek flowed into the river. The city General James Oglethorpe had designed was settled twelve miles northeast of the river's mouth and the creek was known to be a midway point between the colony and the ocean. He arrived at the inlet at two thirty, a half hour earlier than he had expected.

George Chapman made the trip hoping to find pirate's treasure. He knew it was unlikely, but he had to take the chance. If it turned out to be a wild goose chase, all he would lose was an afternoon on the river. But, if he did recover a chest full of gold and silver, he would retire from the sea and live the rest of his earthly days as a country gentlemen. He would buy a grand house and have servants serve his every need.

Chapman pictured himself sitting in a pillowed chair smoking his pipe on the veranda of a big white house built on the cliff above the river. In his mind's eye, he saw a black servant with a silver platter serving him Jamaican rum in a tall glass. Chapman smiled as he looked out over the river.

He would be sitting on the veranda on a day like this with the flowing water sparkling in the sun. Chapman sighed contentedly as a British warship suddenly came into view; the ship, a frigate, was in full sail moving up the river toward Savannah. He imagined a uniformed officer waving to him from the bridge as the sixty-gun ship passed him. The captain's daydream ended abruptly when an oyster-covered sand bar suddenly emerged in front of the bow. He jerked the tiller to the left barely missing the bar.

His dreams of wealth had begun the previous morning. It was at first light when he saw the folded note under his front door. He still had the note in his jacket pocket, although he knew every word of it by heart. Chapman patted his pocket for the fourth time, making sure the piece of paper was still there. Worried that the buttoned pocket might somehow come open, he could not keep his hands from touching it.

The note was poorly written and full of misspellings according to his wife, Martha. She had read it to him since his own use of the King's English included few if any reading or writing skills. George Chapman could only sign his name, which he said was quite sufficient for a man of the sea like himself.

The note consisted of only five lines. He repeated them to himself. "I saild with u in th war an no ur a onerabl man. I no wear a pirat chest is in shalo watr. Haf for u if u sail tomorro to Augustine Creek at 3. Com bi urself an tie up at th reck."

His wife advised him to ignore the note, but, despite her disapproving glare, he could not stop thinking about the chest and what it might contain. Martha told him he would be foolish to think there was any truth to the note. "There's no pirate's treasure there! It's an act of trickery, George," she warned him. "Don't you see it's a ruse to get you to go down to that creek? You'll be at the man's mercy there in that remote place."

"I'll be fine," he declared. "I'll go well armed with my pistol and sword."

"At least have one of your crew accompany you. He could hide in the skiff's cargo hold or ride down early to see who turned up at the wreck. Either way, the man could hide nearby and watch for trouble. Listen to me, George, don't let greed lead you astray. You've been fortunate once, now be satisfied!"

Gritting his teeth, Chapman struck the kitchen table. "I don't need anyone to watch over me. I'm a grown man, not some boy who needs his father to hold his hand crossing the street."

Chapman, of course, did not admit his real reason for refusing to bring another man along. He wanted whatever wealth that might be found and did not want to share it. He worried that if anyone else knew of the treasure, rumors would spread like wildfire through Savannah and there would be inevitable claims to its ownership. Chapman wanted to avoid that possibility at all cost and therefore his voyage to Augustine Creek would be a secret shared only with his wife. Before leaving that morning, he told Martha to say nothing to anyone, not even to her mother, about his trip to the creek. Chapman spoke sternly, pointing his finger at her. At the door where she stood looking glum, he softened and kissed her on the cheek. "I'll be careful," he assured her. Now as Chapman sailed the skiff into the marsh, he fingered the loaded pistol tucked in his belt.

The tide in the creek was running in and, lowering the sail, he let the river current carry the *Beacon* deeper into the marsh. He spotted the wreck about a hundred feet ahead and, in less than a minute, he reached the upper portion of the mast that remained above the surface of the water. The wreck was a sunken schooner that stood almost half out of the water when the tide was out. Now, at nearly high tide, about five feet of mast and a cross spar could be seen.

Chapman tied the skiff to the mast and looked around. There was little to see except salt stunted trees, marsh grass and three large alligators basking in the sun. The alligators lay in a row on the far bank across from the sunken schooner. "The damned alligators can live anywhere," he thought, "even in brackish water."

Near the stern of his skiff, he saw a small clearing in the marsh surrounded by sea oats and a copse of wind-bent trees. As his eyes moved over the clearing, Chapman noticed a broken wooden box in the sand. Squinting in the sun, he looked at his watch and saw that he had twenty minutes to wait. He decided to explore the clearing and examine the box. Chapman doubted the box held anything, but he wanted to inspect it anyway. He used an oar to turn the stern toward the clearing. Two feet from the shore, he jumped onto the sand that bordered the creek. Holding the sword in his right hand, he placed his left hand on the pistol as he walked to the box.

Chapman turned the box over with his sword and two fiddler crabs scurried away into the marsh grass. There was nothing else inside in what he now realized was the broken bottom of a fish crate. The captain checked his watch again and frowned to see there were still ten minutes to wait. "Well, the wait will be well worth it, if the chest is full of coins or jewels," Chapman reassured himself as he walked over to the trees. "If so, it's a dream come true."

He went to the largest tree and stood in its shade. The sun was hot even with a cool wind blowing in off the sea. He felt drops of sweat trickling down his neck into his collar. "Damn it, where is he? It's time!" he said aloud, again looking at his watch. The captain stepped out from beneath the tree and looked in all directions for the man he hoped would lead him to the treasure. He saw no one and shook his head in exasperation. Chapman hated to return home and admit to Martha that she had been right all along. Finally, not knowing what else to do, he stuck the point of his sword in the hard sand and wrote his initials.

Hearing a rustling sound in the stand of sea oats behind him, Chapman swirled around, his sword pointed forward. The sound had come from the left and he pivoted quickly, ready to thrust his sword in that direction. But the blow that struck him on the back of the head came from the right. As Chapman turned, the end of a thick branch appeared from behind the right side of the tree and he was clubbed to the ground. A second blow to his head knocked him unconscious.

At dawn the next morning, two Indian boys saw the skiff as they paddled their canoe up the creek. The boys, both twelve years old, had built the canoe by themselves and were using it to catch crabs in the marshes near their village. They had just entered the creek when the stern of the boat came into view. The boys slowed their paddling and approached it cautiously. They had been repeatedly told to stay away from the white man's lands and possessions, but seeing the apparently empty vessel, they were too curious to ignore it. They waited impatiently for the sun to light up the vessel and, when no one appeared on deck, the boys paddled nearer. They finally dared to climb aboard, but spent only a few minutes looking around. Frightened of being seen even near the boat, the boys hurriedly paddled up the creek. Avoiding a treacherous oyster bar, they paddled hard to pass the skiff's bow and the mast of the sunken ship. They looked neither to their left nor right in their hurry to reach the bend in the creek where they soon would be out of sight. But just as they turned the canoe about, the boys looked back and, to their horror, saw the mutilated head and upper body of a man tied to the mast of the sunken wreck.

"Why are you so certain the same man murdered Captain Chapman?" Oliver Palmer sat with his legs crossed to the side of the desk as he questioned Morgan. It was 8:30 in the morning and they were drinking tea together in the attorney general's office. To Morgan's amazement, the Englishman offered him a cup of his costly East India tea and even poured it from the teapot that Thackery brought to the desk.

"There are a number of similarities that stand out. First, the same bindings – corduroy, were used to tie up both men. The cloth probably came from old discarded breeches. The only difference was the color. The bindings used on Sterling were brown, those on Chapman looked like faded gray."

"Is there any way to determine whose breeches they were?" The attorney general leaned back in his chair, sighed irritably and intertwined his fingers over his stomach. He was tempted to make Morgan use each man's proper title, but decided not to waste the time. Palmer had been summoned to meet with the governor at ten o'clock and he wanted to be thoroughly prepared for their meeting. He knew Governor Wright would expect a scrupulous report of his progress in the murder investigation that now included another victim.

"The only possibility that has occurred to me is that the breeches might have come from old clothing given to the churches for the poor and new immigrants in Savannah. Stockwell is now making inquiries about both donations and handouts."

"That makes sense. Of course, the corduroy might have come from the man's own old breeches. Do continue, Major."

Morgan nodded. "That's true, but it's worth the effort to ask around town." The attorney general nodded in agreement. "The same method of binding was used in both murders; the men were tied at the forehead, neck, chest, arms and waist. Sterling was also bound at the knees and both ankles and that's why the murderer hammered twenty stakes into the ground. Chapman's knees and ankles were probably tied as well, but since the alligators took off both legs, we can't be certain of that conclusion – though obvious."

Palmer made a face and clucked his tongue. "It is indeed. Do continue."

"The clothing of both men also was cut apart in the same way and left to be found. The captain's clothes were neatly piled in the bow of his boat, while Sterling's were similarly piled near his body. And, of course, each of the victims was left to die completely naked."

Palmer furrowed his brow. "I wonder if the manner of the two murders has anything to do with that much quoted verse in the Bible, 'We come into the world naked and naked we leave it.' As I recall it's from Proverbs."

Morgan shook his head. "No, it's from Ecclesiastes and is worded, 'Naked a man comes from his mother's womb, and as he comes, so he departs. He takes nothing from his labor that he can carry in his hand.'"

Palmer carefully studied Morgan's face, but saw no sign of triumph in his expression. "I would never have suspected you had any familiarity with the Bible."

Morgan nodded. "My mother made me read the Bible every morning as a boy and I was required to read memorized verses to her. I also was required to read the classics. She borrowed the books from a wealthy neighbor when we lived in town and I read them before going to bed."

"My mother made similar demands upon me, but I was a recalcitrant child who refused to comply with her wishes. As a result, I have little memory of the biblical verses I was expected to memorize. Well, let's continue. It may be that this murderer is a Christian fanatic and the nudity of his victims has some religious meaning. What are the other similarities you found?"

Morgan nodded. The possibility of a religious fanatic had not occurred to him and it was something to think about. Seeing Palmer's impatient frown, he replied to his question. "The use of the victim's horse after each murder is also the same. After Chapman was tied to the mast, the murderer rode the captain's horse into town and let him loose somewhere about Johnson Square. He was found the next morning grazing across from Christ Church…"

"Another religious connection?" asked Palmer as he held his cup to his mouth.

"Possibly. What we don't know is how he went to each of the remote sites. Since he rode back to town on his victims' horses, it's obvious he didn't ride his own horse."

"He could have taken his own horse out and then ridden back with the other one in tow."

Morgan shook his head. "Stockwell talked to the guards at the two gates and no one led a horse into town the afternoon or night of Chapman's murder."

"Yet, he left Assemblyman Sterling's horse outside the city gates."

"Yes, because his stallion was well known in town. Incidentally, we found out how the horse entered town without a rider. A trapper by the name of Miles McClung saw him grazing in a field outside the gates and brought him into town. McClung piled furs and hides on the horse's back and that's why he wasn't recognized. Once inside Savannah, he let him run loose so no one could accuse him of horse theft." Morgan smiled. "When McClung heard about the murder, he told a tall tale at the *Cup and Keg* about how he knocked the murderer, a big Englishman, off the horse and brought him into town."

Palmer laughed loudly, showing a space where a molar was missing on the lower left side of his mouth. "Oh, the Irish! They are storytellers, aren't they? And they have never forgotten England's conquest of Ireland. Perhaps, they never will."

"Nor should they," thought Morgan, who condemned the English for what he considered to be their endless conquests and colonial empire. "Stockwell heard about the drunken trapper's story and chased the man down. He had to ride out to his trap line to talk to him. McClung was sober at the time and told him how he actually found the horse…"

"Wait a minute." Palmer held up his hand to stop Morgan from speaking. "I understand the murderer rode Sterling's stallion, but how could he ride Chapman's horse back to town? The captain didn't ride to the rendezvous at Augustine Creek, he sailed there."

Morgan nodded. "That's right, he did. But the night before sailing, Chapman rode down to the creek in his carriage with a horse in tow. He was seen on the south road by the squad of soldiers returning from a reconnaissance mission. The captain obviously wanted to make sure he could get back to town if something unforeseen happened to the skiff. He was also wary enough of an ambush to arm himself with a pistol and sword. He took the horse there and tethered him in a thick stand of trees near the wreck. Chapman tried to safeguard himself as best as he could, but sadly it was not good enough. The murderer must have watched his movements that night."

"So it seems. What more is there about the murder of Assemblyman Sterling?" Palmer drank the last of his tea and, with a flip of his wrist, signaled Thackery to make another pot. He sighed in exasperation as the little man tripped on the rug, almost dropping the ceramic pot.

"The murderer left nothing at the lake except the wooden stakes and we're now trying to find the carpenter who made them. Stockwell has been interviewing the city carpenters since last week, but, so far, no one recalls any recent order for stakes. They did tell Stockwell that those he showed them were made from slats used to cage animals.

The cages are common enough around town and the slats have been made by every carpenter at one time or other – but not recently."

The attorney general sighed. "So, the stakes tell us nothing about the murderer."

"They do tell us that the man is meticulous. He cut all twenty stakes to more or less the same length, carved similar points on each of them and hammered them into the hard ground so precisely four inches stood above ground!" Morgan emptied his cup as Thackery returned with the second pot of tea.

"I hope that knowledge will be useful eventually, but, for now, I can't see how. I assume the guards haven't identified any suspicious persons passing through the gates." Palmer leaned forward and filled the two cups with hot steeped tea.

"That's unfortunately true. Stockwell said the guards at the southern gate recalled seeing Sterling ride out of town. But none of the guards saw anyone they regarded as suspicious. One of them told Stockwell, "We don't keep lists of them that comes and goes, you know."

Palmer snorted. "It's unlikely the man could write one anyway. I am surprised he was so surly with the sergeant. Given Stockwell's size, he doesn't look like the kind of man who would put up with such insolence."

Morgan smiled. "I didn't ask Stockwell what he did or said to the sentry, but I'll wager the man won't be insolent to him again."

"Well, Major, do tell me what your *friend*, the esteemed medical examiner, discovered at the murder site that was useful?" Palmer put his hands behind his head and grinned at Morgan.

Morgan narrowed his eyes and returned the smile. "I'll be delighted to tell you what he discovered." He then related the observations the doctor had made about the murder. Morgan, however, did not tell Palmer about the discovery of the honey pot or the unusual knots used by the murderer to bind his victim to the stakes. The major ended with the doctor's description of how the murderer had knocked Sterling down at the bottom of the hill and then dragged him by his feet to the clearing where he was staked to the ground.

"A sound investigation, I must say." Palmer nodded, his jowls shaking.

"There's one more observation he made that might surprise you. The doctor thinks the murderer stayed and watched the fire ants kill the assemblyman."

"My God in heaven!" Palmer sat up straight in his chair.

Morgan told him about the doctor's discovery of the shoe marks below the rock seat and his belief that the murderer sat there watching Sterling's suffering as he died.

Palmer's face paled and he swallowed several times to keep the bile from rising into his mouth. It took him a moment to speak and then he muttered, "What a fiend!"

"A fiend, indeed!" Morgan sipped his tea and waited for Palmer, his face beaded with sweat, to compose himself.

"Well, ah, what have you learned about the murder of Captain Chapman?" Palmer wiped his face with a handkerchief. He still looked shaken.

Morgan noted that Palmer's white handkerchief had his initials embroidered in blue in one corner. "Except for the similarities we discussed, I haven't much to report yet. We only learned about the captain's death yesterday and it wasn't until seven-thirty last night that I saw his body. The alligators left little more than half of him and not much that is recognizable. The doctor is examining his corpse now and I intend to talk to Chapman's wife and crew when we finish our meeting. I've already talked with the two Indians who found Chapman's body, but they told me little that was helpful."

"You don't think they had anything to do with it, do

you?" Palmer had finished two cups of tea and he looked better, though he continued to wipe the perspiration from his face.

"No, they're twelve-year-old boys. They were terrified not only by what they saw, but by the punishment they expected for boarding the skiff."

"What did they expect?"

"To be scalped and hung!"

"What stupidity! Well, I suppose that's to be expected from uncivilized people. I heard they found the captain's remains in the morning. Why did it take so long for you sail down to Augustine Creek?"

"I didn't hear about the body until four o'clock. The boys paddled as fast as they could to their village, but it still took an hour to get there. Their village is north of Augustine Creek and they had to paddle against the current. When they told their chief, he took them to the main Creek village, some six miles away, to tell Chief Toonahowi what they had found. Toonahowi then rode into town with a party of his braves and reported the discovery. By that time it was late in the afternoon. I'm sure you know Toonahowi is the nephew of Chief Tomochichi, who sailed with General Oglethorpe to England some thirty years ago."

"Ah, yes." Palmer nodded. "The Creeks were given a reception at court by King George and the royal family. I was but a boy at the time and wanted desperately to see the Indians from America." He sighed, looking at the portrait of the king on the wall. "But, of course, my father's meager income did not allow a child's capricious trip to London. Oh no!" Suddenly realizing his distraction, Palmer returned his eyes to Morgan. "Do continue."

"Toonahowi brought the boys with him and let me talk to them in his presence. With his help, I heard their account of the discovery. The chief had accompanied his uncle on the voyage to England and learned a little English – at least enough to translate what the boys said to me."

"But didn't you say earlier that you learned nothing from them."

"I said they told me little that was helpful. But they did tell me something that we might have missed. Since the boys saw Chapman's body from west of the sunken ship, they had a view of it that we did not. We approached the wreck from the east. It was faster to go there by boat than horse so we sailed on the river where the prevailing wind blows southeast."

"Of course, I understand the obvious." Peeved, Palmer glared at Morgan. "What did the Indians see from their perspective that you might have missed?"

"They saw that the Captain's head had been bound to the mast so that his eyes looked to the south toward St. Augustine."

Palmer frowned. "What do you mean?"

"The murderer tied Chapman's head so he was forced to look southward. His body faced forward, but his head was turned and tied to the side so his eyes looked toward St. Augustine and Spanish Florida."

"Ah, I see." Palmer pursed his lips. "I wonder what that suggests? You're quite certain that was deliberate?"

"Yes, the binding on his forehead was tied tightly and left a deep indentation in the skin. The man had no choice, but to look south." Morgan paused for effect. "And… the captain's body was hung on the mast with his arms stretched out on the cross spar…"

"Like Christ on the cross!" Palmer slapped his hand on the desk. "I told you there was something religious about these murders."

CHAPTER FOUR

SAVANNAH: TUESDAY, JUNE 3 – TUESDAY, JUNE 10, 1766

Morgan thought about his conversation with Oliver Palmer as he descended the stairs to the first floor. He wondered about the attorney general's argument that the murderer's religious beliefs played a part in the deaths of Sterling and Chapman. Morgan realized he had led Palmer to that conclusion when he described the way Chapman's body hung on the crossbar. Of course, that position did seem to suggest the crucifixion, as did Sterling's body with its outstretched arms and legs staked to the ground.

But the more Morgan thought about the similarity, the less he believed it. He saw more differences than similarities in the comparison. Both victims had been bound nude unlike Christ and their heads were positioned differently. The head of Christ always appears leaning down to the right in death. Sterling's head was staked so his eyes looked directly forward and Chapman's head faced left. Neither of the murdered men fit the paintings or sculptured figures of Christ on the cross. They had none of his bodily wounds or a crown of thorns. Their bodies were bound by cords; Christ was nailed to the cross. The more Morgan visualized their nudity, the more he doubted it had anything to do with the biblical verses that he and Palmer had remembered. By the time Morgan had reached the last step, he knew the murderer had not intended to copy the crucifixion in his killings. His sole purpose had been to hold them firmly in place so they would suffer as much excruciating pain as possible.

The two killings actually were more unlike than similar. Besides the different positions of their heads, Sterling's legs had been bound so they lay apart while Chapman's legs had been tied together. Though the alligators had taken most of the captain's left leg and half of his right, Morgan had noticed one of the murderer's cloth bindings still tied around Chapman's thighs and knew his lower limbs had been bound together as well. To hold his victim firmly to the mast, especially as the tide went out, it was necessary for the murderer to bind the man's legs together before tying them to the mast.

As Morgan walked down the corridor to his office, it occurred to him that the murderer had employed animals to kill both men. He had not considered that similarity earlier and now wondered if there was any significance to it. Whatever his method, the man obviously hated his victims and must have had an implacable grudge against them. Morgan then realized why both men had been stripped bare. Nudity allowed the ants and alligators easy access to their flesh. It also allowed the murderer to see every detail of their torturous deaths.

Morgan found Stockwell sitting at his small, scarred desk, an empty cup in front of him. The sergeant had his elbows on the top of the desk and, leaning forward, he seemed to be looking into the cup. He sighed loudly when the justice entered the office.

Morgan grinned. "If you're reading tea leaves, let me know what's in store for you. If it's something good, you can read mine next."

"I'm not reading the leaves. Even if I could, I wouldn't do it. I don't want to never know what's in store for me. I'm sitting here like a stone because it's too damned hot to move myself anywhere. This office is like a baker's oven." Stockwell wiped his brow with the sleeve of his shirt and slowly leaned back in his chair.

"It is miserable in here. There's no good reason for us to stay inside and we won't. I'm leaving in a while and I have an errand for you that will take you outside for the rest of the day." Morgan wiped his own face with a torn and wrinkled handkerchief he pulled from a pocket. He shook his head. "It's only June and already hot as Hades."

"God, don't be reminding me. Where am I going? Someplace out of the sun I hope?"

"That depends if you know a way to ride down to Augustine Creek through the woods." Morgan saw Stockwell make a face.

"That's next to impossible as you well know, but I'll find the best way down there." He gave Morgan a lopsided grin. "You can be sure I'll find some leafy tree along the road where I'll rest my bones and maybe even take a nap. What do you want me to do at the creek?"

"I want you to look around the shipwreck and see if the murderer left anything behind. I know it's unlikely, but we must make sure we leave no stone unturned." Morgan sat against the edge of his desk. He could feel sweat dripping down his back.

"Let's hope I find more than I did walking through the woods on that clay path. That turned out to be a waste of time. But I've been wondering if there wasn't something there the first time I rode along that trail. You know, Major, I have a suspicion that one of them two fools did find something the day they went with me."

"What makes you think that?"

"As you know, I rode the first time I searched the woods. The two hunters, Canfield and… what's the other one's name?"

"Colby." Morgan crossed his legs at the ankles.

"Right. Anyway, as I rode along the path, Canfield and Colby was behind me babbling on and on. I ignored most of their foolish talk and, now and then, looked behind me to see what they was doing. One time, I seen one of them bend over with his hand out. I don't know who it was. Course, I asked if he seen something and he said, no. The other one was ahead picking his nose. We then went on looking and found nothin' at all. Now, the more I think on it, I wonder if he did find something in the bushes and kept it from me. I'll break his scrawny neck if he did."

"He may have found something and it's not too late to find out if he lied to you. Talk to them both and see what comes of it. We desperately need any scrap of information we can find. This fiend is as clever as he is cruel. Do whatever you need to do to get the truth from them."

"I will." Stockwell stood up and shook his shoulders. He nodded to Morgan and left the office, his limp prominent as he took his first steps toward the door.

Morgan smiled as he watched him walk away. It occurred to him that Stockwell's limp added to his menacing appearance. As he limped along with his long muscular arms swaying at his sides, he looked like some feral beast from a faraway jungle.

Morgan ate lunch at his desk before leaving the courthouse for the two interviews he had planned that afternoon. He ate a stale piece of bread, a chunk of dry cheese and a small batch of blackberries. He bought the berries from a street vender on his walk to his office that morning. Morgan washed down his meal with three glasses of red wine. He kept a corked bottle of wine in his lower desk drawer to quench his thirst during the day.

Morgan left the courthouse after lunch and rode to Chapman's house. There were few trees on the streets leading to Reynolds Square forcing him to ride in the hot sun the entire way. The wine had warmed him and he felt like he was in a flaming fireplace as the mid-day sun beat down on his shoulders. Adding to his misery, the humidity seemed to rise up and take his the breath away. Morgan could find no relief from the heat even when he urged his horse to a trot, hoping for at least a slight breeze. He was drenched in sweat as he rode into Reynolds Square and reached the captain's house.

Chapman's home was the smallest building in the square. The white clapboard house, although modest in size and ornamentation, appeared well maintained and in meticulous order. Morgan, whose own home showed years of neglect, could see that the captain had spent days, not hours, keeping it up. Every surface had several coats of paint and not one slate was out of place or warped. He knew if he boarded the captain's ninety-foot schooner it would surely be as shipshape and seaworthy.

The grounds around the house showed the same scrupulous care as well as the owner's fastidious attention to every tree and plant. A colorful flower garden surrounded the front porch and vegetables grew in a plowed area, Morgan noticed as he walked toward the building. A row of flowers also extended from the front of the house along both sides of a stepping-stone walk to the painted post where he tied his horse. As Morgan started toward the front door, he saw that Pheasant's Eye and Gold Buttons had begun to bloom beside the stone walk. He also recognized the leaves of Daylilies and Black-eyed Susan, which he knew would appear later in the month.

Quickly responding to his loud knock, Martha Chapman nodded to Morgan and invited him inside. As he expected, the inside of the Chapman house looked as orderly as the outside. The walls had been recently whitewashed and he could smell the honey mixture used to polish the wooden furniture. He was ushered into a small sitting room where the strong smell of honey suggested the polish had been applied that morning.

Martha Chapman nodded her thanks for his few words of condolence and then withdrew to the kitchen to make a pot of tea. The widow, a gray-haired woman with piercing green eyes, returned a few minutes later with the tea and a plate of steaming biscuits and orange marmalade. She looked composed, but the redness of her eyes told Morgan that she had been crying.

"I hope my visit is not improper at this time." Morgan sat with his hat in his lap.

"No, Major Morgan, it's not. But from what I have heard about you, propriety would not have stopped you from coming to talk to me, no matter the circumstances. Isn't that so?"

"That's true. I'm here to…"

"I know exactly why you're here and I'll tell you everything I know. I want the man who murdered George arrested and executed as soon as possible. This afternoon if possible! That's why propriety means nothing to me now." The widow's chin quivered, but she did not weep as Morgan expected. Instead, she sipped some tea and passed the plate of biscuits over to him.

"I want the same thing, I assure you." Morgan spooned marmalade on a biscuit.

"My husband was a gullible fool and his insatiable greed led him to his death. We had no need of money then. We owed nothing and lived as well as anyone in this colony. We had more money than we could possibly spend in the next thirty years. Yet, that greedy fool had to go out looking for pirate's treasure. Only he could believe such utter nonsense!" Tears welled up in her eyes and she dabbed them with a lace handkerchief.

"What nonsense did he believe?" Morgan looked up after taking a bite of the biscuit.

"The nonsense in that note." She saw the puzzled look on Morgan's face. "You don't know about it?"

"What note?" he mumbled, the piece of biscuit still in his mouth.

"He had it with him when he left the house that morning. It was in his jacket pocket and buttoned up." Martha Chapman sighed and again dabbed her eyes with her handkerchief.

"We didn't find any note. He was completely undressed and all his clothing was left on the shore." Morgan worried that he might have had said too much, but Mrs. Chapman seemed unaffected by the mention of her dead husband's nudity. She paused only briefly to look at her wedding band and then told him about the discovery of the note under the door.

"I read it so many times I can easily repeat it from memory. Excuse me a moment, I'll get a bit of paper and write it down for you."

"That would be helpful." Morgan saw her hold her back as she rose and walked from the room. He drank half the tea in his cup after swallowing the biscuit and marmalade.

"Here it is." She handed him her handwritten copy of the note. "I may not have repeated every one of the misspelled words, but I'm sure most of them appear as they were written."

Morgan frowned. "What do you think of the note?" He looked up after reading it twice.

"It's absolute rubbish, of course. I knew it was rubbish when I first read it. There's no pirate's chest at Augustine Creek and there never was." She sighed. "The note was written to lure George there. I think the man who killed George knew he couldn't resist it."

"Many men would have been lured by the note. Not only Captain Chapman."

"Yes, but the note was pushed under our door. The man who wrote it knew George well; he knew him well enough to predict he would take whatever risk was necessary to find a pirate's treasure. He knew all about George's greed and counted on it to lure him to Augustine Creek." Martha Chapman leaned forward and refilled Morgan's teacup.

"So, you're suggesting the murderer knew your husband."

"Yes. That's why he said George was an honorable man. He knew that would convince him of the veracity of the note. Yes, I'm sure of it, that man knew George – knew him well!"

"What do you think of the note itself – the way it was written?" Morgan sipped his tea.

She grimaced. "The man who wrote it wanted George to think he was an illiterate sailor. But I don't believe it for a minute. No, I think those misspellings were deliberately made to fool George. If you look carefully at the four sentences, you can see that they are properly structured and grammatical." She pointed to the piece of paper in Morgan's hand. "Only the words are misspelled, nothing else is wrong."

Morgan read the note again and nodded. "Yes, you are indeed correct."

"I was well tutored as a child and I know that poorly spelled note was written by someone who knew better.

My father was a stickler for properly spoken and correctly written English and he tutored me and my sisters to make certain we used it correctly." Martha Chapman paused to sip her tea. "There's something else about the original note that you should know as well. It's not evident in the copy I made for you."

Morgan looked up after rereading the note. "What is that?"

"The letters appeared to be drawn on the paper rather than written. I think the man who wrote the note wanted to make sure no one knew he had written it. So, he went to the effort of disguising his handwriting."

"I see."

"Yes. The letters were little more than unadorned lines. There were also a number of ink smudges on the paper I suspect to make it appear that the writer did not know how to use a quill properly. It was all a ruse."

"Very clever."

"Yes, but not to one who would 'look a gift horse in the mouth.' I tried to tell George the note was not to be believed, but he wouldn't listen to me. No, that man was hopelessly beguiled by greed. He had to find another treasure." She closed her eyes and sighed.

"Another treasure?"

"Yes, he found a broken chest full of gold and silver bars in a sunken wreck somewhere near Savannah. It was three years ago last April. That's what he used to have the *Brazen* built. George spent at least half of it on that ship. The rest he exchanged for a chest of coins we have hidden here in the house. It was a secret that only I knew. Now, there's no reason not to speak of it." Her chin quivered again and, this time, tears fell from her eyes.

Giving Martha Chapman time to compose herself, Morgan looked down at the note and pretended to reread it. Morgan looked up after he heard her blow her nose.

"Mrs. Chapman, by any chance, do you know who built the *Brazen*?"

"Yes, of course. The Parker brothers. It took them eleven months to satisfy every one of George's demands."

An hour later, Morgan rode to the northern end of Savannah where the Parker Brothers had situated their littered shipyard on a narrow strip of land next to the river. He found Joseph Parker standing over a sawhorse sawing deck planks alongside a partially built schooner. His younger and much bigger brother, James, kneeled above him on the half-finished deck, nailing oak planks into place. Neither wore shirts and their muscular upper bodies were wet with sweat. They both stopped work and watched the justice as he rode into the shipyard.

Morgan tied his horse to a split board that leaned against a shed where the brothers stored their tools at night. The shed was the only well-built building in the yard. Their house, several feet away, looked like it had been put up with unfinished logs hastily fitted together. The major could see unfilled spaces between the logs at seemingly every level of the walls. He assumed the building leaked when it rained and could picture standing puddles inside after the recent storms. The outhouse at the rear of the house was no better built and leaned precariously to one side.

The shipyard itself looked like a dumping ground for anything that could be used on a ship. Wherever he glanced, Morgan saw piles of beams, keels, masts, planks and wooden pieces of all shapes and sizes. The largest, a twelve-foot pile of unfinished logs stripped of branches, took up one-third of the yard and stood near the entrance. There were also barrels of tar, ships' rudders and rows of coiled rope.

Folded canvas sails of a variety of sizes hung on one side of the house and steering wheels leaned against the other. Morgan had to walk a zigzag path through the maze of ship materials to reach Joseph Parker.

"Major." Parker reached out a callused hand to Morgan.

"Parker." Morgan shook the man's huge hand, immediately aware that it totally engulfed his slender fingers. He noted that Parker's right arm looked to be almost twice the size of his left arm. It occurred to him that the strong shipwright would need no more than three strikes with a heavy hammer to drive stakes into hard ground. His brother, who had an even bigger right arm, might have been able to do it in two strikes.

"I'm here to inquire about Captain Chapman's schooner, the *Brazen*." Morgan saw the brothers look at each other.

"We expected you'd be along sometime soon, Major." replied Joseph. "It's too bad what happened to the captain. He was a good man for sure."

"A good man?" Morgan crossed his arms over his chest.

Parker nodded. "He treated everybody right. Paid on time. Never complained about the costs and trusted us to build him a good ship."

"That's right." James Parker spoke from the deck above them. "He was one of those who wanted the best and was willing to pay for it. Never tried to barter with us. Never faulted us."

"I understand he made a lot of demands." Morgan moved his eyes from one brother to the other. "Isn't that right?"

"He did, but all he wanted made sense and made him a sound ship." Joseph, the older of the brothers, responded. "He never said no word of complaint about how much this or that cost. He wanted the best ship we could build him and his crew."

"How did he pay you?" Morgan watched them warily.

"He paid us a third to start." Joseph answered again.

"A third more when we done half and the rest when we finished. It took the best of a year to build her. She was a big schooner, you know, 115 tons and 90 feet long."

"When was the ship built?"

"Sixty two . . . three?" Joseph looked at his brother. "Do you recall?"

"Three, I think." James stroked the stubble on his cheeks, which were covered with scars from childhood acne.

"Your bill of sale would show the exact date." Morgan saw Joseph shake his head.

"We don't keep no papers. We shake a man's hand and he pays. That's the way we do it. Never had a problem with nobody in more than ten years."

"I see." Morgan assumed that neither of the brothers could read nor write. "Did Captain Chapman pay you in English coins?"

Again the brothers exchanged looks. "He did," answered Joseph. "Most of it went for all what was in the ship. We made no more than a hundred pounds or so and then lost it when the river flooded and warped all our oak."

Morgan knew Joseph Parker was lying about their profit, but he did not dispute what the shipwright said. He knew the brothers had made a fortune in their shipyard and probably had it hidden somewhere among the piled ship materials. Much of England's merchant fleet had been built in the American colonies and the shipyards in Carolina were busy all year long. The Parker brothers were the only shipwrights in Savannah and made sure they attracted buyers by charging three pounds less per ton than their Charles Towne competitors. It was well known in town that the brothers had plenty of money, though they dressed shabbily and poor mouthed whenever the subject of their income came up. Morgan heard that Joseph spent little and hoarded his money, while James drank heavily and gambled much of his earnings away. He recalled seeing James lose £220 one night playing cards in the *Nip and Tuck*.

"You said Chapman paid in coin. Is that right?" Morgan looked at Joseph. The widow had said her husband paid the Parkers in gold and silver bars. She said the captain spent half the treasure he found on the ship and the remainder he exchanged for coins. "You're sure of that?" Morgan saw Joseph pause before nodding his head.

"Yes, I remember we kept it in our money box until the flood. Then we used the coins to buy us new lumber. Isn't that right, James?" Joseph looked up at his brother.

"That's right – that's what happened." James stood with his arms crossed over his chest.

The Parker brothers waited until Morgan was gone before returning to work. "We can't ever tell nobody about them bars." Joseph sighed and picked up his saw.

"Never. Not with what was on them." James looked down at his brother, who turned his eyes up, nodded, and made a face.

Reverend Bartholomew was eating his lunch when Morgan arrived at Christ Church. The major walked into the church and, finding it empty, went out the back door to the pastor's house. Bartholomew sat outside his house under a maple tree. He had placed a wide board on the arms of his chair and set his bowl of soup and bread in front of him. The Reverend had a half glass of wine in his hand and a bottle of wine at his side on the ground.

He smiled when he saw Morgan come out of the church. "Well, what do you know, two visits from the Morgans in the same month. It's good to see you, James." He held out his hand, but did not get up.

"Reverend." Morgan shook his hand. "I assume we can

talk while you eat your lunch."

"Of course. I'm eating out here after being cooped up inside for an endless meeting with the warden and the entire vestry. It lasted three hours! I assume God was punishing me for my gluttony. However, he did spare me Willington, who was absent for some unknown reason."

Morgan sat on a tree stump in the shade across from Bartholomew.

"How about some delicious fish stew? Elizabeth made a pot and it's sitting inside on the kitchen table. She's gone shopping, but go get yourself a bowl – it still should be hot – and some bread. It was baked this morning. You'll also need a glass for the wine. Oh yes and do bring me a couple more slices of bread." He spoke to Morgan's back as the major walked toward the door of the house. "You'll also need a chair."

Morgan needed four trips to carry everything outside, but he finally sat down across from the minister on a stool. He set the bowl of soup, bread and wine glass on the tree stump. "The stew is delicious." Morgan smacked his lips after his first spoonful.

"It is, isn't it? Elizabeth is a very good cook and that's only one of her many virtues. I'm a lucky man. I expect you would be too if you married. I assume this visit is about the recently deceased Captain George Chapman," mumbled Bartholomew, chewing a mouthful of bread.

Morgan stared at Bartholomew, but ignored his comment about marriage. "I also want to ask you about a possible religious element in the murders." Morgan waited until his mouth was empty before speaking. His mother had insisted on good table manners in her house.

"A religious element? Tell me about it." Bartholomew used his napkin to brush away a fly that landed on his makeshift table.

Morgan described the way the bodies had been arranged

and the attorney general's belief in a religious connection. "I have my own opinions about it, but I want to hear your thoughts on the matter. You know more on that subject."

"Hmm. There might be something to Palmer's argument. I assume he continues to be a pompous prig." Bartholomew saw Morgan nod his head. "As my old father, God rest his soul, would say, 'A vicious dog in the past will be vicious in the present as well as in the future.'"

"It appears your father was a wise man."

"He was indeed. Well, let me continue. I doubt that the killer deliberately arranged the bodies to approximate the crucifixion – there are too many differences. The most obvious one, of course, being the placement of the heads. But it occurs to me that the murderer might very well have put his victims in a somewhat similar position as our Lord on the cross without ever thinking about it. He may be a man who has a long and strong Christian past and so he arranged the bodies from a memory he has never lost."

"Would that make him a Catholic?" Morgan rose from his chair and stood in front of Bartholomew as the minister refilled his wine glass.

"Not necessarily. Some of our churches still display the crucifix and even use it during Sunday service. Ours does not, of course. If you can recall any of your early teaching in this church, you should know why we do not and will never display a crucifix or statues of the holy family. We do not need physical things – we need only our prayer and faith to reach God."

"But some Episcopal Churches do display the crucifix."

"Yes, but I can recall only one I saw in England some years ago. But, keep in mind, all Christians, regardless of the church they attend, have the Lord's crucifixion in their mind's eye. It's there throughout their lives. I'm sure it's in yours as well, despite your present disinterest in his church and teachings." He smiled at Morgan and then sighed. "Although I would not like to think it possible, any Christian, a devoted parishioner or one like you, could kill those men and unintentionally place their bodies in a manner to suggest the crucifixion."

Morgan nodded. "What you say makes sense. By the way, what do you know about Captain Chapman?" He told Bartholomew about the dead man's treasure and how he had been lured to his death.

"So, the sin of greed led him to his death. I didn't know the man except to acknowledge him on the street. He was a lapsed Anglican like you and your father and apparently attended Christ Church before I arrived in Savannah. His wife, I believe, is a Presbyterian."

"Do you know if Chapman and Sterling were friends or engaged in any business ventures together? I assume Chapman sailed for the Sterling Shipping Company at least sometime in the last four years." Morgan drank the remainder of his wine and waved off Bartholomew's offer of another glass.

The minister shook his head. "I don't think so. I recall hearing that Chapman sailed for one of the Scottish shippers. I believe it was Hugh Douglas, now that I think about it. I seriously doubt that Chapman ever shipped goods for Sterling."

"Chapman never sailed for Sterling? I'm surprised to hear that, Reverend. I thought all the shipping companies hired any vessel that was available when they had enough cargo to fill a ship's hold. None of them wanted to store anything perishable for too long."

"That's right. But Douglas was much busier than Sterling and always seemed to have a cargo ready to go. So, he kept Chapman and several other captains at sea throughout most of the year. By the way, I believe your father uses Douglas to ship his rice. I would assume Chapman has also carried a load of his rice at one time or other as well."

"That may be, but I have no knowledge of it. I don't

keep up with my father's business. Let's return to the captain. Even if Chapman did not sail for Thomas Sterling, do you know if he had any other business dealings with him?"

"I wouldn't know." Bartholomew shrugged.

"I ask because both men came into a lot of money about the same time. The source of the money was unknown, but, with it, one bought a new ship and the other built a new dock."

Bartholomew put his spoon down. "I knew of both events, of course, but never thought of the similar timing. Hmm. Did you know that Chapman had nothing before he bought that ship? He served as a common seaman for years and only occasionally as a mate. Chapman never was given a command nor ever hired on as first mate in all those years at sea."

"So, like Sterling, Chapman's new money almost immediately changed his fortunes."

"Yes, and I wonder if that was coincidental." Bartholomew carefully moved the board with the empty bowl and spoon to the ground near his feet. He poured the last of the wine into his glass and dropped the bottle beside the board.

"I am suspicious of such coincidences – especially when both men became wealthy at the same time and then were murdered within days of each other. That's much too coincidental for me." Morgan leaned forward and pointed his finger at the minister. "'Something is rotten'… not in Denmark, but here in Savannah, to misquote Shakespeare."

"I do agree." Leaning back in his chair with his legs crossed at the ankles, Bartholomew twirled the stem of his empty wine glass in his fingers. "But I must remind you, James, that the two men lived much different lives. Thomas Sterling was a Presbyterian who saw the light and joined our church and then lived a good Christian life. George Chapman, on the other hand, was a coarse seaman and lived a selfish and probably sinful life as such men are wont to do.

I could add that he abandoned the church as well, but you would find little meaning in that."

Morgan glared at Bartholomew. "You don't know that Chapman lived a sinful life. Nor do you know Sterling lived a virtuous one. All you know is that the man became very wealthy, joined your church and donated money. That doesn't reveal how he lived his life. No, not at all! And, when more is known about his murder, we may discover that Sterling's life was blighted by some hideous deed he did in the past. A deed so hideous his murderer tortured him to death."

"That may be; we shall see." Bartholomew stood to end the conversation. "But despite what you may say, Thomas Sterling followed a much different path than George Chapman after achieving prosperity. Thomas Sterling shared at least a part of his wealth with this church and its Christian mission – no matter what you think of it! While the captain, from what we know, kept all his wealth to himself and never shared it. It may be that his death from greed may have been a fitting ending for the man."

Morgan rode home to change his clothes, sweat-soaked from the day's heat. He wiped his face on his sleeve as he approached the stable at the side of his house. Reaching the path to the stable, he slowed his big stallion to a walk. Suddenly, without warning, the horse reared up, his front legs pawing the air. Morgan fell from the saddle and landed on his wounded side, his face striking a stone on the ground.

Dazed and bleeding from a cut on his forehead, he lay prone on the ground for a several minutes before trying to stand. Feeling dizzy, Morgan first got up on his knees, where he rested, waiting for his vision to clear. Still on his knees, he took a handkerchief from his coat pocket to wipe off some of the blood and dirt from his face. He withdrew his sword from its scabbard and stood slowly, supporting himself with the sword, the point pressed into the ground. He grimaced as he felt pain in both his ankle and wounded shoulder. More concerned about his shoulder, he gently ran his hand over it and, though sore to the touch, he was relieved there was no bleeding. His left ankle had been twisted and he limped when he took his first step.

Morgan turned and saw his horse standing about ten feet behind him, his eyes wild with fright. He wondered what had frightened him and looked toward the stable. He saw nothing there that should have terrified the stallion. Still using the sword as a support, Morgan limped toward the stable looking along the ground. He shook his head, puzzled by the horse's behavior. Close to the stable door, Morgan was about to turn and call his horse when he heard the distinct sound of a rattle. Without moving a muscle, he looked toward the stable door and saw the snake lying in the pile of leaves beside the stable door. The big brown diamondback blended into the rotting leaves and had been almost impossible to see. But now, less than ten feet away, Morgan saw the curled rattlesnake clearly. The snake was at least six feet long, as thick as a man's lower leg and poised to strike.

Morgan exhaled loudly, wishing he had his pistol with him. With one arm and a twisted ankle, he worried about trying to kill the snake with his sword. He was not a skilled swordsman. For a second, Morgan considered trying to scare the rattlesnake away, but then he thought of his neighbors' young children and knew he had to kill it. Listening to the rattle, he felt a shiver run down his spine.

Morgan rolled his right shoulder to make sure it was limber and slowly sidled toward the snake. He held the sword in readiness in front of him. He hoped he could use the sword to parry a strike and escape being bitten. As he closed the distance to four feet, Morgan saw the snake's huge head move back and knew it would strike when he took his next step.

Morgan slid his right foot toward the snake and tried to jump to the side as it struck. The snake's head shot toward his foot and one of its fangs scraped the side of his shoe. At the same time, Morgan swiftly brought his sword down to sever its head at the neck. He missed the snake completely and the edge of the sword struck the ground, spraying dirt in all directions. Morgan jumped back and stood trembling, fearful of a second strike. He felt the hair rise on the back of his neck as he watched the rattlesnake recoil and once again poise for an attack, its forked tongue flicking in and out of its mouth.

Morgan knew then that he would be bitten if he tried again to kill the snake. Even if his ankle had not been twisted, he was too slow and inept a swordsman to do it. He needed a pistol and his was inside the house. Morgan backed up slowly, keeping his eyes on the rattlesnake as he retreated. He limped to his horse, tied him to the post in front of his house and, after one last look at the snake, went inside for the pistol his father had given him on his fourteenth birthday.

When he returned to the stable, the snake was gone. Pistol in hand, Morgan searched the stall, the hay and water trough in the stable, but could find no sign of it. He then looked outside, cautiously stepping around the stable and through the piles of leaves left from the fall. Morgan gave up the search a half hour later and limped tiredly back to the house. Inside, he continued to worry that the snake might be hidden somewhere nearby and, on his way to visit Claudia Barclay that evening; he stopped to warn his neighbors.

Morgan did not return home that night. He stayed with Claudia and stabled his horse at her house. For a week afterward, he examined every foot of the path before returning his stallion to the stable. At the end of each day, he would dismount in the road, loaded pistol in hand, and slowly walk up the path himself, looking in all directions.

Claudia Barclay made Morgan soak his foot in hot water when she saw him limp into her house that night. An hour before visiting her, his ankle was so swollen he had trouble buckling his shoe. He had even more difficulty mounting his stallion. He cried out in pain when he put his left foot in the stirrup to heave himself up into the saddle. Dismounting at Claudia's house had been nearly as painful. He had bitten down on his leather glove to keep from cursing as his foot touched the ground.

"Ay, mi amor, you look terrible." Claudia gasped when she saw him. "Who you fight?" Morgan knew he looked like he had been in a brawl. He had an inch-long cut and a large bump on his head as well as a black eye. His left side ached where he had fallen and his shoulder was bruised and scratched where skin had been scraped off the stump. He looked at the abrasions for the first time when Claudia took off his shirt and cleaned his wounds. She dipped a towel in hot water and gently washed his wounded arm and shoulder with soap. After sponging his face and neck with warm water, she held a towel cooled with well water against the bump on his head.

"Qué cosa! (What a thing!)" She shuddered when he described his encounter with the snake. "Gracias a Dios, Jaime, you are no bit. Las serpientes kill much people in Florida. A serpiente de cascabel (rattlesnake) kill a boy near the house of my father when I live in San Agustín."

Morgan began to feel better after Claudia served him a full bowl of fish stew and a bottle of Spanish red wine. He drank three glasses of wine with the stew and finished the bottle when he moved to the sitting room to recline on the sofa. He fell asleep five minutes later.

Morgan met with Dr. Nunes Ribeiro on the following morning. He waited an hour and a half in the sitting room while the physician treated patients in his surgery. Morgan did not mind the wait, but was disturbed when he heard a child's scream a few minutes after entering the door.

María Adela was busy assisting the doctor, but she came into the house and spoke to him between patients or when not needed. Nunes Ribeiro signaled her by ringing a tiny bell when he required her help. During one lengthy period, they talked while she prepared lunch.

"I'm concerned about him, María Adela. He doesn't look well. Am I mistaken?"

"No. He's not well, but denies it. He tires easily and has pain. He thinks I don't see him close his eyes and grit his teeth – that's when the pain strikes him."

"Where is his pain?"

"In the stomach. I see him bend over and hold his hand there."

Morgan sighed. "I'll try to get him to tell me about it."

"Good." María Adela carried a kettle of water over to the fireplace and began cutting up vegetables at the kitchen table. She said nothing more. María Adela never said much to him or to anyone else, according to the doctor. She did not even comment on his bruised face.

After a few minutes, Morgan asked her if she knew Claudia Barclay. He knew the girl also had come from St. Augustine and spoke Spanish. In that small settlement, he assumed they must have known or at least encountered each other at one time or other.

"Yes, but not well. We have spoken a few times in the street and market."

"Did you know her in St. Augustine?"

"No. We did not live near each other."

Morgan suspected, though María Adela did not say it, that her family was not wealthy like Claudia's family and lived in a different part of town. He could not think of anything else to say to her and she left the room carrying a pan of hot water into the surgery. María Adela returned a short while later and, after making a pot of tea, poured a cup for him.

The bell then tinkled and she went back into the surgery and did not come out again until the last patient had gone. The doctor followed her into the sitting room a few minutes later. He looked tired and there were dark circles under his eyes.

"Ah, James, I'm sorry to keep you waiting. Don't get up." He frowned when he saw his friend's face. "You do look a sight. What happened to you?"

Morgan described his encounter with the rattlesnake, while the physician examined him. Removing his shirt, he felt his ribs and gently touched his shoulder. "Your shoulder is fine and the bruises and scrapes will heal soon enough. You're certain the snake's fang did not penetrate your shoe?" he asked, gesturing for him to put on his shirt.

"Yes, I was lucky he missed me. It appears neither of us was very accurate, though his strike was much closer than my sword." He held up his shoe and showed the doctor where the snake's fang had grazed the top.

"You were fortunate. Rattlesnake bites are more often fatal than not. Well, we should talk about Chapman's murder. I have a patient coming in an hour." He looked at his watch.

"I thought you were seeing only a few patients a week now." Morgan tucked his shirt in his breeches and sat down.

"I am, but I just happen to be busy today. Are you hungry?" He turned to look at María Adela who was sitting at the kitchen table, cutting up carrots.

"No. The tea is all I want."

"What did you discover down at Augustine Creek?"

"Nothing of importance. Stockwell will take another look to see if anything was missed. What about Chapman's body? Did it suggest anything useful?"

"No. As you know, the alligators took the man's legs and crushed his body; his face was squashed almost beyond recognition. I'm amazed they left his body on the mast. From the size of those I saw on the bank, I'm sure they could have pulled him into the water and devoured him. Why they didn't, I don't know."

"How do you think the alligators were attracted to Chapman's body? I wonder if his legs hanging in the water would have been enough to bring them to his body."

"Perhaps, but that might take too long. I can think of two other ways to entice them to the body. One would be to smear fish bait on his legs and feet and the other would be to cut his legs to make them bleed in the water. The smell of either would attract the alligators to him."

"It would be easier to bleed him. Of course, the murderer may have brought fish bait and spread it on Chapman's body in the same manner he spread honey on Sterling. Whatever he did, I expect he stayed to watch the man suffer as the alligators tore his legs from his body."

"That would be consistent with what he did with Sterling. What hate he must have felt for his victims. I wonder what provoked it. Somehow I can't believe it's a cruel nature alone that makes him kill so fiendishly." The doctor paused to take a cup of tea from María Adela. "Please forgive us for talking so plainly."

"Don't worry, I am fine." María Adela patted his hand. "It is necessary to know why those men were murdered in such a way."

"Exactly." The doctor turned his eyes to Morgan. "What we have concluded, of course, is that the murders come from hate and…"

"Vengeance!" added Morgan. "I've come to think that the two men were murdered for some foul deed or deeds they did in the past – perhaps together. But, so far, I can't connect them in any way except that they came into a lot of money around the same time. They seem to have had little, if any, contact with each other in Savannah and Captain Chapman did not even sail for Sterling." He told the doctor what he had learned from Bartholomew.

"How does the pastor know so much about the shipping business in Savannah?"

"He seems to know almost everything that happens here. Though not a gossip himself, he hears most of what is said in and about town. But I intend to ask Sterling's sons about Chapman this week. They must have shipping records of the vessels carrying their various cargos. I also want to talk to them about the construction of the new dock. Since they worked with their father over the years, one or both of them should know where he got the money to pay for it."

"What about Archibald Willington? I recall you told me he might have loaned Sterling the money for the dock." The doctor sipped his tea.

Morgan shook his head from side to side. "I doubt that now. Sterling's will was read last Friday and, since Willington made no claim against the estate, I must assume he didn't lend him the money. However, he's another one I must interview soon. Willington was a friend of Sterling and apparently the shipper met with him often."

"What has the Sterling family said about their friendship and financial arrangements?"

"That's another question I intend to ask his sons. And that brings to mind something else that bothers me. Chapman's wife told me the treasure he found was in gold and silver bars, but the Parker brothers said he paid for the *Brazen* in coin. I believe the woman, not the men. It's well known that the Parkers lie about their earnings; they have been building boats for years and surely have a fortune hidden somewhere in that cluttered shipyard. I can easily understand why they would lie about what they earned from Chapman's ship – that's typical of them. But why would they lie about what kind of payment they received?"

"Could it be that the gold and silver bars were contraband?"

"That's what I've come to think. Even before he built his own ship, Chapman may have been engaged in illegal trade, maybe with pirates or those outlaws who live at New Hanover. I surely don't believe the captain found a sunken treasure near Savannah. It sounds much like a children's story. His wife believed his story, however, and she's a very intelligent woman."

"Yes, women are all too trusting of their men." The doctor turned to look at María Adela. He saw her smile knowingly.

"It may be that women let men think they believe their stories." María Adela smiled.

The doctor laughed. "You're probably right. My wife would have said the same thing."

"That may well be." Morgan nodded. "I'll have to visit the widow again and ask her to describe the bars. Last time, I was too surprised to hear about Chapman's discovery to think of what I should ask her. I didn't even ask her the number of bars he claimed to have salvaged."

"It is an incredible story. I don't recall hearing of a sunken treasure ship anywhere near Savannah." The doctor sighed. "Keep in mind, I've lived here thirty-five years."

Morgan snorted. "It was all a lie. And isn't it ironic that Chapman was killed believing someone else's lie about a sunken treasure."

"It is indeed. By the way, did Stockwell find anything significant at Augustine Creek?"

"He found the captain's pistol on a high piece of land in the marsh. The land is little more than a sand bar that has built up over time and now stands above the water even at high tide. It's covered by sea oats and sand spurs. Stockwell said it's accessible from the stern of the skiff and Chapman had gone ashore there. He saw distinct marks in the sand where the captain stood and that's where he found the pistol; it was loaded and cocked. His sword also lay there in the sand."

"So, Chapman was wary about his meeting with the note writer."

"Yes, but it did him no good because he was struck on the head by a thick branch – in the same manner as Sterling. The branch was stripped of leaves and twigs like the one you found at the lake. Stockwell found the branch in the sand. It had a small trace of blood on the thick end – obviously Chapman's blood." Morgan drank the last of his tea.

"Did Stockwell see any marks in the sand where the murderer stood?"

"He didn't mention any, but he did say the spot where Chapman fell was easy to discern. Stockwell also found a track in the sand where Chapman's body was dragged to the creek."

"I assume it was the width of his shoulders?"

"Yes, he dragged him by his feet. The creek was at least thirty feet away, but Chapman was a slight man, no more than 130 pounds, and certainly easier to drag than Sterling. Once in the water, I guess he simply floated the captain out to the mast. All he had to do was to hold one hand on the boat's gunwale and pull the man along the side with the other. I'm sure Chapman's arms and legs must have been bound before he was dragged into the water."

"That would be essential in the event that Chapman regained his senses in the cold water. How do you think he got his body up on the crossbar?"

"Ah, that's the question, isn't it? I must say it took me quite awhile to figure out how it was done. This murderer is very, very clever! What he did was make sure Chapman sailed into the creek near or at high tide. At that time, most of the wreck's mast is well below water, but the crossbar is only inches above the surface and easy to reach. All he had to do then was pull the man to the mast and tie one arm after the other to the crossbar. The outgoing tide would expose Chapman's upper body, but leave his legs below the water. It was that easy."

"How did the murderer tie his arms to the crossbar? One arm at a time would have to be untied to do it and therefore free to fight his captor. Chapman could have regained his senses in the water before being bound to the crossbar."

"I think the murderer planned for that possibility, too. If Chapman gave him any trouble while one of his arms was untied, all the murderer had to do was push his head under water until he gave up his resistance." Morgan smiled. "I must admit it's hard not to admire his planning."

"I don't know if *admire* is the appropriate word for such a cruel killer, but his mind and planning are quite exceptional." He saw the major looking at his empty teacup. "Do you want some more tea? María Adela will make us another pot."

"No, don't bother, María Adela." Morgan stood and looked at his pocket watch. "I must be on my way to the courthouse and your patient will be here in a few minutes. I'll be back here on Friday as usual and, who knows, I might even win a game of chess."

The doctor stood. "Before you go, I don't want to forget to tell you the same knots were used to tie up Chapman and Sterling. One more thing. María Adela reminded me that

Thomas Sterling came here a week or so before his death. He brought his daughter, Margaret, to see me. She also reminded me that I was his family physician in the past when his children were young." He sighed and Morgan saw the sadness in his eyes. "I'm getting more and more forgetful these days. One day soon, I fear I'll forget my name."

Where does Nelson live? That question was the last one needing an answer. Thanks to Sterling, the red-haired man finally had a name. William Lyman Nelson was the man who wore the jaunty feather in his hat and talked incessantly. It had taken three years to learn his name, but it would not take long to find out where he had gone with all his treasure. Nelson was the only one who did not live in Savannah and neither Sterling nor Chapman had known where he went. In their final moments, they would have gladly revealed his whereabouts. There was nothing, not any secret, they would have hesitated to disclose if they thought it could possibly save them from their suffering. They did not know, but someone in Savannah knew and, sooner rather than later, Nelson's location would be discovered. His time would come and none too soon.

But, for now, there was still much work to be done. The fat fool and the greedy little man could be forgotten. They got what they deserved and no longer walked the earth. Let those in town spend their time looking in vain for explanations of why they were struck down. There was not much chance that they would find them, no matter how hard they looked.

CHAPTER FIVE

SAVANNAH:
WEDNESDAY, JUNE 11 – WEDNESDAY, JUNE 25, 1766

"We are quite concerned, Major, about your slow – very slow – progress on these murders." Palmer frowned as he peered at Morgan over his glasses. He had summoned the justice to his office at three in the afternoon following his meeting with the governor. "As you can certainly comprehend, Governor Wright is anxious to see this vicious murderer arrested. And, the sooner the better! The colony is still in an uproar over the Stamp Tax and these murders will inevitably worsen the situation. There already have been complaints that the king's men have no right to tax the people, especially if they can't keep law and order in the colony."

"Such complaints should have been expected once parliament passed the Stamp Act."

"The Stamp Act was repealed so pray tell me why should they still complain?" Palmer made a face. "And for the life of me, I cannot imagine why the tax was considered so onerous by the colonists. The taxes on contracts, deeds, notes and ship manifests affected only those who could well afford them." He shook his head in disgust.

"You forgot to mention those taxes that affected everyone in the colonies. The tax stamps were to be affixed to almanacs, books, newspapers, pamphlets and even marriage certificates and university degrees. It's a wonder parliament didn't want them put on death certificates."

Palmer ignored Morgan's sarcasm. "It was only a trivial tax and the colonists should have been amenable to pay it. The king has kept the American colonies in good order, protected them from the French and Spanish as well as the Indians – and even fought a long and extremely hard war for their security. But still the colonists are not satisfied. No, instead they constantly carry on about England's so-called injustice."

"I doubt many colonists would agree that England fought the Seven Years War for them. I think England went to war for the sugar islands in the Caribbean and control of trade in India, even though here in the colonies it was called the French and Indian War." Morgan sat with his hand in his lap. It was balled into a fist.

"Surely you know that isn't true." Palmer cocked his head to the side, looking at Morgan as if he had gone mad. "That war was fought to keep the Ohio Territory out of French Catholic control. You colonists were terrified of the pope's influence in America. England came to your aid and removed both France and Spain from all the land north of the Gulf of Mexico. But when parliament passed a petty tax to help pay for the war, then England became unjust and the king a tyrant. The colonists remain ungrateful even though England maintains a standing army here to defend them against foreigners and Indians." Palmer shook his head. "It defies understanding."

"It's easy to understand, if you look at it from the colonists' point of view." Morgan saw Palmer make a face.

"England acquired Spanish Florida and French Canada and all the territory east of the Mississippi River from the war. Those lands with all their products and trade benefit England, not the colonies, so why should they be willing to pay taxes for a war that profited King George and his rich aristocrats? And let's not forget the English merchants."

"Be careful, Major! You sound like one of those *Sons of Liberty* or should I say Sons of Licentiousness as Governor Wright appropriately named them. I would have called them Sons of Cowardice myself. Let's not forget what happened to their reckless attempt to seize the tax stamps. They scattered like rats in a sinking ship when the governor and fewer than fifty soldiers stood up to them – a mob of more than two hundred strong!"

"What happened to them has nothing to do with the injustice of imposing taxes on people who have no representation in parliament." Morgan felt himself getting angrier by the moment. He had been tempted to join the *Sons of Liberty* and had attended several of their meetings. But too much talk and too little action ultimately ended his interest in their activities. While Morgan agreed with their criticisms of English exploitation of the colonies, he was frustrated by the few acts of defiance they carried out in Savannah. He wanted them to do much more than hang the governor and the tax collector in effigy. Despite his disappointment with the *Liberty Boys*, he believed their cause to be just and resented Palmer's contempt for them.

"That argument makes no sense in a monarchy, even though it's a constitutional monarchy." Palmer leaned forward and pointed his finger at Morgan. "Surely you know better than to say something so – disrespectful." He stopped himself from saying *stupid*, knowing that would have humiliated Morgan and given him grounds for a duel. "Whatever else you colonists think you are – you remain subjects of the king. You should keep that in mind!"

Furious, Morgan was tempted to reach across the desk and knock Palmer out of his chair. He knew exactly what the arrogant Englishman intended to say and, at that moment, he hated the man. Morgan glared at Palmer, but said nothing for a long moment. Finally, gritting his teeth, he said almost too softly to hear. "So are all the people in England subjects of the king – yet they have representatives in parliament."

Palmer saw the fury in Morgan's face and, with Thackery out of the office on an errand, he was wary of the scowling man sitting across the desk from him. Well aware of his reputation for violence, Palmer replied in a more conciliatory tone of voice. "Because, Major Morgan, they are *Englishmen* and not colonists, that's why." His stomach churning, he took the risk and said with finality. "And that's the way it will remain."

Morgan again felt like reaching across the desk, this time to strangle the smug Englishman. But he held his anger in check and said, "I wonder. As we both know, Parliament was forced to repeal the Stamp Act in the face of so much opposition in the colonies."

"That was due to that weakness of Lord Rockingham and his crafty accomplice, William Pitt. When those two fools are out of the way, you can be sure other taxes will be forthcoming. Parliament declared as much in March when it announced the colonies were under its control 'in all cases whatsoever.' So much for colonial politics; we should be talking about the murders."

Morgan nodded. He knew there was no point in arguing with the Englishman. Palmer like the other English officials looked down upon the colonists as lesser beings only one station above the Indians and African slaves. The Englishmen said everyone served as subjects of the king, but thought of themselves as special subjects because of their English breeding.

"So, Major, do you have anything new to report on the murders?" Palmer had leaned far back in his chair, his hands forming a steeple on his stomach. "You might also tell me what has happened to your face. I hope it wasn't from some tavern brawl."

"No." Morgan sighed. He told Palmer about his battle with the rattlesnake.

"My God!" The attorney general sat up straight in his chair. "They're even around our houses in town. What a godforsaken place!"

"It's the time of the year. They seem to be more active in the spring after a cold winter." Morgan was amused to see fear in Palmer's face. "If I were you, I would warn your children not to play in the leaves. Your wife also might want to keep them inside the house for a few weeks until the snakes migrate back to the woods." He saw Palmer nod his head and knew the presence of the children in the house was bound to make his home life difficult, if not miserable. Morgan had met the man's wife once and knew she was not a patient woman.

Morgan then told Palmer about his meetings with Chapman's widow, the Parker brothers and the medical examiner. He described in detail the way Chapman had been bled to attract the alligators and was pleased to see the attorney general's annoyed reaction. Morgan did not tell him about his meeting with the Anglican minister. He intended to keep Bartholomew as a secret source of information.

"The sudden acquisition of wealth of both, ah, victims, is most interesting. I assume you will question Mrs. Chapman again about the supposed sunken treasure."

"Yes, and I intend to interview Sterling's friend, Willington. He's one man I don't recall ever meeting, though I've seen him in town now and then. I understand he is an especially generous supporter of the church."

"I know Archibald Willington from church. He appears

to be quite the concerned junior warden and has convinced several Catholics to attend our Sunday service. Willington has even helped Bartholomew convert one of them. But I must say that I find him too unctuous for my taste. And then there's that mannerism Willington has of shifting his eyes when he speaks to you – he never looks you in the eye. I will be very interested to hear about your interview with him."

"I intend to talk to him in the morning." Morgan was aware that Thackery had returned and was signaling Palmer.

The attorney general rose from his chair. "I must attend to other pressing business now, Major. But, before you leave, I need to stress the governor's concern about the slowness of your investigation. We need some results and soon!"

Archibald Willington returned home after an unusually long vestry meeting that evening. One of the men at the meeting drove him in his carriage. Willington did not own a horse because of a torn Achilles tendon that made it much too painful for him to ride even a short distance. He claimed to dislike horses and refused to buy a carriage horse, saying it would be too troublesome to maintain. He had hired men to remove his stable when he bought his house. Willington said it was healthier to walk anyway and he usually limped around town with a fixed frown on his face. Despite his claim to enjoy the freedom of walking, the junior warden never refused an invitation to ride in someone else's carriage

It was eleven o'clock when he unlocked his front door. Inside, he lit the oil lamp on the wall and had taken only two steps toward the kitchen, when he heard a loud knock. "Who can be calling at this time of night?" he thought to himself. Willington took his sword from its scabbard and turned toward the door. "I'll be there in a moment," he shouted. Relieved to see that he had remembered to engage the door bolt when he entered the house, he turned up the lamp to clearly illuminate the entrance. Willington then withdrew the bolt, but held his foot against the bottom of the door before opening it. With the sword firmly held in his right hand, he reached forward with his left hand and lifted the latch. He peered out cautiously, ready to thrust the sword into the person entering the door.

"Oh, it's you, is it?" Willington nodded knowingly, relieved to see the familiar face in the doorway. "It's 'bout time you came to pay your debt." He smiled seeing the silver coins in his visitor's hand. "It's late, but not too late to get a bit of silver. Do you want a dram of rum?"

He put his sword and scabbard in a stand that stood beside the door and turned to get the bottle he kept in the kitchen cupboard. The club struck him on the back of the head before he took his first step. When Willington regained consciousness, he found himself sitting naked in a wooden chair.

He could not move any part of his body below his shoulders. Tight bindings completely encircled his chest and waist, holding him securely to the chair. There must have been at least fifteen of them around his body. They had been tied so tightly Willington could feel them biting into the soft flesh of his chest. His arms and hands were held taut against his sides and his ankles and calves were tied to the legs of the chair. One additional binding, running over his thighs and under the chair, held him to the seat.

Once awake, Willington realized he was in the kitchen. The room was completely dark, but he could feel the kitchen's coarse wooden flooring under his bare feet. His body felt warm and he was sweating even though a cool breeze wafted in through an open window. There was not a sound in the house and for a few moments Willington thought he had been left alone. He tested the bindings on his arms trying to think of a way to free himself. "There must be a way to do it," he thought. "The important thing is to keep calm and not panic." Willington had escaped any number of life-threatening situations before and he felt confident he could survive this one, too.

His hopes of escape ended with the words he heard from the darkness. The voice came from behind him near the door that opened out the side of the house. Willington turned his neck to look, but could see only a glimmer of light from the hallway where the lamp hung on the wall.

"You will not escape. If you shout, I will club you senseless again. Do you understand?"

"What do you want from me? I've four hundred pounds hidden in my bedroom you can have if you let me go, now. I'll show you where it is." Archibald Willington had never known anyone who could not be manipulated by an offer of money.

"I know where your money is – under the loose board in your bedroom, but money isn't what I want. I want to know where Nelson lives."

"I've much more hidden elsewhere. I'll give you all of it, if you untie me."

"I will not waste words with you. I want to know where Nelson lives."

"If I tell you, then will you untie me? Will you let me go?"

There was no reply from the darkness and Willington heard footsteps moving away. He turned his head toward the sound, but could not see anything in the darkness. Seconds later, he heard the footsteps returning to the kitchen and saw the light of the lamp moving along the hall. The lamp was placed on the kitchen table and Willington now was aware that he had been bound to the new maple chair that Homer Moore, the best carpenter in Savannah, had made for him. It was only six weeks old.

The oil lamp had been dimmed, but it still cast light in a circle that included a portion of the table, his chair and a small area of the floor where his feet were tied. Looking down at his bound body, he saw newspapers, broken pieces of his wooden furniture and twigs piled around his chair. Everything had been arranged carefully, twigs and balled-up newspaper on the bottom and pieces of furniture on top. Several fireplace logs from his woodbin also had been placed on the pile. He then noticed the large jug of lamp oil, which he knew was almost full, sitting on the floor only a few feet away from his chair.

"You wouldn't do it," he mumbled weakly, terrified by the sight of the woodpile that had been built up to the height of the chair seat. Willington now knew with certainty that his wealth, which had bought him so much in the past, would not buy him his future. "I'll tell you where he is; I'll tell you anything you want to know. But, for God's sake, don't do it!"

The fire on Abercorn Street was not seen until one o'clock in the morning. A neighbor, on the way to the outhouse, saw the flames shooting through the roof. By the time the ten men of the water brigade arrived, the fire could not be put out. They found the building engulfed in flames and, full buckets ready in hand, they stood in the center of the street avoiding the intense heat. Along with a hundred or so spectators, the men watched first the roof and then one wall after the other fall in flames to the ground. The best the brigade could do that night was water down the area around the burning house and prevent the fire from spreading to the other houses on the street. At first light, Morgan arrived to find little left of Willington's house, except some still smoldering timbers and the blackened stones of the foundation. The stench of burnt flesh lingered where the kitchen had once stood.

Three days later on Sunday, Morgan left town at dawn to ride to his father's plantation. It had rained heavily the previous night and a humid mist hung in the air as he followed the muddy road south along the Savannah River. The sun did not appear until almost noon and, with dark clouds overhead, he rode slowly, scanning the ground for anything that might trip his horse. In some places, Morgan had to ride into marsh sand to get around washed out sections of the rutted road. At the oyster-shell mound that marked the halfway point to the plantation, he halted his horse to watch a water moccasin slither across the ground ahead of him. His shoulder still sore to the touch, Morgan waited a few more minutes to be sure the snake was gone before urging his stallion forward. The typical hour-long trip through the lowlands took nearly two hours and he arrived at the plantation a little after eight o'clock.

Morgan could see the house he had helped build a half-mile before he reached it. The sprawling log building stood on the highest point of land south of Savannah and was visible from the tidal tributaries of the river as well as the road. Matthew Morgan had built the house with the help of his wife, Rachel, and his two sons, seventeen-year-old Joseph and fifteen-year old James.

The Morgan family was one of the original forty families who made the long sea voyage to Georgia with Oglethorpe. They spent their first nine years in the new settlement of Savannah and then moved eight miles south of town to a 3,000-acre tract of land along the river. Oglethorpe granted the land to Morgan ten days before he returned to England. Matthew built his house on an inlet he called Morgan's

Creek. In the spring of 1742, when the Spaniards in St. Augustine no longer threatened Savannah, he moved his wife and two sons to their newly built home in the wilderness. The Morgans survived the first harsh winters by living off the land and the waters that were within a stone's throw of their house.

Most of their food came from the marsh, which teemed with fish, crabs and shellfish, but they also hunted deer, rabbits, turkey and other game in the woods. Rachel's canned vegetables from her garden added virtually everything else they needed. Flour, spices, sugar and imported food were purchased or traded in town for animal pelts. They also traded with the neighboring Indians. Within four years, the Morgans' dependence on hunting and fishing ended as they began to produce rice as a money crop. The first season's sales in Savannah alone earned them enough money for a year's supply of food and, by the spring of 1745, they were too busy to hunt or fish. Rice production increased to a point where all of their effort was focused on its cultivation. By the end of the decade, the family lived comfortably, working diligently in the spring and summer and only periodically tending to the plantation during the rest of the year.

Their rice production soared in the next two years and they became the leading exporter in Savannah. The talk in town said the Morgans were now rich and, when Matthew heard it, he simply smiled. In the autumn and winter, while the townsmen worked every day at their trades, many from dawn to dusk, the rice planter was often seen strolling through the streets or along the riverfront smoking his pipe. On cold days, Matthew sometimes would spend afternoons, sitting near the fireplace at the *Fox and Fiddle* drinking tea. He did not drink spirits of any kind after a difficult childhood with a drunken father.

When African slaves became available in 1749, Matthew Morgan took advantage of their labor and put more of his property into cultivation. Eventually most of his arable land was in use and he decided to buy additional land. With production and profit increasing every year, in 1761, Matthew approached the two neighbors whose property adjoined his plantation. He sought 1,000 acres from each of them. Aware of his mounting wealth, Arnold James and John Harrison made Morgan pay dearly for the land he wanted. Too proud to bargain, Matthew paid their prices even though the purchases put him in debt for the first time. But, by the end of the French and Indian War, Matthew Morgan was one of three largest landowners in the Georgia colony.

In 1755, tragedy struck the Morgan family. Their oldest son, Joseph, drowned when his canoe overturned on the river and he and a friend from town were swept out to sea. A ship from England approaching the mouth of the river discovered the canoe and the body of his companion entangled in fishing line. But Joseph's body was never recovered.

The family was heartbroken and Matthew, seemingly inconsolable, spent almost a month inside his house. He sat in the kitchen drinking tea or paced the floors for hours, day and night. Matthew lost not only his favorite son, but the one he had chosen to succeed him upon his death. Those who saw him when he returned to town said Joseph's death aged the planter a decade. In time, Matthew resumed his supervision of the plantation, but he no longer showed the enthusiasm and excitement of the past. He went about his work with a disgruntled look on his face.

Rachel never recovered from the loss of her first born and she grieved for him until the day she died. She spent all her time at home by herself, refusing to ride into town. The few women who knew Rachel made the hard carriage ride to Morgan's Creek to offer their condolences, but found she had little to say and made no effort to welcome them into her home. She seemed even distant to her husband and other son on his occasional visits to see his parents.

"When my brother died, my mother lost all interest in life," Morgan told the doctor one evening many years later. She seldom went outside and went about the house as if in a trance. It was obvious she was waiting to die. "Unfortunately for her," he muttered, "she had more than a decade to wait."

Morgan ate breakfast with his father on the porch of the house as was customary when he rode out to Morgan's Creek. The Portuguese housekeeper served them a crab and cheese omelet with freshly baked bread. His father spiced his omelet with hot pepper seeds he traded from his Indian neighbors. They finished their breakfast with strong English tea imported from London.

"I see you have a new housekeeper. What happened to Beatriz?" Morgan sat back, his arm lying on the porch railing. He studied his father and noticed the weight he now carried. His father's face seemed fuller and his stomach protruded over the top of his breeches. Matthew had always been proud of his hard muscular body, but he now looked soft and flabby. His father also had rheumatism, which made him drag his left leg as he walked. A sense of sadness struck him as he saw the signs of aging in the strong man he had wanted so desperately to be like as a boy.

"She left a week or so ago to care for her ailing mother in town. I'll miss her. She was a wonderful cook." Matthew would eat only Portuguese food, claiming that English food was no better than animal feed. "God, I'll miss her arroz de marisco."

"How's the new one doing? What's her name? You didn't introduce her to me."

"Catalina. I will when she comes to pick up the dishes. She's Beatriz' cousin and also a Portuguese widow recommended by the doctor. Catalina's Jewish, of course, and a pretty good cook. She needs to spice up her food a bit." Matthew smiled. "You know how I hate subtle tastes."

"I do. I trust she'll satisfy you."

"I think she'll be fine. She has a couple of young children; they're now with a sister, but will be coming here next week. It'll be good to have children about the house again. It's been a good many years since I've heard the cries or peals of laughter of little ones and I can surely use some playful company around here. But, tell me, son, what are you doing about those murders in town? Do you think they're connected?"

James nodded and then told his father everything he had learned about the murders. He considered his father a wise man and respected his thinking, although he did not often agree with his views – especially his political views. Matthew was an ardent supporter of English rule.

The Morgan family had prospered under the king's colonial system and Matthew believed the complaints about England's exploitation of the colonists were foolish. He argued repeatedly that the colonists should consider themselves fortunate to have England as their mother county. "Who else would have protected them from the foreigners and Indians?" he had asked the other planters who complained about the Stamp Tax. "Keep in mind, everything you enjoy and own, you owe to England's control of the seas and the safe passage of your goods abroad. You should thank God for George III in your prayers every night."

Matthew listened carefully to his son's description of the murders and said, "I agree with you. It seems the murders were done by the same man." He fixed his son with an eye-to-eye stare. "Do you have no idea who that man might be?"

"No." Morgan shook his head. "Now there's Willington's death and, though I have no reason to say it, I think he was murdered by the same man."

Matthew frowned. "Why do you think that?"

"Because Willington like Sterling and Chapman had unexplained wealth in his possession. He claimed his riches came from growing tobacco in Virginia, but Reverend Bartholomew lived in Richmond and never heard of a wealthy planter named Archibald Willington. I've written to Richmond to inquire about him and also to Charles Towne to learn if anyone knows of him there. So, I should know more about him soon."

"That's a weak argument for him to be a murder victim. Was there anything remaining in his house after the fire to support your intuition?"

"No, but there's one other connection." He ignored his father's use of the word intuition, which he knew was a subtle criticism. "Willington apparently enjoyed a friendship with Sterling – they met frequently and talked privately in Christ Church, but there's no known explanation for it. No one seems to know how or when they met. Neither Sterling's sons nor his wife had ever met Willington and did not know the friendship even existed. Stockwell asked the family about their friendship when Sterling's will was read a week ago." Morgan leaned forward and tapped his fingernail on the weathered table. "There's one more interesting fact – despite the friendship they supposedly shared, Willington did not attend Sterling's funeral."

Matthew nodded. "That is interesting. Have you told Palmer about your suspicions?"

"No. Without any proof of Willington's murder, Palmer would see his death as simply a coincidence. So, for the time being, I'll keep my suspicions to you and myself. Of course, I'll tell Stockwell as well and talk to the doctor."

"That makes sense. That old Jew is a wise man. You'll have to excuse me, James. It's my time for the outhouse. I'll be back in a few minutes."

Morgan watched as his father struggled up from his chair and hobbled, with the aid of his cane, toward the outhouse behind the building. It pained him to see his father, who had walked so fast in the past, grimace as he cautiously took one step at a time down the stairs. He recalled when he was a boy and had to run to keep up with him. Morgan sighed, realizing his father's rheumatism had advanced even in the short time since his last visit.

Morgan finished his tea while he waited for his father to return. He introduced himself to Catalina when she appeared to remove the dishes. He stood to greet her and held her hand. The housekeeper blushed at first, but, when he told her of his friendship with Doctor Nunes Ribeiro, she talked to him as if she had known him for years. Catalina was talkative and spoke English with a distinct Portuguese accent. She smiled easily and seemed to be the kind of warm woman his father needed to care for him. James liked Catalina immediately and grinned in amusement as he watched the stout woman waddle away with the dishes in hand.

"What's so funny?" His father frowned as he slowly climbed the stairs to the porch.

"Nothing. I just met Catalina and I think you found a jewel."

"Is that so? Well, we'll see. You know what they say, 'a new broom sweeps clean.'"

Breathing hard from the exertion of walking to the outhouse, Matthew slumped into his chair with a sigh. "Tell me, what else do you know about Willington? Was he a friend of Chapman, too?"

"We know little about Willington except that he came to Savannah a few years ago with a lot of money. I haven't yet discovered if he had any contact with Chapman. What surprises me is that George Chapman never sailed for Sterling. It seems that once the *Brazen* was launched he sailed exclusively for the Douglas Shipping Company."

"I can understand that preference. Sterling was known to be a miserly man who paid his captains poorly. And you know what I think of that."

"You have always said, 'a well-paid man will always give

you a good day's work.'"

Matthew smiled. "I'm glad you remember. And that's why I use Hugh Douglas to ship my rice. I pay him well – probably more than any other planter in this colony, and he pays his captains well. The man is honest and reliable. In all these years, Douglas has lost only one of my shipments and that was in that terrible storm three years ago."

"Wasn't that the ship that went down without any survivors?" James saw his father nod his head. "I assume Chapman was one of the captains who carried your shipments."

"He carried any number of them, but it was Hugh Douglas who selected the captains and ships to carry my products. I do know that Douglas favored Chapman and often said he was one of his three best captains. I understand he has made Mrs. Chapman a very generous offer for the *Brazen*. That's a stout ship."

"It is. Douglas has the schooner docked in front of his office now and I've seen it from the riverfront. He also had his men retrieve Chapman's skiff from Augustine Creek."

"I assume the skiff will be included in his offer to the widow." Matthew stood and leaned heavily on his cane. "Let's take a bit of a walk around the place. It'll do us good after all that food. I've made a few changes I think will interest you. Oh, yes, and I want to tell you about a trip I've planned to Charles Towne. Don't look at me that way – I am able enough to do it."

Morgan met with the Sterling brothers the following Monday. He arrived at their office at eight o'clock to avoid riding there in the late morning sun. A slight and unexpected breeze off the river cooled his face as he rode along River Street.

The crew of the *Stalwart* was busy loading cargo when he tied his stallion in front of the Sterling Company building. The Savannah River flowed twelve feet below the bluff where the town had been settled and Morgan stood beside the company office watching the men lowering bales of tobacco into the hold of the ship. Luke Sterling, the older brother, sat astride a stool on the deck, supervising the loading. Morgan found Mark Sterling inside the shipping office. He sat at his desk pressing the company seal on a thick envelope obviously full of ship's papers.

Mark looked up inquiringly. "Good morning, Major. I wasn't expecting a visitor. I'll be with you in a minute or so. I must take the manifest down to the captain. He's sailing while the tide is high."

Morgan nodded and sat down in a chair across from the desk. He watched as the shipper dipped his quill in an inkpot and hurriedly recorded numbers in a ledger. Sterling's notations fit neatly into columns that had been made by vertical lines drawn down the page. The cover of the thick leather ledger was scratched and worn and more than half its pages had already been filled. When Mark finished writing in all the columns, he closed the ledger, nodded to Morgan and left the office. From the open window overlooking the dock, the justice watched him run down the stairway and hand the sealed envelope to his brother. They spoke briefly and his brother looked up at the office. Morgan smiled, knowing Mark had told Luke about his arrival.

Morgan turned away and walked over to the desk. He picked up the ledger and opened it to the first page, which had a heading of Shipping Ledger and the date 1755 written beneath it. Morgan turned the pages to the one with 1763 on top. He began with that year since he assumed the *Brazen* had been launched that year or the next. He ran his forefinger down the left side of each page looking at the first and second columns, which listed the names of the sea captains and their ships. Morgan did not see Chapman's name or the *Brazen* anywhere on the first four pages. He had reached December 1765, when Mark entered the office.

Morgan looked up from the ledger when Mark closed the door. "Did George Chapman carry any cargo for the Sterling Company?" he asked, his finger still on his place in the ledger.

"I don't think so. I don't recall him sailing for us in the five years I worked with Father. You can ask Luke when he arrives. Or – you can continue to look through the ledger yourself." Mark's flushed face betrayed his irritation.

Morgan closed the ledger, unconcerned his inspection of the ledger had angered Mark. "I'll wait and ask Luke. How many years did he work with your father?"

"He started three years before me and…" Mark turned as Luke came into the office.

"Major." Luke placed a sheaf of papers on the desk and reached over to shake Morgan's hand. "What can we do for you?"

"He wants to know if George Chapman ever sailed for us." Mark spoke before Morgan could answer his brother.

Morgan glared at Mark. "Don't speak for me again!"

Luke quickly spoke to avoid the justice's anger. "Not as captain of the *Brazen*, but he served under a number of captains who carried our cargo. You probably know he was first a seaman and then a mate before he built his ship. As a third mate, he usually was in charge of cargo storage and we worked with him innumerable times on the dock."

Morgan nodded. "Were you both working with your father when he extended the dock?"

"Yes. The new dock was built in the summer of 1763 and we both were here at the time. Why do you ask, Major?"

Morgan ignored his question. "How did your father pay for it? I know the company had financial problems at the time."

The brothers exchanged looks and Luke replied. "We were doing well enough. I don't know where you heard that rumor."

"It doesn't matter. What I want to know is how your father paid for the new dock."

"I have no idea." Luke shrugged.

"Neither do I." Mark shook his head.

"Are you telling me that you worked every day with your father in this office and yet you don't know how he paid for the construction? That's hard to believe." Morgan glared at them.

"We are being truthful." Now Luke's face was flushed. "For the first few years I worked here, I spent nearly every day on the dock supervising the loading and unloading. When I wasn't so engaged, I was required to clean and maintain the dock. I also managed the dockworkers. I rarely came up to the office in those years. Mark performed the same duties when he arrived. I was given paper work responsibilities only three years ago when Father put me in charge of the shipping ledger and the records of ship arrivals and sailings. Father always kept money matters in his own hands."

"Unfortunately, we still don't know all we should about the company because Father kept so much of the figuring in his mind." Mark made a face. "He left us few written records and it's been near impossible trying to sort everything out. We've had to learn what to do by ourselves."

Morgan held up his hand and spoke softly. "Enough said—I understand. Before I leave I want to see whatever records your father kept. They might reveal some reason for his murder. By the way, do either of you recall seeing gold or silver bars in his possession?"

The brothers exchanged bewildered looks. "What kind of gold and silver bars?" Luke shook his head, a puzzled expression on his face.

"Bars of bullion like those that might be found on a sunken ship."

Both brothers shook their heads, still looking bewildered.

"Did either of you know Archibald Willington?"

"No sir, at least not well enough to have a conversation." Mark looked at his brother and Luke shook his head. "Sergeant Stockwell already asked us that at the reading of Father's will."

"Well, I'm asking you again." Morgan scowled at Mark.

"We never met the man outside of church." Luke looked at his brother. "As you know, he was the junior warden at Christ Church. We saw him there, but never anywhere else."

"He never came here to the office to visit your father?"

"No, never." Luke shook his head.

"So it came as a surprise to you when you heard he was a friend of your father?"

"It did." Luke frowned. "He didn't seem the kind of man who would be his friend."

"What do you mean?" Morgan saw the brothers exchange looks again.

Luke clucked his tongue. "He seemed… common."

"He was coarse and uncouth," interrupted Mark. "Even with all his money he spoke like a man from the streets and had deplorable manners. At a church supper, I once saw him eat with his hands and afterward wipe them on the tablecloth. And he never would look you in the eye—even when saying, 'God bless you.' There was something… unsavory about him."

"Are you saying he wasn't a man you would trust?"

"Yes, quite so. I was astonished when the vestry made him junior warden." Mark shook his head. "Of course, it was well known that he had given a lot of money to the church."

"That must be the reason why Father spent time with him." Luke pointed his forefinger at his brother. "Father probably was the one who persuaded Willington to donate his money to the church. I can see him doing it."

"So can I." Mark nodded. "I'm sure that's why Father spent time with that man."

Morgan rode away thinking about his interview with the brothers. He doubted that their father's friendship with Willington had anything to do with donations to Christ Church. There was something else involved and he suspected it had resulted in the murders of the three men in Savannah. Even though he had not yet discovered a connection between Sterling and Chapman or Chapman and Willington, he was certain the three men had been involved together in a secret enterprise that made them all rich. Whatever the venture, he knew it had to be criminal in some manner and probably had cost at least one man's life. If someone had been killed in the process of carrying out the enterprise, it would explain their murders. A vengeful relative, most likely a father or son, would have had good reason to kill the three men. The vicious way in which they were slain might have something to do with the cruel manner the murderer's loved one had been killed. Morgan thought of God's Law for the punishment of wrongdoers he had read in Exodus 21:24-25. He remembered it word for word from his childhood.

Life for life, tooth for tooth, hand for hand, foot for foot,
Burning for burning, wound for wound, stripe for stripe.

Could Oliver Palmer's religious explanation for the murderer's merciless killings be correct after all? Morgan still doubted it, but he would have to keep the possibility in mind. As the justice neared the courthouse, he wondered if Sterling, Chapman and Willington had been the only men in the enterprise. If so, hopefully there would be no more murders. He needed time to look into the many possibilities that already existed and he worried that Palmer would not give him the necessary time to find the murderer. The attorney general and, probably the governor as well, were already impatient with the pace of his investigation. He would be replaced if he did not show some significant progress soon.

When Morgan arrived at his office, he found Stockwell standing at the one window in the room, fanning himself with an old issue of the *Georgia Gazette.* His shirt soaked with sweat, he was making a futile attempt to sweep some of the slightly cooler outside air into the office. He turned with the rolled newspaper in one hand and, with the other, pointed to a soiled envelope on Morgan's desk.

"It's from the Justice of the Peace up in Richmond." Stockwell announced, as he resumed his fanning. "I'll wager he says Willington wasn't from Virginia. He was no more a tobacco planter than me. I once heard him talking in a tavern and he sounded to me like one of them that knocks heads on the docks of London. I doubt the man could read or write."

Morgan tore open the envelope. The letter inside was brief.

Richmond. June 16th. 1766
Major James Morgan
Justice of the Peace
Savannah
His Majesty's Colony of Georgia

Sir,

This letter is in reply to your inquiry of June 6th. 1766. No known man with the name of Archibald Willington has resided in His Majesty's Colony of Virginia. My clerk examined the census for the years 1740, 1750 and 1760 and found no subject of His Majesty with that name in Virginia. The President of the Planters Association also has informed me that no such man ever possessed land in this province.

With due respect,
Jeffery Bottomly, Esquire
Justice of the Peace
His Majesty's Colony of Virginia

"You were right." Morgan handed the letter to Stockwell. "Now, let's see what we hear from the justice in Charles Towne."

"It'll be the same. I wager he was an outlaw in the past and never lived in one place for long. Willington came here from who-knows-where with a purse full of coins and that's all there is to know about him. There's no wife or children about and he lived alone without even a whore to keep him company. No one ever seen him with a wench and I'd guess he was an outlaw who lost his balls in a fight. I'd say when you know more about him, you'll find he was a nasty rascal who done a lot of brutish things in his life. I expect he got what was coming to him."

"Perhaps. Willington was probably old enough to have been a pirate when they were all over the Caribbean." Morgan sat on the edge of his desk. "I never met the man, although I saw him about town. He looked like he was well past fifty."

"I would say he was older. I saw a lot of him in taverns when he first came to Savannah. Then he found the church and he was no longer seen in his cups. Probably drunk himself dumb at home. Anyway, Willington didn't wear no wig and you could see the long hairs that old men get sticking out of his ears, nose and the top of his bald head. All the hair he had was white, too. I'd say he was the other side of sixty."

Morgan nodded. "Old men often go to church more and it's not only the Catholics who give generously when they see death around the corner. They think they can buy their way into heaven after a past full of sins." Morgan shook his head. "The fools expect God to forgive them if they purchase a few new pews in the back of the church."

"Of course, a poor man can't make those arrangements."

"No, and that's what's foolish about their expectations. They think that Christ, who cared more for the poor than the rich, will be concerned with them because of what they give. Those few wealthy who do read the Bible conveniently forget what Matthew said, wasn't it in 19:24?"

Stockwell lowered his fan. "Yes and even I know that one. 'It is easier for a camel to go through the eye of a needle, than for a rich man to enter the kingdom of God.'"

"That's it! What's more that has nothing to do with a past life of sin, which the rich also conveniently forget stands against their hopes to enter heaven. Well, so much for our look at the Bible. You know I don't believe a word of it." Morgan sighed and flipped one hand upward as if to sweep the Bible away.

"I do, and I fear you'll pay for it when the time comes."

"That may be." Morgan stood, dismissing his comment. "I'm going to see Chapman's widow again and I want you to do a dirty task. The ruins of Willington's house must be searched to see if there's anything that might tell us more about his death. What little that remained of the man has already been removed by the undertaker so it shouldn't smell too bad. But wait until the sun is almost down – it's too hot, now."

Stockwell groaned loudly. "Dirty, you say? Ha! That's a task that deserves at least a pint of rum. You know that stench will still be there, never mind the flies and smell of fire."

"You'll get the pint if you find anything useful."

"Before you go, I want to tell you about my talk with that little toad, Canfield." Stockwell laid the rolled newspaper on Morgan's desk. "I didn't hurt him much at all – I only boxed his ears a time or two. But he stuck to his story and said he didn't pick up nothin' on the path. He said he bent over thinking he seen a Morel mushroom, but then seen he was wrong. That was all there was to it. I scared the shit out of him and I don't think he lied to me."

"I doubt it, too. Well, it was worth a try anyway." Morgan saw Stockwell nod his head. "One more thing. I suggest you take a shovel when you go over to Willington's house." Morgan grinned. "Who knows what you might find – maybe even some of the man's money. No one has found it yet, you know."

"I got as much chance of coming on that outlaw's hoard as the captain finding treasure at Augustine Creek."

Martha Chapman served Morgan freshly baked biscuits with his tea. Despite his obvious impatience to talk to her, she made him wait while she blessed the food. The widow then made him wait longer while she spread blackberry preserves on his biscuits. She permitted him to ask questions only after Morgan had eaten two biscuits and finished one cup of tea. There was a faint smile on her face as she watched him hurriedly eat the biscuits.

"In this house, Major, we bless God for our food, share our bounty and then talk business. I'm sure your mother made you follow the same good manners."

"She did indeed. Did you know my mother?"

"Not well. She seldom came to town, although I did

see her now and then at the market. After your brother's tragic death…" Mrs. Chapman closed her eyes momentarily, thinking of her husband. Her eyes were wet when she opened them. "I heard she secluded herself at Morgan's Creek. I certainly never saw her again."

"It's true. She spent all her time at home alone."

"I can surely understand the pain she felt after her loss. I have one son, John, and I don't know what I would do if I lost him." She sighed. "No parent should have to suffer the loss of a child, especially a son who survived the worst years of childhood."

"She never got over the death of my brother – not until the day she died."

"Such losses are very hard." She sighed again. "But I don't intend to wallow in self pity. I will mourn at home for a decent period and then I will find something else to occupy my time. Now, Major, what is it you want to ask me?"

"The last time we talked, you told me your husband found a chest of gold and silver bars in a sunken wreck."

"Yes, that's what George told me. But, now, I don't believe a word of it! I have thought a lot about that treasure since we talked and I think he acquired it – I do not know what other word to use – some unlawful way. I think he lied to me rather than face my disapproval. I remember now how agitated he was at the time. He was up to no good – I'm sure of it!"

"I think you're right. What I don't know is what he was up to. Did you see one or more of the bars?"

"I saw two bars, one gold and one silver. George had a leather pouch full of them. He said he had twenty-four of them, but he showed me only two. I don't know how many of each."

"Do you remember anything about the bars? Can you describe them?" Morgan felt his stomach tighten as he saw her frown in thought.

Martha Chapman placed a finger on her cheek. "They were about half a foot long and a little over a half-inch wide. There was writing on them and seals of some kind. There also was a capital letter stamped on one end of the bar. What was it? I'm not certain… maybe an 'M?' I'm sorry, that's all I can recall."

"That's fine. Can you recall anything else?"

"Yes, I think the writing might have been in Latin or Spanish."

Morgan spent that night with Claudia Barclay. They ate dinner with Carolina and her son and then, trying to find some elusive breeze, they sat in the walled-in patio that had been built at the back of the house. They spent only a short time outside. Not one leaf stirred in the trees and a dark cloud of mosquitoes seemed to descend upon them as soon as they sat in their chairs. With conversation continually interrupted by the need to slap or wave off mosquitoes, they gave up the evening in the night air and retreated into the house.

Carolina and her son Felipe went upstairs to their room and Claudia and Morgan sat in the living room fanning themselves. They sat in darkness. As the church bells chimed at eleven o'clock, a wind blew in from the west, signaling the arrival of a summer storm. In only minutes, they felt the first cool air flow into the room and put down their fans. With the welcome wind, the sweet fragrance of night-blooming jasmine wafted into the room. They went outside into the patio again and watched lightning light up the dark clouds in the western sky.

The wind increased in strength and, when the window shutters banged against the house, they knew the storm would soon strike Savannah. Claudia went back inside with the first drops of rain and Morgan followed her a moment later when he saw lightning overhead. As he stepped back into the house, brilliant streaks of lightning and explosions of thunder filled the evening sky and Morgan knew everyone in town was now wide awake. Claudia had left an oil lamp lit in the living room and he walked toward it as the rain began to fall in torrents outside. Morgan quickly closed the windows on the first floor and went upstairs to close the two in Claudia's bedroom.

He and Claudia then lay on the couch, her head resting on his chest and one arm around his waist. Neither of them spoke and Morgan stroked her soft hair with his hand. Claudia had removed her shoes and stockings while he was closing the windows and now she rubbed her bare feet against his legs. Morgan sighed with satisfaction. Claudia then pulled his shirt out of his breeches and, moving her hand beneath the shirt, she spread out her fingers to mimic a spider's legs and went walking up and down his chest.

"You're tickling me." He laughed and twitched as she moved her fingers over his chest.

"There is more I do." She nipped at his neck with little bites.

Claudia slowly walked her fingers down to his breeches and unbuckled his belt. "Look what the spider do," she said, unbuttoning his breeches and moving her fingers over his stomach.

"I hope the spider doesn't hurt me." Morgan spoke in a shrill child's voice.

"No," she giggled, "The spider no hurt you."

Claudia continued to walk her fingers down to his pubic hair. She then stopped abruptly. "The spider not know what to do ahora." She giggled again and began nibbling on his ear.

Morgan laughed. "I think it knows what to do." He spoke softly in the child's voice.

Claudia then grasped him firmly and moved her hand

rhythmically up and down.

"Oh, my God," Morgan moaned. He turned Claudia's head upward and kissed her nose, her cheeks and mouth. He pressed his lips against hers and pushed his tongue into her mouth.

"Ay," Claudia gasped and rolled off his body. She stood up and stripped with a frenzied speed. Claudia then pulled his breeches down and mounted him with an anguished cry. Bent over him with her breasts in his face, she moved up and down in unrestrained passion. Closing her eyes, she was lost to all sights and sounds and felt only him inside her and her body on him. She cried out at the end and then fell onto his chest, her hair in the crook of his neck.

Later, when they went upstairs to bed, they cuddled with him behind her, listening to the rain beating on the roof above them. They lay that way without moving or speaking as the storm passed overhead and moved out to sea. After the rain had ended and they had taken turns going outside to the outhouse, Claudia told him what was on her mind. Morgan tossed and turned and slept little that night.

CHAPTER SIX

SAVANNAH AND CHARLES TOWNE:
THURSDAY, JUNE 26 – MONDAY, JULY 21, 1766

Morgan spent Thursday evening at the house of Doctor Nunes Ribeiro. He arrived to find that María Adela had gone out and left them a rabbit stew that was still lukewarm. She also had cut up two tomatoes from the garden and saved half a loaf of the bread for their meal. The plates were covered by towels to keep the flies off the food. The major drank a glass of wine while the doctor set the table.

"I think María Adela has someone courting her." The doctor glanced at Morgan as he put their plates on the table. "She's been out and about in the evenings these last few weeks and only smiles when I ask if she has met someone. She's not only shy, but now is being secretive. I'm not surprised, of course. It was inevitable she would meet someone sooner or later."

"Aren't you concerned about María Adela going out alone at night? I wouldn't expect her to have a chaperon, but at least a friend to accompany her. There are many unsavory types in Savannah."

The doctor shook his head as he removed the towels and motioned for Morgan to sit at the table. "What you say is true about the scoundrels in town, but don't forget María Adela has Indian blood and knows how to take care of herself. Woe to the rogue who chooses her for his mark. Not only does she carry a knife hidden somewhere in her bodice, María Adela is much stronger than she looks. Keep in mind, she's the one who chops our firewood and cuts up our meat. Any man who has seen her use a cleaver would know she's not one to be bothered."

Morgan nodded. "That's good to know. Do we need a blessing tonight?"

The doctor shook his head. "No, when the cat's away, the mice can play." He chuckled. "We're like two children with our mother away."

"Yes, we are. Though they say this is a man's world, men always seem to be submitting in one way or other to women's wishes."

"It's true. Well, we can be the mice once again next week when María Adela is away. She's going to St. Augustine to visit her family for a few days."

"Do you need any help in the surgery while she's gone?" Morgan continued to worry about the doctor. The elderly man's face not only looked drawn and pallid, he now seemed to grimace as if in pain every time he stood up or took a step.

"No, I'll be fine. I'm not nearly as frail as I look." He smiled as if reading Morgan's mind. "Please pour another glass of wine for me."

They finished their meal and, while the doctor washed the dishes in a pail of well water, Morgan cleaned the table with a wet towel. He took the pail outside and sprinkled the dishwater over the vegetable garden. When the major returned, he found the doctor seated in one of the two cushioned chairs near the door. Another bottle of red wine and

Morgan's glass stood on the table beside him. Morgan sat in the other cushioned chair and stretched his legs out in front of him.

"You know Claudia Barclay is welcome here any time." The doctor smiled at his friend.

"I know." Morgan sighed. "I now have a problem with her – a serious problem."

"I see." The doctor said nothing and waited for Morgan to continue.

"Claudia is with child." Morgan rubbed a hand over his mouth.

"Ah, and you don't know what to do?"

"No. I know what to do, but it… frightens me." Morgan looked at the doctor and sighed again, this time in exasperation. "I love her and I know she is the woman for me. But…" He paused and then said nothing.

The doctor again waited patiently for Morgan to continue.

"I worry about what will happen to her when it's her time."

"What do you mean?"

"I never told you about my wife – her name was Elizabeth. We were married when I was young – only twenty. I met her in Virginia while away at the College of William and Mary. We were married less than a year. Elizabeth died in childbirth and so did the baby – a boy." Morgan exhaled his breath loudly and looked down at the floor.

"Ah, so that's why you're worried about Claudia."

"Yes. I know it's not sensible, but I fear I will lose Claudia – like Beth—if she has a child. So many women seem to die in childbirth."

"That's certainly true. But most of the women who die when giving birth, die because of incompetent midwives. Even if I'm gone, there are several good doctors now in town, who can help Claudia through the birth of your child. Dr. John Morris is one I would recommend."

Morgan glared at the doctor. "And, where are you going?"

"You know very well I'm failing. I see it in your eyes. I don't feel well and I don't think I have long to live."

"You don't know that." Morgan continued to glare at his friend.

"I do know it. I have abdominal pain and there's dark blood in my stool." He raised his hand to stop Morgan from speaking. "I don't want to talk about it anymore. Now, what you must do is to make sure a physician is with Claudia when her time comes and she has birthing pains. It's not assured she will do well, but she will have her best chance with a physician present. Do you hear me, James?" He saw Morgan shake his head.

"I'll see to it at the time," he mumbled. The doctor's description of his illness remained on his mind. Morgan felt closer to the old man than his own father. He dreaded the possibility of the doctor's death and he didn't want to believe it. Yet, he saw the signs of his sickness and knew the time would come – probably much sooner than he could imagine.

"So, what do you intend to do for now?" The doctor sipped his wine.

"I must go to Havana and ask Claudia's father for her hand in marriage. I haven't asked him before now because I knew our marriage would mean child bearing..." He exhaled his breath loudly. "I dreaded what might happen to Claudia when her time came."

"But when you bedded her you surely knew the risk of pregnancy."

"Yes, of course. But since she had not been with child during her marriage to Barclay, I thought it might not happen with me either. I also tried, when with her, to withdraw at the final moment. I didn't always succeed, however, as you can imagine." Morgan gave the doctor a wry smile.

The doctor laughed heartily, showing several gapes in the back of his mouth where he had lost teeth. "The Catholics have tried that futile practice for God knows how many centuries. And you know who has the largest families." He shook his head from side to side. "I'm sorry James, I know it's not funny to you."

"I know I've been a fool, especially with a passionate Spanish woman." Morgan threw up his hands. "But I couldn't do without her, could I? Well, it's too late now for regrets and, as they say, there's no sense 'crying over spilt milk.' I'll make sure a physician is present when it's her time. But that's in the future, for now I must sail to Havana. Since the war is over, it shouldn't be a problem entering Cuba."

"I wouldn't think so. You should go as soon as possible before Claudia shows any signs of her pregnancy. Her father won't be aware of anything different about her, but her mother and the other women in the family might well see something he wouldn't ever notice. As you know, women always see things in other women that men never see. It's as if they have another eye to the world that men completely lack."

"That eye sees hidden things in men, too."

"It does indeed, but I think that eye watches women more closely." The doctor chuckled. "I recall my Rebecca warning me that a female patient was flirting with me and I would tell her she was imagining things. Then sometime later, the woman came see me about an invented illness and began removing her clothes. She suggested I give her an intimate exam."

"Did you?" Morgan smiled.

The doctor's face reddened. "No, of course not, but a year or so later another woman used false symptoms to undress and approach me. It was quite an awkward experience and I've never forgotten it."

"Of course, you never told Rebecca about either of them." Now, it was Morgan's turn to laugh and he chuckled seeing the doctor's pained expression.

"No, I did not! That's definitely not something you tell your wife," he said, his face still flushed. "By the way, I didn't know you had gone to college."

Morgan suppressed a smile when the doctor changed the subject. "For only two years. I didn't complete my studies. My father wrote and told me I was needed at the plantation. I was glad to leave Williamsburg. I had buried Beth and the boy there only a month earlier."

"I see. Well, let's talk about your trip to Havana. Will Palmer approve it?"

"I don't know. He's becoming impatient with the murder investigation. He may remove me from office, whether I go to Cuba or not."

"It would be foolish for him to remove you and, no matter how pompous, Palmer is not a fool. As I recall, he once thought of removing you and then thought the better of it."

"That's because he couldn't find anyone willing to wrestle vomiting drunks and disarm angry gamblers. But I think I have a good reason to go to Havana, one that should appeal even to Palmer." Morgan told him about Chapman's gold and silver ingots. "I assume they're Spanish."

"From her description of them, there's no doubt. Especially with the 'M' on them." The doctor saw Morgan's puzzled look. "The 'M' stands for Mexico where they were minted."

"How do you know that?"

"During the war, a Spanish ship was seized near St. Augustine and brought to Savannah. It had been in a convoy struck by a summer storm and blown off course on its way from Cuba to Spain. The ship carried about fifty or so bars and the Spanish captain told us the meaning of the engraved symbols. I was asked to translate what he said to our officials so I learned a little about Spain's minting methods. The Spanish captain – I've forgotten his name, was held prisoner here until he was eventually exchanged for one of our captains." He refilled Morgan's glass. "So, you plan to tell Palmer about Chapman's bullion and the necessity of a trip to Havana to learn where he acquired them."

"Precisely. I think Palmer will release me, albeit reluctantly – especially when he hears that Willington was another victim of the murderer. I think I can convince him with the three pieces of proof I now have thanks to you and Stockwell. One by itself wouldn't convince him, but three should do it. The tiny scrap of corduroy you found stuck to Willington's burnt flesh, the charred bit of binding that Stockwell pulled out from the iron chair support and the Phoebe lamp found near the remains of the body."

"What makes the lamp one of your proofs?"

Morgan pointed to a Phoebe lamp on the wall near the closed door. "Lamps like that one hang on the wall, not sit on a table. The Phoebe lamp Stockwell found was in the center of what had been the kitchen. It was in the burnt debris beside the body where the table and chairs would have been. It was well away from any wall in the room. Though blackened, the metal lamp was still intact even with its collection cup; the glass dome was gone of course. I think the murderer tied Willington to a chair in the kitchen and used the lamp to set fire to him."

"That makes sense. Meu Deus! (My God!) What intense hatred that man feels toward his victims." The doctor shook his head and then excused himself to go to the outhouse.

Morgan drank the rest of his wine and refilled his glass while he awaited the doctor. He thought about Claudia and decided to visit her after playing their game of chess. He looked at his watch and saw it was already 8:30. They probably would not have time for a chess game that night since the elderly man went to bed at nine-thirty.

"There's been one more important discovery," Morgan told the doctor, when he returned.

"What was discovered?" He spoke slowly, a bit out of breath from his walk outside.

"I told you that the justice in Richmond reported that

no man with the name of Archibald Willington ever lived in Virginia. Well, today I received another letter from the justice in Charles Towne and guess what he wrote about Willington?"

"Willington never lived there either." The doctor took a sip of his wine.

"Yes, but he told me something even more important." Morgan looked up at the ceiling. "I can repeat it word for word.

'We have no knowledge of a man named Archibald Willington in this province, but we do have a report from army headquarters about such a man. It has the date of August 26th, 1760, and states that a suspected brigand by the name of Archibald Willington has been seen residing in the outlaw settlement of New Hanover.'"

"Ah, so everyone's suspicions of the man were warranted. It seems that men cannot hide their pasts no matter what they do in the present. You, of course, know what Shakespeare wrote, 'Foul deeds will rise, though all the earth o'erwelm them, to men's eyes.' Wasn't New Hanover that illegal settlement set up by the notorious Edmund Gray and his band of outlaws? As I recall, it was south of the Altamaha River and defied both English and Spanish officials for years."

"Yes, that was the settlement. It was occupied by criminals, debtors, and outlaws. Gray moved there sometime in the middle of the last decade and his men built some log houses on the site and called it New Hanover. The settlement expanded in time and almost a hundred outlaws eventually lived there; apparently Archibald Willington was among them. It became a location for illegal trade, smuggling, the sale of stolen goods and who knows what other criminal activity. Even though our English officials as well as the Spaniards knew of its activities, they did nothing to destroy it – why, I don't know. In fact, the settlement lasted ten years until the end of the war in 1763, when the king established the boundaries between East Florida and Georgia. New Hanover was abandoned a year or so earlier and that's when Willington came to Savannah. I recall seeing him at the time – limping about town. He must have been wounded in the midst of some crime."

"That makes his friendship with Sterling even more interesting."

"It does. I think those two along with Chapman were involved in some illegal enterprise that made them all quite wealthy. It probably happened before the end of the war and obviously involved Spanish bullion. It's easy to assume the bullion was seized or stolen somehow. But from where? That's a question I haven't been able to answer."

"A seizure at sea? Could they have been aboard a pirate ship that seized a Spanish ship bearing gold and silver bullion?" The doctor drank the last of the wine in his glass.

"I doubt it. The English navy controlled the seas all along this coast during the war, even beyond St. Augustine. Any captured Spanish ships would have been seized by the navy – in the manner of the ship you mentioned earlier. Besides, most of the gold and silver bullion from the New World was mined and removed in the sixteenth and seventeenth centuries. I doubt much is produced now in Mexico, though I've heard that silver is still mined in quantity in Peru. These days, as you know, the Spaniards ship mostly foodstuffs and timber from their colonies."

"That leaves only a theft on land." The doctor tried to stifle a yawn.

"It does." Morgan saw the yawn and knew he should take his leave. "Whether by land or sea, I should be able to learn in Havana where they procured the bullion. It's not likely they got it in Mexico. Incidentally, I suspect there were more than three men in the enterprise."

"Why do you think there were more than three men involved in the scheme?" The doctor yawned and this time he could not hide it from Morgan. "Forgive me for yawning, James. As you well know it's not from boredom."

"I know." Morgan smiled. "We can finish another day."

"No, I want to hear everything now." The doctor sighed. "I'll have time to sleep later."

"There's really not much else to discuss for now. As to why I think there were more than three men, I have no good reason to say it. I simply think there were more. It's a notion I have that I can't explain."

The doctor shook his head. "I have had those moments when there were no symptoms for a patient's illness, but somehow I knew what it was. In the end, I found I was right and I suspect you will find you were right as well."

"We'll see. Whatever the number of men involved, I'm certain they killed one man, if not many, as they carried out their scheme. I'm also sure they killed viciously. That's why they had to suffer such horrible deaths. They were not simply killed. No, the murderer wanted them to die slowly and in excruciating pain. They were first securely bound and made aware of their fate and then, helpless to save themselves, they faced a death only the devil himself could design."

"Yes, and not only did the murderer want them to be aware of what they would suffer, he watched them in their misery." The doctor shook his head. "I can't imagine such cruelty."

"What kind of man could be so cruel? A madman?"

"Perhaps. If not mad, he is a man who has little or no regard for civil or religious law or morality. He is merciless and apparently so moved by hatred and vengeance that he may not be of sound mind. If these terrible killings had taken place in Spain or Portugal, I would think the man might be a religious fanatic or one of the Inquisition's torturers. But here in Savannah, it's hard to imagine someone even conceiving of such cruelty. Yet, here he must be, unless he came from outside for the killings and now has gone."

"Something tells me he's still here in Savannah and walking casually among us. He may well be mad, but, if so, he hides his madness well enough to escape notice. I know of no one in Savannah who seems mad with anger or shows such viciousness. Do you?"

The doctor shook his head. "I know of no such man, nor have I ever seen one in town."

Morgan nodded. "There are a few witless people in town, but they're under the scrutiny of their families and rarely out of their sight. There's that old bearded man who sits on the river bank mumbling to himself, but he couldn't ride a horse if his life depended on it."

"I doubt the murderer is a madman. He's much too clever to be mad. The man may have his mad moments, but I think he's consumed with hatred and vengeance and those moods all too often have been behind the murder of men."

"That's very true. Well, whatever he is, we need to find him soon!" Morgan noticed the doctor rubbing his eyes. "I should leave." He raised himself from the chair.

"Sit, sit." The doctor waved him down into the chair. "Before you go, I want to know the current mood in town. Since I don't leave the house much these days, the only news I ever hear comes from the few patients who still come to see me. As you know, María Adela tells me little of what she hears in town."

"We are very fortunate the townspeople know so little about the murders or there would be panic in the streets. For now, they don't know there were three murderers nor do they know one man is the murderer. Since we so often have drunken men dying from fistfights and knifings in the taverns, few people seem concerned. Stockwell tells me that there are even those who think Sterling and Chapman probably got what they deserved."

"One of my patients told me he heard that Sterling was killed by someone he had cheated in business. It seems Sterling had a reputation for dishonest dealings."

"That's the rumor around town. Stockwell also told me the tavern talk is that the captain was killed by Indians. It's said he hated them and insulted them whenever they crossed his path. Of course, no one knows what happened to Willington. There was nothing unusual about the fire that killed him, especially since it followed the fire that destroyed the Elliotts' house the previous night. Let's hope the town remains ignorant until we find the fiend. I assume you've told María Adela to say nothing about our discussion of Sterling's murder."

"María Adela never mentions what she sees or hears in the surgery or with you when we discuss matters of the medical examiner's office. As you well know, she is not much of a talker anyway. I sometimes wonder what she says to those who court her."

"Sometimes it's like pulling teeth to get her to say anything. Well, I'll take my leave. I intend to talk to Palmer when he returns from Charles Towne. He's gone a week. We'll know then what he thinks about my proposed trip to Havana." Morgan stood and stretched.

"It shouldn't be too late to find a game of faro somewhere in town." The doctor's eyes twinkled as he teased Morgan about his gambling.

"I'm not playing tonight. Everyone's gone. Williams has been sick all the week with a stomach ailment, probably from some tainted oysters he ate out of season. Cameron went to see his father in Charles Towne on some business he wouldn't talk about. To tell you the truth, lately I haven't felt much like sitting in a smelly tavern drinking and playing cards."

"What about Claudia? I'm sure she would welcome you."

"Later tonight. She and Carolina are with the other Catholics. There was a baptism and a confirmation, I think."

The doctor stood up and hugged him. Morgan patted the smaller man on the back. The Portuguese custom of hugging men always made him feel uncomfortable, but he accepted it from his friend. Morgan turned around as he reached the door.

"You know, there are times when I wonder if we will ever identify, never mind arrest, this clever fiend."

The doctor smiled. "I have a notion it will all be over by the beginning of autumn."

Nelson had been dozing in the sitting room when he heard the rapping on the front door. He rose with a sigh, pushed his feet into his slippers and paused only long enough to drink the last of his brandy. "I'm coming," he shouted, scuffling to the door as the knocking continued. He noticed the pouring rain when he looked outside and saw the man standing on the stoop.

"Well, what a pleasant surprise." He smiled and shook the man's hand. "Come in, you look soaked to the skin."

"I am a bit wet. My hat blew off and I got drenched chasing it down." He walked into the house as Nelson stepped aside.

Nelson looked out into the rain before closing the door. "Where's your horse?"

"I came by coach; it will be back in about an hour."

"I see. A short visit, eh?"

He nodded. "I have another man to meet this afternoon."

"I'll get you a towel. Are your feet wet?"

"No, just my head and shoulders."

"Come, sit down. I'll get you a towel and make us a pot of tea."

Hesitant to sit until he dried his face and hands, the visitor stood while his host was gone.

Nelson returned and handed the man a white towel. He gestured him to a chair. "Well, how many years has it been?"

"Two years or so." The visitor ran the towel over his face and neck and briefly rubbed it over his hair. He used the dry end of the towel on the shoulders of his jacket. He kept his eyes on Nelson the entire time.

"That long?" Nelson pointed to the floor when his guest held the towel out to him. "You haven't changed much – a little more gray in your hair."

"A little more belly, too." He dropped the wet towel on the floor.

"Well, I've got more than a little of that." Nelson smirked. "Too much more!" He was a thin narrow-shouldered man with a protruding stomach that drooped over the top of his breeches. He had red hair flecked with gray and a pale face badly pitted from the pox. "I'll get the tea and be back in a minute." He again gestured his guest to a chair.

The visitor looked around the room while he waited. It was hard to see very much since only one small table lamp lit what seemed to be a spacious sitting room. There were surprisingly few pieces of furniture in the room. There were only two upholstered chairs, the table and an oil lamp. In the dim light, he could see little beyond where he now sat across from his host's chair. Spectacles, a pipe, a cracked plate full of pipe ash and an open book were on the table. He reached over and saw that Nelson was reading *Robinson Crusoe.*

Nelson returned at that moment with two steaming cups of tea. "Drink up, I don't want you to catch your death of cold," he said with a smile. He sat in his chair, sipped his tea and then picked up his pipe. Leaning back, he looked at his visitor. "Well, I trust you are still doing well down in Savannah." He reached into his pocket for a packet of tobacco.

"I'm doing quite well. What about you?" He sat erect and watched his host use his pinky to dig out the burnt tobacco from his pipe.

"Oh, I'm all right." Nelson busied himself refilling the pipe.

"Has anything unusual happened in the last few weeks?"

"No, why do you ask?" He stared at his visitor, his brow furrowed.

The visitor's answer was lost in a burst of thunder that seemed to reverberate throughout the house. He held his hand up, signaling he would speak when the noise subsided. The thunder exploded every few seconds and they sat looking at the brilliant streaks of lightning though the windows. As the thunder began to abate, they heard the creaking of shutters and rain pelting the side of the house. Minutes later, the noise finally ended as the storm moved away to the south.

"It's one of those evening storms we get here all summer long. I assume you get them in Savannah, too."

"We do, especially in August and September. So, your circumstances remain the same?" The visitor carefully watched his host's face.

"I'm still in debt, if that's what you mean. Much the same as I was when I saw you last." The host made a face. "I sometimes think I'll never be free of it." He held a thin stick to the oil lamp and, when it flamed, he lit his pipe.

"The last time we met, you needed money to pay for your wife's funeral." The other man finished his tea and set the cup and saucer down on the floor beside his chair.

"Yes, and I thank you for your loan. I hope you're not here to ask for repayment because I can't give you anything now. My debts have grown like weeds after a heavy rain, and whatever I pay to cover the interest, there's still more, never mind the outstanding principal. I've sold my best horses and most of my furniture. My creditors have recently threatened me with jail."

The visitor stared at his host, a look of disgust on his face. He knew Nelson, as usual, was poor mouthing so he would not press him for money.

"I'm not here to ask you for money. When I loaned you the £100, I never expected to get it back. But, for God's sake, what did you do with all your share? With what you got you should have lived like an English lord for the rest of your life. You got the lion's share after all."

"I deserved every bit of it. It was my plan, my leadership. It never would have happened without me. You sound like that miserable little weasel, Willington, who wanted what I got. The greedy bastard – all he did was make us trouble. It's a wonder we escaped. After what he did, I should have killed him on the spot. Instead of slicing his Achilles, I should have cut his throat."

"Probably so. You know I never complained about my share. It was enough for me as I told you at the time. But what happened to all of yours?"

"I pissed it all away. Drinking and gambling, that's where it went. Damn it, that's what I did, pissed it all away – every bloody bar and coin." Red-faced, Nelson struck the wooden arm of his chair with the palm his hand. He stood abruptly and took a brandy bottle and two glasses down from a shelf behind his chair.

"Would you like a brandy?" He banged a brandy bottle down on the table. Uncorking the bottle, Nelson filled one glass and, waiting for a response, looked at the other man.

"Not for now." The visitor intended to keep his wits about him. There was the possibility that Nelson was the murderer and he needed to be watchful. He had a knife hidden in his sleeve, which he could withdraw swiftly if the man made any menacing movement.

"Well, if it's not for money, what brings you all the way up here on such a foul day? Is it Sterling's death? I heard he was murdered. We got some sketchy news about it several days ago. Something about a brutal killing. Do you know what happened? Did that miserly bastard refuse to pay someone what he was due?" He chortled loudly and drank half the brandy in one swallow. "Yes, I still drink too much." He looked for disapproval in the other man, but saw none.

"Sterling wasn't the only one killed – George Chapman was murdered as well." He saw his host's eyes widen and his mouth drop open. "I'll tell you about it."

"My God! Both Sterling and Chapman murdered!" He gasped when he heard what had happened to them. "What a way to die! Who could be so damned heartless?" He drank the rest of his brandy and refilled his glass. "Do they have any idea who murdered them?"

"None at all. The murderer has never been seen. He's very clever and has left nothing of meaning to trace. They were lured out to remote places where he took his time killing them." The visitor expelled his breath loudly. "What he did to them is… beyond anyone's worst fears."

"Who could be so damned cunning? Willington? I wouldn't put it past the cruel little weasel! You've seen his sadism. I wouldn't dare turn my back on him. I heard he killed a man for winning a few coins from him in a card game. He stabbed the poor fellow as he got up from the table. That's why they threw him out of New Hanover."

The visitor glared at him. "Then, why in damnation did you bring him in with us?"

"He's the one who gave me the notion for it all, but you can be certain I watched him the entire time. I scarcely slept and kept a loaded pistol in readiness. Do you think he's the man? I suppose the greedy bastard wants everyone's cache. Well, I'll cut him to pieces if he ever shows his ugly face here."

"Willington's dead, too. His house burned down and he died in the fire. It happened less than a fortnight after Chapman's murder and it's too coincidental to be an accident. There's only one conclusion to make of the murders and I'm frankly… concerned." He would not admit his fear to Nelson. "I think our lives are in danger as well."

"Good God! So that's why you asked me if anything

unusual had happened in the last few weeks." Nelson looked deadly white in the lamplight. His hand trembled as he reached down to pick up his glass. "All three of them murdered!" Nelson thought it over for several seconds. "It means that someone knows what we did. But how?"

"I've asked myself the same question many times over in the past two weeks and I have no answer. But I've come to the conclusion that how someone knows is not important. No, what is important is that someone not only knows, but also intends to kill us. The murder of the others leaves just you and me and we are marked for death." He knew Nelson was not the murderer; the man's shocked reaction to the murders ended any worries he had about him. Completely unnerved, the man now sat shaking in his chair. "I came here to warn you so you can do whatever is necessary to safeguard yourself. I expect he'll soon be coming for us and I doubt we have long to wait."

"God, yes, that leaves only you and me." Nelson wrung his hands as if to warm them.

The visitor nodded.

"Is it money? I haven't much left, a bar or two, but I'll give him everything – the house, the horses…" Tears appeared in his eyes and Nelson wiped them away with his shirt sleeve.

"He doesn't want our money. He wants our deaths."

Nelson locked and bolted the doors that night and put a loaded pistol within reach on his nightstand. The next day he had a carpenter install stronger locks on the doors and latches on the windows and shutters. Within a week, his house was closed up and he had transferred his horses to a neighboring farmer's barn. He paid the farmer's son to feed and exercise the horses for a six-week period with the possibility of longer employment. All the activity around his house quickly came to the notice of his neighbors who assumed he intended to embark on a long journey. They were surprised a few days later to see him still coming and going and then mystified after a week to see him still at home. They knew the closed-up house would be intolerable in the July heat.

"It must be like an oven in there," one neighbor said to his wife. "How can he possibly stand it? He'll dry up like a potato in the fireplace."

Nelson survived the sweltering heat by spending most days down in his now empty wine cellar. He moved one of his sitting room chairs into the damp cool room and there he sat reading and drinking, only occasionally going up to the main floor. Nelson continued to eat his meals in the kitchen and, at night, he slept in his bed on the second floor. Since no high trees stood beside his house allowing access to the upstairs windows, he would open the two in his bedroom and let in whatever breeze blew in from the river. He used a chamber pot at the bottom of the stairs and emptied it every morning in the outhouse. Whether in the bedroom, cellar, kitchen or even in the outhouse, he carried a loaded pistol. By the end of his first week of vigil, the former officer felt completely secure in his newly safeguarded house. He named it *Nelson's Fortress* and drank half a bottle of brandy to celebrate his efforts.

Whenever Nelson left his house, he carried his pistol and knife for protection. Though unnoticed when he walked about town, he had the pistol inserted in the top of his breeches and a sheathed knife attached to his belt. Either could be drawn in less than a second. The wool jacket he wore to hide his weapons did provoke some quizzical stares, especially during the third week when the temperature soared to 98°, but Nelson pretended not to notice. As was customary, he would raise his hat and smile politely to those who passed him on the street. The townspeople, he assumed, would think his jacket was simply an eccentric affectation like the feather in his hat.

After a month, Nelson began to resume his normal life. By that time, without seeing any sign of danger, he left the damp cellar and once again padded unarmed around the house. Nelson did not doubt his life might be at risk, but when so much time elapsed without incident he began to think he might not be a marked man after all. It occurred to him that the murderer might not know his name or where he lived. The other killings had taken place in Savannah and the cruel brute might also be ignorant of his role in the enterprise. There had been no attempt to lure him out of town, like Chapman and Sterling, and since his house was now locked and secured, he no longer worried that the murderer could get in and set fire to it.

After a miserably hot weekend in his fortress, Nelson decided it was time to reduce some of the security measures he had put into place. He intended to be cautious, but he would not let fear rule his life. "I'll not let my guard down," he assured himself, "but I'll not hide in here like some scared rabbit in his burrow." Nelson once again opened the first floor windows in the early mornings and late afternoons and, during the day, he kept the doors locked, but no longer bolted. The wary man continued to keep a pistol at his side wherever he sat, but, as time passed, he often forgot where he put it. The pistol would be left beneath an opened book or newspaper, much like his spectacles, which he also misplaced. His silver-hilted officer's sword, which stood beside his favorite chair in the sitting room fell over and lay on the dusty floor beyond his reach.

Six weeks after hearing about the murders in Savannah, Nelson changed his routine in the evenings and began opening the windows and shutters around eight o'clock.

That was what most residents in Charles Towne did in the summer months. After years of living in the province, the townspeople realized they could keep their houses cooler if they let the night air in after dusk and then closed the windows and shutters in the morning to keep the heat and sun out during the day. They also hoped for an evening thunderstorm or a random wind off the river to keep their homes cool and perhaps limit the number of mosquitoes that flew in at night.

Still cautious before going to sleep, Nelson continued to close and latch the windows on the first floor and made sure all the bolts and locks on the doors were secured At twelve o'clock, when he habitually retired to his bedroom, he would hold his pistol at his side and walk through every room in the house before mounting the stairs. Once in his bedroom, Nelson bolted the door to the hall and lit the lamp on his bedside table. He then lowered the wick so the light would last throughout the night. The last thing he did before undressing was open the bedroom windows as wide as possible in the hope of a breeze from the sea. A cool night's sleep would be well worth a few mosquito bites in the morning.

On Saturday evening, Nelson walked to the *White Stallion* and drank a bottle of rum with a couple of retired army officers. He carried his pistol to and from the tavern. He walked home after midnight and staggered inside, telling himself it was time to bring one of his horses back in the morning. Maybe he would bring them all back. Before going upstairs to bed, he bolted the doors and latched all the windows except the one in the kitchen. He had just finished latching the sitting room windows and was on his way to the kitchen when he had to relieve himself.

Nelson had been drinking steadily for three hours and suddenly felt the urgent need to use the chamber pot. He turned from the sitting room and hurried into the hall.

Standing unsteadily over the white pot and groaning in pain, he finally managed to open his buttoned breeches. When Nelson finished, urinating more on the plank floor than in the pot, he stumbled up the stairs and, too tired to undress, hurled himself on his bed. He did not think to bolt the bedroom door and completely forgot about the unlatched window in the kitchen. His only thought was the return of his racehorses; he pictured himself on his big black stallion leading them home. Seconds later, Nelson was asleep and snoring loudly. Sleeping deeply, he did not hear the rasp of the kitchen window as it was lifted nor did he see a hooded figure climb over the sill.

Nelson awoke from a nightmare in which he had fallen into the sea and could not move his arms to swim. As his eyes opened in the dark room, he realized the right side of his face was pressed into the coverlet on the bed. Nelson knew that was the way he had fallen asleep and, in fact, the way he often slept with his right arm extended straight out and his left arm hanging over his stomach. He had slept in that position since childhood. But now as he tried to move his arms, he realized they were not where he expected them to be. Neither were his hands; they were tied behind his back so tightly his fingers tingled. His legs also had been bound tightly together at the knees and ankles. It occurred to Nelson that he had been trussed up like the hog carcasses he so often saw hanging in butcher shops.

Aware of a faint light at the foot of the bed, he tried to slide his body in that direction. He thought it might be possible to slip off the bed and stand up, even though hampered by the tight bindings that held his legs together. He then could shuffle to the bedroom door, turn his back and cut the bindings by rubbing them against the door's edge. A sharp blow to the back of his knees brought tears to his eyes and he immediately stopped moving.

"Don't move!" said an unfamiliar voice. "I'll move you

when I'm ready."

Nelson opened his mouth to speak, but before he had a chance to say anything a cloth ball was stuffed into his mouth and held in place by a binding tied around his cheeks and neck.

"Don't try to speak. If you make a sound, I'll hit you again, this time harder."

Nelson remained motionless for what seemed at least an hour. Tied down on his stomach, he could not see above or behind himself. The light came and went and he knew the oil lamp was being moved in and out of the room. Every few minutes, he heard footsteps coming up the stairs and the creaking of the next-to-last step before the landing. The warped board had creaked all the years he and his wife, Marian, lived in the house and he could not count the number of times she had asked him to fix or replace it.

For a second, Nelson saw Marian standing in the bedroom, hands on her hips, asking him if he intended to wait until she was dead and buried before he did something about that step. He recalled her criticizing him with that irritating voice of hers. Marian's voice would rise to a high-pitch tone that ran through him like the sound of a screeching child. In the end, of course, he had done nothing with the bloody board, though it would have taken him no more than a half hour to hammer in a replacement. The creaking step had never bothered him before, but now the sound made him grit his teeth every time a shoe stepped on it.

Suddenly, Nelson heard the din of his downstairs furniture being broken. Even with one ear pressed hard into the bedcover, he recognized the sound of splintering wood. The noise came from the kitchen and he pictured his captor wielding the firewood axe to smash his kitchen table and chairs to pieces. The chopping continued for some time and then Nelson heard the footsteps on the stairs and entering the bedroom. A load of what Nelson assumed were broken pieces of his furniture was dropped on the floor and then the footsteps went back downstairs. Not a word was spoken to him on that trip to the bedroom or during the five others that followed. He heard only the footsteps on the stairway, the noise of the wood falling on the plank floor and the grunts of someone carrying heavy loads. Nelson knew the six trips up and down the stairs had only had one purpose – to pile the broken pieces of the furniture on the bedroom floor.

Apparently neat and orderly, the intruder piled the pieces of wood on all three sides of the bed and beneath the headboard, which stood against the wall. After the sixth load was dropped on the floor, he heard heavy breathing from the hall. Nelson knew how hard it was to make one trip with anything heavy up the narrow stairway, never mind six of them. He realized the last load of wood had been brought upstairs when the lamp was held up to light the room and he heard a sigh of satisfaction. The footsteps then left the room and walked slowly down the stairs. He wondered if the pot of tea he had made that afternoon and left standing on the kitchen table would be drunk after all the hard work.

When the footsteps did not return for a time, Nelson tried to crawl quietly off the bed. But he quickly discovered the bindings that bound his arms also tied him to the bed. They had been run around and under the bed a number of times to make sure he could not get up or move very far in any direction. The murderer had thought of everything.

William Lyman Nelson was no fool and knew he had little time left to live. He also knew the awful suffering that awaited him. He would die the same way as Willington, in terrible pain. The thought of what was coming made him shiver and he started to cry. As the tears ran down his cheeks, Nelson wondered if there was anything he could do to stop what was to come. He could only hope he would be given the chance to plead for his life. There had to be a way for him to say something – beg for forgiveness, plead for mercy, beseech in God's name. Nelson would say or do anything to save his life. If only he could speak to this man, he could say something – something to prevent the torment that had been planned for him.

A few minutes later, Nelson heard the footsteps on the stairs and the creak of the second-to-last step. The light reappeared and he felt the weight of someone on the bed behind him. He could tell that person was kneeling over him and he felt his body released from the bindings that had held him to the bed. His hands and legs remained tied and he was rolled over like a log onto his back. Nelson cried out when the full weight of his body fell on his bound arms. The searing pain was excruciating and remained when the bindings were run over his chest and under the bed to hold him in place.

A face appeared over him, but it was too dark in the room to make out any features or the color of the eyes. The bedroom lamp had been placed somewhere near the doorway and gave too little light for him to see anything clearly. Nelson guessed the wick had been turned down lower than he set it at night.

The figure looked down at him. "You wouldn't know my name even if you saw my face. But I'll tell you and my words will be the last you ever hear."

Nelson tried desperately to speak, but could do little more than mumble incoherently.

"Don't try to speak! It's of no use and I don't want to hear anything you would say."

The figure stood beside his bed and talked to him for several minutes. The story was told in a few short sentences and Nelson gasped when he heard it all. He now knew his fate and what was in store for him. He tried again to speak, but his captor moved out of sight.

Nelson smelled wood smoke before he saw the flames. He struggled to slide off the bed, but was immediately stopped with a vicious blow between the legs. Almost breathless, he closed his eyes in agony. Seconds later, when Nelson opened his eyes again, he saw the flames leaping up at the foot of the bed. The fire began to spread to the woodpiles on both sides of the bed and the smoke burned his eyes. He tried once more to slide off the bed, this time over to the left side where he saw the lowest flames rising from the floor. Again, Nelson was struck hard in the groin and he groaned in pain. He doubled-up, bringing his knees to his chest, and when he recovered enough to look around him, he could see the end of the mattress burning where his feet had been. His eyes wide with terror, Nelson tried desperately to scream for help, but choking on the cloth ball in his mouth, he only managed to croak weakly. The fire quickly consumed the goose-down mattress and no matter in which direction he twisted the flames relentlessly followed him.

Before leaving, the murderer stood momentarily in the hall and waited until the writhing man on the bed no longer moved. The bedroom was completely engulfed in flames by that time and the heat and smoke had become intolerable. Certain the entire upper floor would be ablaze, the murderer hurried down the stairs and set fire to the two piles of broken furniture in the sitting room. The wood slick with lamp oil instantly burst into flame. A few seconds later, the murderer, once again hooded, climbed over the windowsill in the kitchen and jumped down to the ground. Though resistant to the first two efforts to pull it down, the window finally closed on the third try and the hooded figure disappeared into the darkness.

For the next few minutes, Nelson's house looked as serene as the other houses on Maiden Lane. It took the fire awhile to burn through the wood-shingled roof, but, once outside fed by the fresh air, the flames swiftly devoured the upstairs rooms. The downstairs fires spread throughout the first floor soon afterward and, within a quarter of an hour, everything inside was burning. By then, Nelson's neighbors, awakened by someone's hysterical shouts of fire, stood in front of the blazing house waiting for the fire brigade to arrive. They watched the spreading flames consume the building, knowing nothing could be done to save it.

The hooded figure meanwhile had walked to nearby Cumberland Street and mounted the horse that had been hidden in a thicket of oak trees. No one noticed the horse or its cloaked rider leave the neighborhood. Hearing the fire wagon's clanging bell, the residents on the street were running to see the burning house. They ran past the oak trees unaware of the horse and rider. The hooded rider waited until everyone had gone before spurring the horse toward the city gates.

Leaving the city was routine, requiring the usual bribe for the guard and, in no more than a minute, the rider moved the horse through the gates. An empty road appeared ahead and, though long and tiring, the ride to Savannah would be finished in two days' time. Once on the road outside of town, the rider glanced back at the darkened city and saw an orange glow in the night sky. It was situated where Nelson's house stood in the wealthy section of the community. The rider nodded knowingly and put the horse into a canter that soon left Charles Towne far behind.

As in the past, there was no feeling of elation, only weariness and worry. Everything had gone as planned and yet the dread of discovery haunted the rider. Even in the dark of a moonless night, it was possible that someone had seen something that could lead to exposure or arrest. The most perilous moment had been the entry into the house through the noisy window and, since no one had raised an alarm, there really was no reason to worry. Yet, the uneasiness could not be so easily dismissed. It remained even after a fortnight had passed.

It was now time to think of the last man. The fourth man had finally paid his debt. Only one more remained and he would be the hardest to bring down.

CHAPTER SEVEN

SAVANNAH: MONDAY, JULY 28 – WEDNESDAY, JULY 30, 1766

Morgan found Martha Chapman waiting for him in his office when he arrived Thursday morning. She sat in Stockwell's chair, which he had placed beside the open door. The sergeant, always shy with proper women, stood well away from the prim widow near the window. Before Morgan's arrival, they had been discussing the recent invasion of biting gnats that had come like a biblical plague to Savannah. The justice greeted Mrs. Chapman and gestured for Stockwell to wait outside in the hallway.

"Well, Mrs. Chapman, it's certainly a surprise to see you here this morning. We don't see women very often in the courthouse." Morgan saw her amused smile. "How may I help you?" He walked over to his desk and leaned back on the front edge facing her.

"You may not help me at all, Major Morgan. I am here to help you." She smiled like a little girl with a secret. Mrs. Chapman opened the large purse she held in her lap and, rummaging inside, removed a long object wrapped up in newspaper. She looked up at Morgan before slowly unwrapping the paper, one folded piece at a time. When the final fold was reached, she paused to smile at him and, then, with a theatrical flourish, produced a gleaming gold ingot from the paper.

"It was in the same place where George had put our savings." She leaned forward and handed it to Morgan. "I found it last night and cleaned it up with brass polish."

"My God!" Morgan exclaimed as he inspected the gold bar in his hand.

"It's five and a half inches long, a half-inch wide and almost as thick. I measured the bar this morning at home." She smiled smugly. "It's Spanish as I suspected."

"So it is." Morgan continued to stare at the bar in his hand.

"You can keep it temporarily for a proper examination, if you like. But I will definitely want an official receipt with a statement promising its return and a written date to that effect. Is that understood, Major?"

"Of course. But I doubt we will keep it for more than a day or so. We will only hold it long enough to decipher the letters, stamps and symbols."

"Fine. When you are finished, I will want to know what you have discovered."

"Yes, of course, Mrs. Chapman. If you wish, I'll put that in writing as well."

"That's not necessary, Major. Your word is good enough."

Morgan turned, went behind his desk and sat in the chair. He took a piece of plain paper from the top drawer and, dipping his quill in a pot of ink, began to write the receipt. When he had finished writing, he signed the receipt and handed it to her.

"I trust that will be satisfactory." He stood behind his desk and watched her read though the receipt once and then reread it more slowly a second time.

"Correctly written, Major," she announced. "It is written without any grammatical errors, which as we both know is not at all typical of the reports prepared in this courthouse."

Morgan chuckled. "I can't argue with you, Mrs. Chapman. Thank you for your help."

"You're indeed welcome." She smiled obviously pleased with herself and put the receipt in her purse. She nodded to him and started to stand.

"Before you take your leave, I want to make sure I recall correctly the year that Captain Chapman brought home the gold and silver bars. I recall you telling me it was three years ago in April. Is that correct?"

"Yes, I am certain it was the last week of April in 1763. That's when we put out seeds in our vegetable garden. There is little fear of frost then. George was not here to help. That year I planted the seeds myself."

"So, this gold ingot has been in your home ever since that time?"

"I expect so. George handled all money matters; he was very clever with money. I did not know the amount or value of our savings until last night, when I counted the coins he kept in the money chest. That's when I found the gold bar; it was buried beneath the coins."

"Didn't you also tell me he showed you twenty-four bars?'

"Yes, he counted them as he pulled them from that filthy leather bag he brought into the house. I can see them now in my mind's eye… laid out in rows on the table. Now that I think about it, I believe there were many more silver than gold bars – perhaps twice as many."

"You of course know he brought home an enormous fortune in bullion."

"Oh, yes!" She smiled broadly, showing small, uneven teeth. "I'm a rich widow and, if I let that be known in town today, I would have a long line of suitors at my door tomorrow. So, I trust you will be discreet, Major, and keep my wealth from the town's ears. I hope you also will instruct all others of my wishes." She pointed to the hallway where Stockwell stood out of sight.

Morgan nodded. "I'll tell only the attorney general and advise him of your wishes. The fewer who know, the better. I hope you have the chest of coins well safeguarded."

"I do. My son, John, came home for George's funeral and is still with me. He now lives in Perth Amboy. John is a Presbyterian minister, you know. He studied at the College of New Jersey." She spoke with obvious pride.

"What will you do when he leaves? How will you safeguard the money then?"

"My older sister, Betsey, and her husband will be coming from Philadelphia to live with me. He was a soldier in the king's army and he is nearly as large as your man, Stockwell."

"Good. If there is a gap between your son's departure and your brother-in-law's arrival, let me know and I'll have someone watch your house during that time."

"Thank you, Major." Mrs. Chapman stood up and walked to the door. She turned in the doorway. "You do need someone to tidy up this office. It's quite dirty and there's no place for a decent person to sit."

Morgan nodded, a slight smile on his face. "I'll have the sergeant escort you to the outer door. He can take you home as well." He saw the sergeant standing in the hall and knew he had heard their entire conversation.

"That will not be necessary. My neighbors brought me here in their carriage and they are waiting for me outside the courthouse. Good day, Major."

"Good day, Mrs. Chapman." Morgan watched her walk through the doorway and shook his head as she went down the hallway with Stockwell trailing awkwardly behind her.

Oliver Palmer could not take his eyes from the gold ingot on his desk. He kept looking back and forth between the gleaming bar and Morgan who sat across the desk watching him. He finally settled his eyes on the justice, though his fingers still touched the bar.

"So, Mrs. Chapman brought this into you yesterday morning? I don't suppose you know what all the symbols mean?"

"I do now. Doctor Nunes Ribeiro gave me a full explanation of everything stamped into the ingot. I showed it to him last night. I knew he would be the most likely man in this colony to identify the markings."

Palmer sighed as if exhausted by Morgan's explanation "Yes, Major, I know the old Jew is intelligent. They all are – especially about money. If you are looking for my praise of him, I will say he has his special uses for us. I think that's more than enough to say about him." Palmer leaned back with a smirk on his face. "Now, Major, do tell me what is stamped on the bar."

Morgan nodded. A muscle in his right cheek twitched as he gritted his teeth, but he made no retort. "The 'M' on the left end indicates the ingot was minted in Mexico City. The crowned stamp beside that letter bears the monogram 'PVS' of Philip IV of Spain. He was king from 1621 to 1665, as surely you must know." Morgan doubted that Palmer knew the dates of Philip's reign as monarch and he was pleased to the see attorney general glare at him. "Philip's monogram also indicates that the quinto or the fifth-tax had been paid to the crown. Spanish kings have always received twenty percent of everything, including bullion, found or produced in America as well as all assets and income."

"And you colonists complain about the petty little stamp tax that good King George asks of you!" Palmer shook his head and sighed. "Do continue." He picked up the ingot and waited for Morgan to continue his explanation.

Morgan again gritted his teeth. "The small round 'p' beside the king's title is the initial of the assayer who evaluated the coins and bars during much of the last century. Next is a large 'V', which signifies the bar weighs five Spanish ounces – actually five and a half ounces according to our weight assessment. The year the gold ingot was molded, 1659, appears in the round crowned stamp. Finally, the two large round stamps on the right side are the king's coat of arms, assuring the 22-carat bar to be worth eight escudos."

"What's the value of an escudo? I only handle coin of the realm." Palmer held the bar in the palms of his hands. Morgan thought he looked like a supplicant offering a gift to his lord.

"The Spaniards minted gold coins with the value of two, four, six and eight escudos. The two-escudo piece, which we call a doubloon, was worth about £50-60 during the last century and certainly much more today. The gold ingot in your hands was worth four doubloons or £200-240 at the time it was minted. Now, I would estimate it has double the value or at least £450."

"Good Lord! So Chapman was as rich as Croesus! Certainly richer than most men in this colony. Didn't you say he had twenty-four bars?" Palmer sat back in his leather chair, the gold bar still held in his hands. He rubbed his hands over the bar again and again, almost fondling it.

"Yes, and Sterling and Willington probably had as many. However, keep in mind, at least half the bars were silver and worth much less." Morgan was amused to see Palmer so enthralled with the gold ingot in his hands.

"How much less?"

"I would estimate about twenty-five percent of the value of a gold bar."

"Chapman was still quite wealthy." Suddenly aware that he still held the ingot, Palmer leaned forward and carefully placed it on his desk. "Do we know where the bullion originated? We do know he procured it some three years ago –

isn't that what Mrs. Chapman told you?"

Morgan was irritated to hear the attorney general's continual use of we to describe what he had discovered. Of course, when the investigation seemed stymied with no new information, then Palmer used the pronoun you in his complaints about the lack of progress. "Like it or not," Morgan reminded himself, "that was the way of officials – probably all over the world."

"She said the captain brought the bullion home in April of 1763 – the same time Sterling was away. I spoke to his sons on Monday and they recalled him taking an unexplained trip that lasted twelve days. He was gone from April 19 to April 30. They found the exact dates in their father's payment ledger. The older son, Luke, made the entries while Sterling was away. Luke showed me those dates in the ledger in his own handwriting. The lad's writing is much different; Sterling wrote in a tiny script, the son in a bold one."

"So, both men left Savannah at about the same time. That's too much of a coincidence considering what else we know about them. But what about the source of the bullion?"

"At this time, we have no notion where or how they acquired it." Morgan pursed his lips. "And, we need to answer both questions to learn the identity of the murderer. We have to know what Sterling, Chapman and Willington did to get the bullion. When that's known, the reason for their murders will be understood and the murderer revealed."

"You again include Willington in the bullion robbery – I don't know what else to call it, although we don't yet know if that's indeed what happened. All we know about Willington is he seemed unsavory, possessed a lot of money and died in a house fire."

"Much more now is known about Willington – and I know he was murdered." Morgan tapped his forefinger on Palmer's desk. "Murdered by the same man who killed Thomas Sterling and George Chapman."

Morgan saw Palmer frown and knew the attorney general doubted what he had said. "Let me tell you what I've ascertained about Mr. Archibald Willington." He then related Willington's reputation as a brigand, his residence in the outlaw community of New Hanover and the reasons why his death did not appear to be accidental. As he finished, Morgan saw Palmer nod his head and knew he was convinced.

"Well, I must say it does appear that the three men were involved in some illicit scheme together; one that brought each of them a fortune in Spanish bullion." Palmer glanced at the gold ingot on his desk, with a look that Morgan later described as longing. "It also seems their scheme brought about their murders. Our concern now, of course, is the murders and not the bullion. We need not be concerned with whatever criminal act was perpetrated to acquire the bullion, unless we find it was pilfered from the king's holdings or one of his majesty's subjects. As I see it, we must seek the source of the bullion to apprehend the murderer. I assume neither Mrs. Chapman nor the assemblyman's sons know where the bullion came from?"

"What a pompous prig!" Morgan thought. "So many words to state the obvious and what already had been said." He barely managed to keep the contempt he felt for Palmer off his face. "That's correct. I'm certain Mrs. Chapman told me all she recalled and I believe Sterling's sons did the same. They apparently never saw any gold or silver bars in their father's possession."

"I would think the shippers here are typically paid in coin of the realm." Palmer spoke in an authoritative tone. "But the question that remains is how and where the bullion was acquired."

"I believe I have a way to answer that question without any cost to the crown." Morgan knew Palmer would never authorize an expenditure of the colony's funds for a trip to Cuba.

"Oh! Do tell me what you have in mind." Palmer leaned back in his chair with his plump hands clasped over his stomach. He beckoned to Thackery who entered the room at that moment. "Do get us a pot of tea, Thackery, and some biscuits. You know it's late for my morning tea."

Morgan grimaced as he watched the little man hurry from the room. "Shall I continue?"

Palmer saw his expression. "You don't approve of the way Thackery serves me, do you? Well that's the way of the world in the king's service. You are fortunate to have a rich father so you have never had to survive in such a system." His face reddened. "Well, I have survived and served for more years than I want to remember. I had to put up with tyrants whose demands and insults would have shattered Thackery. One even boxed my ears for being one minute late with a report. God, how I hated that man and when he died of apoplexy I rejoiced. He was raging at a clerk at the time." He smiled, recalling the man's collapse. "I suspect someday Thackery will be in a position like mine and I expect he will have some subordinate serving him the same way or with even more demands." Palmer frowned. "Well, do continue; I have other concerns today."

Thackery arrived with a silver tray in his hands. He made a face as he set the heavy tray down on Palmer's desk. The tray held a Leeds teapot, two cups with saucers, a matching creamer and sugar bowl, a jar of orange marmalade, three spoons, six baked biscuits and three white linen napkins. Thackery was about to pour the tea, when Palmer waved him away.

"I'll do it. Thank you." Palmer started pouring the tea and did not see the surprised look on Thackery's face as he turned away.

"Now, let me hear your plan." Palmer looked at Morgan as he handed him a steaming cup of tea. "Try the marmalade. My wife made it from Florida oranges. I assume you are aware of Jesse Fish's citrus plantation in St. Augustine."

Morgan nodded and spoke when he saw Palmer waiting with his teacup in hand.

"Since the bullion is Spanish, the Spaniards are the only ones who would know where the bullion originated. Whatever is said about them, we know the Spaniards are good record keepers. The records for their lands in America are in Cuba and that's where I think the information about the bullion can be found. Everything is in the Building of Records or what they call the Archivo de las Indias in Havana. Fortunately, I am acquainted with a prominent Cuban who can enter the archives and find the information we need to know about the bullion. He also knows the treasury officials and can make discreet inquiries for us. I hesitate to correspond with him since I don't know if English mail is under scrutiny. I therefore suggest a trip to Havana to meet him and ask for his assistance."

Obviously suspicious of the proposal, Palmer stared at Morgan. "Who is this prominent man in Havana and why would he be willing to help us?"

"His name is Miguel López Moreno. The man made his fortune shipping goods between Spanish ports in the Caribbean Sea. He would help us because he holds a long-standing grudge against the Spanish officials for their trade restrictions and admires us because we give the same trading rights to Englishmen and colonists alike. In the Spanish colonies the Peninsulares, those Spaniards born in Spain, hold the highest and most important positions in their government and severely restrict the rights of the Criollos, those Spaniards born in the New World colonies. The restrictions facing the Criollos also include trade and shipping. In order to ship their goods, they not only must pay the requisite fees, but exorbitant bribes as well. The king's officials make the Criollos pay dearly for every bit of business they conduct."

Palmer sat up and raised his finger. "The tyranny of the

Spanish monarchy is well known. It has been that way for centuries. Their kings are quite unlike the enlightened kings of England who permit a functioning parliament. They rule with absolute authority. So, it's no wonder their colonists suffer such restrictions and penalties."

Morgan listened to Palmer without speaking. In his opinion, there was little difference between the two monarchies and the oppressive rule of their colonies. The English colonists also endured restricted trading rights as a result of the previous century's Navigation Acts. Morgan, however, hesitated to offer his opinions. He wanted Palmer's approval for his voyage to Havana and would not risk offending him.

"Above all," he said, "it's the regulation of Criollo trade that most infuriates shippers like López Moreno. Apparently, they are forced to relinquish half their profits in bribes to evade the restrictions. For that reason, they hate the Spanish officials and the Casa de Contratación (House of Trade) in Spain."

"Ah, I see. So that's why this man, López Moreno, would be willing to help us." Palmer mumbled, trying to speak with half a biscuit in his mouth. "I can understand his disgust with that corrupt trade system."

"Yes. Keep in mind, he would provide the information only for the murder investigation. He would provide no other information. López Moreno would never engage in espionage."

Morgan knew Palmer believed him. He had convinced him with the doctor's knowledge of the Spanish colonial system. His description of the operation of Spain's empire was the only accurate part of his account. The rest was a pack of lies. Morgan did not know Miguel López Moreno and had never met him, although he expected him to be his future father-in-law. He had no idea what Claudia's father thought about Peninsular control of the colonies nor did he know if the man criticized the restrictions put upon Criollo trade. Neither did he know if López Moreno paid bribes to the king's officials to conduct trade in the Spanish colonies. The man had been a prominent shipper, but Morgan could only hope he would help him in his search for information. Whether or not the old man, now quite ill, could or would enter the Building or Records for him, Morgan would not know until he made that request in Havana.

"Tell me, Major, are you proposing to make the trip at your own expense? I recall you said there would be no cost to the crown." Palmer studied Morgan carefully as he sipped his tea.

"I am. I want this vicious murderer arrested and executed."

"I see. So, you would be willing to pay for everything, even if the man wants to be paid for his service?" Palmer cocked his head to the side as he stared at Morgan.

"Yes, I want this investigation finished before I leave office." Morgan knew the attorney general was suspicious of his explanation since the Englishman would never think of spending his own money on any colonial matter.

"I wonder, Major, if your generosity has anything to do with your hope to be reappointed justice of the peace?" Palmer smiled like a father who had just caught his son taking a forbidden sweet from the cookie jar.

Morgan laughed heartily. "No, that's not why I suggested it. When my term is up, I'll be delighted to end my days and nights dragging town drunks to the stocks and punishing people for breaking laws I find ridiculous. I look forward to a time when I am free of such obligations. You probably don't believe me, but so be it."

Palmer pursed his lips. "Whether I believe you or not doesn't matter, Major. What matters is that your suggestion has merit and I will consider it. Fortunately, the town is not in an uproar about the murders so we have time to pursue such a plan. If there's another murder that would no longer be true. How long do you think you would need to be gone?"

"Less than a month. I will not need much time in Havana, maybe ten days. Most of the time will be spent at sea. With smooth sailing, I should reach Cuba in eight or nine days and return in less time through the Bahama passage. Of course, in this storm season, it's hard to know."

"That's a long time. Who would take charge of your office while you are gone?"

"I would suggest Thackery." Morgan looked over at the little man writing at his desk.

Thackery raised his eyebrows in surprise. He looked at Morgan to see if he was serious.

Morgan nodded. "Yes, I recommend you." He then turned to Palmer. "Stockwell knows what to do with the ordinary lawbreakers, but Thackery would be the one to continue the murder investigation. I would leave him a list of tasks to do and naturally he would keep you informed of his progress."

"Well, what do you think of such an assignment, Thackery?" Palmer smiled benignly at his assistant.

"That would be fine." Thackery nodded his head in agreement.

Morgan smiled, thinking that Thackery would appreciate the time away from the attorney general. He drank the last of the tea in his cup.

Palmer stood, ending the meeting. "I'll let you know in a day or so." He watched Morgan casually reach over and pick up the gold bar as if it were a scrap of paper on the floor.

Morgan left the office knowing Palmer would speak to the governor before announcing his decision. At the top of the stairs, he heard him say to Thackery, "Fetch a cup for tea and try one of these biscuits with Esther's homemade marmalade."

Palmer met with Governor Wright at his home that afternoon. The governor's old slave, Judah, greeted him and guided him into the sitting room just inside the front door and to the right of the entryway. Sir James Wright used the spacious room as an office and meeting room for his staff, colonial officials, petitioners and complainants, as well as other townsmen who came to him for advice and assistance. Oliver Palmer had never been invited elsewhere inside the governor's enormous mansion, which he heard had as many as eighteen rooms.

According to the workers who built the house for the governor, it had a second and much larger sitting room, a library with shelves for more than 2,000 books and a large ballroom. The mansion also boasted eight bedrooms, all with fireplaces, a kitchen with piped-in water from the well and two indoor toilets. The toilets emptied into metal containers, which were tended by the governor's slaves. Wright's house also had an inside bathtub and a bath closet built outside for use in the summer months. It was the first such residence to have both inside and outside bath facilities in town, if not in the entire colony.

The governor's spacious mansion created little concern in Savannah since he and his wife, Sarah, brought eight children to the colony. But many of the prosperous families in town were envious of the governor's novel plumbing improvements, especially the new bathing facilities. Bathing had become important in Savannah as the wealthy now dressed more elegantly with well-made wigs, white silk gloves, satin bonnets and colored suits and dresses. In the winter months, those who bathed used basins in their bedrooms, but, in the warmer seasons, even the wealthy often went to ponds and rocky streams to wash themselves. Preferring to bathe inside or outside in bath closets close to their houses, the wealthy colonists soon duplicated the governor's coveted innovations. The carpenters no sooner had finished the governor's house than they were hired to include similar bathing facilities in almost all the best houses in town.

Palmer did not envy the governor his improved plumbing. His resentment was reserved for those who received invitations to the governor's mansion for dinners and entertainment. He and his wife had never been invited even though he was an Englishman and the guests, with the exception of army officers, were wealthy colonists and visiting foreigners. It infuriated Palmer that he and Esther had only once been invited to his house in Charles Towne when the governor was attorney general and he was serving him as his assistant. Palmer could not understand why he had not become more than Wright's valued assistant. He was an Englishman after all and like the governor he had been born and educated in England. In fact, James Wright had become the governor of Georgia in 1760 on the same day as Oliver Palmer's birthday, November 2. They drank toasts to each other that day.

As Palmer looked around the unadorned sitting room, with only a long meeting table and chairs in the center, it occurred to him that the room had been whitewashed since his last visit. Everything looked cleaner and smelled better. The governor's pipe smoke usually lingered in the meeting room along with the odor of his old dog, Ulysses. Ulysses, a fifteen-year-old terrier, had an animal scent that Palmer found revolting. The odor was not in the room now, but he knew it would be eventually since Ulysses always accompanied the governor wherever he went, even to assembly meetings in the courthouse.

Governor Wright entered the room as Palmer rubbed a sore spot on his left shoulder. The governor motioned him to remain seated as he started to rise from his chair. Ulysses followed his master and, as usual, ignored the attorney general. The dog ignored everyone who visited the governor and would growl or show his teeth to those who tried to pet him.

"Sit, sit, Palmer." The governor sat in a chair at the table across from Palmer. He faced a huge portrait of King George III hung on the wall behind the attorney general. The gilded-framed portrait was the only decoration in the room. Wright put his pipe and tobacco pouch on the table beside the pot of ink, quill and several sheets of paper he always kept at hand. The governor was a forgetful man and, at meetings, he wrote notes to remind himself of important information.

"I trust you and Esther are doing well, Palmer, as well as the children." He smiled at the attorney general and pressed tobacco into the pipe with his thumb.

"Yes, sir. Everyone is in good health. Esther, of course, complains about the heat."

"My own dear Sarah, God bless her soul, also complained of the heat. Though she's now gone three years, I can still hear her say, 'We surely can't go to hell when we die, we've already been there living through summers in Georgia.' " The governor chuckled.

Palmer laughed politely, having heard the story any number of times. He watched Wright light his pipe and thought the governor had aged little in all the years he had known him. He was now fifty, but still had a full head of brown hair with only streaks of gray. The governor did not wear a wig at home and looked much younger without it. His light complexion was completely clear and he even had color in his cheeks. The only signs of his long life were a few lines around his mouth, the beginning of a double chin and an expanding paunch at his middle.

"The children are all in good health I hope, Sir James." Oliver Palmer could hear crying from an upstairs room and knew the boys were fighting.

"Oh yes, they drive me to distraction." The governor

grimaced and pointed to the ceiling above his head. "Well, Palmer, what progress is there to report about these awful killings? We shall discuss the other matters afterward." Wright paused as Judah entered the room, carrying a decanter of sherry and two wine glasses on a silver tray. "Thank you, Judah. I trust it isn't too early for a glass of sherry? As you know, I think a glass of sherry in the afternoon and a whisky before bedtime will give a man good health and long life."

"Thank you, Sir James. I'll have just half a glass."

Judah placed the tray between the two men, bowed to the governor and, without a word, left the room.

"Fine." He poured the wine and then reached down to his dog, gave him a treat from his pocket and patted his head. "I know I spoil him, but he's a loyal fellow and Sarah loved him like a child. We purchased Ulysses in Ireland, you know… in a tiny town called Killarney in County Kerry. They call these dogs Kerry Blue Terriers in Killarney."

Palmer smiled politely. The origin of Ulysses was another story he had heard many times. He vowed never to tell the same stories over and over if he lived to be a hundred.

"Well, Palmer, I do ramble on, don't I?" He held up his hand. "You don't have to reply. Let me hear your report."

Palmer informed him of everything that Morgan had told him. In his account, the justice had been the one who found the known facts of the investigation, but it was he who had directed Morgan's movements and had interpreted his findings.

"So Willington was murdered, too, and apparently by the same man." The governor blew pipe smoke to the side away from Palmer.

"Yes, sir. That's how I assess it. The remnants of corduroy bindings, like those found on the other victims, and the burnt wall lamp on the kitchen floor brought me to that conclusion."

"Good thinking, Palmer. Well, what do you propose should be done now?"

"Since the town is currently quiet, I think it might be worthwhile to send Morgan to Cuba to find the source of the Spanish bullion in question. He has an acquaintance in Havana who has the authority and willingness to help us. Once we know how the three murder victims suddenly became wealthy, we should be better able to identify and arrest the murderer."

"Yes, that does seem sensible." The governor scratched Ulysses between his ears. "Even if Morgan is impertinent, he is intelligent and should be able to discover what we need to know in Havana. We must give the devil his due – Morgan has been a successful justice in Savannah. We may not like his surly manner, but he has made the commoners toe the line. He surely has done better than the previous one… I can't think of his name."

"His name was Captain Conrad, Sir James."

"Yes, of course. Conrad was such a likable fellow, but not at all cut out to be justice. On the other hand, Morgan is not very likable, especially with that terrible temper of his. I suppose it comes from his missing arm. I've heard he was an angry and opinionated young man, but not nearly as mean as he is now. Yet, the man, like him or not, has kept peace in this difficult city. What do you think about him?"

"He has been adequate as justice. His dalliance with Barclay's widow has been a source of continuing gossip, but at least he does not flaunt it in town. He has done as well as can be expected under my direction."

"I too have heard about his scandalous involvement with that Spanish woman. Sometime soon, Palmer, you will have to say something to him about it. We can't have one of our officials, even a low level one, engaged in any such shameful behavior. Well, where were we?"

"We were talking about sending Morgan to Cuba." Palmer knew that Wright's increasing forgetfulness was a sign of his aging.

"I see no reason why we shouldn't send him there. The cost of the trip would be little."

"Morgan says he will bear the cost himself."

"Why is that?" The governor rubbed his hand over his chin.

"Morgan says he wants to end his term of office with the arrest of the murderer." Palmer smiled. "But I suspect he hopes to be reappointed justice for another two years."

"Well, that would be a reasonable result of a successful investigation, would it not? The major should be rewarded for his efforts, especially if he ends his involvement with that woman. That is unless you think otherwise and have another man in mind for the office." Wright looked across the table at Palmer as he tapped the burnt pipe tobacco into his empty glass.

"I have no one else in mind at the moment, Sir James. I suggest we wait and see how the investigation turns out."

"That seems sensible." Wright nodded. "In the meantime, send Morgan off to Cuba with instructions to return as soon as possible. Everything here appears to be calm for the time being. The province has quieted down after the repeal of the Stamp Tax and should remain peaceful for awhile – that is until the next inevitable tax imposed by Parliament."

"Do you know of a new tax being prepared, Sir James?"

"Yes, I do. Of course, what I'm telling you is quite confidential. I hear from London that a new tax is currently under consideration in Parliament. It will be applied to all imports brought into the colonies and I fear an outcry here worse than we suffered with the Stamp Act. We will need additional soldiers to enforce the tax, but I doubt we will get them." Wright sighed wearily. "Parliament is quite successful passing laws that affect the colonies, but not nearly as successful supporting those who must enforce them. What is it they say? 'Policy made in England, cannot often be put into practice in America.'"

"That means we have a difficult time ahead of us." The new tax worried Palmer. He had intended to stay in office until 1770 in the hope the governor would recommend him for a higher position in the colonies – perhaps even a governorship. At the least, he hoped to be given a minor title upon his return to England. In his daydreams, Palmer often pictured a sycophantic servant addressing him as Sir Oliver as he strode about his huge estate, an hour's ride from London. The possibility of an outbreak of violence in Savannah over the new tax could change everything and jeopardize all his hopes. Palmer said nothing to the governor, but he felt sick to his stomach.

"Yes, indeed. I think we have less than a year before the new tax is levied. Well, to return to the murder investigation, I must admit I was quite surprised to hear that Thomas Sterling was involved – an assemblyman at that! He seemed like such a sound man. I didn't know Chapman at all. As for Archibald Willington, I found him quite common in both speech and manner. I was surprised he became the junior warden at Christ Church. I can't imagine it was his wealth alone that won him that position. I intend to speak to Bartholomew about it this Sunday."

"I had the same impression of Willington, Sir James." Palmer made a face. "I also was surprised to learn about Thomas Sterling. Perhaps Morgan's trip to Cuba will offer us another explanation of his death."

"Let's hope so. I'll look forward to hearing about it."

"Palmer approved the trip to Havana," Morgan announced to Stockwell as he strode into his office on the following morning. "I must say he was quick about it."

"I'll say. Knowing Palmer, I'm surprised." Stockwell sat beside the open window with his shirtsleeves rolled up to his elbows and his forearms extended over the sill. It was pouring outside and raindrops blew into the room. An afternoon storm had come in off the sea, bringing both rain and a cool breeze into Savannah. "I would have expected him to keep you swinging like a puppet on strings till it suited his fancy."

"I'm surprised as well." Morgan shook the water from his clothes and leaned back on the edge of his desk. "Of course, he gave his usual instructions about being a proper representative of the king. Morgan mimicked Palmer's soft voice with a falsetto affectation. "*Ah, Major, do keep in mind, you will represent King George and should behave in a dignified manner. If at all possible, you must put aside your colonial tactlessness while in Cuba.*"

Stockwell laughed. "Does that mean you don't fart at the dinner table?"

"Among other things. He said, 'It might also improve your reception in Cuba if you had a pleasant expression on your face.' He also suggested I have a tailor make some *decent clothing* for the trip. Of course, I didn't tell him I already had a new suit tailored for the wedding. Well, what's important is his approval." Morgan chuckled. "Can you imagine his anger if he knew of my marriage to Claudia?"

"I take it Palmer has no notion that López Moreno is Claudia's father?" Stockwell blotted the raindrops on his arm with the soiled handkerchief he kept in the pocket of his breeches.

"No. Palmer thinks I met him when those Spanish officials came here last year. He made that assumption since he saw me talking to one of their officers at the governor's reception."

"I don't guess you argued with his assumption." Stockwell smiled.

"No. I let the pompous fool continue to think he knows everything. The man can't speak a word of Spanish so he had no idea the officer was from Spain, not Cuba. He thinks it is quite *unnecessary* to speak anything but the King's English in this world. After all, Oliver Palmer is an Englishman, you know.'" Morgan again mimicked the attorney general.

"What did he say about how long you're to be away?"

"No more than a month, but even Palmer knows my time away depends on the seas. This is the beginning of the storm season, so who knows how long the trip will take. I don't want to be gone longer than a month myself."

"You worried about your father?"

"Yes, and the doctor. Neither of them looks good. My father talks of sailing to Charles Towne to see a tobacco planter there, the same man he met a while ago. He wants to buy seeds to start a tobacco crop at Morgan's Creek. But I doubt he has the strength to go anywhere outside of Savannah. He had to rest in bed for almost a week after the last trip."

"I saw him boarding a ship at the time and wondered where he was going. He didn't have his cane with him and he looked like he was trying to appear as if he didn't need it."

"That's my father for you. 'Never show the world your losses or wounds,' as he always says. I tried to talk him out of the trip and told him I would go in his stead, but he's hardheaded as ever and wouldn't hear of it. He insists he has to talk to the man himself."

"The doctor don't look good neither; he's white as a ghost. I seen him to treat the spider bite I got in the outhouse. It infected my leg – the bad one, of course. That's always the way."

"I didn't know it was that bad. How is the leg now?"

"I'm like your father. No need to tell anyone your problems – everybody's got them. I'm fine now. I guess I must now watch where I put my bum." Stockwell guffawed.

"So it seems." Morgan smiled. "I'll see the doctor tonight; it's our evening to play chess. I agree, he doesn't look good – worse in fact every time I see him."

"You know, he wouldn't let me pay him for the treatment. He said he expects deer meat or trout in the fall. That's what he always says when I go see him at his office… and he knows I don't never go hunting or fishing."

"That's the kind of man he is. The doctor never takes money from those he knows have little, but he will accept vegetables from their gardens, eggs or baked bread and cakes. Everyone knows the doctor has a sweet tooth and he gets more sweets than he can eat. Whatever money he needs, he gets from his wealthy patients, who still come to him for treatment. That includes the governor's family and Palmer's wife and children." Morgan smiled. "He doesn't leave home to see patients anymore, but, as you know, he's still the medical examiner and will go to wherever an unexplained death is reported."

"I suppose that gives him an extra bit of money, too."

"No more than a bit, you know how cheap the crown is. Well, has Thackery come down to talk to you yet?"

Stockwell smiled. "He did, yesterday. The 'lil rabbit told me he would not 'interfere with my functions' while you're away. Those was his exact words. I had all I could do to keep from laughing in his face. He never looked me in the eye the whole time he was here."

"Thackery's afraid of you. You know that. I expect him to do little more than sit here in the office and avoid Palmer as much as possible."

"Just as well. He wouldn't know what to do anyhow."

"I gave him a list of tasks to do for the investigation, but I doubt if he will come up with anything new. I told him to talk to Sterling's sons again as well as the Parker brothers. But, who knows with his lawyer's words he might wring something out of them about the bullion that they didn't tell me."

Stockwell shook his head. "He'll get nothin' from them Parkers. I talked to those two and if I couldn't get anything out of them, you can be sure Thackery won't neither." At the boatyard, Stockwell hit Joseph in the stomach when he insisted Chapman had paid them in English coins. Regaining his breath, Joseph repeated what he had said and vehemently denied ever seeing any Spanish bullion. He remained steadfast in his denial even when Stockwell threatened to beat him with a two by four. The big man gave up when the Parkers would say nothing more.

"I also told Thackery to try to find out more about Willington before he moved to town."

"He might do better at that. Do you think Willington's the last one to die?"

"I think so. Sterling, Chapman and Willington were all killed at about the same time with only a week or so between the murders. Since Willington's death, almost a month has passed and no one else has been murdered. That's why I think there won't be another. It may be that those three were the only ones involved with the bullion. But, as they say, time will tell."

"You think there might have been more men in on it?"

Morgan shook his head. "I just don't know. If the Spanish records in Havana mention the amount of bullion, which was probably stolen, I can figure out the number of men involved."

"Tell me how." Stockwell used his wet handkerchief to wipe his face.

"We know Chapman had twenty-four bars. So, if I find there were a total of seventy-five or even eighty, it would suggest only three men were involved. I assume each man would have about the same number as Chapman. A load of more than thirty bars would be too heavy for one man to carry whether on foot or horseback. Therefore, if many more than eighty are mentioned in the Spanish records, then we'll know others took part in the scheme."

Stockwell nodded. "Makes good sense."

"I'll notify you of what I discover in Havana. It will be in a coded message. If I succeed, I'll say, 'It's much hotter in Havana than I expected.' I'll not mention the weather if I fail to find information about the bullion. Palmer will receive the same message, but I doubt he would deign to tell you what I've written. Be sure to tell the doctor the situation."

Stockwell nodded. "That fat hog would never think of telling a mere commoner the likes of me anything important. Thackery's most likely the same. As my dear ol' dad, the drunken sod, would say, 'they think their chamber pot smells better than mine.'"

Morgan smiled. "That's certainly true of Palmer. I don't know about Thackery."

"Don't matter as long as Thackery stays out of my way and don't tell me to fetch his tea."

"I'm sure he knows better. Thackery is a toady, not a fool."

The doctor looked better than the last time Morgan saw him. There seemed to be more color in his cheeks and his dark eyes sparkled with an amusement he had not shown for weeks. He clapped Morgan on the back when the younger man brought out the chess set and he smiled an hour later when it seemed his game was lost.

"Do you think I should resign?" The doctor pointed to the pawn that stood in the way of Morgan's bishop and the check that would follow.

Morgan nodded. "The pawn will only delay the inevitable and you know it. Checkmate is no more than six moves away, no matter what you do. I played well for a change."

"You did and I thought you might be preoccupied with your sea voyage on Saturday."

"I thought so, too. Well, this was the first game I've won in quite awhile." Morgan put the elaborately carved pieces away in the wooden box that came with the chessboard. Governor Oglethorpe had given Dr. Ribeiro the chess set before he left the colony. It was a gift for helping the first settlers survive the plague of 1733. Now, it was the doctor's prized possession.

"You win many more than..." The doctor's words were lost in an explosion of thunder that burst over the house. "Another thunderstorm; this has been a summer of storms." He stood and closed the two windows in the room.

"I'd rather have the rain than the insufferable heat." Morgan filled their wine glasses as the doctor returned to his chair. It was the major's third glass that night.

"Well, what are your plans for the trip to Havana? That is beside the marriage to Claudia."

The doctor patted Morgan's good arm. "I'm not making light of your marriage, my friend. You know I am delighted that you and Claudia will be married."

"I know. I recall that it was you who arranged for us to meet. As for the voyage, I intend to stop off at St. Augustine in the hope that someone in town knows something about the mysterious Spanish bullion. I'm sailing on a ship bound for Havana with a one-night stay in St. Augustine. Incidentally, the ship is carrying a shipment of my father's rice to Florida."

The doctor laughed. "What a coincidence! But what do you hope to learn in Florida? All the Spanish officials left St. Augustine and only a few of the former residents are still there. I'm sure you know that their king, Charles III, urged all their people to leave Florida when the colony was ceded to England after the war. It's said that some 3,000 colonists, including Christianized Indians and former slaves, left St. Augustine, Apalache and Pensacola. I've heard the Spaniards even took their recent dead away to Cuba. They feared their souls might be tainted by the heresy the Protestant settlers would bring to the colony. It's astonishing what some people believe."

"It is. I know it may be a waste of time for me to go there, but there might be someone in St. Augustine who knows something. Even if only a few of the Spaniards are left, I hope one of them might have heard of the bullion. I'm anxious to meet María Adela's father for that reason. I recall her saying he spoke English and, if nothing else, he could assist me with translations."

"True. I forgot María Adela's family lives in St. Augustine. We must ask her when she returns. She's gone off, I assume with her suitor, whom I've yet to meet. I expect her soon; she wants to wish you a smooth sailing." The doctor reached for the bottle to refill Morgan's glass.

Morgan shook his head. "No more for me. I have decided to limit myself in the future. It's not because of my marriage. I just don't like feeling miserable every morning after drinking so much the night before. Lately, I have had no more than two glasses at night and I feel better."

"A wise decision. Well, what about your plans in Cuba? How do you intend to proceed?"

"I'm uncertain at this time. Obviously, I'll need someone to enter the Building of Records and search for documents describing lost or stolen bullion in 1763. I must assume the murdered men acquired the ingots illegally." With heavy rain beating on the roof, Morgan had to raise his voice to be heard.

The doctor nodded. "That's the only sensible assumption to make since everything was kept secret. Perhaps, someone in Claudia's family has the needed authority to enter the Building of Records. I would think any official, army officer, or even someone in the king's service would have that authority. If no family member serves in such a capacity, perhaps a friend. Whoever is sent into the archive will have to read and copy the critical documents for you."

"That's true. I can read a little Spanish, but not enough to understand an entire document. Claudia has a large family and I would think there must be at least one man in the king's service. If so, he would be the one to ask for assistance. I worry less about finding the man who can enter the building, but more about his willingness to search and copy the documents for me. I wouldn't think it would be a treasonous act to assist an English murder investigation, but I just don't know what a Spaniard might think of it."

"I understand your worry. The Spaniards may well consider your request as a request for espionage. You will need to be completely candid and yet quite circumspect when you approach someone to help you. He will have to be a man you trust who will not report you to the Casa de Contratacíon (House of Trade). If a Casa official hears of Spanish bullion in Savannah, he might insist on the return of the ingots or their equivalent in English coin. You could also be arrested as a spy. You will need to be very careful in Cuba, my friend."

"I know." Morgan sighed. He shook his head, his brow furrowed.

"Assuming you acquire the significant documents, how will you report your information to Palmer? You obviously can't send him copies or translations in the mail. I assume Claudia will make the translations for you."

"She will. Palmer will be notified of what I find in a coded message. But the document translations will have be carried aboard ship upon my return. Stockwell will inform you of what I find; he will also receive the coded message."

"A sound plan. When is Claudia leaving? I assume she will leave before you." Trying to hide a yawn, the doctor brushed a hand over his mouth.

"Claudia is already gone; she left this morning." Morgan saw the yawn and knew he should leave soon. "You will be amused to hear that Palmer is worried I will cause an international incident in Cuba. He said if I'm arrested while there, the crown will deny sending me on the mission and make no effort to repatriate me. 'Expect no help from us,' he told me. 'If you are arrested, you can expect to rot the rest of your life in one of their disgusting dungeons.'"

The doctor shook his head. "That Palmer has so much compassion." He turned to look at the door as María Adela entered the door. A puddle formed on the floor where she stood to take off her sodden cape.

"You look drenched. Change your clothes and join us for a cup of tea."

María Adela nodded and went to her bedroom. She returned a few minutes later and sat across from the men in a chair she carried from the kitchen. Her hair was still wet from the rain that had soaked through the shawl she had used to cover her head.

"María Adela, Major Morgan will be sailing to St. Augustine on Saturday and would like to talk to your father." The doctor told her about Morgan's proposed voyage to Havana and what he hoped to discover. "He hopes your father will help him meet and speak to the Spaniards still living in and around St. Augustine."

"My family will help you, if they are still there. When I last visited them, they talked of moving to Pensacola. It's hard now to live in St. Augustine or anywhere else in English Florida. There's little work for the residents. The army makes their soldiers do most of the work."

The doctor noticed the puzzled look on Morgan's face. "Before Spain gave up Florida, her father worked for a wealthy family – the Puente family as I recall." María Adela nodded. "But Puente abandoned St. Augustine along with the other Floridians and, since that time, only a few English settlers and the army have moved into colony. So, now there is little work for him there. With three children, the family has had to live on hunting and fishing. Farming has always been poor on the Florida coast. It's hard even to grow vegetables there."

Morgan nodded. "I've heard the Spaniards in St. Augustine had to import food for years. They even purchased foodstuffs from Savannah."

"It is true." María Adela got up and went into the kitchen for her tea. She added a large dollop of honey from a covered pot that stood on the table. Stirring the tea, she drank a spoonful before carrying it back to her chair.

The doctor looked at María Adela. "So, your father talked of moving to Pensacola. Was that when you visited your family a few weeks ago?"

She nodded. "He doesn't want to leave East Florida. He has lived in St. Augustine all his life, but, without work, he must go where he can find more food for the family."

"Of course. I've heard it's easier to grow crops in the Florida interior. But, without the large garrison of British soldiers, I suppose Pensacola has more opportunity." The doctor again tried to hide a yawn.

"Yes, but he could still be in East Florida. I haven't heard the family has moved as yet." María Adela looked at Morgan. "I'll make a map to show you the pueblo where my family now lives; it's only five miles northwest of St. Augustine. There's a rutted road leading to the pueblo and you should have no trouble finding it. My family's house is the one with a wooden roof."

María Adela went into the surgery where the doctor kept his writing materials. He had his quills as well as paper and a pot of ink on the cluttered table he used for his desk. She returned a few minutes later with a well-drawn sketch of St. Augustine and its immediate surroundings. The drawing included several villages north and west of the presido as well as the huge stone fortress, the Castillo de San Marcos, that stood on the bay to defend the colony. Her sketch even showed the inlet that flowed into the bay where the two hundred year old city had been built.

The villages appeared as a line of tiny boxes representing houses. María Adela circled the one where her family's house stood and the home itself was marked with an X. It looked to be in the center of the village with several tiny boxes on either side of the building.

"Well done, María Adela. The map shows me exactly where to go. I hope I find him and he remembers what happened in 1763. By the way, what is your father's name?"

"Miguel Macías. I'm certain he will remember the year. It was the year my little brother, Felipe, was born. If you find him, he will tell you everything you need to know."

CHAPTER EIGHT

SAVANNAH, ST. AUGUSTINE AND HAVANA:
THURSDAY, JULY 31 – FRIDAY, AUGUST 9, 1766

A day before he left for St. Augustine, he rode out to see his father at Morgan's Creek. It was a sultry day, the first in a fortnight without afternoon showers. As usual, Morgan arrived at six in the evening. In the summer, he always avoided a ride in open country under a full sun.

Following a dinner of spicy fish soup, Matthew and his son sat in the portion of the porch protected by woven mosquito netting. They sat in silence and watched the sun, a brilliant orange ball, fall into the western woods. When the daylight was almost gone, James lit the two oil lamps his father kept on the porch. He then opened the bottle of Spanish wine he had brought with him and poured each of them a full glass.

He saw his father frown. "I know your views on drink, but the doctor says a daily glass of wine would be to your benefit."

"Is that so? And does the good doctor follow his own

advice? I never saw the man take more than a sip or two in all the years I've known him. But that doesn't stop him from giving me such advice. Damned doctors think they know everything. They tell their patients nothing they want to hear. The gluttons are told to lose weight, the drinkers to limit their drink and teetotalers like me to drink. And, tell me, is there anything in his old medical volumes that says alcohol will help with rheumatism or aging? I'll wager the next harvest there isn't."

"I see you're out of sorts tonight. What happened today?"

"I'm not out of sorts," Matthew raised his voice. "Just disgusted – the damned rheumatism keeps me from doing what I want. I think I'll hire a man to help me get about better."

"That's probably a good idea. You want tobacco seeds from Charles Towne, don't you?" His father nodded.

"I told you I'll go there for you when I return from Cuba. You can put the seeds in next spring and have your first crop in the summer."

Matthew made a face. "Enough about me and my complaints." He looked at his son and smiled. "James, I want you to know I'm very glad you are marrying Claudia. I'm certain she will make a fine wife. She's probably not as strong as your mother, but full of affection for you. Her eyes were on you the entire time of your last visit here. It's certain she loves you."

Morgan chuckled. He knew his father's lifelong belief that a woman's eyes showed her emotions, especially love. "She is a good woman and will make a good wife."

"Claudia will be a good mother, as well! You know, I'm pleased she is with child – very pleased! I don't give a damn about the Church and what that sanctimonious ass Bartholomew would say if he knew about it. Though I wish I could see his face when he hears you married a Catholic woman in a Catholic church." He laughed until tears formed in his eyes. "Oh, what a wonderful sight it would be." He continued to snicker. "I can see it clearly in my mind's eye."

James laughed with his father. "So can I."

Matthew wiped away the tears with his shirtsleeve and sipped some of his wine. "Well, I shall surely look forward to the birth of the child. You know, after we lost your brother and your wife, I feared we would never have a grandchild. Now, I can at least hope the child will be a boy to carry on our family name."

"We can only hope. Although there's no way to know, Claudia is certain we will have a boy. You know how women seem to see and know much more of the world than men."

"It's true. I surely hope Claudia's right. The Morgan's line must go on into the future."

"Yes and, of course, continue our pirate heritage."

Matthew guffawed. He claimed half in jest and half with pride to be a descendent of the Welsh pirate, Henry Morgan. The seventeenth-century pirate terrorized the Spanish Caribbean, plundering cities and fleets and was eventually knighted by Charles II.

"I doubt Claudia's family would be pleased to know of our heritage or that the boy would have pirate blood. Of course, our name will be carried on, only if she has a boy."

"Even if not, I expect you will continue to do the hard work to father a boy in the future." They laughed together. "So, here's to a Morgan in the years to come." Matthew reached over the arm of his chair to touch glasses with his son. He smiled and finished all the wine in his glass.

"I regret that I can't sail to Havana with you. I'd like to see you married, you know."

"I know." His father and mother had both journeyed from Savannah to Williamsburg for his first wedding, as well as the later funerals for his wife and child. James always knew Joseph had been their favorite son, but they had tried not to show it.

"Well, we'll have a celebration here when you return."

Matthew smiled. "We'll spruce the place up and have a grand time. Now, tell me about the inquiries you're planning in Cuba."

Morgan left the plantation at first light. His father was still asleep when he quietly closed the front door and went to the barn to saddle his horse. The first rays of sunlight had reached the nearby creek and colored it golden as he nudged the stallion onto the road to town. Knowing his father would awaken when the light struck his bedroom window, Morgan turned to look back at the highest point on the road. He smiled to see the familiar figure in his white nightshirt waving from the porch. A flock of screeching crows erupted from the woods as he waved in return.

His mind was on Claudia as his stallion splashed through puddles made by an overnight thunderstorm. He thought of her much of the time now, particularly when unoccupied or alone. Though Morgan had always glibly said that love was a word only women understood, he knew he loved Claudia. He felt the need to be with her more and more often and found a kind of quiet contentment in her presence he had never known before. Claudia had been gone less than a week and he already missed her. He especially missed seeing her mischievous smile and the childlike way she would tiptoe across the room to kiss him when he entered her house.

The more Morgan thought about Claudia, the more he yearned to be with her. He wished his sailing to Havana did not include a one-night stopover in St. Augustine. Morgan wanted her arms around him now, but was well aware he had a long time to wait for that moment. He would have to wait not only more than a week before he arrived at her home in Havana, but who knew how many days afterward until they were married.

Morgan thought about Claudia all during the ride to town. He was so preoccupied that it seemed as if only minutes had passed when he saw the southern gate a short distance ahead. He continued to think about her as the sentry moved the gate aside. It occurred to him that in less than a day, he would be on his way to Havana and his future life with Claudia. He pictured her smiling and waving to him as his ship slowly approached the dock. In his last look at their reunion, he was ashore running toward her.

Morgan arrived in St. Augustine on Sunday, August 3. His ship, an old schooner named the *Saving Grace*, had been delayed by the replacement of a broken mast and, instead of sailing at dawn on Saturday morning, departed six hours later. Under full sail and with a brisk wind, the ship reached the inlet to St. Augustine at 8:30 in the evening. But by that time, it was almost dark and the tide had begun to turn toward the sea. The Scottish captain therefore anchored the *Saving Grace* outside of St. Augustine that night. He would not risk sailing the heavily laden schooner into the treacherous channel unless in daylight and deep water. He knew of too many captains who foolishly tried to take their vessels through the inlet at low tide and had grounded them on the infamous Florida sandbar. With those incidents in mind, he was content to wait until eight in the morning when he could sail into the bay at full tide.

Morgan slept poorly that night in the heaving ship and awoke before dawn. He stood at the bow when the schooner finally sailed into the channel and watched impatiently as the captain slowly guided it into St. Augustine Bay. It was after 9:30 by the time the *Saving Grace* reached the dock and he jumped off the deck as the crew tied up. Morgan had only a day to complete his mission and he worried there would not be enough time to interview everyone he had in mind.

To his dismay, Morgan found only five residents to question in St. Augustine and he had to wait until after ten o'clock to talk to them. The English officials, whom he had written to ask permission for interviews, were in church until that time. He initially met with Governor James Grant and then with Colonel Blaine, the commander of the army's fifth brigade in St. Augustine. Morgan found both men to be gracious and hospitable, but neither knew anything about Spanish bullion in Florida. They directed him to the few Spaniards who remained in the colony following the mass exodus, but only after engaging him in lengthy talks about life in Carolina and Georgia. He patiently responded to their queries about living conditions in Savannah and Charles Towne and even managed to maintain his geniality when they inquired about old friends in the Georgia colonial service. Inwardly seething about the wasted time, he sat courteously for more than two hours, talking, first, to the governor in Government House and then to the commander in Fort St. Marks as England's officials now called the Castillo de San Marcos.

It was after 11:30 when Morgan politely declined lunch with the commander and left his office in the fort. Fortunately, the first Spaniards he interviewed lived only an eight-minute walk away on the Street of Merchants and the second Spaniard lived next door. All were at home that day and they spoke enough English to understand most of what he said. Their clearly enunciated Spanish was also easy for him to understand. And that was the end of his good fortune.

None of the Spaniards, neither the elderly couple in the first house nor the widower in the second, offered him any useful information. They had lived all their many years in St. Augustine, but looked bewildered when Morgan asked them if they could recall anything unusual happening in the colony in the spring of 1763. One of the men could remember only that the year was *muy malo* because of terrible storms all through the summer and early autumn. Morgan hesitated to ask them specifically about missing or stolen Spanish treasure, fearing news of his inquiry would somehow reach Havana before him and ruin his investigation in Cuba. He had hoped they might mention the loss of bullion as a memorable event in the last year of Spanish rule in Florida. But despite his patient attempts to word his question in a number of different ways, the Spaniards did not remember anything remarkable except the storms and the end of the Seven Years War.

They did refer Morgan to two other residents who also had lived in the colony throughout the sixties, but neither was available that day. The prominent landowner, Luciano de Herrera, lay sick in bed and Jesse Fish, the English orange grower, lived as a recluse on the island across the bay. Morgan was told that Fish suffered gout and rarely left his estate.

Fish had come to St. Augustine in the thirties as a youth and it was said he spoke Spanish so well he seemed "more Spanish than English." It was also said that Fish knew within an hour everything that happened in St. Augustine. Morgan thought about taking a canoe across the bay to meet the Englishman, but decided instead to ride out to find María Adela's father. He could always return to Florida and talk to Fish as well as Herrera if his mission in Havana failed.

Unfortunately, María Adela's father also was unavailable to Morgan. In fact, he could not be found. Loaned a horse by the army commander, he rode out to his home north of town only to find the wooden dwelling unoccupied. Morgan knew he had found the Macías house by its cedar shingles. María Adela said it was the only house with a wooden roof.

With the exception of some building ruins, the small village consisted of only nine other houses, all with thatched roofs and unoccupied. Morgan dismounted, deciding to look around on foot. He was surprised to discover that the houses, including Miguel Macías' home, looked as if they had been abandoned long ago. Morgan studied María Adela's map and, though the village appeared to be as she had sketched it, with a distinct X marking the Macías house, it occurred to him that he might have ridden to the wrong settlement. He then rode in concentric circles around the village, but found no other community within a fifteen-minute radius. Returning to the row of empty houses, he went through every one of them, searching for any signs of recent occupancy. Morgan found none and concluded María Adela's family must have lived in the tiny village for only a short time before moving to Pensacola.

Morgan mounted his horse and sat astride him thinking about what to do next. He looked at his watch and saw it was five o'clock. Four hours of daylight remained and he wanted to make good use of his time in Florida. Since there was no one else in town to interview, he decided to cross the bay and talk to Jesse Fish. Morgan did not look forward to paddling a canoe against a moving sea, but it would be worth the effort if the man could tell him something useful.

"Jesse Fish is a miserly man and not at all courteous for an Englishman," Colonel Blaine told him, when Morgan returned the horse and requested the use of a canoe. "They say he's the wealthiest man in Florida and yet he comes to town in shabby patched clothes. Fish also stinks, some say worse than his namesake. God only knows if the man ever bathes."

"But he knows this town and what has happened here in the past?" Morgan stood in the fort's parade ground, the horse's reins in his hand.

"That he does. I'll show you where he lives." Blaine realized the visitor from Savannah was determined to meet Jesse Fish. Out of the corner of his eye, he appraised the one-armed man and doubted his ability to paddle across the bay. "I'll have a man take you over to his house," he said, as if it were a routine army responsibility.

"That won't be necessary. I'll go over alone if you permit me to take a canoe."

"As you please." The colonel turned to his aide, who stood awaiting orders behind him. "Sergeant, provide Major Morgan with a requisition order for a canoe."

Five minutes later, Morgan with a signed requisition order, accompanied Colonel Blaine to the fort's entrance. They walked to the other side of the wooden bridge that extended over the moat and descended a steep stairway to the stone seawall. The two-foot wide wall ran along the bay from the fort to the southern end of St. Augustine. Blaine pointed to a long dock projecting out from the island across the bay.

"Fish's house is back in the trees behind the dock. You can't see it from here. He calls his plantation *El Vergel*, the fruit and flower garden, which is fitting since his orange groves produce hundreds of barrels of oranges and juice every year. Fish claims to own the entire island where *El Vergel* is located and that land extends twenty miles south of the plantation. The Spaniards originally named it Santa Anastasia Island, but he calls it *Fish Island.* He says the Spaniards sold him the island when they left the colony. The king's accountants are now examining his many property deeds, which include most of the houses in the city. Fish even has deeds to the Catholic Church and the Franciscan monastery."

"I thought all Church property belongs to the crown of Spain." Morgan turned to Blaine.

"That's what the accountants have decided despite his deeds. Even without the Church property, Fish probably has more holdings here than King George himself!"

Morgan shook his head from side to side showing his astonishment. "Thank you for your assistance. I'll talk to you upon my return."

Morgan walked along the wall to the city pier, where he

showed the sentry his requisition order. "Take anyone you want, sir." The sentry pointed to the six bark canoes overturned on the ground. "The paddles are underneath." He stared at Morgan and made no effort to hide his doubt that a one-armed man could paddle a canoe across the bay.

Morgan selected the canoe that looked least damaged. He made sure there were no holes in the hull and flipped it over, placing a paddle inside. He paused momentarily to look up at the overcast sky and then dragged the canoe into the shallows. He pushed off, jumping quickly into the canoe as it floated away from shore. Morgan paddled steadily, moving his right arm back and forth across his body to steer the canoe in a straight line.

A brisk wind and white-capped waves buffeted the bay as Morgan began paddling and he quickly found it exhausting to steer the canoe toward the island. Fifty or so yards from shore, he luckily caught an eastward running current that carried him well over half way to the point of land where he was headed. He rested as the canoe glided along on the current, using his paddle as a rudder. His shoulder ached and he leaned back, sighing in relief as the canoe cut effortlessly through the choppy water. As Morgan rested he had the luxury to look about and see a long line of pelicans flying in formation over the bay. He also noticed a number of fins skimming above the waves and he braced his legs against the rough sides of the canoe. Morgan knew well what would happen to him if he fell into the sea.

Within clear sight of a man standing on Fish's dock, he changed course slightly and tried to steer the canoe to the left where a sailboat was tied up. Morgan estimated he had no more than twenty yards ahead to reach the dock. He no sooner had changed his heading when the eastward current disappeared. Morgan immediately paddled with all his strength, but, no matter how hard he worked, the boat seemed to wallow in the swells and barely move at all.

Wave after wave broke over the bow as he struggled to paddle forward. In only moments, the sluggish canoe seemed to be full of water and was pushed aside as if by a huge hand. It then foundered and Morgan fell into the churning sea. The canoe was gone before he rose from beneath the water. Trying to keep his face above the waves, he swam toward the dock. Morgan could see it now and then as he struggled to breath in the roiling water. He swam with a sidestroke, which enabled him to use his one arm and legs to thrust himself forward.

As Morgan struck out swimming, he saw two fins rise up on his left side and expected at any second to feel a shark's teeth seizing him. In the rough sea and without any weapon to fight off the sharks, he knew his life would be taken. It was only a matter of time. His only chance to survive was to keep swimming and hope the sharks might be after other prey. With that thought in mind, he swam on, slowly nearing the dock. Morgan lost all hope when he sensed the presence of a long shape moving along his left side and, for an instant; he felt a slick skin against his foot. He tensed, expecting to be bitten at any time. But nothing happened and he resumed swimming, resigned to the shark's strike that would end his life. It occurred to him that he would never see Claudia again nor would he see the child she would bring into the world.

Suppressing a sob, he swallowed salt water and, for a moment, thought he might choke to death before a shark took him. Coughing up salt water and unable to see above the waves, Morgan continued to swim on awkwardly, unaware of where he was headed. His arm ached and he knew his strength was almost gone. Suddenly, he kicked out with left leg and, to his surprise, his foot scraped the sandy bottom of the bay.

Morgan saw waves running to shore ahead of him and stood unsteadily, waist high in the water. He pushed himself forward through the waves, staggered onto the beach and fell forward, exhausted and panting on the sand. Except for his breathing, Morgan lay unmoving in the sand, his arm flung out to the side, his fingers spread out like the rays of a starfish. He had no notion how long he lay there. Morgan only moved when he heard a voice above him. He rolled over on his back and looked up too see a bearded man smiling down at him.

"I trust you are looking for me. You made quite an entrance. Might you be in theatre?"

"No," Morgan gasped. He was bewildered by the man's jest. "I'm Major James Morgan and I'm lucky to be alive. I thought the sharks would take me at any moment."

"What sharks?" The man looked puzzled.

"Out there!" shouted Morgan, exasperated by the man's obvious ignorance. He pointed weakly toward the waves, which were still crashing into shore. "Don't you see their fins?"

The man shaded his eyes with his hand and looked into the bay beyond the white-capped waves. It took him a minute, but then he saw the black fins, three in all. He threw back his head and laughed heartily. "You saw dolphins, you fool, not sharks. The dolphins own this bay and no shark would dare risk swimming inside."

Morgan sat up and stared at the bearded man, whom he now saw wore faded and patched clothing. His wild hair was blowing about in the wind and Morgan thought the man looked like a goblin from a child's fairy tale. "I don't suppose you're Jesse Fish?"

"I am indeed and I assume you're here to talk with me. I suggest we go to my house. It appears you need some dry clothes and a hot cup of tea. A glass of whisky might also be proper for an Englishman attacked by Florida dolphins."

Morgan was elated as he returned to the *Saving Grace* at first light the next morning. His suspicions had been verified – Spanish bullion had been involved in the Savannah murders. Jesse Fish had told him everything he knew in a few sentences, but it was all Morgan needed to know.

"I don't know much," Fish told him. "It was supposed to be a secret, but I heard a sunken Spanish ship from the 1715 treasure fleet was found in sixteen feet of water outside of Matanzas Inlet. That's the southern ship channel that flows north into the bay out there." Fish pointed out the window, where whitecaps still covered the bay. "They hired Indians to dive for the bars and they brought up several hundred – both gold and silver. A big warship took the salvaged bullion to Spain. It was in 1763. I remember there was no rain that spring."

"The warship took all of it?"

"As far as I know. The ship, I don't recall its name, was anchored in the bay for almost a month. It was either in April or May. It was one of those enormous ships they call a man-of-war with three or maybe four masts and as many as a hundred cannon. Its draft was too deep to dock at the pier. I remember now, it was named the *Favorita*."

"So they had to ferry the bars out to the ship by longboat?"

"Yes, but the bars had been put into chests so no one would know about the bullion. They loaded the bullion into the chests late at night for the same reason. Of course, everyone in town suspected something valuable was carried to the warship. After all, what else would be stored in heavy chests the ship's crew struggled to carry aboard? Tea leaves? And would twenty or more soldiers with muskets be on the dock guarding ordinary cargo or ship's stores? It always amazes me that the colonial officials think they can deceive the townspeople time and time again. The people always know much more than the lying officials think they know. It only takes a dram or two of rum given to the right man to find out any supposed secret in St. Augustine."

"Are you saying the entire town knew about the sunken ship and salvaged bullion?"

"I doubt that everyone knew, but those who didn't know certainly suspected something of great value was taken aboard the warship. Anyone who had lived in St. Augustine for any length of time would have been suspicious of a ship's crew loading cargo in the dead of night and under guard. No other cargo had been carried aboard a ship under such circumstances before – at least not as long as I've lived here."

"What cargo is shipped out of St. Augustine?"

"There is no outgoing cargo, except the barrels of oranges and orange juice I ship to England in the winter. This colony can't even support itself, never mind ship out a crop or some mined mineral. Ships come to St. Augustine to bring cargo in, not out. This city couldn't survive a month without foodstuffs from abroad. This is and always has been a garrison town since it was founded in 1565. There are many residing here who imagine the city has more importance, but it simply doesn't. The colony produces nothing of any worth and has served the Spanish kings as a military station guarding the sea route the convoys take from Cuba to Spain."

"I've heard that the Spanish fleets sail north from Havana through the Bahama Channel to St. Augustine, where they cross the Atlantic toward Spain."

"That's correct. All products from America are taken first to Havana and then are shipped to Spain. The fleets use the Bahama Channel because of the northern current that flows between the Bahama Islands and the coast of Florida. No ship from this colony ever joins that fleet."

Morgan nodded. "So it was obvious to everyone in the colony that something of value was being carried aboard the warship – even if they didn't know what it was."

"Exactly. Their efforts to keep it secret were a waste of time." Jesse Fish ran his fingers through his stringy hair and scratched a bald spot at the back of his head.

"So it would seem." Morgan now knew that anyone in the colony could have been aware of the sunken treasure ship. Since it took a month to complete the salvage, news of the treasure could have easily reached Georgia well before the work was finished. The same news could also have reached the ears of Chapman and Sterling in Savannah and Willington in New Hanover.

Fish held up his hand. "There's even more to the story. In their endless quest for secrecy, the foolish officials sent every soldier involved in the salvage to Spain; they thought the secret of the treasure would go with them." Fish threw his head back and chortled. "What stupidity! As if the soldiers, once back in Spain, couldn't send messages to their wenches and friends in Florida." He crossed his legs, revealing a patch in his faded breeches and several holes in his stockings.

Morgan nodded. "Even if they couldn't write a line, they could send the news with other replacement soldiers on their way to serve in St. Augustine."

"Exactly. But, by that summer, the officials were no longer concerned about the bullion. Their concern was the transfer of all the Spanish townspeople to Cuba and New Spain. As you probably know, the king wanted his Catholic subjects removed from Florida before the arrival of English Protestantism. He didn't want his people to mingle with heretics."

"I heard that the colony was almost completely emptied and I saw very few people in the streets when I walked through town today."

"There are only a few stubborn souls left here and a landowner or two like myself. You can see the results of the evacuation here even three years later. The town is still almost empty and many of the houses have been stripped of much of their wood. Their first winter in Florida, the

English used any wood they could find to keep their fires going. They burned the furniture the Spaniards left behind as well as doors, shutters, shingles and even outside planks. It was an especially hard winter in Florida that year and I lost most of my orange trees."

Morgan learned nothing more of importance from the unkempt, smelly man and he left Fish Island before dusk. By that time, the wind had subsided and the bay seemed as calm as an inland lake. A slave rowed him across the water after he shared supper with Fish and his family. Morgan left the island wearing his own wet clothes; they had been washed while he and Fish talked.

On the way across the bay, Morgan saw a group of dolphins gliding through the water as if in a race with the rowboat. They leaped above and below the surface as they swam. "They're mammals and must rise periodically from the sea to breathe," Jesse Fish had said as he described their differences from sharks. While they walked to his house, he recounted stories of men who fell into the sea and claimed dolphins had saved them from drowning. "Believe it or not, Major, the dolphins pushed them to shore. Morgan felt foolish as he listened to Fish. He had often seen dolphins in the tidal waters near Morgan's Creek and should have recognized their curved fins when he fell into the water.

Morgan was not a man who paid much attention to the fish or mammals that swam in the waters around Savannah. Sea life never interested him, no matter how many times his father had excitedly pointed out wayward whales or mass concentrations of small fish. He avoided the sea unlike his brother who spent hours sailing and fishing in the river and ocean.

Morgan had always looked inland to the forests, sylvan lakes and distant mountains. As a boy, he loved to walk stealthily through the woods, listening to its sounds and looking for hidden animals that shied away from men. He made long treks into the forests in all seasons, whether in the middle of winter when it was bitter cold or in the sultry days of summer when the biting flies and clouds of mosquitoes besieged him with every step he took. In autumn, when the water oaks and sweet gums filled the woods with orange, red and yellow leaves, he would leave his home at dawn and only reluctantly return at dusk. On those days, he longed to be an artist to retain what he saw on canvas.

But now as the setting sun colored the cloudy sky and surface of the bay in shades of pink and purple and leaping dolphins glistened in the fading light, he knew the striking view of the sea compared to any autumn scene he had seen in the past. Morgan had seen many beautiful sunsets before in Morgan's Creek, but none so stunning as the one he saw that evening on St. Augustine Bay. He turned to see how far the boat was from shore and, in the seconds it took for him to look away, the colors in the sea and sky had blurred and blended together. The spectacular sunset was gone and all that remained was in his memory.

As the rowboat neared the pier, it occurred to Morgan that his host never offered him the whisky he had mentioned when they first met on the beach. He doubted Jesse Fish had forgotten his offer, especially when he recalled the meager meal he had eaten with the family that evening. Everyone, adult and child alike, had been served a small piece of fried fish, a slice of tomato and half a cooked carrot. Nothing else had been offered and he had risen from the table still hungry. Standing in the bow ready to climb the stairs to the dock, Morgan smiled, recalling that Colonel Blaine had said Jesse Fish was a miserly man. "Miserly indeed," he thought, "but more helpful than anyone else in St. Augustine."

Jesse Fish confirmed his suspicion that Chapman's gold and silver ingots had come from a Spanish source – probably, the salvaged treasure ship. Morgan then remembered the manner in which Chapman's head had been tied to the mast of the sunken schooner. It had been fixed in a position to stare southward toward St. Augustine. The murderer forced his victim to look toward the city where he had committed his unforgivable offense – whatever that was. Morgan was now certain the three dead men had stolen bullion from the salvaged ship. He had no notion how they managed the robbery with armed soldiers guarding it, but he was sure they had succeeded. How they had stolen the bullion was the question he hoped would be answered in Havana.

Everything now depended on someone trustworthy entering the Building of Records and finding the reports that described the salvage of the treasure ship. Amid those documents, he was certain there would be at least one account of the robbery of bullion. Morgan sighed, worried he would not find a man in Havana willing to make the search for him. Without knowledge of what happened to the bullion in 1763, he doubted the murderer would ever be identified and arrested.

Morgan stood at the bow of the *Saving Grace* looking toward Cuba. The island stood out miles away as a dark mound in the sea. He looked at his pocket watch noting it was four o'clock. If the wind held, he thought, the ship should be docked well before dusk.

Morgan wondered how much time he would spend in the Custom House; with his official credentials, he expected to be routinely admitted into Cuba. He carried two letters addressed to Governor Antonio Maria Bucareli y Ursúa and signed by Governor James Wright. One letter included Wright's cordial greetings and his congratulations for Bucareli's recent appointment as Governor and Captain General of Cuba. The second requested permission for Morgan to enter Havana and reside in the city for a thirty-day stay. Palmer informed Morgan that a month would be enough time to find the information they needed. The two letters had been sealed and placed in an envelope addressed to the governor of Cuba. He carried a third letter written to the customs officials, which requested permission for him to deliver Wright's correspondence.

That letter introduced Major Morgan and described his mission as an effort to learn about the Spanish methods of criminal investigation. Morgan thought the explanation was preposterous and would never be believed by the Spaniards. But Palmer, who thought of the idea, insisted on its use despite Morgan's vain protests and Wright's lukewarm approval. The governor preferred to follow customary international procedure and mail the letters well before the voyage, but there had not been enough time.

The island seemed to have grown larger as Morgan stood thinking on deck. It was a clear day with only an occasional cloud drifting across the sky. He could see far into the distance in all directions. The *Saving Grace* had enjoyed clear skies, southerly blowing winds and smooth seas the entire trip. There had not been a single calm or thunderstorm to delay the sailing; the schooner was slowed only by the current that flowed north along the Florida coast.

Morgan knew the voyage had been unusually easy even before he heard it from the ship's captain. Calum Macauley, a short squat Scotsman, joined him at the bow as the first buildings on the coast came into view. "It's the best sailing I've made in these waters; I never before seen the coast of Cuba in only six days sailing. Thanks be to God."

"How long a voyage is it usually?" Morgan asked to show his interest.

"From seven to ten days even if no storm blows in. The winds on the coast change before you know it and ships face any number of calms south of St. Augustine. But the winds was good to us this voyage. The sails full most of the time. It's a blessing from God."

Morgan continued to stare at the growing landmass in the sea. He was anxious to get off the ship. He had Claudia on his mind and his thoughts of marriage and meeting her family made him uneasy. He began to pace the deck when the captain returned to the ship's wheel.

The voyage to Havana had not only been shorter than Morgan expected, it had given him unexpected information about the murders in Savannah. He finally learned how the victims had known each other. It had happened the third afternoon out of St. Augustine as the *Saving Grace* sailed past Río Seco (Dry Rivert), considered to be the halfway point on the voyage to Havana. Following a card game with the captain and first mate, a burly bearded Irishman named Seamus O'Sullivan, Morgan casually asked if either of them had known George Chapman. Both sailors laughed loudly as if in planned harmony.

"We should." The captain snorted. "He sailed with us on and off for near ten years. He was third mate most of the time. A lazy man, never did more than he had to."

"And greedy," added O'Sullivan. "All the man thought about was money and never took no pride in his work or his ship."

"That's why he never got no promotions. The other captains saw Chapman the same way. It took most of his years just to be a mate and never a first mate." Macauley spit over the railing. "I would take him on only when nobody better was around."

"Then, how did he get his own ship?"

"Now, that's a story, ain't it?" The captain exchanged smiles with O'Sullivan. "The story Chapman told around town was he found a sunk ship with a chest full of gold and silver. Claimed he seen the sunk ship in shallow waters south of Savannah. Now, fact is nobody else ever seen no sunk ship in the shallows. There're any number of ships out in deep water at the river's mouth and along the coast, but them ships are there in nine or ten fathoms of water. You can see them now and then in calm seas. But none are in the shallows."

"So, no one believed his story?" Morgan saw both men shake their heads.

"No!" Macauley almost shouted. "And nobody seen the chest or a piece of gold or silver – except maybe the Parkers. They're the ones built his ship and those two never says nothin' to nobody. They're too busy poor mouthing and complaining about the price of wood and taxes. You can be sure Chapman paid them in coin – them Parkers wouldn't lift a finger without it."

"It's said they get half before they start," said O'Sullivan. "The rest is paid when the hull is done. They do build a good ship – I been on a couple over the years."

"Do you have any idea how much Chapman paid to have the *Brazen* built?"

"No, but I'll give you a good guess." The captain stroked his chin. "Let's see, I'd say the ship was near 120 tons…"

"Actually, 115 tons and 90 feet long. The Parkers told me that much."

"Then, I'd say a ship that size cost some £3,500. I hear them Parkers charge £20 a ton to build a ship with every cleat. That's £5 less than they charge in England. But it costs more to fit it out. The compass, chronometer and sextant together would cost more than £100. Then, there's extra canvas, carpenters' materials, sounding lines and ropes, ballast, a pistol or two, harpoons and a hundred other things—and let's not forget a good size dingy."

"How about provisions for the first sailing?" asked O'Sullivan. "And wages for a crew?"

"That's right." Macauley looked about his ship. "You

know, Major," he said, sitting down across from Morgan, "The more I think on it, Chapman's schooner would cost much more than I said at first – maybe £4,000 or more before it was put out to sea."

"That's a lot of money. If there was no sunken ship with treasure, where did Chapman get the money to pay for the *Brazen*?"

"That's a question for Seamus. He knows more than me about George Chapman. But I'll tell you true, Major, no captain I ever knowed had near enough money to have a new schooner built for himself. Not in all these 30 years I been at sea."

"I've heard ships are usually owned by merchants or shipping companies." Morgan knew about the shipping business from his father, who had considered purchasing a schooner to carry his rice abroad. Matthew changed his mind when he heard the cost of even a small schooner.

"That's right. They're the only ones with such wealth. The *Saving Grace* is owned by a wool merchant in London and if I was captain for a hundred more years I wouldn't have money enough to buy it. Only in my dreams could I ever own a ship. Of course, Chapman on seaman's wages had enough to buy himself a brand new schooner. As they say, it's who you know and Chapman knowed them brigands and cutthroats that was settled there on the Altamaha River." Macauley looked at O'Sullivan, who nodded in agreement.

"Are you saying Chapman had dealings with the outlaws at New Hanover?"

"It's what many a man says. That's how he got his house and ship. The lazy lout didn't get his high station on a third mate's wages, that's for sure."

O'Sullivan nodded. "Nobody believed his yarn about the sunk ship. It's smuggling with them cutthroats got him all that money. Chapman's been thick with them for years, 'specially that sly Willington fella. That one won't be missed,

I'll tell you."

"Ah, so Chapman knew Willington?"

"They was thick as thieves, them two." O'Sullivan shook his head up and down. "There wasn't no time when we came to port they wasn't together at some tavern on the river. I can see them in my mind's eye hunched over their whiskies. They'd be talking quiet and looking round to see if anybody was trying to hear what was said. That sneaky Willington with his shifty eyes was the one mostly looked round. One time he caught me looking, so I gave him a big smile and raised my glass to him. After that he turned away and paid me no mind."

"Was that after Willington came to Savannah?"

"I seen them together many times before that, too. They was together in Charles Towne, Port Royal, Savannah and some other ports along the coast. I can't recall where all they was at one time or other. But, if you seen one, you'd see the other sooner or later." O'Sullivan held up a finger. "I also seen another of them – a gentleman he was, talking with them a time or two."

"How did you know he was a gentleman?"

"He was dressed in a fine suit and had a hat with a white feather… and a walking stick."

"What about a wig?"

"No wig, but you could see he had money. He was the one who ordered the whisky and paid for it from a fat bag of coins. He did most of the talking, too, and they listened hard."

"Did you ever see that man again… in the streets of Savannah or Charles Towne?"

"Not that I recall." O'Sullivan twisted the end of his beard as he tried to remember where he had seen the man with the white feather in his hat. "I seen him no more than a couple times in taverns with the others. It could of been in Savannah or Charles Towne, too, but it was only in Port

Royal I recall seeing him for sure."

"When you saw the well dressed man with Chapman and Willington, was he speaking in a low voice so he couldn't be heard?"

"He was – the same as them others. They was surely up to no good."

"Most us captains knew they was up to something outlawed," added Macauley. "Surely, something that made a lot of money, but was criminal – probably smuggling. Willington was from that thieves' nest at New Hanover so we knowed he was up to no good. So, when we seen Chapman with Willington, we was leery of the man – you know the old saying, 'birds as has the same feathers.' That's again why nobody hired him except when the best mates was too drunk or shipped out at the time. When Chapman needed work he went to the docks for any ship that lacked a mate. That's how he got hired on. Now and then, he even went to sea as a sailor when he was outa money. That's before he met up with Willington and that lot at New Hanover."

"What do you think he and Willington were smuggling?"

O'Sullivan looked at Macauley. "I'd guess it was stolen slaves and goods of all kind. If the cost is low, there's planters aplenty in the colonies don't care a whit where the cheap goods come from 'specially in the wars. That's when things from Europe was hard to come by. 'Money answers all things,' the Bible says."

"Anything made in England would fetch the best prices in the colonies." Macauley again spit over the side. "Those brigands from New Hanover probably stole the slaves and goods and then Willington and Chapman went around selling the booty. I'd guess they had customers all-round the coast and nobody knew nothin' in Savannah or Charles Towne. Course, it all ended after the war when them cutthroats got chased out of New Hanover."

"While they were smuggling, where would they get a ship?"

"Chapman must of captained some pirate vessel, most likely a ketch or sloop. If they had a heavy load, he might have sailed some shipping company's schooner." Macauley snorted, seeing Morgan's raised eyebrows. "What do you think, them greedy bastards wouldn't be doing a bit a smuggling at night to make some fast and easy money? I don't know one that's not done it a time or two." Macauley smiled mischievously. "As you might expect, Major, most captains and crews make a few silver coins now and again carrying a bit of extra cargo into the colonies." Macauley grinned again. "But never no slaves and nothin' stolen."

Morgan smiled, too, amused at the captain's candor. "What about Thomas Sterling?"

Macauley and O'Sullivan again laughed in unison. "Him 'specially!" Macauley snorted. "Sterling was the greediest of them all. The fat hog had the busiest nighttime dock on the river. That's how he paid for the new pier. His shipping business was doing poorly at the time."

"Was Chapman sailing at night for Sterling?"

Macauley shook his head. "I don't know. I only sailed one time for Sterling and he tried to cheat me. When I caught him, the fat bastard said he counted wrong. I recall his lying words even now. 'Oh, do forgive me, Captain, I am at fault for miscounting what is due you,' he said in that snooty way the English talk. The whore's son! I heared he tried the same trick with other captains and I'd wager he was done in by one he cheated. He got what was coming to him."

"Do you ever recall seeing Sterling and Chapman together – talking in low voices?"

"No, can't say I did. What about you, Seamus?"

"No, but they was two of a kind and would of done most anything for money."

"Did Chapman ever sail for Sterling after he built the *Brazen*?"

Macauley shook his head. "I never heared it, if he did.

Chapman sailed mostly for Hugh Douglas. But before he got his own ship, he must have sailed one time or other with them that carried Sterling's cargo out of Savannah."

"Do you think Chapman got all his money from smuggling? Keep in mind, he had more than enough to pay for the *Brazen* and buy that fine house in Percival Ward." Morgan watched both men as they thought about his question.

"No!" Macauley almost shouted. "Even if everything was stolen, he had to share what he got with Willington and the cutthroats in New Hanover." He looked at O'Sullivan who nodded in agreement. "And if they was to sell the goods, they had to keep prices low so what they got in the end was good, but not grand. Seamus, how many years was them two together?"

"Three years or so."

Macauley shook his head vigorously. "No, Chapman didn't build the *Brazen* and buy that grand house with smuggling money. Maybe the house, but not the ship, too."

"That means he had other money to pay for the schooner. So, if there was no sunken ship with treasure, how or where did he get it?" Morgan looked back and forth at the two men.

"He stole it, that's how!" O'Sullivan pounded the table with his hand.

Macauley nodded. "He must have stole it from one of them Spanish ports in the Caribbean. Not St. Augustine – the Spaniards had nothin' there for years, except sickness and hard times."

Morgan could see the walls of the Castillo del Morro as the *Saving Grace* approached Havana. The great fortress stood on the eastern side of the deep passage that flowed from the ocean into the harbor. El Morro was across from another fort, the Castillo de San Salvador de la Punta, built on the western side of the inlet. The two forts guarded the sea entrance into Havana and focused rows of cannons on the channel that ran between them. An enemy ship or fleet that sailed into the Canal de Entrada would face the devastating crossfire from both forts. A third and ever more imposing stronghold, San Carlos de Cabaña, was under construction on the same side of the waterway as El Morro, but closer to Havana.

Morgan saw the unfinished walls of San Carlos as the *Saving Grace* glided slowly on the current toward the docks and the customs house. He stood beside the captain at the bow, while a Spanish naval lieutenant piloted the ship. The Spaniard came aboard from a smaller sailboat that intercepted the *Saving Grace* as the crew lowered its sails just outside the inlet. After greeting the captain and scrutinizing his papers, the Spanish pilot took the wheel and guided the ship through the channel, past the harbor shoals and toward the port-city.

"He's a young one, isn't he?" Macauley nudged Morgan. "Speaks good English, too. I hear they brought new officers from Spain after they lost Havana in the war."

Morgan nodded. "I expect so. I assume that's why they're building a new fort, too. They don't want this port ever taken again. It's their main port in the New World, after all."

"Makes sense. God only knows how long it'll take them to build it. They been at it three years already."

As the *Saving Grace* neared its berth, Morgan saw two Spanish officers emerge from the customs house and walk to meet them. Moments later, everyone aboard the schooner was taken inside to be questioned and cleared for entry. It took only an hour for Captain Macauley and his crew to get their required papers. After paying the port's passage and docking fees, they left the customs house to unload their cargo for transfer to the Cuban merchants.

Morgan submitted his letters to a Spanish lieutenant and was politely asked to sit and wait while the ship's crew went through the entry process. He was still waiting when Macauley and O'Sullivan stopped to shake his hand as they walked by on their way out of the Customs House. Morgan waited another hour, even though no other ship's crew or visitors came into the building. The ten customs officers seemed to be sitting unoccupied at their desks. Morgan noted that none of the officers wore wigs, which surprised him after what he had heard about Spanish formality. Another half hour passed as he shifted uncomfortably in the unsteady wooden chair he had been given. Finally, his name was called and Morgan walked to a cluttered desk where a grim-looking colonel sat watching him approach. It was clear that the colonel commanded the office.

"Please sit down, Major Morgan." The Spanish colonel spoke fluent English. He pointed to a chair in front of his desk. "My name is Colonel Juan Rodríguez y Rivera and I command this Customs House." The colonel was a severe looking man with thinning black hair and a carefully trimmed beard and mustache. As Morgan took his seat, he saw streaks of gray in the Spaniard's hair and suspected he was well over forty. The reading glass on his desk confirmed his suspicion.

"Thank you, Colonel." Morgan sat as straight as possible facing the Spanish officer.

"Major Morgan, I want you to know that I carefully read the letter from Governor Wright addressed to us at the Customs House. As I'm certain you know, it requests our permission for you to take the other letters to Governor Antonio María de Bucareli y Ursúa. Those letters were also opened and read." The colonel smiled, seeing Morgan's surprise. "It is official policy in Havana for us to examine all correspondence of unannounced visitors, no matter to whom it is addressed or if officially sealed. Since you fit into that category, I read all three letters you brought to us. Is that understood?" Colonel Rodríguez stared at Morgan.

"Yes, sir." Morgan had a queasy feeling in his stomach.

"So, Major Morgan, I must tell you I find the explanation for your visit to Cuba hard to believe. In fact, I find it ridiculous! We Spaniards are not fools, Major Morgan, and we do not expect you English to treat us in that manner. Do you understand me?" The colonel spoke softly, glaring at the man facing him.

"Yes, sir." Morgan did not know what else to say.

"I suggest you think carefully about what you next will say. I warn you, Major, if you persist in repeating that preposterous story you will seriously regret it. Not only will you not enter La Habana, you will remain in detention here until a crown attorney becomes available to interrogate you and decide your fate. Is that understood?"

"Yes, sir." Morgan knew it would be futile to insist Palmer's explanation was true. It would also be futile to attempt other lies. The Spanish colonel was too intelligent to be fooled and would see through any fictional story he told. Morgan recognized he would have to tell the truth if he hoped to enter Havana. Everything depended on it, his marriage to Claudia as well as the murder investigation. He also feared being held in detention, even if briefly. Morgan had a vision of a dark dungeon where he was given wormy gruel and foul water.

The colonel watched him without comment, knowing he was thinking about what to do.

"I'll tell you the truth, Colonel Rodríguez. I apologize for the preposterous explanation as you rightly call it; I can only say it was not my idea. You and I both serve other officials and I'm sure you can easily surmise the origin of that explanation."

"Yes, I'm certain I can." The colonel watched Morgan shift uncomfortably in his chair.

Morgan exhaled audibly through his nose. "There are two important reasons why I want to enter Havana, Colonel, and I will inform you of both of them."

"Good." Rodríguez leaned back in his chair to listen.

Morgan spoke for an hour without a pause. He told the colonel about the three unsolved murders in Savannah as well as his planned marriage in Havana. Morgan spoke first about the murders and his suspicion that Spanish bullion was involved. He related all he knew about the murderer and described in detail the cruel methods the murderer had used to kill his victims.

At that point, the colonel held up a hand and stopped Morgan to order a bottle of wine. A lieutenant brought a bottle of Rioja to the desk and filled two glasses, handing one to his superior and the other to Morgan. The major drank down his wine in two swallows and then continued his account. When he finished, the colonel gestured for the lieutenant to pour another glass of wine.

"Dios mío!" exclaimed Colonel Rodríguez. "What a diablo you have in Savannah!" He had gasped in horror when he heard how Sterling and Chapman had been murdered. "God only knows what those men did to deserve such cruelty." The colonel crossed his arms over his chest. "So, Major, what is it you hope to learn in Havana that will help you arrest this devil?"

"I think the three victims were involved in a scheme to steal Spanish bullion and they did something terrible during the robbery that resulted in their brutal murders. I am hoping there is a record of the robbery in the Building of Records, which will help me identity the murderer. It's the only possibility I have." Morgan told the colonel what he had learned in St. Augustine about the salvage of a treasure ship and his suspicion that some of salvaged bullion was stolen.

"So, Major Morgan, why did your governor not tell us the truth? He had only to request permission to search for such information in the Building of Records." The colonel furrowed his brow in bewilderment. "A simple letter requesting entry to search for information about a murder inquiry I am sure would have resulted in a written permit. One of the learned men at the archive would even have accompanied you in the search. That's what happened on my own visits to the archive in the past."

"My superiors feared the officials of the Building of Records would regard any foreigner, especially an Englishman, as a spy and would refuse to let him enter the archive. What worried them most, however, was the possibility that Spain would require England to make restitution for any bullion stolen by English colonists."

"That is also preposterous! Why would they think such nonsense?" Colonel Rodríguez shook his head, obviously exasperated. "Todo el mundo – Everyone in the world seems to think the worst of us Spaniards." He sighed. "It's the *Black Legend*! It never ends!" Rodríguez saw the puzzled look on Morgan's face. "You are not familiar with the *Black Legend*?"

"No. I've never heard of such a legend."

"The *Black Legend* began in the sixteenth century when the Dominican monk, Bartolomé de Las Casas, criticized our colonists for mistreating the Indians. Over the centuries since then, the legend grew as Spain was blamed for the death of millions of Indians during the colonization of the New World. It is true that many were killed in the wars to conquer the vast territories they held. But most died from the plagues, particularly the pox which killed the native peoples in all the colonies, including those under English rule. And let's not forget, the Indians Spain found in the New World sacrificed untold thousands of their own people, including little children, to their pagan gods. They also ate human flesh. Even though Spain ended those heinous practices and brought them Christianity, we are still blamed for what happened then. That is the *Black Legend* and, unfortunately, it has endured beyond those early times and condemns all Spaniards as cruel, greedy and immoral."

"I have heard such criticisms, but never knew of the *Black Legend*."

"I'm not surprised. Yet, you English have also killed many thousands of Indians, taken their lands and pushed them away from your colonies. But no similar legend exists about you." The colonel sighed wearily. "There's no point in saying more. It is getting late and we should talk about the second reason for your visit to Havana – your marriage to a Spanish woman. What is the family name?"

"López Moreno. They came here from St. Augustine after the war." Morgan handed the colonel a piece of paper with the family's name and address written on it.

"Ah, one of the families that passed through here three years ago."

The colonel beckoned one of the soldiers who stood guard at the door to the street. The man immediately strode to the desk and came to attention. "Sí, Señor."

"Ayala, vaya a la casa del Señor López Moreno. El vive en la calle Cristo, número seis. Dígale al Señor López Moreno que el Mayor Morgan está aquí esperando y que mande a alguien a recogerlo." Rodríguez translated for Morgan as the soldier hurried out of the office. "I told Ayala to go inform Señor López Moreno that you are here at the Customs House waiting for someone to escort you to his home. While we wait, we can talk about the joys and miseries of marrying a Spanish woman."

The hooded figure stood among the thick trees beyond the house. There was little left of twilight and the beginning of night obscured everything outside in shadow. Candles already had been lit in the house and the flickering light appeared in the windows. Cautiously staying within the shadows, the figure crept around the house studying it from every side. The stable and other outside buildings had also been surveyed. No one stood or moved anywhere about the house and no sound suggesting a man's presence could be heard.

Standing silently beside the trunk of a leafy tree, the figure thought about what had to be done in the next few days. It was finally time to finish it. No more waiting would be necessary. He was the last one and then everything would be ended. But this one was cautious and it would be much harder to dispose of him.

He knew what had happened to the others and had hired an armed man with a big dog to watch over him day and night. The man slept in the house, accompanied him wherever he went and never seemed to let him out of his sight. The big dog also guarded him. During the day, the dog stayed on the porch except for three walks he took with his master around the property. The walks were scheduled every day at nine o'clock in the morning and one and five in the afternoon. Each of the walks lasted forty-five minutes. At night, the armed man carried a lantern and took his dog on two fifteen-minute patrols around the house; the first at ten o'clock, the second at two in the morning. The man went around the house slowly, extending the lantern into the darkness. He allowed his dog to move about freely, searching for any intruder in the surrounding area. The armed man never deviated from the established schedule or the routes he followed.

He had been wise to safeguard his life, but neither the armed man nor the dog would save him from the death he deserved. They would make it harder to take his life, but it still would be achieved. He was doomed and, in time, a way would be found to strike him down when he least expected it.

CHAPTER NINE

HAVANA: MONDAY, AUGUST 26, 1766

Morgan sat drinking tea in a tavern across from the Customs House. He was waiting for Colonel Rodríguez, who was expected to arrive at eight o'clock that morning. The young sentry guarding the door to the Customs House had advised him the colonel would be there a las ocho en punto (exactly). Morgan knew enough Spanish to understand the fast-speaking soldier and, looking at his pocket watch, saw he had a half hour to wait. The sentry then pointed him to the tavern where he now drank a cup of tepid and tasteless tea.

Morgan rubbed his eyes with the palms of his hands. He had slept poorly again and felt exhausted as he faced the long day ahead. His visit to Cuba had been both sad and disappointing. Instead of the anticipated joy of marriage and helpful information from the Building of Records, he had found sorrow and failure. It seemed all his expectations had been doomed to fail from the start. "What was the saying?" he thought, "The best laid schemes o' mice an' men often go awry." He swallowed the tea, hoping to settle his queasy stomach.

It all began with the wedding. He and Claudia had been married in the rectory of the old Espíritu Santo Church, completed more than a century earlier in 1638. The plain and unadorned church was where her family went for Mass, confession and all ceremonies. Three generations of the large family already had been baptized, confirmed and married in Espíritu Santo and many more would follow in the years to come. Claudia's father had attended only one other church in his lifetime and that had happened during the fifteen years he had lived abroad in Florida. As a boy, Miguel López Moreno had gone to Espíritu Santo and it was where the fifty-seven year old man expected his funeral service would be held when he died.

Despite the family's long history with Espíritu Santo, the marriage did not take place in the church itself. Because Morgan had been baptized Protestant, he and Claudia were married in the rectory. According to Spanish law, a Catholic could marry a Protestant, but the ceremony could not be held in a Catholic church, though an ordained priest was expected to perform the marriage ceremony. Father Fernández, pastor of Espíritu Santo also informed Morgan that their children would have to be raised as Catholics. Morgan scowled when he heard the requirement, but then shrugged, realizing he and Claudia would do what they wished with their children in Savannah.

The wedding took place Saturday, August 17, at four o'clock in the afternoon. It was the time of day a sea breeze usually blew into Havana during the summer, bringing cool air and rain into the city. Fortunately for the assembled wedding party, the easterly wind carried only cool air that afternoon and Morgan found the rectory surprisingly comfortable. He was also surprised by the priest's evident sincerity as he conducted the marriage ceremony. Morgan had anticipated an apathetic recitation of the memorized phrases and platitudes he must have given a thousand times before. Instead, the elderly priest's softly spoken words touched him even though he understood little of what was said. Morgan felt tears form in his eyes and worried they would cascade down his cheeks in front of everyone. His eyes remained moist as Father Fernández finished speaking and gently turned him to face Claudia. They smiled exchanging their vows, received the priest's blessing and kissed to seal their marriage. The crowded rectory then resounded with the clapping and cheers of the more than two hundred family members and friends who filled the room.

At that moment as Morgan stood with his arm around Claudia, he knew he had never been happier in his life. A smile seemed to cover his face as they were surrounded by the boisterous Spaniards all competing to congratulate and embrace them. He was hugged and kissed at least a hundred times and, to his surprise, he enjoyed every moment of it. He let himself relax in the joy that permeated the room. "What wonderful warm people you are," he whispered to Claudia. She nodded as their bodies were pressed together by the crowd of smiling faces. Before Morgan even became aware of it, he and Claudia were separated by the mass of people and each of them was encircled by a throng of men and women taking turns, hugging and kissing them. Even the little children hugged them, clutching their legs. It was a fiesta of affection and warmth Morgan could never have imagined.

Then, as the bottles of red wine were uncorked and emptied, filled glasses were passed from hand to hand and other filled glasses were raised in toasts to the newly married couple, the wedding celebration ended. It ended before the toasts were finished, it ended before everyone could embrace Claudia's smiling parents, it ended before the filled pots and pans of food could be served, it ended before the children were told to wash their hands before eating.

It was over before Father Fernández could move through the crowd and offer his heartfelt congratulations to López Moreno, his lifelong friend. All the happiness and gaiety in the rectory disappeared as if blown out the windows by an unexpected gust of wind.

Morgan saw it happen over the shoulder of Claudia's oldest sister, Esperanza, as her head was pressed against his chest. His eyes met those of Claudia's father who had turned to smile at his new son-in-law. Still smiling, he nodded at Morgan and raised his glass to him, the red wine sparkling in the candlelight. Then, as if he had changed his mind, his smile seemed to collapse, the glass tumbled from his hand and Miguel López Moreno dropped to the floor. His wife, Sofía María, screamed and everyone in the room turned to her. In the silence that followed, a physician rushed to the fallen man and kneeled in the wine and broken glass. He gently placed his hand on López Moreno's chest and bent to the side, his left ear above the man's mouth. A moment later, the doctor looked up at Sofía María and sadly shook his head. Miguel López Moreno was gone.

Morgan had known Don Miguel, as everyone addressed him, for only a week before the wedding ceremony and his unexpected death. He had liked the man immediately when they met and spent one long afternoon talking to him. Claudia's Uncle Rafael, who spoke limited English, translated for them. Rafael, a tall soft-spoken man, was her father's older brother and a printer of royal proclamations and notices. The three men talked in the library where Don Miguel reclined on a settee with a pillow behind his head. He suffered from a heart ailment and was instructed to rest every day by his physician. But Don Miguel decided to attend his daughter's wedding despite the doctor's orders to stay home. "I'll be there for my daughter if it's the last thing I do," he said.

It was with Don Miguel's help that Morgan entered the Building of Records. A day before the wedding, while

Claudia and her mother made final arrangements for the wedding, he sent his future son-in-law to see an old friend who, it was said, knew everyone of importance in Havana. Uncle Rafael accompanied Morgan since Don Miguel did not know if the man, Señor Francisco Serrano Montalvo, understood English. Serrano Montalvo did speak English and also knew the director of the archives. He wrote a letter of introduction for Morgan and, an hour later, he sat in the director's small office. Uncle Rafael sat in a chair alongside Morgan and translated for both men as they talked.

Director José Céspedes de Castro smiled at his guests. "We will be pleased to help you, Major Morgan. What is it that you seek here in the Building of Records?" The director was a short thin man with a surprisingly deep voice.

"I am looking for records of the salvage of a sunken Spanish ship in 1763. It was found somewhere south of St. Augustine." Morgan did not mention that the ship carried bullion.

"Do you know the name of the ship?"

"No. But I do know it took at least a month to salvage the ship."

"Do you know when the ship was sunk?" Morgan noticed that the director had a habit of lightly tapping his fingers on the edge of his desk when he asked a question. The man looked like he was playing a harpsichord.

"Earlier this century – I don't know the year," he lied.

"How much earlier?" The director sighed loudly. "Sixty-five years have passed since the beginning of the century and there are thousands of documents from Florida for that time period. Surely, you can be more precise. Do you at least know the decade?"

"I think the ship was sunk within the first twenty years of the century." Morgan scratched the back of his head as if unsure of the decade. He hesitated to tell him that the sunken ship was from the treasure fleet of 1715.

The director's frown seemed to deepen in his forehead. You will have to be more precise. It would take at least a year to look through twenty years of Florida records."

Morgan nodded, unsure what he should say.

"Who told you about the sunken ship?" The director made a face, obviously irritated.

"A man in St. Augustine – a prominent planter who knew of the salvage."

"How did the planter know about the salvage?" The director's fingers moved faster and tapped louder as he questioned Morgan.

"He saw them loading salvaged goods from the sunken ship to another ship in the bay."

"Ah! I assume *them* were Spaniards and he was an Englishman? What is his name?"

"Yes. His name is Jesse Fish and he has lived in St. Augustine some thirty years. He's a well-known orange planter."

"So, Señor Fish saw the salvaged goods, but didn't know when the ship was sunk?" The director sighed and continued to tap on the desk.

"Yes." Morgan persisted with his lie, though it sounded as ridiculous to him as it did to the director. "He said it happened long ago, years before he arrived in Florida."

"I see." The director pursed his lips. "By any chance, did the very observant Señor Fish see what cargo was salvaged from the sunken ship? Surely, it must have held something worth the effort."

"No. He didn't see it, but he did hear that gold and silver bars were salvaged." Morgan could no longer lie about the bullion. The clever Spaniard had made him admit the sunken ship was one of the lost transports of the 1715 treasure fleet. This was the second time his attempt to lie about his mission had failed. He vowed it would be the last time.

Céspedes de Castro smiled broadly. "So, the sunken ship was a bullion ship, undoubtedly one of those lost in the terrible storm that destroyed the fleet of 1715. I would think everyone in the colonies knows about that terrible tragedy – even Señor Fish." Céspedes de Castro turned his eyes to Uncle Rafael. "Is that not so, Señor López Moreno?"

"It certainly is well known here in Havana." Uncle Rafael nodded to Morgan.

"It is indeed – a disaster no Spaniard will ever forget. Eleven of the twelve bullion ships and hundreds of men were lost in the storm as well as thousands of gold and silver pieces. Only one ship survived and reached Havana safely. There were bodies and ship wreckage scattered all along the southern coast of Florida. The wreckage was found far south of St. Augustine, perhaps 300 miles farther south – but if this Englishman, Jesse Fish, is to be believed, it seems one of the eleven ships was separated from the fleet and sank much farther north near the old settlement."

"Fish made no mention of such a disaster. He did not arrive in St. Augustine until 1732, so he may not have heard about the number of men and ships lost in the storm." Morgan told the truth this time since he had no idea what Fish heard about the destruction of the treasure fleet.

"That seems possible." The director leaned back in his chair and clasped his hands over his stomach, reminding Morgan of Oliver Palmer. "Well, now we know when the ship was sunk and what cargo it carried. Incidentally, Major Morgan, we know the salvaged ship was from the fleet of 1715 because no other bullion ship has been lost along the Florida coast in this century. A bullion fleet was sunk in a storm some fifteen years later – I don't recall the year, but the ships were sunk in the Mártires (Martyrs) or what you English call the Florida Keys."

"Señor, please understand that I am not here searching for lost Spanish bullion."

"Then, do tell me why the salvage of the Spanish bullion ship is so important to you."

Morgan gave Céspedes de Castro a brief account of the murders and told him of his belief that the salvaged bullion was somehow involved. He did not mention Mrs. Chapman's gold bar. The director listened with interest to the translation of Morgan's narrative and grimaced in horror when he heard how the three men had been murdered. Uncle Rafael also looked horrified as he translated Morgan's description of the ant and alligator-eaten bodies.

"Dios mío!" The director gasped, shaking his head in disbelief. "Who could conceive of such cruelty? I can only think of an Inquisition torturer or a madman."

"He may very well be mad, but clever enough to hide himself from our eyes. We have no notion who he is or how to identify him. It is therefore our hope that something identifying him might be found in one of the records of the salvage."

"I see." The director frowned. "So, Major Morgan, you obviously think those men were involved in a plot to steal bullion from the salvaged ship." He saw Morgan nod his head. "That man Willington certainly seems like someone capable of such a scheme."

Morgan nodded. "Yes, Willington would be the likely leader of the plot. His unsavory past suggests he would have been the man the others followed."

"Well, let's see what we can discover." The director rose from his chair and went over to a sideboard, which held a decanter of wine and four empty wine glasses. He filled two glasses and handed them to Morgan and Uncle Rafael. "Please excuse me for what I hope will be only a few minutes. Help yourself to more wine as you require." Céspedes de Castro bowed politely to his guests and left the office. He walked out into a hallway and they could hear his footsteps recede down the stone floor leading to the archive.

The archive, commonly called the Building of Records, was an old church located in the center of Havana. Constructed by the Dominican Order in the sixteenth century, the church fell into disuse in the next century and ultimately became a place of storage for colonial records. The archive eventually accumulated the kings' cédulas (orders), official correspondence and colonial papers for Cuba and the other Spanish colonies in the Caribbean, including Florida. The building contained millions of documents from the earliest years of the conquest of the Caribbean islands through the eighteenth century. Only the spacious archives in Mexico City and Sevilla contained more colonial documents than the Building of Records in Havana.

Morgan and Uncle Rafael each drank another glass of wine as they waited for the director to return. A half hour passed before they heard him walking back from the interior. Céspedes de Castro entered the office carrying a packet of documents under his right arm. As he approached the desk, Morgan noticed that the packet was tied with red ribbon.

"It took me much longer than I expected," he said apologetically and laid the packet on his desk. "This slim bundle contains all the documents we have concerning the sunken ship; it was a brigantine called *Nuestra Señora de la Soledad.* It was loaded in Vera Cruz and carried 60 chests of silver coins, 400 gold and silver bars, 30 chests of Mexican jewelry and 110 chests of Chinese porcelain. The porcelain came from Manila."

"Dios mío!" Uncle Rafael paused before translating what the ship carried. "Que cosa!"

"A king's ransom!" Morgan understood most of what the director said in Spanish.

"That was only a fraction of what the entire fleet transported," announced the director. "I looked at a manifest listing all of the cargo. There were almost 10,000,000 silver coins on board the twelve ships sailing for Spain. The *Captana*, the flagship of the fleet, carried 1,300 chests of coins and the *Almiranta* carried almost 1,000 chests. Each chest held 3,000 coins. The fleet also carried emeralds and pearls, gold and silver jewelry, most with precious stones, hundreds of gold and silver bars and Chinese porcelain. Some of the ships even contained chests of gold dust."

"Qué riqueza! (What wealth!)" Uncle Rafael gaped at the director.

"Yes, and most of it was retrieved. We found the wrecked ships following the storm and immediately began salvaging the bullion. It took three years of effort, but most of the ships were emptied and their riches eventually reached Spain." Céspedes de Castro extended his chin, proud of Spain's accomplishment.

"But not the *Nuestra Señora de la Soledad*." Morgan pointed to the bundle of documents. "That ship was not discovered and salvaged for another forty-eight years."

"That is correct. But we know what it carried from the fleet's manifest which is included in the salvage reports after the storm."

"What about the salvage reports of the Nuestra Señora de la Soledad – three years ago?" Morgan pointed to the documents on the director's desk. "Was there any mention of robbery?"

"Unfortunately, our records only include the ship's manifest from 1715. We don't have any reports of the salvage or any other records from Florida for much of 1762 or 1763."

"There are no records of the salvage here?" Morgan could not believe that Uncle Rafael had correctly translated the director's words. He stared at the Spaniard, his brow furrowed.

"No. Apparently, all the records of the recent salvage in 1763 are in the Florida papers, which are not among our holdings here. The salvage took place in that time we call the foreign occupation, when you English held Havana. As I am sure you know, your soldiers occupied the city for eleven months from the summer of 1762 through the spring of 1763. During that period, the Florida governor did not send any colonial documents to Cuba. That's why there is a gap in our records from Florida."

"What about after the English troops left Havana? There were still Spaniards in Florida until 1764." Morgan looked at Céspedes de Castro, hoping to hear him say there were additional records to examine in the archive.

"Yes." The director nodded. "There are records from Florida at that time, but they relate to the movement of our people from St. Augustine to Havana. As you know, everyone left the colony when Florida was given to England in the treaty that ended the war."

Morgan sighed loudly. "So, there are no reports of the ship's salvage in the building?"

"No. I know it is disappointing for you."

"But there must be Florida records for that year somewhere."

"I certainly would think so." Céspedes de Castro frowned. "They should be here in the Building of Records – where they belong."

"Do you have any idea where the Florida records might be?"

The director shook his head. "Unfortunately, I do not. They might be in the possession of the former governor and captain general of Florida. His name is Colonel Melchor Feliú and he sailed from Florida on one of the last ships to leave the colony. I believe he is still in the king's service and might possibly be here in Havana."

"Who would know if he's here or where he lives?"

"I don't know, Major Morgan. You might inquire at the governor's office… or perhaps with the commandant's staff at the Castillo del Morro. Now that I think about it, unless Colonel Feliú has recently left the king's service, his current position here or abroad should be known to either the governor or the commandant."

"Thank you, Señor." Morgan rose wearily from his chair. He was too disappointed at that moment to think of pursuing the whereabouts of Colonel Melchor Feliú. As he and Uncle Rafael left the building, Morgan decided to wait until after his wedding to try to find the location of the former governor and the critical records from Florida.

Morgan looked at his watch and saw that it was 8:15. He left the tavern and crossed the street to the Customs House. Horse traffic had already begun to fill the street and he dodged a fast moving carriage before reaching the outside door.

"Está aquí el coronel Rodríguez? (Is Colonel Rodríguez here?" he asked the guard.

"Sí," said the guard and opened the door for him.

Colonel Rodríguez was talking to several of his officers when Morgan entered the room. Everyone turned when the door opened and he stepped inside. The commandant looked up from his desk and smiled when he saw Morgan.

"What an unexpected pleasure." Rodríguez held up his hand to stop his meeting. "Please sit down, Major, I will speak to you in a moment or two." The colonel pointed to a row of chairs near the door to the docks and then resumed his morning instructions. Fifteen minutes later, the meeting ended as the officers saluted and walked to their desks.

"Well, to what do I owe this unexpected surprise?" asked Rodríguez, when Morgan had taken a seat in front of the colonel's desk. They reached over the narrow desk and shook hands. "I trust you are now married and living in ecstasy." The colonel chuckled until he saw the grim expression on Morgan's face.

"It's a long story." Morgan exhaled his breath. "I hope you have the time to hear it."

"I think so." The colonel looked across the room at a lieutenant sitting near the door to the docks. "Peralta, have any ships entered the channel?"

"No, mi Colonel. Not in the last hour."

Colonel Rodríguez turned back to Morgan. "The port sentries raise a series of red flags from El Morro all along the entrance channel so we will know when a ship flying a foreign flag has reached the harbor and is approaching the Customs House. Unless the channel is especially crowded, it takes most ships an hour, más o menos, to reach us from the time of its first sighting at sea until it docks here. When we see a red flag raised across the harbor at the Cabana barracks, we know a ship is about fifteen minutes away."

"I assume a sentry tells Lieutenant Peralta when a red flag appears."

"Exactly. Peralta has observation duty today. The officers take turns doing that boring duty every day. We have three shifts a day since the Customs House is always open. But, Major Morgan, you are not here for a lesson on Customs House procedure. What has happened? You look glum, if I may say so."

Morgan sighed. "It seems all my plans have gone awry – that is, except for my marriage."

"What has happened, Major?" The colonel sat back and crossed his arms over his chest.

Morgan told him about the death of López Moreno and the sad ending to his wedding. He described the unexpected death of the man, but did not go into detail about the disappointment he felt in the days following the funeral. He did say the mood in the house remained gloomy and the family's grieving continued unabated.

The week afterward had been a time of family mourning and he often felt in the way and awkwardly out of place. Instead of the intimate time Morgan had anticipated with his new wife, he saw little of her following the funeral. Claudia's time understandably had been devoted to her mother. She would rise from bed at first light and fall asleep as soon as she put her head on the pillow. At night, after blowing out the bedside candle, she would kiss and embrace him absently and then turn away to her side of the bed. She would be asleep seconds after saying, "Te amo." Claudia never heard him say, "I love you, too."

Morgan told the colonel about his failure to find the documents describing the salvage of the sunken treasure ship. He described the director's search in the Building of Records and the few documents he had found referring to the *Nuestra Señora de la Soledad.* The critical Florida records reporting the ship's salvage, he lamented, were missing. They had not been sent to Cuba, during the English occupation and had never been deposited in the Building of Records. Morgan told him Céspedes de Castro was unsure where the Florida records were located, but suggested they could be in the possession of the former governor of Florida.

"His name is…"

"Colonel Melchor Feliú. I know him very well. We served together years ago as young officers in the Canary Islands. I talked to Melchor when he arrived here from Florida."

"After the colony was abandoned?"

"Yes, he stopped by to see me when his ship docked here. In fact, we shared a meal that day. His family had arrived a week earlier. I haven't seen him since then. He has been abroad for a number of months at a time in the king's service."

"Do you know where he is now?"

"I'm not sure, but I don't think he is in Havana. I can ask his wife, Esperanza."

"I would be very grateful if you would." Morgan nodded his thanks to Rodríguez.

"If Melchor is not here, I will ask Esperanza if the Florida records are in his possession. She will surely know if he has them at their home. I'll send a man over to her house. Is there anything else you need to know?"

"No, thank you." Morgan's mood immediately improved. He visualized himself sitting in Melchor Feliú's house, looking through the salvage reports from St. Augustine.

"Por nada." Rodríguez removed a piece of writing paper from a desk drawer and picked up his quill. "Please excuse me for a minute or two, Major Morgan."

The colonel wrote a brief letter to Feliú's wife and placed it in a white envelope, which he addressed and sealed. Morgan watched as Rodríguez held a thick stick of red wax over the flame of his desk lamp. He tilted the stick so the melted wax spilled on the seams of the envelope and, while still soft, he pressed his stamp into it. The wax impression revealed the outline of a shield with stallions and swords inside, which Morgan assumed to be the Rodríguez family coat of arms. After wiping the remaining wax from the stamp, he looked around the room until his eyes settled on the sentry at the door to the street. "Sierra, venga aquí."

"Sí, Señor."

A moment later, Sierra left the customs office with the sealed letter in his pocket. In his hand, he held a map showing him the way to Melchor Feliú's house; the colonel knew the soldier could not read and would not find the house from the written address on the envelope.

"It's a long walk from here to Melchor's house," he told Morgan. "It will take Sierra more than an hour to go and return. Let's go for a breakfast, while we wait. There is a tavern nearby that has good food. Peralta!"

"Sí, mi Coronel."

"I will be at *La Taberna del Mar*. Let me know if a ship is approaching."

"Sí, Señor."

"Send someone if Sierra returns before I do."

Rodríguez stood and reached for an oak cane he kept

behind his desk. He straightened up and steadied himself on the cane as they walked to the door. In the street, he quickened his pace as the stiffness in his bad leg lessened. His limp was less pronounced as they crossed the street at the end of the block.

"The war." Rodríguez was aware of Morgan watching him. "And you?" He pointed to Morgan's left shoulder.

"The war." Morgan nodded. "August 27, 1758. The first cavalry charge in the battle for Fort Frontenac."

"Ah, yes, the English campaign in Canada. I was hit by a musket ball here in the defense of Havana. July 27, 1762. Four years after you."

They left La Taberna del Mar an hour later and found Sierra waiting outside the Customs House. The soldier arrived a few seconds earlier and watched them as they approached. His face was flushed and his chest heaved from his hurried walk. He stood with a white envelope clutched in his hand. When Rodríguez reached him, Sierra, suddenly aware his fingerprints were smudged on the envelope, wiped it on his breeches before handing the letter over.

"You didn't have to run, Sierra." Rodríguez smiled at the soldier. He took a silver coin from his pocket and gave it to the soldier. "Go get some breakfast."

"Gracias, Señor."

Colonel Rodríguez opened the envelope at his desk and translated the letter as he read it. He left out the personal greetings. "'Melchor is in Madrid on a mission for the governor. He expects to return to Havana in November. The Florida records are in the possession of Don Juan Elixio de la Puente. Melchor gave them to Puente for safe keeping."

The colonel looked at Morgan. "I don't know Puente, but there were many from Florida who entered Cuba, but did not come through the Customs House. It was an extremely busy time. Esperanza says Penete was a prominent man in St. Augustine and she included his address. His house is on

San Juan de Dios – one of the streets of los ricos (wealthy) here in Havana."

"Now, I must write to Puente. Mucho trabajo! (A lot of work.)" The colonel smiled. "Do you think I deserve a gold bar from the *Nuestra Señora de la Soledad*?"

Morgan stared at Rodríguez, unsure what to say.

The colonel laughed. "I'm joking, Major. Greed is another sin attributed to Spaniards; it's said we expect payment for everything we do. It's as if no one else in the world expects propinas (fees/tips) for service. But be not concerned; I expect nothing from you."

"I had no such expectations."

"Good. Please excuse me again while I write to Puente. If he has the Florida records, I will accompany you to meet him. I think it will help if an officer of rank introduces you to him. If you go alone to meet him, even with a letter from me, he might regard you with suspicion. He might, in fact, refuse your request to examine any Florida records, never mind those concerning the salvage of a bullion ship." Rodríguez smiled. "I would if I were Puente."

Morgan nodded. "Let's hope he has them in his possession."

"Verdad. (True.)"

Morgan waited two hours while another soldier was sent with a letter to Puente's house.

He returned shortly after noon, but Colonel Rodríguez, busy interviewing a Dutch captain and his first mate, did not read Puente's reply until the two seamen had gone and the office emptied.

"He has the records!" Rodríguez said as he read the first sentence.

"Splendid!" Morgan was relieved. He had feared that Puente had given the documents to someone else in Cuba or even sent them to Spain. Now, he worried the salvage reports might not be among the Florida records in Puente's possession. And, if they were there, Morgan wondered, would they inform him of what he needed to know. Would they report a robbery of the bullion? More important, if the records did report a robbery would they mention who was involved and what had happened? His mind full of worries, Morgan almost missed the colonel's next words.

"He will see us at three o'clock. Until then, I hope you will accept my invitation to my home for our midday meal."

"Yes. Yes, thank you," Morgan replied after registering the invitation in his mind.

Following a meal with the colonel's wife, Alicia Rosa, and their three children, they rode in Rodríguez' open carriage to Puente's home. An approaching afternoon rainstorm clouded the sky and kept the tropical sun off their heads as the colonel drove along the busy streets. But even under a cloudy sky, the stifling humidity made Morgan's shirt stick to his back. He was wet from sweat by ten o'clock every morning and waited impatiently through midday for the cooling wind that blew off the ocean. It was only then that the city of Havana seemed bearable to him.

Puente's house, large and imposing, looked much like the other costly houses built on the street. It stood out with fresh whitewash and recently painted red shutters. A well-tended flower garden interspersed with a variety of citrus trees faced the street and two men were weeding the garden when their carriage approached the gate. Another man, a servant, greeted them at the gate, tethered the horse and escorted them along a stone walk to the front door. Morgan noted that the door was made with inlaid pieces of rosewood fit together to create a labyrinth leading to the center where a treasure chest of coins and jewels had been carved.

The servant ushered them inside and led them directly to a large library full of rolled up maps, piles of documents, strange lettered scrolls as well as hundreds of books. The books had titles in many languages and seemed to be on every conceivable subject. They not only filled the ceiling-to-floor shelves built around the room, but were also strewn about on the wooden floor, as well as on a wide table located to one side of the room. Other books had been opened and piled, one atop the other, on what Morgan assumed was Puente's a desk, which stood close to the table. Morgan wished he had the time to stroll about the room and at least look at the book titles on the shelves. An avid reader since childhood, he often read in the middle of night when he awoke and could not go back to sleep.

The only light in Puente's library came from two dimmed oil lamps on the desk and much of the room remained in darkness until the servant turned up the wicks. But, even with brighter flames, the higher sections of the bookshelves and lower corners of the room were still hidden in shadow. Morgan suspected the strong musty odor that permeated the room came from unseen mold in the dark corners and unlit shelves. As his eyes adjusted to the dim light, he saw the library had two windows, both locked and shuttered. The light also revealed five water-stained chests standing in a corner of the room.

Seconds later, Puente greeted them and gestured them to two cushioned chairs standing in front of the table. He went behind the desk and sat facing them in his chair. No sooner had they taken their seats, when another servant arrived with a decanter of white wine and crystal glasses. He also carried a cup of hot tea, which he placed on the table in front of Puente.

"I don't drink spirits." Puente said in precise English. "I assume you would prefer if we speak in your language, Major Morgan." Puente spoke very softly, only slightly above a whisper, forcing both his visitors to lean forward to hear him clearly.

"Yes, thank you," Morgan replied.

Puente was a slender, bearded man with a severe expression seemingly engraved on his long, narrow face. He never showed even a hint of a smile the entire time they spent with him; his lips remained compressed in a tight line as he listened to their explanation for visiting him. Puente sat straight in his chair, his long slender hands pressed together as if in prayer. Morgan noticed his face and hands were as white as snow. He looked like someone who had not been outside in the sun for years. Morgan wondered if Puente was a scholar who spent his life studying inside his house.

Except for a white collar, Puente was completely clothed in black and looked like he was in mourning. He reminded Morgan of a grim, humorless man from Massachusetts he had met in the war. He, too, dressed in black. Later, when they left Puente's house, Rodríguez told Morgan that Puente reminded him of the famous portrait of a Spanish knight painted by El Greco in the sixteenth century. Morgan, who had never heard of El Greco, could only picture the dour man from Massachusetts. He recalled the man had constantly quoted passages from the Bible.

Puente seemed to have little interest in either the bullion ship or the murder investigation. He seemed to be listening to Morgan's account, but showed no expression of surprise or horror at any of the descriptions that shocked everyone else who heard them. When Morgan inquired if he remembered the salvage of the treasure ship south of St. Augustine, Puente nodded, saying the event obsessed the townspeople for years afterward. The terse man said nothing more no matter how Morgan prompted him for more information. Puente eventually looked at his pocket watch, politely excusing himself from the meeting. He said other important matters required his attention.

"The records you seek are in the chests there." Puente pointed to the corner of the room. "I assume you wish to view them for information regarding the *Nuestra Señora de la Soledad*."

"Yes, sir, with your permission," replied Morgan.

"I see no reason why you shouldn't examine them. Governor Feliú left them without any instructions. His only request was to transfer them to the Building of Records when I was done with them." Puente saw the puzzled look on Morgan's face. "I took them to examine the property records, which will be included in our petition to the crown for recompense. Most of our people left Florida before they could sell their lands and they now need financial assistance."

"How has the petition been received?" Rodríguez spoke to Puente as he walked away.

Puente exhaled his breath loudly. "The Council of the Indies is now considering it. Well, I will leave you to your search of the records. Whenever you wish something, whether assistance or food, rap on the door and someone will serve you." He pointed to the decanter. "Should you require more wine, rap on the door for that as well. I will return when you are ready to depart."

"Gracias." Colonel Rodríguez frowned as Puente turned to leave.

"Por nada." Puente bowed stiffly and left the room.

Rodríguez shook his head. "A strange man," he said when Puente had gone. "He never introduced his wife or family to us. I wonder if he has sangre pura (pure Spanish blood)? Well, let's see what we can find here. Let's hope the records are stored in a month-to-month order."

"That would be helpful." Morgan dragged one of the chests into the lamplight in front of the desk. He waited while Rodríguez dragged another into the light. "Where will I find the date on Spanish documents?" he asked, lifting up the hinged top of the chest.

"The date should appear at the beginning of all the documents, whether reports or letters. It will be written in words rather than numbers. I assume you know those Spanish words."

They both got down on their knees to look through the chests. Rodríguez put his hand on the desktop for support and grimaced as he slowly lowered himself to the floor. A red woven rug in front of the desk spared them from direct contact with the wood floor. But, even with the rug, the oak planks made their knees ache and they changed positions every few minutes. Morgan finally took the soft cushions from the chairs and put one under his knees and handed the other to Rodríguez. "Let's hope that helps a little."

The colonel thanked him with a smile. "After all the work on this floor, Major, you will have to double the number of gold bars you give me from the bullion ship."

This time Morgan smiled in reply.

They found nothing useful in the first two chests. All the enclosed documents were dated 1762. The third and fourth chests contained records from both 1762 and 1763 but, after an hour painstakingly sorting through them, they found no mention of the *Nuestra Señora de la Soledad.* Rodríguez saw Morgan's disappointment as they pushed the chests back to the corner. Opening the fifth and last chest, they divided the bundles of records and began scrutinizing one document after the other.

By that time, Morgan doubted they would find anything. It appeared as if the tragic death of Claudia's father had not only ended the wedding celebration, it also ended his good fortune in Cuba. Afterward, everything he had tried seemed futile and doomed to failure. He could picture himself standing before Oliver Palmer, as the fat man smirked with self-satisfaction at his failure. He knew the pompous Englishman would revel in his misery.

Morgan had gone through more than half of his pile of records and had reached a colonial census made in 1763, when he heard a grunt from Rodríguez. He kept his forefinger at his place in the report and looked at the man beside him. The colonel nodded his head and a smile spread across his face.

"I found it! It's all here."

CHAPTER TEN

HAVANA AND SAVANNAH:
MONDAY, AUGUST 26 – THURSDAY, SEPTEMBER 5, 1766

"Actually, there are two bundles of documents that mention the salvage of the *Nuestra Señora de la Soledad*." Colonel Rodríguez handed Morgan the documents as he struggled to his feet and sat in the chair nearest the desk.

Morgan stood at the same time and shifted the other chair to face the colonel. He waited while Rodríguez, grimacing, crossed his legs. Morgan then passed the bundles back to him.

"Let's see what we can discover." Rodríguez reached across the desk to move an oil lamp close to him. "Which one should I read first? According to the notes on the cover, the big bundle describes the entire salvage and will be more thorough. It's dated three weeks after the report of the robbery. The other describes the robbery alone." He raised the wick to get a brighter flame.

"The report of the robbery. It looks to be only five or six pages long."

Rodríguez untied the red ribbon that held the report together. "There are seven pages." He counted them out in his lap and showed Morgan the title page.

"So, the report was written on the eighth of April."

"Yes, and the robbery took place the day before the report was written. That is unusually fast work for our officials." Rodríguez quickly scanned the first page. "I won't translate every word – that would be a waste of time. I think a summary of what I read will be more useful."

Morgan nodded.

"You need not memorize any of it. I will have the document translated and copied at the Customs House. Several of my officers have a command of your language. Unlike you English, we make certain that many of our colonial officials learn other languages."

"It's true. Too many Englishmen think everyone else in the world should speak English. But that's not true of us colonists. Many do know other languages, especially the merchants who ship goods abroad. Unfortunately, I'm not one of them, but now with my new wife, I expect I'll quickly learn Spanish."

"Por cierto." Rodríguez chuckled and shook his finger at Morgan. "I'm certain you will. Now, as for the report, once it is translated you can take it with you to show to your superiors. I will stamp it with my seal to make it official. Of course, any portion of the report that might be considered treasonous by the Council of the Indies will not be included, though I cannot imagine what that would be after all this time."

"I can't either. It has been three years since the salvage."

"We shall see. The document is simply entitled, *Report of Lost Cargo from La Nuestra Señora de la Soledad*." Rodríguez turned the pages to the last one. "Lieutenant Emiliano Lerdo Palacios wrote the report. He was with the First Infantry Regiment of Havana and I assume was sent to St. Augustine for a four-year tour of duty. That's the typical length of duty in Florida. I also assume he was assigned to some phase of the ship's salvage, probably the transportation of the bullion from the sunken ship to St. Augustine."

"I would think the robbery took place during the transfer." Morgan looked at Rodríguez. "The site of the salvage would have been too well guarded with troops; I would guess there were more than a hundred men. So was St. Augustine where the bullion was put aboard the warship. Jesse Fish said there were soldiers everywhere during the salvage."

"You are probably right, but let's now see what Lerdo Palacios says." Rodríguez returned to the first page of the report and began to read. He read the first page twice before looking up at Morgan "Lerdo Palacios was sent to the salvage site itself, a place called La Costa de Mosquitos, some twenty or so leagues (fifty-two miles) south of St. Augustine."

"What a terrible place for the salvage." Morgan could picture the clouds of mosquitoes hovering over the nearby swamps. Any man who left the shore, where the sea breezes blew the mosquitoes inland, would be covered with bites before he took ten steps into the interior. "What torment those soldiers must have suffered!"

"I can imagine." The colonel looked up. "Havana is bad enough this time of year. Well, Lerdo Palacios was assigned the responsibility of listing and counting the salvaged items as they were carried away on mules and packhorses. His inventory was the third made at the site. One was done as divers brought the bullion up and it was taken ashore; another followed as the horses and mules were packed. The lieutenant made his salvage inventory just before the pack animals were led away to St. Augustine. One final count was completed when the caravans reached town. Of course, all the inventories had to tally. They are included in the long salvage report."

"An impressive system! With four inventories, I can't imagine anything was stolen."

"You certainly would think so. The crown has used the same or variations of that system for at least three centuries. It is called the sistema de cuatro cuentas (system of four counts). We call it simply el sistema. The system was instituted in the sixteenth century with the first bullion shipments from the New World. As you know, enormous quantities of gold and silver were taken out of New Spain and Peru. The Council of the Indies established the system to assure the crown received its quinto real (royal fifth) of everything discovered or produced in America. I assume you have an understanding of the quinto."

"Yes. As I understand it, those who profit from the crown's lands in the New World pay a fifth percentage of their profit for the use and products of those lands. That's the quinto."

"Exactamente. And since that quinto had to be protected, the system had to be infallible. It was for a while, but in time, losses of bullion were discovered. Small losses at first, but then larger and larger losses over the years. Even with the addition of other safeguards, countless numbers of gold and silver coins and even bars disappeared during transport from America. The king's officials, still convinced of their infallible system, were sure it only needed to be altered. One of their changes included the use of locked chests, opened with three different keys held by three trade officials aboard each of the ships. The chests were then locked in front of a group of customs officers and lowered into the ships' holds. The holds, of course, were likewise locked. And what do you think happened? Bars and coins were still missing when the shipments arrived in Cadiz! The Casa de Contratación (House of Trade) next sent the three key-bearers on three different ships bound for Spain and still bullion was stolen." Rodríguez chuckled. "I suppose you could say the failure of the system indicates man's ingenuity."

"And avarice."

"Yes, that, too. Anyway, the officer in charge of the salvage, a Major Morales Lastarria, used that system to safeguard the bullion from the *Nuestra Señora de la Soledad.* He transported everything of value from the sunken ship in small caravans, each with four pack animals, four soldiers and a sergeant leading the way. All of the men were well armed. The caravans left the site every two hours from first light to midday. No others were sent afterwards, even though the divers brought up more bullion during the afternoons. The major would not risk sending any caravan on the route in the dark. He plotted a passage north along the coast to keep the caravans away from wooded areas where ladrones (robbers) could be hidden. The major also scheduled rest stops in open country with clear vistas of the surrounding terrain. He set up two well-armed camps for overnight stays and stationed squads of fifteen men at each camp to guard the bullion. Ten soldiers were ordered to stand guard duty all night. Finally, the major set up two patrols of five cavalrymen to ride the caravan route each day; one rode from the salvage site and the other from St Augustine."

Morgan smiled. "The major was a cautious man."

"Yes, he took every precaution expected of him. I am sure there was an inquiry after the robbery and I would assume he escaped blame for it. Lerdo Palacios' report certainly would have helped him if he was charged with dereliction of duty."

"Surely, he wasn't blamed for the robbery. I don't know what else he could have done to safeguard the treasure."

"Not much unless he had more soldiers available to accompany the caravans." Rodríguez read the second page. "Ah, as you suspected, the robbery took place during the transportation of the treasure. It happened during the final week of the salvage. By that time, most of the bullion and the Chinese porcelain had already been transported to St. Augustine. The robbers struck on April seventh and waylaid the second to last caravan of the day. It happened between the second and third rest stops in an area with sparse undergrowth and several wind-bent trees. The robbers were hidden in the undergrowth. They lay in shallow trenches they had shoveled out and covered themselves with branches, leaves and palmetto fronds. There were six of them and…"

"Six?" Morgan had always suspected that the three men from Savannah were not alone in the scheme, but was surprised that twice that number had been involved. He wondered if any of the others lived in Savannah and worried there might be more murders in town. Perhaps, one or more of them had been killed after he sailed to Cuba. The thought of Thackery or worse, Palmer, leading an investigation into their deaths made him feel ill. He realized whether or not the report revealed the murderer's identity, he now would have to return to Savannah as soon as possible.

"Does the number of robbers suggest something significant to you?" Rodríguez noticed the concern on Morgan's face.

"Now that I know the number of the robbers, I wondered if more men had been murdered in Savannah since I left."

Rodríguez nodded and returned to the report. "Lerdo Palacios explained that his account of the robbery came from the interviews he held with the sergeant and the four soldiers. None of the men from the caravan could write, so they made no written statements. He said that except for few minor details, their descriptions of the assault and robbery were remarkably alike – perhaps, too alike. The similarity, particularly the words they used, made him suspicious of them. For a time, he wondered if they had stolen the bullion themselves and made up a false story of robbery to fool their superiors. But, as the lieutenant sorted through his findings and interviewed them a second time, he became convinced the men were telling the truth." Rodríguez grinned. "He said two of the caravan guards were too dull-witted to concoct such a story. The lieutenant therefore recommended no disciplinary action be taken against them."

"Lerdo Palacios appears to be a good officer." Morgan stood up and reached for the wine bottle. He poured wine in their glasses and handed the colonel his glass as he resumed his seat.

"Yes, it seems he was quite thorough." Rodríguez sighed. "Unfortunately, all too many of the officers we see these days are careless and lazy. They think their commissions entitle them to do little more than strut about like peacocks in the plazas, impressing the unmarried girls."

"It's the same in the English army as well. I guess it's the times. Too many spoiled and arrogant aristocrats are in the army now. They have little concern for king or country and appear to be in uniform only to serve themselves. They long for fame and fortune, but won't do what it takes to get such rewards."

"Exactamente. God help them if they ever go into battle." He made a face. "According to the soldiers' statements, the robbers leaped up from the underbrush as the caravan passed and overpowered them before they could draw their weapons. The robbers used cudgels to strike the soldiers and they were struck senseless for a time. When the guards did regain their senses, they found themselves lying face down on the ground. They were tightly blindfolded with their arms and hands bound behind their backs. One of the soldiers, a young Cuban named Pedro Ramírez, was able to push the lower portion of his blindfold up far enough to watch what the robbers were doing. He rubbed his face repeatedly against the ground until he could see beneath the blindfold. Ramírez remained motionless so they would not know he was watching them."

"There's a lad who deserved a promotion." Morgan leaned forward and held his glass up the colonel. "Salud." He raised his glass to the Spaniard.

"Salud." Rodríguez touched glasses with Morgan. "Lerdo Palacios, in fact, did make that recommendation; it was the last statement in his report. Ramírez watched the robbers the entire time they were there. He saw them remove the bullion from the pack animals and fill their saddlebags. The robbers took only bars and coins. They then laid out canvas sheets on the ground – he thought the sheets were pieces of sailcloth, and they also filled them with gold and silver. They tied the sheets into bundles, which they hung over the pummels of their saddles. One of the men filled a leather bag instead of a canvas sheet. Ramírez said the robbers packed and were on their way in less than a half hour."

"They wasted no time and took all they could possibly carry on horseback. They knew a long hard ride was ahead of them to evade the Spanish cavalry."

Rodríguez looked up from the report. "Exactly! They were too clever to try to take away all the bullion loaded on the pack animals. The robbers took only what their horses could bear to carry along with their own weight. That's why they ignored the costly Chinese porcelain carried by one of the mules. It was too heavy and bulky and not nearly as valuable as gold and silver."

"The robbery was well executed and obviously planned. I would guess they had watched several caravans passing before they struck that particular caravan. They probably arrived there a day or so earlier and scouted the entire route to find the best place to ambush the caravan."

"That was Lerdo Palacios' conclusion as well," said Rodríguez, reading a page ahead. "He observed that the site they selected was the most remote and had the thickest underbrush."

Morgan nodded. "I would think it was also the farthest

point from the salvage area to the south and St. Augustine to the north."

"Verdad. Well, here is a section that will especially interest you. Lerdo Palacios quotes the soldier's descriptions of the robbers. I will read this part to you word for word:"

There were six ladrones. Five were white and one was an Indian or Mestizo. They tried to hide their faces, using their hats and kerchiefs tied behind their necks. But their eyes and skin color could still be seen beneath the brims of the hats they wore. Three of the men had blue eyes and light hair. They wore colonists' clothes that looked like those worn by the Englishmen who live in St. Augustine. One of the ladrones, a tall man, wore a hat with a long white feather. He did not speak, but motioned to the others with a walking stick.

Morgan nodded his head vigorously. "The man with the white feather in his hat and the walking stick – he was seen with both Willington and Chapman before the robbery in Georgia! So, he was there in St. Augustine, too. I wonder where he is now."

"Ramírez also mentions the horses ridden by the robbers. He said three of them were big stallions, much bigger than any he had ever seen in or around St. Augustine. In fact, the soldier said he had only seen horses of that quality ridden by los ricos in Havana and running at the races. We have horse races here every year in early December."

"Ramírez has a good eye. It's the same in the English colonies. Only the rich or highest-ranked officers in the army have such stallions."

Morgan realized he was one of the rich who could afford to own a stallion. His father had given him the stallion when he received his appointment as justice of the peace. "You will need a good strong horse to chase down brigands," Matthew said as he handed his son the reins.

"Ramírez had one more memory that may help you. It seems that one robber suspected the soldier had seen them as they loaded the bullion on their horses. He was the last man to leave and he looked about the site before following the others into the woods. The man appeared ready to ride away, when suddenly he turned his horse and walked him to where Ramírez lay prone on the ground. The man stared down at him and the young soldier said he could almost feel his hard eyes upon him. Pedro Ramírez, of course, had closed his own eyes tightly and hoped they looked completely covered by the blindfold. The man on horseback waited above him for what seemed like an hour. Ramírez said he had the feeling the man was thinking of killing him. He recalled a cold shiver ran down his back as he expected any second to die. The man had his hand on the hilt of his sword when he walked his horse toward him. Ramírez then heard one of the other robbers shout something and the horseman rode away. Even after he heard the horse galloping into the distance, Ramírez waited awhile before opening his eyes again."

"That's quite an account. I have even more admiration for Ramírez." Morgan paused to take his next drink of wine. "Did Ramírez say what the other robber shouted?"

"Yes, but it was in English and the soldier had no knowledge of your language. He knew only that it was English after hearing it spoken in St. Augustine."

"Too bad. It would have been helpful to know what was shouted. I assume the robbers avoided speaking so the Spanish soldiers wouldn't know they came from the English colonies."

"Yes, they were clever. The shout was lost except for a few indecipherable words that the lieutenant included in the report. The painstaking Lerdo Palacios spent time with Ramírez trying hard to identify the shouted words. In the end, all he could do was write down a number of letters to represent the sounds that the soldier recalled hearing. It was a good idea, but I doubt it could be accurate; the lieutenant interviewed the soldiers more than six hours after the robbery. Lerdo Palacios admitted the words made no sense to him, but he included them for others to read later. He said his understanding of English was limited. As I look at the words, they make no sense to me either and I spent five years in England." Rodríguez removed the sheet from the report and handed it to Morgan. "See if you can read or understand them."

"So, that's where you learned to speak English so well." Morgan held the sheet in his hand. "I had wondered."

"I was in London with my family in the forties. My father was a military attaché to the Spanish ambassador who was sent to England to arrange a peace treaty to end the so-called War of Jenkins' Ear." Rodríguez made a face. "I'm sure you must know of that stupid war."

"It was a stupid war. England used the supposedly severed ear of Robert Jenkins, captain of the *Rebecca*, as an excuse to start a war with Spain. Jenkins claimed the Spaniards cut his ear off and, months later; he displayed his ear, apparently pickled, at the House of Commons. What nonsense! Nevertheless, the famous ear became a pretext for England to attack the Spanish fleets and ports in the Caribbean. Of course, all the English efforts to defeat the Spanish forces ended in dismal failure. The war, however, dragged on for a number of years."

Rodríguez raised his eyebrows. "An accurate, but surprising account by an Englishman."

"You should know, Colonel Rodríguez, that I am an English colonist, not an Englishman who favors the expanding empire. Many of us in the colonies resent England's long domination of our lives and lands."

Rodríguez nodded. "There are many here in Cuba, as well as in the other Spanish colonies, who have similar complaints about Spain. I for one…"

Puente's servant entered the room with a platter of food. He laid the platter on the table and set out two places with tableware and linen napkins. He then dished out servings of shellfish, sizzling plantains and rice. A loaf of freshly baked flat bread was put between the place settings, along with a pot of tea and another bottle of Spanish wine. The servant filled two cups with tea and bowed before leaving the room.

"Señor Puente sends his regards." The man said as he left the room.

Rodríguez shook his head. "This is not our way with guests, Major. We welcome them in our homes and delight in sharing our food and lives with them. I am certain you found that to be true in the house of López Moreno." The colonel looked with distaste at the food on his plate.

"I did. Tell me Colonel, how old were you when your father went to England?" Morgan changed the subject, hoping Rodríguez would eat as they talked and finish his meal. Morgan was anxious to look at the English words Lerdo Palacios had written, but he knew it would be better to delay the task until after they had eaten. Claudia had made him aware of Spanish customs and the Spaniards' practice of avoiding controversial discussions during dinner.

"I was a young man in my early twenties. My family stayed in England well beyond the treaty negotiations because my mother fell ill and became bedridden. Despite the good and kind care she received from the Scottish physicians, especially Dr. Angus MacDonald, she eventually weakened and died in London. I credit those physicians for keeping her alive for months beyond our expectations. I, of course, learned English at that time. Since then, I've improved my use of the language over time in the Customs House. Of course, I've been well assisted by the necessity to interview many English seamen and inept liars seeking entry into Cuba." The colonel's smile broadened when he saw Morgan smile with him.

Still full from their heavy meals at the colonel's home, the two men picked at their food, but drank the wine. The colonel did finish his plantains. "I cannot leave them," he said. "They are one of my favorite foods and these are better than Alicia's."

"I must remember to tell her your observation." Morgan spoke without smiling.

"You would not dare." Rodríguez laughed and pointed his forefinger at Morgan. "Well, I am interested to see what you make of those words the lieutenant left us."

Morgan picked up the sheet as the servant entered the room to clear away the plates. He carried everything away with the exception of the wine bottle and their wine glasses. The table was cleaned with a thorough wiping of a wet towel. Hoisting the heavy platter on his shoulder, the manservant nodded instead of bowing as he left the room.

When the servant was gone, Morgan and Rodríguez moved their chairs to one side of the desk so they could sit side by side. Before sitting, Morgan retrieved the wine bottle and glasses from the table. The colonel placed the report on the top of the desk between them and turned the pages to the second to last page. He then repositioned the oil lamp to ensure its light encircled the sheet of paper.

Morgan found the words in the fourth and last paragraph on the page. There were four of them. *Ariapeleñatn nelzansz dapatrolzan dall.* He read the words over and over again, but could make no sense of them. He finally tried to speak the words aloud, but they sounded like the incoherent mouthings infants make before learning speech.

"I can't make heads or tails of them." Morgan looked at Rodríguez. "You were right – they make no sense at all."

"They are incomprehensible."

Morgan continued to stare down at the words. Suddenly, he held up a finger. "Colonel, didn't the report say that Major Morales Lastarria ordered two patrols sent out along the caravan route each day?"

"Yes, it did." The colonel bent over to look at the words.

"Look at the third word. See patrol there!"

Rodríguez shook his head. "I do."

"I think that word as well as the two other long words are actually a blend of two or three smaller words. You know when we speak quickly, we often blend our words together. I'm sure it's common to all of us, no matter the language. "

"Yes, it is especially true of those who live in cities or ports. We say about the porteños, 'They speak fast and say nothing that's understood.' So, that third word might be three words."

"Yes, exactly."

Rodríguez mouthed the first letters of the word. "I think I know what the *da* means – *the*. As you know, there is no th in Spanish, so Spaniards would probably hear the as *da*. That means we can make the patrol out of the first seven letters of the word, *dapatrolzan*. The word *da* or *the* is also in the last word."

"Well done! So, we have 'the patrol *zan* the ll." Morgan studied the five words, trying to find meaning in them.

"I have part of it." Rodríguez' eyes gleamed with excitement. "The *z* must be *is* and *an* is *on* and we have the patrol is on the…"

"Way! The patrol is on the way – that's all it could be."

"That makes sense. In Spanish, the double *ll* would sound like the *y* in English. As for the *wa,* Ramírez would not have heard the w since we don't use that letter in Spanish and I think he simply did not hear the *a* spoken. Of course, he also could have forgotten it in all those hours before he was interviewed by Lerdo Palacios. After his fright, it's astonishing the soldier recalled anything at all."

"Indeed. Now, for the second word. I wonder if the first six letters, *nelzan*, is the name *Nelson*?" Morgan looked at Rodríguez. "What do you think?"

"Ah, yes. The man who shouted might have used his name. Nelson is a common English name." The colonel ran his forefinger under the last three words. "If so, the sentence then might read, "Nelson says the patrol is on the way."

"Very good! Thanks to Ramírez and Lerdo Palacios, I think we've found the name of a fourth robber. That leaves only two others unknown. It may be that Nelson and those two killed the men in Savannah. Vengeance might not have been involved at all; they may have been killed for their shares of the bullion. If so, the remaining robbers would have doubled their booty. One single share might not have been enough for them. I'm sure you know the old saying, "He who is greedy is always in want?' "

"I do; it's a saying by the Roman poet, Horace." Rodríguez grinned pleased with himself. "What you suggest is indeed a possibility. Perhaps, the first word includes the name of another of the robbers. It would make sense since we know one of them shouted to him."

"That does make sense, but I can't find a way to break up that long word into other words that make any sense. And I don't see a name in it." Morgan stared intently at the twelve letters. The word *Ariapeleñatn* defied understanding.

The two men spent another hour trying to find some meaning in the word. But despite all their attempts to add or take letters away to make other English words, no series of letters could be grouped together in any reasonable way. By that time, they had finished the bottle of wine left by Puente's servant and were weary of staring at the unintelligible collection of letters. Two long pauses in the effort had not helped them and they were no closer to understanding what the word meant. Almost simultaneously, both men leaned back and sighed in frustration.

"I suggest we stop for awhile." The colonel sighed. "We can continue trying to decipher it in the morning. It should be much easier to do in the light of day. For now, I think it best if I finish the translation for you. We are near the end of the report and I wish to leave this gloomy house and its inhospitable host." Rodríguez made a face as he looked around the room.

Morgan nodded, rubbing his eyes with his fingers. "A new look in the morning might be more successful. I'm also anxious to hear the rest of the report and what the robbers took away from the caravan."

"I understand." Rodríguez turned to the last page. "They emptied one chest of gold coins and half a chest of silver coins. I suspect they could not carry any more in their saddlebags since there were 3,000 coins in each chest. They also took 136 ingots – 38 gold and 98 silver. I assume the robbers carried them in the sailcloth bundles. Thus, each man would be entitled to 750 coins and 22 bars más o menos if they divided the bullion equally. Since the bars weighed six ounces, their horses could carry both the bars and coins. A sixth share of the bars alone would be worth some 10,000 pesetas. Dios mío! They had more than enough to live in luxury for life."

"One would think so." Morgan nodded. "But it may well be such wealth was not enough for one or more of them – beguiled by greed!"

Nine days later, Morgan was aboard the schooner, *Bountiful,* headed for Savannah. He sat on the deck in the stern as the sleek ship sailed smoothly along the Florida coast. The schooner coasted on the current flowing north and, assisted by a strong wind from the southwest, it moved swiftly through the sea. Morgan could see the vague outline of the faraway shore and one of the sailors told him the ship was in waters five leagues south of St. Augustine. The voyage had been unremarkable so far, but the sight of a long bank of dark clouds to the west now worried him. He stood beside the mainsail mast, shading his eyes with his fingers, and studied the ominous clouds moving toward them. Even from afar, Morgan could hear thunder claps and see bright streaks of lightning every few seconds.

It was September third and Morgan knew he had boarded ship in the middle of the storm season. There had already been three severe storms in the Caribbean that summer and one passed by the northern coast of Cuba while he was in Havana. Morgan had seen all too many hurricanes along the coast of Savannah in his lifetime and he dreaded the fury of the powerful winds and the devastation they left in their wake. One hurricane in the fifties had completely flooded Morgan's Creek and all the rice fields, ruining the summer crop and contaminating the land with salt. Only their house had remained above water as the storm sent countless waves into the marshland and over the lowlands.

The sinister clouds Morgan saw to the west looked similar to those he had seen two hours before the destructive storm struck Savannah in 1753. That hurricane also had appeared in early September. Morgan felt his stomach tighten as he watched the thick, dark clouds advance rapidly across the water. The sky was now alight with streaks of lightning and the explosions of thunder seemed louder than any cannon fire he had heard in battle. He glanced about the ship and saw the sailors nearest him hauling down the mainsail. One of the mates had his eyes fixed on the clouds.

He turned to Morgan. "It could be a bit of a blow, Major. You ought to get yerself below deck and hold tight to something."

"I'll stay up here on deck and tie myself to the mast." Morgan knew if he went below, he would be tossed about in the stifling darkness and the swaying ship would make him vomit.

"Then be quick – the squall's 'bout on us." The mate threw him a length of rope.

Morgan wound the rope around the mast, brought the ends together at his waist and, with his one hand, tied a square knot in the rope. He no sooner had secured himself to the mast when the storm struck the ship broadside. The crew had barely enough time to drop the other sails and tie them down before the black clouds were overhead. The jib had only been partially tied down and, seized in the sudden wind, a length of its loose line appeared to slither along the deck like a venomous snake preparing to strike.

The storm came and went quickly. It seemed to Morgan that the black clouds he had seen far away were suddenly over them and the light in the sky extinguished as quickly as if someone had thrown a blanket over the ship. Except for the streaks of lightning, which lasted only seconds, the vessel was now in complete darkness. The wind suddenly struck and the *Bountiful* was forced over on its side as if a huge hand pressed its palm against the masts and pushed them down to the water. The masts appeared to be pressed almost horizontal to the waves and Morgan thought the *Bountiful* would surely capsize. Terrified, he worried the ship would suffer the same fate as the *Nuestra Señora de la Soledad* fifty years earlier.

If the schooner sank, there was nothing he could do. Tied to the mast, he would be one of the first men to drown. Even if the ship remained afloat, with his feet dangling over the churning sea, he expected at any moment to fall overboard. To his relief, the *Bountiful* then righted itself as the fury of the storm temporarily subsided. But no sooner did he lean back to relieve the pressure of the rope against his chest than the ship was blown over on its side once again. It happened again and again as the wind strengthened and abated capriciously. Meanwhile, a hard rain drummed on deck as if volley after volley of musket shot had been fired into the wood.

The pelting rain stung Morgan's exposed face and head;

his hat had blown away with the first blast of wind. He could even feel the rain peppering his skin through his clothing. Morgan put his hand over his eyes and brought his knees up to his stomach, but the rain still battered his body. Only his back and buttocks pressed against the wooden mast were spared the punishment. Afterward, Morgan would say that he felt like someone who had been beaten with a whip.

Moments later, the winds subsided and the rain ended as the bank of clouds moved away to the east. A bright, shining sun once again lighted the sky and the schooner, its sails billowing in the wind, sailed smoothly into the late afternoon. Standing up and looking about the *Bountiful*, Morgan could see no obvious signs of damage and, except for the sodden deck, it almost seemed as if there had never been the sudden squall that came so close to sinking the ship. A sailor told him no one had been lost and nothing of value had been lost overboard.

Thoroughly soaked, his shoes full of water, Morgan went below to change his clothes. In a mirror, he saw the welts from the rain on his face and the rope burns on his chest and stomach. He sighed, thinking the few bruises he suffered were little to pay for surviving the storm. When Morgan returned topside, most of the deck had dried and the spot where he usually sat beside the mast was only slightly damp to the touch. He sat with his back against the mast and stretched his legs out on the deck. He turned his head to look to the east and saw the dark clouds already miles away as they raced on toward the Canary Islands.

Morgan no longer worried about the possibility of other murders in Savannah while away in Havana. His mind had been put to rest several days earlier when he spoke to a merchant on a passing ship heading to Cuba. The ships sailed within ten feet of each other and they were able to speak briefly without shouting. A bearded and mustached Scotsman Morgan knew by sight told him all was quiet in town.

He wanted to question the man further, but the *Bountiful*, moving swiftly with the current, sailed by too quickly to ask anything else.

With that worry out of his mind, Morgan could leisurely think about Claudia. He wished she were with him now. She had remained in Havana to care for her mother, who had fallen sick following the funeral. At first, the family thought Sofia María, in tears since her husband's death and seemingly inconsolable, suffered from grief, but a fainting spell and sudden fever brought a doctor that evening. She was seriously ill with something the doctor could not diagnose. Claudia and her sisters remained at home carrying out the physician's instructions. They were well aware of the peril their mother faced after losing her husband of forty years.

Claudia told Morgan her worries about her mother the same day he and Rodríguez read the salvage report. Though anxious to return to Savannah with his new wife, he knew Claudia should stay on until her mother felt better. Sofía María's fever did abate a day later, but she was still too weak to get out of bed. Claudia told him she had never seen her mother in bed in her entire life. Sofia María was usually the first one to rise in the morning and the last to go to sleep. Now, she spent most of the day lying in bed looking out the narrow window that faced the red-tile roof of her neighbor's house. She remained that way despite all the efforts her daughters made to cheer her up. Sofía María had little to say and tended to speak only when one of the girls spoke to her. It was obvious she suffered a deep sadness that they could only hope time would heal.

Knowing Claudia would be tormented by thoughts of her mother if she left for Savannah, Morgan urged her to stay in Havana without him. Although he wanted her to come home with him, he suggested she return to Georgia when her mother's health improved. Claudia reluctantly agreed and he decided to leave on the next ship headed to

Savannah. Uncle Rafael made arrangements for his departure and he boarded the *Bountiful* two days later.

Claudia was attentive and loving to him during his last week with her. She seemed more like herself. Claudia still dressed in black every day, but she appeared to have begun to accept the loss of her father and now showed her need for him at night. She would have him hold her close, his body behind her, his arm around her waist. He would lightly stroke all of her body he could reach with his hand until she fell asleep. Many nights, Claudia would twitch and whimper as she lay sleeping against him. Awakened, he would gently rub her back until she slept quietly.

A surge of warmth ran through Morgan as he thought of her coming to him at night and he yearned for her closeness at that moment. He thought of his love for her and how he would shiver simply from the touch of her tiny fingers on his face. Claudia had become more essential to him than he had ever thought possible. He now could not think of living without her.

His last two nights in her home, Claudia had thrown herself on top of him, seizing him in a frenzy. She wanted him immediately and gritted her teeth impatiently until he was inside her. Claudia closed her eyes, spread her hands over his chest and shuddered as she moved frantically against him. She bit his lips and dug her nails into his back as they finished and then instantly fell asleep with her head on his chest. Claudia slept like a child and never knew it when he slid out from beneath her and cuddled her from behind.

Morgan's only worry now was the future birthing of their child. He could not dismiss the fears from his mind and he worried about all that could go wrong every time Claudia appeared in his thoughts. Most of all, he feared losing her in childbirth even in the presence of a physician. Morgan knew he would live in dread during the birth and would not find peace until Claudia and the baby had survived the ordeal. The image of Claudia with a tiny baby in her arms warmed his heart and brought tears to his eyes. Morgan realized he already missed her and it had only been eight days since he left Havana.

At that moment, a group of porpoises swam alongside the *Bountiful.* Morgan stood and watched them rise and fall in unison as they swam past the schooner veering westward toward the coast of Florida. He kept his eyes on them, their sleek bodies glistening in the late afternoon sun until they were out of sight.

Morgan resumed his seat on the deck against the mast and turned his thoughts to his last meeting with Colonel Rodríguez. They met at his office the afternoon he sailed from Havana. Claudia rode with him in the family's coach and they hugged and kissed openly in the street in front of the Customs House. She sadly bid him goodbye, brushing the tears from her eyes as she stepped up into the coach. For a moment, he stood in the street and watched the coach as it moved away into the distance. He turned to the Customs House only when it was out of sight.

Morgan talked to Rodríguez while he waited to board his ship for Savannah. He found the colonel unoccupied and they spoke for more than an hour. A Spanish convoy arrived from Cádiz delaying the movement of foreign ships along the channel.

"Have you figured out the meaning of the first word yet? I've had no luck myself. It has evaded me." Rodríguez showed Morgan a sheet of paper almost covered with words he had tried to extract from with the twelve senseless letters – *Ariapleñatn.*

Morgan shook his head. "No, I've also made similar lists, but to no avail. I have thought about the word almost every waking hour without any success."

"The only word I could come up with is the name 'Harry,' which I got from the first three letters. But I strongly doubt its meaning or use." Rodríguez shook his head from side to side.

"That's more than I could find in the damned letters."

"By the way, it may interest you to know the method Lerdo Palacios used to preserve the robber's words was the same used by the monks to learn the history of the Aztecs. They listened to the Indians as they spoke and wrote down what they heard in our alphabet. The Indians wrote in pictures, and their pictures accompanied by the monk's writings, tell us how their people lived before the New World was discovered."

"I did not know that. I assume you read history."

"I do whenever I have the opportunity. The Customs House interviews are not enough to keep my mind occupied. In fact, I find myself bored most of the time. My appointment here was bestowed upon me after I was wounded. I'm no longer qualified as an infantry officer and, while no one has officially informed me, I know I will never be given a command of troops again. My future in the king's service will be in some office at a desk doing clerical work. I'll undoubtedly go to my grave with some trivial order clutched in my dead hand." Rodríguez smiled. "I'm not looking for sympathy. I could resign my commission any time I choose and be awarded a pitiful pension – after all, I am a wounded war hero. The pension means nothing to me – I own a finca (ranch) with cattle and pasture lands south of Havana. The reason I don't retire is that I would be bored even more at home or on the finca. I have no wish to be Don Juan the wealthy hacendado (landowner) of San Felice – that's where my lands are located. So, at least for now, I will remain a complaining clerk in this office."

"I understand completely. This is the last year of my term of office as justice of the peace and I don't know what I will do in the following years. My father isn't well and he wants me to manage his lands and, though that's the last thing I want to do, I fear I will end up in his service."

"So, such are the rewards of being wounded in the service of king and country. Enough self-pity! I will continue trying to find meaning in these senseless letters. Incidentally, the study of these documents is the most interesting activity to occupy my mind in months. It's a wonder my mind hasn't withered away like the muscles in my bad leg."

"I'm pleased to hear that. I've received more assistance from you than I expected from anyone in Havana." Morgan smiled. "I guess a good lie has its virtue."

"It was a bad lie – you were just lucky!" The colonel, chuckling, patted Morgan's arm.

"Yes, it was. My lies apparently only succeed with pompous English officials."

"So it seems. Here is your copy of Lerdo Palacios' report." Rodríguez handed Morgan a thick envelope sealed with the wax impression of the colonel's stamp. "My stamp is also on the last page. I wrote a brief letter verifying the copy is authentic; it's written in English so Attorney General Palmer will find it easy to understand. Quien sabe, perhaps Palmer will appreciate your efforts here in this enemy land."

"Muchas gracias, Colonel. I wouldn't expect Oliver Palmer to appreciate anything except his own achievements or mine that he claims are his."

"I did not copy or translate the full report of the salvage. It included too much information about Spain's navy and armaments."

"Even though the *Nuestra Señora de la Soledad* was sunk fifty years ago?"

"Yes, I asked an admiral I know to advise me and he told me to send it to the Building of Records. Apparently, our naval armaments have not changed much in all those years."

"I understand. What about the section concerning the robbery?"

"There were more reports, statements, inventories and

additional interviews with the five guards, including the sergeant, but not much new that I could see. The Lerdo Palacios report was the best of the lot. I did learn the sunken ship was found by a lone fisherman who snared his net on the mainmast. The one useful piece of information was in the sergeant's statement. He said he heard one of the ladrones speak Spanish. The sergeant didn't remember what the man said, but he was sure the man wasn't a foreigner speaking Spanish; rather he was someone who spoke our language his entire life. Apparently, the robbers had the man speak Spanish to make the soldiers think that Spaniards had robbed the caravan – not Englishmen."

"He must have been the dark-skinned man Ramírez mentioned."

"That was my thought, too. He might well have been a Spaniard from St. Augustine who advised the brigands of the sunken ship's discovery and the bullion it carried. He also could have been a Mestizo. After all the years Spaniards have lived with Indians, Mestizos are as common in St. Augustine as everywhere else in the Spanish empire."

Morgan nodded. "We even have Mestizos in Savannah." He thought of María Adela and the other house servants who had come from Florida in the English colony.

"You might be interested to know the salvage of the *Nuestra Señora de la Soledad* – even with the robbery – was quite successful. They retrieved fity of the sixty chests of coins; the others had broken open in the wreck and their contents were lost in the sand. They found all but five of the four hundred gold and silver bars and all but a single chest of jewelry. Every one of the chests of Chinese porcelain was brought up from the wreck, but, as expected, much of the porcelain was broken or badly cracked."

"That's understandable in a sinking ship, no matter how well the porcelain was packed."

"Yes, especially since the ship split in half when it sank

into the sea. That was why the salvage was so successful. The two sections of the ship were lying close to each other and their storage holds were open with the bullion in full view of the divers. Many of the chests, in fact, were found in the sand between the two sections."

"That was fortunate."

"It was. There is one report relating to the salvage I have not yet seen. I missed seeing it with the other documents at Puente's house. It's mentioned at the end of the principal report and I will look for it as soon as possible. The Florida documents are now in the Building of Records. Puente wrote to me, stating he sent them there the day following our visit." Rodríguez frowned. "He instructed me to do the same with the reports I took from his house. He said it was time for all the Florida records to be secured in the Building of Records. An annoying and officious man! As you will recall, he required me to sign for the reports before we left his house."

Morgan smiled. "I suspect he's been wealthy all his life and treats everyone like a servant."

"Probably so." Rodríguez paused, seeing one of his men signal him from the door to the docks. "A ship is in the channel so we will have to close our conversation shortly."

"I understand. I must board my ship soon anyway."

"Well, I am glad we did get some time to talk. I hope we will meet again."

"I do, as well. I have enjoyed our time together."

"Yo también (I also). I will advise you of the contents of the final report when I read it in a day or so. I am too curious to wait much longer to read it."

"I'll keep you informed of our search for the murderer in Savannah. We will meet again when Claudia and I visit Havana to show her family the beautiful baby. Of course, that will happen only if the child is fortunate enough to look like her mother."

Rodríguez smiled and stood. He walked around his desk to shake hands with Morgan. "I wish you good fortune, my friend. I will look forward to hearing you have arrested and executed the murderer. Hasta luego."

Morgan nodded. "Thank you for all your assistance and hospitality. You have made my trip to Cuba successful. Without your help, I would have returned to Savannah empty handed."

"Por nada." Rodríguez embraced Morgan briefly. "My only hope is that you will leave Havana knowing we Spaniards are not the villains the *Black Legend* says we are."

"You can be certain of that."

Three hours later, Morgan stood at the stern of the *Bountiful* watching the sun set over the sea. The sky at dusk was full of feathery clouds colored in orange, pink and purple and he remained on deck even when the lush colors were replaced by the somber blues and grays of the coming night. Morgan wondered if the afternoon storm had given the sunset its striking beauty.

Still on deck in the last light, Morgan again thought about the twelve-lettered phrase that still eluded his understanding. No matter how many ways he had manipulated the letters, he had failed to find their meaning. He had discarded countless sheets of paper in the process. Now, as Morgan thought about the hours of wasted effort, the twelve letters appeared, uninvited as usual, in the front of his mind. Powerless to stop himself, he began to think of new ways to move them about as he went below for the night.

The man pushed open the door and stumbled out of the outhouse. He took three unsteady steps and fell to the ground. His breeches and underwear were twisted about his ankles, leaving his stark white buttocks bared to the air. He tried desperately to crawl forward, but even when he dug his fingers into the dirt, he moved no more than a few inches. His legs were of no use. The pain behind the knee of his good leg kept him from using it to propel himself ahead. Barely able to move, he finally shouted for help. At first, he could do little more than croak weakly. Then, he found his voice and bellowed loudly. He shouted twice.

The big man was walking his dog on the other side of the house when he heard the shout. He turned, thinking the shout came from inside the house, and ran to the front door. The dog ran beside him. He had his pistol cocked and ready to fire as he turned the door knob. A second and weaker shout stopped him as he was about to rush inside. He turned and ran around the house to the outhouse with the dog ahead of him. The dog stood panting beside the fallen man by the time his master reached him.

"What happened?" He kneeled down beside the body.

The man mumbled a few incoherent words and then fell silent. His right hand twitched, but he made no further movement. He lay, as if dead, on the ground.

The big man felt his breath on the back of his hand and knew he was alive. Relieved, he looked him over to see what had happened. He saw no blood on him and knew the man had not been shot or stabbed. Then, he spied the two bites behind the knee of his right leg. He quickly pulled off his belt and tied it tightly around the man's thigh above the bites. Pausing only briefly to take a deep breath, he picked up the heavy body and carried it in his arms into the house.

The hooded figure watched everything from a high limb of a live oak in the woods. The perch was some fifteen feet from the cleared land around the house. The watcher waited until the man and his dog had gone inside and then climbed down to the ground. It was only a short walk through the woods to where to the tied horse had been hidden. The return trip to town turned out to be uneventful and not one person rode or walked either way on the road that morning.

It had all gone exactly as planned. The doomed man had been bitten and collapsed outside the outhouse, leaving the unlatched door open wide enough for the water snake to slither back into the woods. The snake escaped well before the big man and his dog reached the body. If the man was not dead already, he would eventually die, suffering the pain he deserved.

CHAPTER ELEVEN

SAVANNAH:
MONDAY, SEPTEMBER 9 – WEDNESDAY, SEPTEMBER 11, 1766

The *Bountiful* arrived at the mouth of the Savannah River in the first light of dawn. There was an unseasonable chill in the air as Morgan stood at the bow, watching the sunlight spread out on the eastern horizon. He wore a blue wool sweater loaned to him by the captain.

The Dutchman, who spoke little English, gestured for him to put on the sweater when he saw him on deck in only a shirt and breeches. Morgan was the only passenger on the ship and he and the captain had spoken nightly since leaving Cuba. The captain always took the early night watch until midnight and they would talk for a while when Morgan came topside before going to sleep. Communication had been initially difficult, but they managed with the few words each of them knew of the other's language aided by hand and facial gestures. Now, the captain pointed to the east and waved his hands toward his chest, indicating a storm was blowing in from the sea.

The chilly wind felt refreshing and Morgan hoped the approaching storm would be one of the summer Northeasters that would cool off Savannah for a few days. He cleared his nostrils to inhale the fresh air. Morgan felt invigorated and looked forward to the day ahead. If the morning with its bright orange sunrise and brisk breeze was an omen, he knew everything he had planned would succeed, even his meeting with Oliver Palmer. But, before walking to the courthouse, he intended to eat a big breakfast of ham, hot biscuits, blackberry preserves and strong English tea, all of which he had sorely missed at sea.

Morgan felt especially good that morning because he had finally figured out the meaning of "ariapleñatn." It had come to him in the middle of the night as he lay swaying in his hammock. Morgan awoke suddenly with the solution in his mind. He had gone to sleep, thinking of the one word the colonel had extracted from the senseless assortment of letters. The word was *Harry*, a name Rodríguez doubted had any meaning. Morgan, however, continued to think about it. The name seemed to be lodged in his mind and he repeated it aloud over and over again. Then, as he lay listening to the sound of water lapping against at the sides of the ship, the meaning of the first five letters came to him. Morgan realized if he changed the vowel *a* to *u*, the first word would be *hurry* and it would follow that ariap actually meant *hurry up* and leñatn was *lington.* And since *w* did not exist in the Spanish alphabet, the rest of the word was – Willington. The Spanish soldier heard the man shout, "Hurry up, Willington, Nelson says the patrol is on the way."

Morgan smiled as the ship turned into the Savannah River. He was pleased with himself and looked forward to getting off the ship and walking on dry land once again. It was good to be home. He made a mental note to write Rodríguez and tell him the full meaning of the shout.

An hour later, as the *Bountiful* carefully approached the

Douglas Company dock, Morgan was surprised to see the broad figure of Stockwell leaning against one of the mooring posts. The sergeant looked severe without even a trace of a smile. Morgan sighed, thinking that Palmer had done or said something stupid to infuriate the big man.

"What, Stockwell, not even a smile of greeting for me?" Morgan asked him as he leaped ashore. He threw the leather haversack with his clothes over his left shoulder. The sealed letter to Oliver Palmer, which held the copy of the robbery report, was in the pocket of his breeches. "I suppose Palmer has made your life miserable while I've been gone."

"Palmer hasn't bothered me at all. I haven't seen the man, but twice since you was gone." The big man shook Morgan's hand. The sergeant's expression remained stern, his mouth a tight line. "I'm afraid I have some bad news for you, Major."

Morgan stared at Stockwell, but said nothing.

"I'm sorry to be the one to tell you, but your father's dead." Stockwell saw the surprise in Morgan's face. "It's been ten days now. It happened on August 30th – in the morning."

"What was it, his heart?" Morgan dropped his haversack on the dock and stood motionless as if fixed to the spot.

"Snake bite. Rattlesnake, most likely. It happened in the outhouse when he went there in the morning. He was bit twice."

Morgan exhaled his breath loudly. "Did he die immediately or linger?"

"Sorry to say, he lingered a time – some two and a half days. The doctor was there with him the entire time, even though he's not doing well himself."

Morgan nodded. "So he suffered a lot of pain?"

"Afraid so."

"I suppose Bartholomew officiated at the funeral?"

"Yes, he did that and much more. Stayed with your father

for most of his last day and made all the arrangements. He told your father's man what to do till you returned."

"You mean Abraham Cabot, the plantation supervisor?"

"No, that big German who's been at his house for most of the month. Claus Bruckmann is the man's name. A big brute, he is."

"I assume he was there to help my father get around."

"That's what he said. The man can't speak much English, but says little anyway. I did hear him say he was hired to watch out for your father."

"You mean more than help him get about?" Morgan stared at Stockwell.

"Don't know. I do know he walks about like a sentry on guard duty. Armed to the teeth, he is. Better than most soldiers in the field. Carries a loaded pistol and a long knife hanging on his belt as well as a sword. He looks to be a man who knows how to use every one of the arms, too. Bruckmann also has a dog that follows him around. He's a big beast, must be close to 120 pounds and looks to have some wolf in him. Bruckmann calls him, 'Kaiser.'"

Morgan sighed. "Well, I better get out there. He's buried at Morgan's Creek, isn't he?" He swallowed the sob he felt form in his throat and picked up his haversack.

Stockwell shook his head and saw Morgan's eyes glisten with tears. "The pastor put him out there right next to your mother. He said that's where your father would want to be."

Morgan grunted in reply. He was afraid he would sob if he spoke.

"I got your stallion tied up on the hill. Palmer says take whatever time you need. He's the one sent me here. Said he heard you was aboard the *Bountiful* from a captain on a schooner that passed by a week ago at the tip of Florida."

Morgan nodded. He recalled shouting a few words to the captain as his much faster ship sailed past the *Bountiful*.

"Do you want me to come with you?" Stockwell turned

to Morgan as they trudged side by side up the stairs to River Street.

"No, I need to go alone."

Morgan stood looking down at the mound of dirt that lay on top of his father's grave. He was glad he had gone to visit him before his voyage and remembered seeing him standing on the porch in his nightshirt as he rode away in the morning. They had enjoyed their time together the evening before. It always amused his father to talk about the family's pirate heritage. He told his son he hoped Claudia would bear a boy. "We need a boy to carry the pirate bloodline into the future." Matthew laughed and clapped his son on the knee.

Tears filled Morgan's eyes as he recalled his father's words. Now, if a boy was born, his father would never see him and never be a grandfather to him. Morgan's shoulders shook as he began to cry. In the woods behind the house, he made no effort to suppress his sobs.

He was all alone now – the only Morgan left. His father, his mother, his brother Joseph – they were all gone. The remains of his mother and father lay buried beneath his feet. His father had created the small cemetery when Joseph disappeared at sea. Morgan recalled him clearing a rectangular area and placing stones around it.

"It's for all of us," Matthew told his son, "when the time comes." He made a dirt mound the length of a grave and laid Joseph's headstone on it. Rachel's grave lay next to Joseph's and Matthew had been buried beside his wife. His headstone, carved in the same style as those of his son and wife, stood on the freshly dug grave. They all lay there in the dark earth now and, in the not too distant future, Morgan knew, he too would lie beneath the ground in the little graveyard. And, unless Claudia bore a son, there the Morgan line would end forever. He dried his eyes on the sleeve of his jacket and breathed deeply. It was time to take charge of Morgan's Creek.

Morgan got down on his knees between the graves of his mother and brother and brushed the dirt from their gravestones. He then began pulling the accumulated weeds that had grown on the graves since his father's death. Every week, even when suffering excruciating pain from his rheumatism, Matthew had hobbled to the clearing to trim the holly bushes and marsh lavender he had planted and remove any leaves or weeds that desecrated the gravesite. His son now assumed his father's task and, an hour later, the cemetery looked as tidy as when Matthew had tended it.

Morgan felt the wind blowing on his back as he stood and brushed his dirty hand against his breeches. The storm he had seen at sea had reached the coastal lands. Dark clouds covered the sky and he felt the first drops of rain on his head and shoulders.

On the way to the house, it occurred to Morgan that the newborn child could be named after his father. In fact, the boy, if Claudia brought a son into the world as she predicted, could be named after both their fathers. Matthew Miguel Morgan sounded fine to him. It was a good strong name for a man with pirate blood coursing through his veins. In spite of his sadness, he smiled to himself.

Morgan stopped abruptly a few feet from the back door. He was struck with the sudden realization that he was not alone. He had a new family now. He had lost those who brought him into the world, but he was fortunate to have a beautiful woman who loved him and a child soon to enter his life. He had no reason to feel sorry for himself.

Morgan knew the sadness he felt for the loss of his

father would stay with him for a long time, but his grief would eventually lessen as the days and weeks passed. It happened that way when his mother died a year ago. His parents would forever remain in his heart, but in time, he would think of them only now and then when they reappeared from memory. He remembered his mother and father often speaking of what their parents did and said. His father would say, "My father would grip an axe handle one inch from the end" and his mother would remember her own mother saying, "A stitch in time saves nine." Morgan nodded. It was time to straighten up and face the world like a man. That's what his father would have said. Oblivious to the rain, Morgan stood in the open as the drizzle became a downpour and soaked his jacket.

Catalina, his father's housekeeper, had a cup of tea waiting for him when he walked into the kitchen. "You eat breakfast, Major?" She handed him the chipped orange cup he always used when he visited his father.

"No, I'll just have some tea and bread." Morgan removed his hat and put it on the table. He shrugged out of his jacket and Catalina took it from him.

"It's wet and I dry it by the fire." Catalina took his jacket and hung it on a hook near the fireplace. She brought back a towel for him to dry his face and hand.

"Where are your children, Catalina?" Morgan nodded his thanks as she put freshly baked bread and blackberry preserves in front of him.

"They now staying with my sister, Fabiola, in town. Fabiola come and take them a week after your father die. I leave them with her until you come home. I don't know what you will do with the house."

"I would like you to bring the children back and stay in the house – if you are willing. I don't know yet where I will live now that I'm married, but I would like you to take care of the house the same way as you did for my father. I will pay you the same salary and buy whatever food and other supplies you and your children require. Will that be satisfactory?" He sipped his tea and eyed her over the rim of his cup.

"Yes, Major." Catalina beamed. "My children, they like it here at Morgan Creek."

"Good. I do, however, require one important task from you. It is absolutely necessary if you are to remain here." Morgan looked very severe as he stared at her.

Catalina stopped smiling, worried what he would ask her to do. "What is that, Major?"

Morgan scowled at her. "Every once in awhile, I would like you to make the same arroz de marisco that you made for my father. Claudia can't make it that tasty, but of course I would never tell her that."

Catalina studied Morgan for a brief moment and then laughed heartily, her plump cheeks shaking. "You just like your father. You joke with angry face."

Morgan smiled faintly. "Now, tell me about Abraham. I assume he still comes here to the house every morning?"

"He comes at first light. That's when Abraham and your father sit on the porch and speak about the crops and the colony. They sit there for a half hour no matter the rain or wind and drink tea. Now, Abraham drinks his tea here in the kitchen with me."

"His family is well?" Morgan spread preserves on the two pieces of bread.

"They all well. The children get bigger every day. The boys, of course, fight every hour about one thing or other."

Morgan sighed. "I will ride over to his house this afternoon. Whether I like it or not, he will insist that I see the plantation and all the improvements he has made."

Catalina smiled. "He tells me about everything now your father is gone. He misses him very much – we all do!" Tears suddenly streamed down her cheeks and she abruptly turned her back to Morgan. Catalina stood that way for several seconds, her shoulders heaving.

Morgan, who also had tears in his eyes, got up and patted Catalina's shoulder. "Sit with me," he said, "I want to ask you about Claus Bruckmann."

"The German is gone now." Catalina dried her eyes on her apron and filled two cups with tea. Handing Morgan his cup, she sighed and sat down across from him. "He goes soon after the funeral. I hear from my sister he lives with his mother in town. They come down here from that old colony upriver."

"You mean the German settlement at New Ebenezer?"

"Yes, he is one of them." Catalina's face showed her distaste. "They say there are two thousand of them there."

"What do you know about him?"

"He is a soldier in the war."

"He was in the war?" Morgan had not known of any Germans fighting in the war.

"That is what he said. He come here a day after you left for Havana. Your father told me he is here to help him get about. As you see when you come here, your father he sits most of the day. It was very hard for him to walk even with his cane."

"So, my father leaned on Bruckmann when he walked?" Morgan ate the last of the bread and preserves and then sipped his tea.

"No. Your father still walked with his cane. The German never helped him walk anytime I saw. I didn't know what to think and asked myself what he is here to do."

"Then, what did Bruckmann do?" Morgan frowned.

"He went everywhere your father went with that awful dog, even to the cemetery the days he pulls the weeds there. The German walks close to him, but does not give him his arm to hold. Whenever he goes outside the house with your father, he looks all around – I don't know what he looks for." She shrugged her shoulders. "I see them walk from the window and think he worries Indians might run at them out of the woods."

"To attack them?"

"Yes. The German walks with one hand on the handle of the pistol he has in his belt."

"I see. So, it looked like Bruckmann was guarding my father?"

"Yes, that is what he does." Catalina nodded. "He sleeps on the floor at the door – one night at front door, the next night at back door. That smelly dog sleeps at other door. They both smell bad, like moldy meat." She twitched her nose in disgust.

"You mean, at night, the man would sleep at one door and the dog at the other?"

"Yes. I don't know why. The Indians are friends to your father. They smoke with him and trade goods all year long. An old one I see many times has tears in his eyes when I tell him your father dies."

"I don't think Bruckmann was worried about Indians. Did he do anything else at night in the house?" Morgan raised his voice to be heard above the noise of hail striking the roof and the east side of the house.

Catalina looked puzzled. "No, no, nothing I see. The German he closes and locks all the windows on the first floor at night. I think he closes them to keep the mosquitoes outside – they are terrible this summer."

"What did my father say about Bruckmann staying downstairs at night?"

"He says the German and his dog smell too bad to sleep in beds upstairs. Your father tells me to keep the children away from him and the dog. I don't know why."

"Did Bruckmann ever bother you or the children?" Morgan drank down the last of his tea and raised his hand to stop Catalina from making more.

"No. He says few words. His English is very bad. I only see him in the house at night before we go to bed. He stays outside and eats on the porch. The German he eats two plates at every meal. Your father tells me to give him all he wants – probably he gives half to that dog."

"Did Bruckmann kill the snake?"

"No. He carry your father inside the house and rides to get the doctor. The next day, the doctor looks at the outhouse and says the snake is gone. I do not go to the outhouse. Too many spiders. The chamber pot is better." Catalina blushed.

Morgan smiled. "When did Bruckmann leave?"

"He goes four days ago. Abraham tells him to go. He does not want him here and sends his house slave, Able, to guard the house at night. I pay the German from the cookie jar."

Morgan nodded. His father always left money in the cookie jar for household needs. As boys, he and Joseph had stolen many a coin from the jar. "How much was he paid?"

"Your father never tells me. The German says he is owed three pounds and eight pence. I do not know what that money is for. He does not say. Abraham says to pay him what he asks. He leaves when I give him the money. Did I do right?"

"Yes, you did fine and so did Abraham. The question is what Bruckmann did to earn the money he demanded."

Morgan rode to town the next morning in the rain. A stiff wind drove the raindrops into his face and he had trouble seeing much farther than a horse length ahead. It had rained heavily off and on all night and he tossed and turned listening to the fastened shutters clattering against the sides of the house. Morgan's thoughts of his father would have kept him awake even if there had been no storm. He got up before dawn and saddled his stallion in the dark. The first light of day was breaking through the clouds as he led his horse to the road to town. Morgan could not see well enough to ride when starting out and he walked a half hour in the rain before mounting his horse. He had trouble seeing even then and he was forced to get off and on his horse several times to guide him along the pitted and washed out road.

Morgan arrived at the courthouse a few minutes before eight o'clock and he had to stand and wait for a clerk to open the door. He was soaking wet by that time and, once in his office, removed as many of his wet clothes as possible. He spent three hours in the courthouse looking irritably through the thick stack of papers that accumulated while he had been gone. Stockwell told him what had happened in town and gave him a list of the men who had been put in stocks or jailed for wanton drunkenness, disturbing the peace and destroying community property. He was relieved to learn there had been no murders or suspicious deaths during his absence. Only old people had died while he was away and the last deaths were from natural causes, with the exception of a farmer's wife who got a chicken bone stuck in her throat and choked to death. A doctor had been summoned from town, but he arrived too late to save the woman.

After Stockwell finished his account, he left the office to find Claus Bruckmann. Morgan then glanced hurriedly through the report Thackery had left conspicuously on his desk. Palmer and Thackery were both away from the office that morning attending a meeting of the assembly with the governor.

By noon, Morgan was somewhat dry and decided to visit Reverend Bartholomew. It was still raining hard, but the wind no longer blew with the same intensity. He rode his horse without needing to remove his hand repeatedly from the reins to keep his hat on his head. Bartholomew was meeting with a group of women when Morgan arrived at the church. He waited impatiently on a back bench while the women talked to the pastor about the upcoming harvest festival. They seemed to be quibbling about the amount of food to be served.

The details were finally settled at two o'clock and the six women trooped past Morgan on their way out of the church. Those who knew him stopped to offer condolences. Abigail Sterling was one of the women in the group and there were tears in her eyes when she patted his hand in sympathy. Morgan thanked her quietly and bowed his head.

"Please accept my sincere condolences, James." Bartholomew got up from where he had been sitting and hurried to meet Morgan as he walked down the aisle. He put his arm around the major's back and squeezed his shoulder. "You know how sorry I was to see your father leave us for his final rest. Even though he left the Church, I always thought of him as a close friend. I'm sure you know that."

Morgan nodded, although he doubted the man's sincerity. He sat across the aisle from the pastor who showed his concern with a crease between his eyebrows.

"Of course, in the end, he came back to us and made his peace with God. I know you are of little faith, James, but you should be glad to know his last moments were serene. He was truly penitent and I'm sure he is now with God."

Morgan sighed, determined not to express his contempt for Bartholomew's words, which he suspected were given similarly to all his parishioners whose loved ones had died. Instead, he thanked him. "Reverend, I want you to know I appreciate all your efforts for my father. I heard what you did for him before he died and I am very grateful. I also thank you for the funeral and other arrangements you made afterward – especially the carved headstone for his grave."

"You know I was happy to help, James." Bartholomew hoped that Morgan's sigh meant the usually perverse justice was touched by his words and might someday return to the fold. "I trust you found everything in order at Morgan's Creek when you returned."

"I did, thank you. Abraham and Catalina are as helpful as ever and I am fortunate to have them with me. But tell me, Reverend, what did you think of that man, Bruckmann?"

"I was frankly surprised your father hired him. He's a Lutheran, you know. I found him an unsavory man – quite unclean and bereft of any language fluency. I spoke to him in German, but he seemed little more expressive in his native language than in English. I told him what to do until you returned, though I wondered if he was competent enough to carry out my instructions. I was glad to hear that Abraham Cabot sent him packing a few days ago."

"Do you know why my father hired him?"

Bartholomew shook his head. "No, I do not. I would have expected your father to employ a man of quality with a good mind. Bruckmann has little more mind than a dumb beast. The man served as a soldier in the last war and walks about armed as if ready to do battle at any moment. I cannot imagine what your father thought he could do for him."

"I can't either."

"I must say he did have mind enough to tie his belt above the snake bites. The doctor said your poor father would not have lasted through the day if that had not been done. As it was, the unfortunate man had very little time left."

"Did he say anything before he died?" Morgan felt his stomach tighten as he waited for Bartholomew to reply.

"Only a few words now and then. He lay in a daze most of the time." Bartholomew put his hand on Morgan's shoulder. "I'm truly sorry, James."

Morgan did not shake off the pastor's heavy hand. He knew this time Bartholomew was sincere in what he said.

"I'm sure you know all your father's legal papers are in the hands of his lawyer, Clarence Blake. I saw him at the funeral. He said you should come see him at your earliest convenience. Blake wants to go over your father's will and settle his affairs."

"I'm sure he does – so I can pay him for his services." Morgan threw his hand out as if to swat an insect. "That's what the greedy bastard wants to go over. I'll see him when I'm damn good and ready."

The sun peeked out of the clouds as Morgan left the church and rode over to the doctor's house. As he rode, he noted the clear skies to the east and north and knew the storm would be gone by evening. Tomorrow, the relentless heat and humidity would return. He started to frown, but brightened realizing that fall was not far away.

Morgan found his friend looking much worse than when he had seen him last. Despite his obvious effort, the doctor's smile did not hide the physical deterioration that Morgan saw in him. The sick man had lost a lot of weight, maybe as many as thirty pounds, and he now looked shrunken as if denied food in a dungeon. His face was ghostly white and he had deep dark circles around his eyes. He made no attempt to stand when Morgan entered the house and he waited for him to reach his chair before grasping his hand. Morgan leaned over to embrace him and noticed how light his body seemed as he held him momentarily. There was also a noticeable odor about him that reminded Morgan of Fort Frontenac's infirmary where he had almost lost his life.

"You are a sight for sore eyes." The doctor held his smile, although Morgan could see it took an effort. "I know this is a bad time for you and I appreciate your taking time to visit me."

"The time I'm taking with you here is far more important than anything else I have done since coming home. I have lost my father and now I fear losing you." Morgan decided there was no use pretending his friend would survive his illness. In the war, he had seen so many wounded men slowly waste away and die. He saw the same signs of approaching death in the doctor. The dullness Morgan saw in his once sparkling eyes struck him most of all and he remembered it was one of the signs that comrades of the wounded men at Frontenac dreaded to see.

"Your fears are well founded; I don't have long to live. But I prefer not to dwell on it, so let's talk about your trip abroad. I'm anxious to hear all about the wedding and what you learned in Havana. But let's have some wine first. Please pour us a couple of glasses. The wine is in the cabinet – you know where it is, of course."

"Where is María Adela?" Morgan took a wine bottle from the bottom shelf of the cabinet. There were four bottles of red wine on the shelf. He opened the silverware drawer and removed the corkscrew.

"She's in town buying some Bayberry powder for me."

"Does it help?" Morgan asked when he handed the doctor a glass of wine.

"It helps with the diarrhea, but not with the bleeding. I think it's cancer. Have you heard of the illness?"

"Yes, but I don't know much about it." He touched wine glasses with the doctor.

"No one else does either, but enough about my illness. I want to wish you many happy years with Claudia…"

"Thank you." Morgan smiled as he sat in the chair next to the doctor.

"I'm not finished with my toast. So, you will have to hear the first part again. I want to wish you many happy years with Claudia and many mischievous children who will eventually fill your lives with joy."

Morgan chuckled. "Thank you. I wish the same for us." He sighed, still worried about Claudia's birthing of the baby. Morgan then told the doctor everything that had happened in Havana. He began with the wedding and the unexpected death of his father-in-law and ended with the robbery report and his last meeting with Colonel Rodríguez.

The doctor sat up in his chair and listened intently as Morgan described his month in Cuba. Morgan thought his eyes looked a little brighter as he interrupted occasionally to ask questions or make comments. Typically polite, he waited until his friend finished his story and picked up his glass before he sipped any of his own wine.

"Well, you certainly had a memorable trip. I am sorry to hear how your wedding ended. What a shame! I hope Claudia's mother survives the loss of her husband. After so many years of marriage, many elderly people die when they lose their spouses. I think it was wise of Claudia to remain with her mother at such a time. I say that even though I know you will miss her."

"Yes, I will indeed, but I understand her need to stay with her mother. I am hopeful she will be able to return to Savannah at least by the middle of next month. It is odd, is it not, that we both lost both our fathers following our marriage? Their deaths in fact were only days apart."

Morgan shook his head in amazement.

"It is indeed." The doctor drank the remainder of his wine and Morgan refilled both their glasses. "My friend, we need to talk about your father's death – there was something about it that bothers me. It has been on my mind ever since I left Morgan's Creek."

"Does it have anything to do with Bruckmann?"

"It does, but only partially. We will talk about him in a moment. What bothers me more is how the snake got into the outhouse. The outhouse, like every one of the structures your father either built himself or had built for him, was tightly constructed. It was set into a mortared stone foundation. There were no spaces or cracks in its sides or at the wooden base. Neither were there any holes or sizeable openings in the ground around the building. I walked around it a number of times and found the ground hard and firm against the foundation. So, how then did the snake get into the outhouse?"

Morgan stared hard at the doctor, but made no reply. He sat with his elbow resting on the arm of the chair and his chin cupped in his hand.

"The door was always latched and Bruckmann told me he remembered latching it when he went to the outhouse the night before. I believe the man…"

"Why do you believe him?" Morgan had his doubts about Bruckmann.

"I believe him because everyone here knows better than to leave any outhouse door open. No one wants to confront a wild animal when in a hurry to relieve oneself. Anyway, Bruckmann said the door was closed when he walked his dog around the outhouse the next morning. He did not use it himself at the time because he pees in the woods during the day. Bruckmann told me he only goes to the outhouse at night. Since only your father used the outhouse in the morning, that leaves only one possible conclusion. The snake was put inside by someone during the night after Bruckmann had been there." The doctor paused to wait for his friend's response.

Morgan sighed. "So you think my father was murdered? That's hard to believe. Why? There are those who envy his success, but… Ah, I see. You think he was another of the murderer's victims, don't you?'

"I'm afraid it looks that way."

"I don't believe it." Morgan raised his voice. "My father

had property, wealth and was well respected in Savannah. Why would he rob the bullion caravan? For what reason would he do it?"

"I am sorry, my friend, but there are a number of things about his death that bring me to that conclusion. Please let me continue."

His face flushed, Morgan nodded without enthusiasm.

"Let's begin with what we know about his use of the outhouse. According to Catalina, your father went to the outhouse every morning after breakfast. Is that correct?"

"Yes, every day of his life, unless he was sick."

The doctor nodded. "Let's keep that fact in mind as we proceed. Even if you doubt he was murdered, how do you explain the snake's presence in the outhouse? How and why would the snake enter that confined space?"

"The why is easy for me to answer." Morgan scowled. "The snake probably entered the outhouse to escape the heat or pursue its prey – a field mouse for example. There are many such incidents in Savannah. I myself have been fetched on occasion to remove snakes from buildings in town. Last year, I killed a copperhead in the governor's carriage house. This summer, as you know, I had my own encounter with a rattlesnake outside my stable."

"The snake that struck your father was not a land snake – it was a water snake."

Stunned, Morgan was briefly silent and then he asked, "How do you know that?"

The sick man held up a trembling hand. I'll tell you shortly, but for now let's talk about how the snake entered the outhouse. Assuming the outhouse door was closed, how did the snake get into the building? The only openings other than the door are the air vents in the upper walls, which are much too small for a snake to crawl through – that is, if the snake somehow slithered up the outside wall to those openings."

"It's possible that Bruckmann lied about seeing the door closed. He might have forgotten to close it the night before and would not admit it."

"That is possible, but I doubt it after talking to the man. Bear with me a moment and, for now, accept his statement as true and the possibility that someone put the snake in the outhouse."

"All right." Morgan shook his head reluctantly agreeing to listen.

"Let's now return to the fact that your father went to the outhouse every day after eating his breakfast. If, as I suspect, the murderer put the snake into the outhouse, he would have known of your father's morning visit. That means he must have watched the house for at least a couple of days, including a night or two. As a result, he would have observed your father going there in the morning and Bruckmann at night. Is that right?

Morgan nodded, but his frown showed his doubt.

"We have seen that careful preparation before, haven't we? It's the mark of the clever fiend who murdered the others. The use of an animal to carry out the killing is also consistent with two of the murders we now know about. And, James, I am sorry, but I must point out that he showed the same callous cruelty to your father that he did to the others. The murderer made certain your father suffered an excruciatingly painful death."

Morgan clucked his tongue. "What you say makes sense, but I'm still doubtful."

"Let me ask you a question. Do you remember if your father was away at the time of the robbery?" The doctor watched Morgan's face as he frowned in thought.

"I do recall he was away in the spring, but I'm not certain if his trip was in 1763 or 1764. Now that I think about it I'm sure it wasn't 1764. My mother fell ill in February of that year and she rarely left her bed thereafter; she got weaker and weaker and my father never went anywhere until after her death." He sighed. "Yes, he was away sometime in the spring of 1763, but I don't remember in which month he was gone."

The doctor saw him still in thought and waited without speaking.

Morgan sighed again. "I recall now he told me he was riding to Charles Towne to meet with some other rice planters. He said they were considering the possibility of jointly purchasing a ship to transport their rice abroad. He expected to be gone for a fortnight and asked me to ride down to Morgan's Creek one day while he was away. He wanted to make sure everything at the plantation was in good order. I recall the year because that spring was wetter than usual and the pain in my shoulder was incessant; it was the worst pain I had suffered since the amputation. Of course, it was at that time I rode to the house, cursing my father all the way. The pain was awful and became unbearable with every step the stallion took on the road. I felt faint and could barely stay in the saddle."

"You came to see me upon your return from Morgan's Creek. I remember giving you laudanum for the pain. It's is in my records and I can find the day it was given."

"That's unnecessary. I now know he was away the same time as the robbery. But it's still hard for me to believe he was involved with the likes of Sterling and Willington."

"It's hard for me, too, James. I knew him all the years I've lived in Savannah. In fact, he was one of the first colonists to greet my people and welcome us here. Your father also helped us build temporary shelters. As you know, he was one of my patients." The doctor smiled. "A cranky and contentious one at that."

"That he was. You know, it never occurred to me he might have been murdered. Nor did it occur to me he might have been one of the men who robbed the bullion. I still can't believe it."

"I understand your doubts. It's not a fact one would like to know about his father."

Morgan shook his head and smiled wryly.

"What do you find amusing?"

"My father always spoke of the pirate blood that runs in our veins. It seems the Morgans are distant relatives of the infamous pirate, Henry Morgan. At least, that's what he believed and enjoyed with great pride." Morgan paused to think. "I wonder, with what you now suspect, if he decided to follow in his footsteps and become the pirate, Matthew Morgan."

"I doubt it. I cannot imagine him taking such risks simply to be like his ancestor. He was much too practical a man." The doctor grimaced, obviously in pain, and pressed a hand over his stomach. "I fear I must ask for your help, my friend."

Morgan stood immediately. "What can I do?"

"Please get the chamber pot from my bedroom. It's clean, thanks to María Adela. I also need a kettle of hot water and some cotton strips." The doctor's eyes were full of tears.

Morgan nodded and had turned toward the bedroom when he heard a horse's hooves on the stone path outside. "Wait!" gasped the sick man. They both looked at the door. A moment later, María Adela entered the room and immediately went over to the doctor.

"Please excuse us for a few moments." The doctor grimaced from pain.

Morgan went outside and leaned against the wall. María Adela joined him a while later. She stopped him from going inside and spoke quietly, almost whispering.

"He is asleep. It often happens after one of these attacks. He's in much pain."

"How often does he have the attacks?" Morgan also

spoke softly.

"At least once every day." María Adela shook her head sadly. "He will sleep for an hour or so and then he'll awaken feeling better. Please wait. He has looked forward to your return."

"I will wait out here until then."

"I'll bring you a bowl of carrot soup; I made a pot this morning." María Adela saw him nod and went back inside the house.

Moments later, María Adela returned with an old tarnished silver tray that held two bowls of soup, a half loaf of bread, silverware and cloth napkins. Morgan held the tray, while she swept acorns and leaves off a warped pine table and wiped it dry. She also cleaned the two half-barrels used for chairs. They ate and talked about the doctor's worsened condition and then María Adela asked him about his trip to Havana. Morgan told her about his brief wedding, the sudden death of Claudia's father and her mother's unexplained illness. Afterward, as they sat in silence for a few minutes, Morgan asked about her family in St. Augustine.

"I could not find your family anywhere there. I went to the house you described north of the city, but no one was living there."

"That is so. They stayed in town until they moved on to Pensacola. When I visited them in July, my father told me they would return to the house, where we lived before the war. But he later changed his mind and they went to Pensacola. In his last letter, he told me they already had settled there. The letter came the day after you left for Florida."

"Ah, so that's why I couldn't find them. How does your family like Pensacola?"

"My father says the fishing is better – he tells me it is easier to fish in the calm waters of the gulf. At his age, it was hard for him to take a boat out through the waves at St. Augustine."

"I understand. Tell me, María Adela, did you learn to speak English in Savannah? You speak it well – like an English colonist."

"Thank you, Major Morgan. No, I learned English in St. Augustine. The doctor taught me to write English, but I learned to speak it in the house of Jesse Fish."

"Jesse Fish?" Morgan raised his eyebrows in surprise. "I met Jesse Fish in St. Augustine. How did you come to know him?"

"I worked as a criada (servant) in his house as a girl. I was ten years old when Señor Fish took me in and I worked five years there. I learned English with his children, Jesse and Phoebe. Señora Fish gave us lessons every morning. She was very kind to me and always waited until I finished my chores before beginning the lessons."

"I met the children while there. They are fine looking children."

"I'm not surprised – they were fine looking then, too." María Adela nodded, pausing to think. "Jesse must be fifteen now and Phoebe almost thirteen. They were so little then." She smiled, recalling Phoebe's giggles when she was found hiding in their games of hide and seek.

"Jesse's a big lad, now; I'm sure he will be much taller than his father. Phoebe is a very pretty girl and soon will turn the heads of all the young men in St. Augustine." Morgan looked at his pocket watch and saw that more than hour had elapsed. "Do you think the doctor might be awake now?"

"I will see." María Adela stood and opened the door a fraction to look inside. She held up her hand, signaling Morgan to wait, and tiptoed into the house. Moments later, she opened the door and waved him inside.

"Well, it seems I left you for quite a while." The doctor smiled weakly when Morgan was once again sitting beside him. He looked exhausted even after his sleep.

"Are you feeling better?" Morgan asked the question

even though he knew his sick friend would say he felt fine. He saw that María Adela had put a pillow behind the doctor's head.

"Yes, indeed. I feel much better. Well, where were we? Ah yes, we were talking about your father and I said he was a very practical man – a man whom I would never expect to risk his life or reputation to be involved in such a venture. Surely, he didn't need any more money."

Morgan shook his head. "No, I wouldn't think so. It is hard to imagine him taking such foolish risks capriciously. The more I think about it, the less it seems he would take such risks to follow a whim. There must have been some other reason for his involvement in the robbery."

"That would be my assumption. You will need to know what that reason was sooner or later. For now, let us look at the murder itself – if it's not too soon for you to talk about it."

"No. I want to know about it – as much as possible, especially if it will help me find the murderer. I want to see him hung! His death will not lessen my grief, but it will, I hope, satisfy my wish for vengeance."

"I understand. Well, then, according to Bruckmann, your father went to the outhouse that morning as usual after eating breakfast. Bruckmann said he watched him walk to the door before turning away to take his dog around the house. A moment or so later, he heard him shout for help and found him sprawled out on the ground several feet from the outhouse door. He was lying on his stomach with his breeches and underwear about his ankles. His buttocks and legs were bared and Bruckmann saw the bite marks behind his right knee. There were two of them and he tied his belt above the bites. Though certainly not a quick-witted man, he did know what to do with snakebites. The belt probably wasn't tied fast enough to save your father, but Bruckmann did the best he could for him. He carried him into the house and rode to fetch me. Bruckmann hitched up my wagon in what seemed like seconds and drove me as fast as possible to Morgan's Creek."

Morgan nodded. "It's hard to find any fault with him after all his efforts. I was suspicious of him at first, but it seems he did everything that could be expected of him."

"I agree. Bruckmann is a simple man without any affectations or subtlety. He is exactly as you find him. He was hired to watch over your father and he did that to the best of his ability. Your father told Bruckmann to guard the house day and night and accompany him wherever he went. The man carried out every one of your father's instructions and brought that big beast of a dog to make sure no one unknown came near your father or the house."

"Did Bruckmann tell you why my father hired him?"

"Your father told him there was someone who would take his life if given the chance. He said nothing more that Bruckmann remembered."

"That's all?" Morgan scowled. He had hoped his father told Bruckmann something about the man who worried him.

The doctor nodded. "Like everyone else, he thought your father's death was an accident. They all assumed the snake had somehow gotten into the outhouse at night on its own accord."

"An easy assumption to make. What about the snake bites?"

"They were three and a half inches in width, which suggests the snake was about four feet long." He showed Morgan the width between his thumb and forefinger. "A very large snake!"

Morgan shuddered. "What a thing to find in an outhouse," he thought aloud. "My poor father. Surely, he didn't deserve such a death."

"Shall we stop for now?" He saw the tears in Morgan's eyes.

"No, no. I need to know everything."

"There is nothing else I know for certain. What remains are my assumptions."

"Let me hear them, even if unpleasant." Morgan sighed. "Please continue."

"The snake, I would guess a venomous water snake, was probably curled up in the corner when your father sat down and shut the door. The snake obviously lay to the right of him."

"Why do you think it was a water snake and not a rattlesnake? There're many more of them in the woods and one killed our dog when I was a boy. I remember seeing my father cut off its head with a machete. The snake's body was at least six feet long and its head appeared to be as big as my father's hand when he held it up to show me." Morgan nodded as María Adela motioned to the teacup she handed the doctor.

"Thank you." The sick man carefully took the cup in his trembling hand. "After seeing so many snakebites over the years, I now recognize most of them. Since venomous snakes killed so many colonists when I first arrived here, they hunted them for at least six months. At my request, the hunters brought me specimens including copperheads and I studied their mouths and fangs to learn the differences. Rattlesnakes have longer fangs than the water snakes, some as long as two and a quarter inches. So, I usually can tell from seeing the bite. Though the bites on your father's leg were wide, indicating the big head of either a rattlesnake or water snake, they were not deep which told me he was struck by a water snake."

"I see." Morgan nodded his thanks to María Adela who had returned with a cup of tea.

"There is another reason why I suspect it wasn't a rattlesnake. A rattlesnake would have rattled the second the outhouse door opened. Your father then would have moved backward or, if too slow to move quickly enough, he would have been bitten on the front of his leg, not on the back of his knee. In any event, I can't imagine any situation in which he would have the time to enter the outhouse and drop his breeches and underwear before hearing the snake's rattle. It's an unforgettable sound most of us have heard at one time or other."

Morgan exhaled his breath. "So, he was unaware of the snake until it struck him."

"It appears that way. He had time to enter the outhouse, turn to sit on the wooden seat and drop his breeches and underwear. He apparently didn't see the snake or touch it with his foot – even in that confined space."

Morgan nodded.

"So, now the question is who would be able to catch and handle a water snake? I know of no one who could do it, do you?"

Morgan shook his head. "The Indians are the only ones I know who catch snakes. They hunt them for food in the winter when game is scarce."

"I have eaten snake meat myself. It's quite tasty in a stew or cooked over a fire. María Adela has made it a number of times. Isn't that right, María Adela?" The doctor looked at her over his shoulder.

"Yes." María Adela sat at the kitchen table cutting up vegetables for their evening meal.

"You have eaten snake yourself, Major Morgan, in several of the stews you have praised. A few had rattlesnake in them." She smiled at him when he turned to look at her.

"That's a surprise. I had no idea I was eating snake. I thought I was eating chicken."

"Let's continue," said the doctor. "Not only would the murderer have to catch the snake, he would have to keep it hidden somewhere near your father's house – probably in the woods. He must have kept the snake in a woven bag or box, but not for too long or it would die in the heat. It wouldn't be sensible for him to hunt for a snake the same day he planned for the killing." Morgan nodded. "No, unless he knew with certainty where and when he could capture the snake. I assume it would be possible for someone who spends a lot of time in the woods."

"There was one way to make certain the plan could be executed without such knowledge. He could have waited until the day the snake was caught and, that night, taken it to the outhouse. In that way, the snake would not have to be hidden for long nor would the murderer have to spend much time waiting in the woods."

"That's surely what happened." Morgan was glad to see the doctor so animated; he was obviously engaged and thinking about something other than his illness. "At night, there would be much less chance of being seen."

"Exactly. I assume he waited until Bruckmann's last night patrol and then moved out of the woods. At that time, there was no one to see him when he carried the snake to the outhouse. Everyone, including the dog, was asleep inside the house. The snake, left in the dark, undoubtedly did what it would do in the swamp – it curled up and awaited a way to escape the enclosure."

Morgan stared at the doctor. "So, when it was all over, the snake slithered out the open door and into the woods. What a clever fiend! It seems he thought of everything."

"Yes, the murderer thinks through every move he makes. Though his vengeance is surely conceived in hate, he hasn't let his hatred distort his thinking. His mind is firmly fixed on what must be done. The murderer knows precisely what misery his victims must suffer as they die and he makes certain they realize it."

Morgan met Bruckmann the following morning. Stockwell brought the big man into the office a few minutes after eight o'clock. He stood awkwardly in front of Morgan's desk, his odor filling the room. Stockwell remained in the doorway behind the big man. When Bruckmann was seated, the sergeant smiled and held his nose with forefinger and thumb. He saw Morgan trying to hide a smile and then quickly sidled out of the room.

"Tell me, Mr. Bruckmann, where did you serve during the war?" Morgan had moved his desk chair back against the wall to be as far away from the man as possible.

"I kämpfen (fight) at Fort Duquesne in der vest. I come hier after der var."

"What have you done since the war?" Morgan watched the big man move his hand to his scabbard and then to his empty knife sheath. Stockwell made him give up all his weapons when he entered the office. Bruckmann initially resisted until the sergeant, nearly as tall, but broader, warned him he would put him in stocks if he refused to comply with the courthouse regulations.

"I vatch das dock nacht."

"You guard the docks at night. For which shipping company?"

"I vork für Herr Douglas."

"Ah, you guard the docks of the Douglas Shipping Company."

"Ja." Bruckmann rubbed the stubble on his chin.

"How did you come to work for Mr. Morgan?"

"Herr Douglas tells mir."

"He told you to go see Mr. Morgan?"

"Ja." Bruckmann nodded his head several times.

"So you rode down to Morgan's Creek to talk to him?"

"Ja."

"What did he say?" Morgan sighed. He thought talking to Bruckmann was harder than talking to a four-year-old child.

"He vant mir to vatch him. Pay mir five shillings a day mit

essen (food) für me und mein hund, Kaiser."

"He asked you to watch over him for five shillings a day and meals for you and the dog?"

"Ja." Bruckmann sneezed and wiped his nose on the sleeve of his faded army jacket.

"Why did he want you to watch over him?"

Bruckmann looked puzzled by the question. "Vy I vatch Herr Morgan?"

"Yes, why did he pay you to watch over him?"

"He say somvon vant him tot."

"Tot?"

Bruckmann pointed down at the floor.

"In hell? Oh, I see, you mean dead! He said someone wanted him dead."

"Ja." Bruckmann was pleased with making himself understood and smiled, showing four missing teeth in his wide mouth.

"Did he say who wanted him dead?"

"Nein." Bruckmann shook his head from side to side. "He say somvon – nichts mehr."

"All he said was someone and nothing else."

"Ja."

Morgan looked at Bruckmann, realizing he would learn nothing more from the German. His father had not told him anything about the murderer. Morgan wondered if it was because he thought Bruckmann did not need to know or because he did not know himself. He answered the question as soon as it entered his mind. His father didn't know the man's identity. He knew only that someone was intent on killing him.

CHAPTER TWELVE

SAVANNAH AND CHARLES TOWNE:
WEDNESDAY, SEPTEMBER 11 – FRIDAY, SEPTEMBER 20, 1766

Morgan met with Palmer later that morning. Stockwell saw him arrive in his carriage and enter the courthouse with Thackery following at his heels. The sergeant, lingering in the hallway after Bruckmann left, watched as the attorney general struggled up the stairs. Oliver Palmer had become much heavier in the last several months and everything he wore looked stretched to the point of tearing at the seams. Now, he huffed and puffed with each step he took upward.

"His nibs just came in," Stockwell announced as he walked into Morgan's office. "He's as wide as a wine barrel, now." The sergeant immediately went to the window and opened it as far as it would go. "God, it stinks in here. You would think Bruckmann sleeps in a hog pen." He picked up a *Georgia Gazette* and, using it like a broom, tried to sweep the odor out of the room.

Morgan nodded in agreement. "Sergeant, I need you to go over to Mrs. Chapman's house and ask if I can visit her this afternoon. Tell her I'll come over at whatever time suits her. I also want you to talk to Moses, the old slave who works down at the Sterling Company dock. I think he stays there at night, probably in the stable. Make sure you speak to him without the Sterling brothers about. I want to know if he remembers when the elder Sterling was gone in the spring of 1763. If so, ask him if there was anything unusual about the man upon his return. Give him a couple of shillings and promise him Sterling's sons will never be told of your conversation."

"I'll have to wait until this evening to talk to him in private."

"That's fine. Sterling's sons leave at six o'clock at night."

"Then, I'll talk to him after they leave and when it's getting dark." Stockwell sniffed the air and nodded with satisfaction. "That's a lot better than it was with Bruckmann here."

"It is indeed. Let's meet again before you go over to the docks tonight. I want to talk to you about the murderer and what yet needs to be done to arrest him."

"Good. I want hear what you found out in Havana."

"I understand." Morgan stood and walked toward the door. "I wonder what Palmer will have to say?"

"I'll wager he 'll be less a prick now that you are master of Morgan's Creek."

Morgan smiled and walked into the hallway.

"I'm terribly sorry about the loss of your father, Major Morgan. Please accept my sincere condolences." Oliver Palmer stood as Morgan entered his office and extended his hand. He had a pained look on his face as they shook hands. "I do hope you know it was not necessary for you to come see me so soon. We can talk about your trip when it's convenient for you."

"It's convenient now. I want to continue my pursuit of the murderer as soon as possible. I want this matter resolved before I leave office."

"I am indeed happy to hear your decision."

Morgan stared blankly at Palmer, but did not reply.

"The governor and I recently spoke about the current situation and we both were worried that you might not want to finish your term of office. Of course, such a decision would be quite understandable under the circumstances. But I am indeed delighted to hear you will carry on and hope you will consider another two-year term."

Morgan tried to keep from smiling. Only a few weeks ago, Palmer had reprimanded him for his impolite remarks to the Sterling family. He could still recall his words,"Major, this is the last time I will tell you to mend your ways. I don't want to hear any more complaints about your behavior or lack of respect. As you surely know, I can replace you before the end of your term and will do so without hesitation the next time I hear one word of criticism. You only remain in the office now because of my respect for your father. However, I think you would be ill-advised to expect reappointment for another two years."

"I have no such expectations and do not want another term of office. As I've told you earlier, I only hope to arrest the murderer before leaving office."

"I recall what you said, but I hope you will reconsider your decision." Palmer waved him to the chair facing his desk. "Thackery is on his way with tea and biscuits. Ah, there he is now."

Thackery came into the room carrying a tray which he placed on Palmer's desk. "Good morning, Major Morgan. Please accept my condolences, I am very sorry for your loss."

Morgan nodded.

"We will need two more cups and plates, Thackery."

Palmer gestured to the cupboard. "Please join us; we can all have a chat over tea. I think we have more than enough biscuits."

"Yes, sir." Thackery placed the cups and plates on the desk and poured tea for everyone. He sat to the left of Morgan and passed him the plate of biscuits after Palmer had been given his on a separate plate. A jar of pear marmalade stood on the desk within everyone's reach.

"Do tell us what you discovered abroad, Major Morgan. We know from your brief letter, 'brevity is the soul of wit,' of course, that you found the source of the Spanish bullion. We also now know the murder victims were indeed involved in the robbery. As you predicted, most of our questions were answered in Havana. Well done, Major."

"Stockwell as usual knew what to expect from Palmer," thought Morgan. "Now that I'm the master of Morgan's Creek, I've suddenly become brilliant. What a weasel!" Morgan resisted the temptation to tell Palmer his contempt for him, but instead, he simply smiled. "We would not know so much if it were not for the help of the Spaniards. In fact, without their help we would still be ignorant of the robbery."

"Is that so? I must say I'm surprised."

Morgan gave the Englishmen an abridged account of his discoveries in St. Augustine and Havana, but one that emphasized the assistance of Colonel Rodríguez. He did not mention his marriage to Claudia, the death of her father or what he had learned about his own father. Except for the doctor, no one else would ever know about his father's role in the robbery. Morgan spoke only of his search for the records of the robbery in Havana. When finished speaking, he reached into his jacket pocket and produced the signed copy of the report. He handed it across the desk to Palmer, who bowed his head to Morgan.

"Splendid work, Major. You achieved everything you had

intended." Palmer opened the envelope, placed the robbery report on his desk and quickly perused the letter written by Colonel Rodríguez. "I assume you have seen the enclosed report, Major Morgan?"

Morgan nodded and picked up his teacup.

"I think then, for the purposes of this meeting, it would be helpful if you would summarize it for us now. I will read the report thoroughly later."

Morgan reviewed everything of importance in the Ramírez report and told them about the shouted words and their meaning in English. He did not bother to describe the effort involved in translating the incoherent words. Morgan doubted either of the Englishmen would be impressed with what he and Rodríguez had accomplished, although the newly appreciative attorney general might offer some insincere praise. He already found himself wincing when Palmer flattered him. Morgan almost preferred the arrogant official he had come to hate rather than the sycophant who sat beaming at him across the desk.

"So, we now know there were six robbers in the enterprise." Palmer pursed his lips. "The man named Nelson and the one who spoke Spanish, of course, are new to us, but not that villain, Willington. Though now we know with certainty he was among them."

"Yes. As Thackery's report reveals, Willington was an unscrupulous rogue well known in Charles Towne for his crimes and cruelty." Morgan turned to Thackery. "How did you learn so much about the man's criminal activities in New Hanover?"

"I went to Charles Towne and spent an entire day looking through the attorney general's records relating to New Hanover. I've been there before and know the record room quite well. There are three chests of documents pertaining to the settlement and its outlaw activities."

"Well done, Thackery." Morgan saw the little man blush

and look down at the desk.

"Yes, it was a good effort, wasn't it?" Palmer smiled benignly at his assistant. "Well, we now know Sterling, Chapman, Willington and Nelson were involved in the robbery. That leaves two others unknown. Do you know anything about this man, Nelson, except that he looks like a gentleman? I must say it is hard for me to imagine an English gentleman involved in such acts."

"No, I know nothing else." Morgan ignored Palmer's comment about English gentlemen. "To my knowledge, there is no man with that name or description in Savannah. Of course, with the arrival of so many new people every week, it's certainly possible Nelson is indeed living here and we don't know it."

"There is a register of new arrivals here in the courthouse." Thackery spoke softly. "It's compiled from the passenger records of the shipping companies. It's done once a month by an official of the House of Trade."

"Quite so." Palmer nodded, showing his awareness of the process. "Thackery will look for Nelson in the register. I suppose we should look back at least a year."

"I suggest two years to make quite sure." Morgan looked at Thackery. "Do you agree?"

"Yes, that should be sufficient. That was when new people began arriving in numbers. It was after the war, of course."

"If we can find Nelson, he could lead us to the other two robbers." Palmer wiped biscuit crumbs from his mouth with his napkin. "It may very well be that one of them is the murderer we seek. The wealth of bullion in each man's share would tempt any one of those scoundrels to add to their fortune. Such men could kill their comrades without the slightest regret."

"But…" Thackery hesitated and then continued, "by 1766, three years after the robbery, I would think much if not most of the bullion already would have been spent.

Surely, Sterling used much of his share to construct the new dock and Chapman similarly must have spent most of his share for the construction of his ship – the *Brazen*."

Palmer gave Thackery a disapproving look. He resented being contradicted by his clerk.

Morgan saw the silent reprimand and spoke up to spare Thackery any criticism. "That's true, but I'm sure Sterling didn't spend all his share on the dock or in donations to Christ Church. We know Chapman still had an abundance of coins as well as that gold ingot when he died. We don't know what Willington did with his part of the bullion, except for the contributions he made to the church. But, like the others, I doubt he spent it all before his death."

Palmer smiled, seeing the disappointed look on Thackery's face.

"However, I don't think the murderer is interested in the bullion."

"Why ever not, Major?" Palmer frowned in surprise.

"Because neither Mrs. Chapman nor Sterling's sons have come to any harm. If bullion is what the murderer seeks, he would have struck at least one of them by this time. Stockwell has kept his eye on them and they have not reported any suspicious movements about their homes or lands. There haven't been any similar concerns at the Sterling Company either. Of course, the Sterling boys wisely hired two armed men to guard the dock at night and one during the day."

"Well, where does that leave us then?" Palmer looked at his watch. "I dislike ending our meeting, but I must speak to the governor this morning."

"We still don't know the reason for the murders, though it obviously had something to do with the robbery." Morgan looked from Palmer to Thackery. "We need to find Nelson and look for any man in Savannah, who like the others, suddenly came into wealth in 1763."

Palmer looked at Thackery. "Major Morgan of course is

quite correct. You will therefore begin an investigation into both, ah, possibilities today. Leave no stone unturned."

"Yes, sir." Thackery stood and turned toward his own desk.

Palmer smiled at Morgan as he stood. "Thank you, Major, for all your diligent work in St. Augustine and Havana. We wouldn't be so far along with this murder investigation without such effort. By the way, the governor insists that you submit an expense account for your trip abroad. We want you to be properly remunerated."

Morgan rode to see Mrs. Chapman at two o'clock that afternoon. She informed Stockwell the justice would be welcomed at that time for tea. Morgan felt a cool breeze on the back of his neck and he knew autumn was on its way. He noticed the leaves on the sweet gums were starting to change color and the air about him somehow seemed fresher than before his voyage to Cuba. Morgan thought his stallion also sensed the changing season as he shook his head playfully and cantered along without any urging.

"My sister and her husband are off to the market for tonight's meal," Mrs. Chapman said as she poured Morgan a cup of tea. "I assumed you wanted to speak to me in private. Make sure you try the blackberry preserves, Major. I don't serve them to everyone, you know." She gave him a commanding look.

"Thank you, Mrs. Chapman, I will. I trust you are doing well, today." Morgan spread the preserves on one of the biscuits she had baked that morning.

"I am indeed. I miss George, of course, but I have come to enjoy my time without him. I like coming and going as I please all the time rather than only when he was at sea. And now I have made a number of changes in the garden that George surely would have disputed. With my sister and her husband here, I have all the company I need – at times too much, in fact. So, I am doing just fine. What about you? I was sorry to hear about the loss of your father."

"I'm fine, although I miss him and the time we spent together, especially in these last few years. With both my parents now gone, I somehow… seem unconnected to the world. I don't know if that makes any sense." Morgan was surprised to hear himself speak so personally to the widow, but he did not regret it when she nodded with understanding and put a comforting hand on his knee.

"It is certainly understandable and I had similar thoughts myself when my parents died as well. The death of those who bring us into the world leaves us feeling quite alone no matter who shares our life at the time – even our children."

Morgan cleared his throat, now embarrassed by what he had told her. "Well, it's time for me to explain why I asked to speak to you. And what I tell you must be kept in confidence."

"I am not a gossip, Major Morgan, and you can be assured what you say to me will never be repeated. It will remain with me alone."

Morgan nodded, believing her. For some unknown reason he trusted the plain-speaking widow and knew she would not reveal one word of what he shared with her. He paused to sip his tea and then told her most of what he knew about the murders in Savannah. Morgan did not mention his father nor did he speak of the man named Nelson.

"I must say I'm not at all surprised George was involved in the robbery. My husband was utterly dominated by greed. And, in the end, it was his greed that sent him to his death."

"It seems the others shared the captain's greed and came to the same end."

"Yes, they stupidly thought there would be no consequences to their actions. It's the way of the world, isn't it? So, Major Morgan, you now know the names of three of the victims, but lack the reason why they were so cruelly murdered?" He nodded. "You also lack the names of the other three robbers. Ah, I see. You have come to ask me if I know any of the others."

"Yes. We're at a standstill without the names of the other robbers."

"I am sorry to say that I have no knowledge of any of them – even the two who lived here in Savannah. I never met Thomas Sterling and never would have wanted to meet that vile brute Willington. God only knows why George would fall in with such a villain. He was a good man at heart. His crew thought the world of him… forgive me, Major, I am going astray."

"There's nothing to be forgiven."

Mrs. Chapman sighed. "Well, Major, I'm sorry to say I cannot help you. I know none of the others. There have been very few visitors to our home with the exception of family members and George's crew who came once each summer for a picnic. Pastor Coppinger, of course, has come to dinner with his wife, Sharon, but no one else whom I can recall. Keep in mind, Major, before George found the treasure, we lived quite frugally for many years. He did not go to sea with any regularity and his income was quite meager. We had a very trifling house budget and could not afford to entertain…" Mrs. Chapman abruptly stopped speaking and put a finger to her lips, seemingly lost in thought.

She turned her head toward the dining room, which was to the right of the sitting room. Mrs. Chapman stared into the room without speaking for several seconds. She then returned her eyes to Morgan.

"We did have one dinner guest. A man whom I expect will interest you, Major. He came shortly after we moved into this house. It was after the first of the year – in 1763."

Morgan felt his stomach tighten and he held his breath. He dreaded she would say the man was his father. Morgan waited anxiously, too worried to speak.

Martha Chapman smiled, remembering the evening and the pleasure she had entertaining a guest in her new home. "The man was an English gentleman. His accent and his fine clothes made me think he was an aristocrat. I recall his lace shirt and silver handled walking stick. Oh yes, and he wore a dashing hat with a long white feather."

Morgan let out his breath slowly hoping she would not notice. "Do you recall his name, Mrs. Chapman?"

She bit her upper lip in thought. "Yes, I do recall his name – it was Nelson. A handsome man! I remember him now – William Lyman Nelson. His name had a melodic quality about it. He was quite charming and spoke upper class English. You know, he said 'rahsberry' instead of 'raspberry.' George and I were delighted to entertain such a fine man in our home. He brought us a costly bottle of Sherry which we sparingly consumed in the weeks that followed."

"By any chance, do you remember where he lived?" Morgan tried to inquire in a matter-of-fact tone, but it was futile. He could see it in her twinkling eyes and tiny smile that suddenly appeared. She knew he had come to find out where Nelson lived.

Martha Chapman pointed her forefinger at Morgan. "So, Nelson was one of them, wasn't he? You knew his name all along, you rascal!" She smiled broadly and Morgan nodded. "Well then, Major Morgan, I think you need to tell me what you know about the cunning gentleman named Nelson."

Morgan drank the rest of his tea. He raised his hand to stop her as she picked up the teapot. "I've had quite enough tea for now, thank you, Mrs. Chapman. I learned about Nelson in a report of the robbery I read in Havana." Morgan described the robbery in detail and told her how he and

Rodríguez had deciphered the final words included in the report.

Morgan reached into his pocket and brought out a folded piece of paper. He unfolded the paper and handed it to her. Morgan had written the unintelligible words from the robbery report on the paper along with the translation. The letters appeared exactly as they had been written by the Spanish officer. Morgan knew he would not forget the shouted words as long as he lived.

"Very impressive, Major." Martha Chapman smiled after studying the line of letters and the English sentence they represented. "Yes, indeed – quite clever." She cocked her head to the side as if looking at Morgan for the first time. "I now can see there is a fine mind lurking beneath that scowling face."

Morgan smiled and then laughed out loud. "Thank you Mrs. Chapman, I assume that was a compliment. Well, do you know where Nelson lives?"

"No, Nelson never did mention where he lived. But… he did discuss horse racing with George and I think he said something about running his horses at a track in Charles Towne."

Morgan was on the road to Charles Towne early the next morning. He hoped to reach the old colonial city in three days. Even riding his big stallion, he knew the seventy-five mile trip would require two nights on the road. He did not look forward to sleeping on the ground, but his horse could not cover more than thirty miles a day. With clear weather, Morgan hoped he could reach Charles Towne by noon on the third day. Both he and his horse would be exhausted by that time no matter how he alternated trotting and walking with periods of rest. Fortunately, he stopped at a farmer's house and slept in a bed his second night on the road. The house was only eleven miles from Charles Towne and he had stayed there with his father three years earlier.

Morgan decided to make the long trip to find Nelson rather than write the Charles Towne justice for information. He was too impatient to wait a week or more for a response. If he found Nelson, Morgan hoped the man could be persuaded to answer his questions. There was so much he needed to know and Nelson was one of the only two robbers left who could help him. He had no idea where the other man who spoke Spanish, might be found so Nelson had to be his source of information. It was also possible the so-called English gentleman himself was the murderer.

Morgan had made a mental list of questions he intended to ask him and he repeated them to himself as he rode along. Most important, he wanted to know who murdered his father as well as the three other men. If Nelson appeared to be innocent of the killings, Morgan hoped he knew the murderer's name or at least whom he suspected. He also hoped to learn the reason for all the murders. His mind awhirl with the many other questions he wanted to ask Nelson, Morgan was unaware his saddle's cinch strap had slipped loose until the saddle shifted beneath him.

Morgan stopped briefly to tighten the loose strap and, for those few minutes, his mind was focused on his task. But as soon as he remounted his stallion, his thoughts returned to the murders and the seemingly endless quest for a murderer whose identity remained unknown. As Morgan urged his horse to a trot, he wondered if the man would ever be known.

Whoever the murderer might be, his intense hatred for the robbers had provoked him to kill them with a cruelty that shocked him even after the carnage he had seen in the war. Morgan could not imagine what terrible atrocity they had committed to deserve so much suffering before they died. Whatever had happened to infuriate the murderer to such a vengeance, he could not believe his father had been party to something so heartless. It had been hard enough for him to acknowledge his father had robbed the bullion caravan, never mind consider the possibility he had committed some appalling act as well. But, believe it or not, he had to admit his father had been killed as mercilessly as the others. As the doctor had said, "The murderer knows precisely what misery his victims must suffer and, as they die, he makes certain they realize it."

Morgan knew Nelson would not answer any of his questions unless he was arrested. The Englishman might have been forthcoming in the presence of Stockwell, but he had not asked the big sergeant to accompany him. The severe pain in the sergeant's wounded leg had worsened over the years and he would have suffered too much on the long ride to Charles Towne. Morgan's only way to question Nelson would be to have him arrested at his home and taken under armed guard to the courthouse. For such an act, Morgan needed the assistance of the town's justice and, with that in mind, he carried an arrest warrant for Nelson signed by the attorney general in Savannah. Oliver Palmer dutifully prepared the warrant before leaving his office on the previous afternoon.

Morgan did not arrive in Charles Towne until after sunset on the third day. He had been delayed by taking a long detour around a washed-out portion of the road. Hungry and exhausted, Morgan stayed in the first inn he reached in town. He overpaid the toothless stableman to make sure his stallion was given good care and then knocked on the door to the inn. The innkeeper, a bald man smelling of beer, admitted Morgan and served him stale bread and hard cheese before he went to bed. He slept until eight o'clock the following morning and, after eating a hurried but tasty breakfast in a nearby tavern, he rode over to the courthouse. Morgan grimaced in pain as he dismounted in front of the two-story wooden building. His good shoulder ached from holding the reins for so many hours the day before.

The justice's office was much larger and better furnished than Morgan's austere quarters in Savannah. It even included an anteroom where a wigged and well-dressed clerk sat primly at a small reception desk. He was a youth whose pale skin was marred by acne on both cheeks. The lad looked him over cursorily and Morgan knew he had been found wanting. Even with the new clothes tailored for him before his trip to Cuba, he did not look like one of the well-attired army officers or wealthy English gentleman who came to see the justice.

"How may we be of service to you, sir?" The clerk looked briefly at Morgan and, hearing no immediate reply, returned his eyes to the *South Carolina Gazette* on his desk. He made no attempt to get up from his chair and greet Morgan politely.

"You cannot be of any service to me, young man." Morgan glared at him with unwavering eyes. "I'm here to see Justice Richardson. Now, get up off your arse and inform him that Major James Morgan, the justice from Savannah, is here to see him."

"Y-yes, sir." The young man, his eyes open wide, jumped up from his chair and knocked on the door to his superior's office. His hand trembled as he knocked.

Moments later, Morgan sat across from Richardson in his office. They sat in two stuffed chairs to the side of the justice's elegant mahogany desk. The room was furnished with a portrait of King George, several colorful oriental tapestries and a red, blue and brown rectangular Persian rug. Morgan thought the room looked more like a parlor than the office of a crown official.

"I'll have Nelson brought here forthwith, Major," Richardson said after Morgan told him the reason for his visit. Nathaniel Richardson was a tall stooped man with a pale face and striking blue eyes. He wore a blue velvet suit, an impeccably clean white shirt and a perfectly fitted wig. Everything about Richardson suggested a strict commitment to tidiness.

"Here is the warrant for his arrest." Morgan handed him the sealed envelope.

"I'm sure it's all in order." Richardson opened the envelope. He read the enclosed letter from Palmer and only glanced at the warrant. "I know Oliver Palmer. As I'm sure you're aware, Palmer served Attorney General Wright here in Charles Towne before Sir James was appointed governor of Georgia. He was a hard working and very ambitious man."

"His ambitions have not lessened any in Savannah, I can assure you."

"I'm not surprised." Richardson smiled, showing a full set of teeth. "Well, let's get this man Nelson before us." He walked to the closed door and opened it to the anteroom. "Conway, I need you to go to the record room."

"Yes, sir."

"Find the home of William Lyman Nelson and send some men to arrest him. I want him brought here as soon as possible."

Morgan and Richardson were discussing the rumors of new English taxes for the colonies when Conway knocked on the door a half hour later. "Please excuse me." The justice stood and went to the door where Conway waited.

"William Nelson is dead, sir."

"Come in, Conway, and tell us what you found." Richardson turned to Morgan. "Well, it appears you rode to Charles Towne in vain."

"So it seems." Morgan slumped back in his chair as

Conway entered the office. "All for naught," he thought. "Damn, now I'm left without anyone who knows about the robbery."

Conway stood self-consciously before the two seated men and started to read from a fire report he held in his hand. "On the night of July 21, at 11:45…"

Richardson sighed impatiently. "For God's sake, Conway, don't read the report word for word. Bring that stool over here and tell us what it says in your own words."

"Yes, sir." Conway took the stool from beside Richardson's desk and set it down so he would face both men. His hand shook as he held the report up close to his eyes.

"Can you see well enough there?" Richardson turned to look at Morgan. "Conway needs spectacles, but is too vain to use them. He thinks none of the young girls here will show him any interest if he wears them. Isn't that correct, Conway?"

"Yes, sir." Conway's face reddened. "I haven't read it before, sir, so I must read it word for word."

Richardson frowned. "All right, Conway, let's hear it."

On July 21 of this year, the fire brigade went to the home of William Lyman Nelson and found it in flames. They arrived too late to save the house or anyone inside. The loud noise of the collapsing roof awakened his neighbors, but by the time they notified the fire brigade, the entire building was aflame. No one could get close enough to throw water on it and those watching in the street said there was no use trying. The house was too far gone and within minutes the walls fell into the fire. The stable also burned, but the horses were pastured elsewhere."

"What about Nelson and the other occupants of the house?" asked Richardson.

"He lived alone. There was no one else in the house. His remains were found the next day and it was believed he had been trapped in his bedroom and could not escape out the window or down the stairs. Nelson smoked a pipe and it was assumed he fell asleep with it still lit…"

"Of course, that's how our summer fires start." Richardson sighed. "Some fool drinks too much and falls asleep on his bed with a lighted pipe in his hand. The embers fall from the pipe's bowl onto the bedding and the man burns to death. It's all too typical here."

Conway looked up from the report. "A neighbor saw Nelson going home that night from the *White Stallion*. He was singing loudly, walking unsteadily and obviously drunk."

"Was he the Nelson whose horses run in the races?"

"Yes, sir." Conway laid the report on his lap.

"Those horses are splendid beasts and often win the races here. I wonder who will own them now?" Richardson thought of the possibility of purchasing the stallion and running him in the spring races. "Is there anything else pertinent in the report, Conway?"

"Only some comments by his neighbors, sir."

"And what were those?" Richardson made a face. "I have little regard for the gossip of neighbors. There's always some old woman in an upstairs window that watches the street like a hawk and, of course, sees every petty sin below her. God help the young couple that holds hands within her sight. But do go on, Conway."

"Yes, sir. It seems that Mr. Nelson hired a carpenter to install a variety of bolts and locks on his doors as well as new latches on the windows and shutters. He then closed and locked up his house for quite some time before the fire. He…"

"Why did that deserve commentary? I assume he closed the house and went on a trip."

"No, sir, that's what was strange – he did not leave. He continued to live in the closed-up house despite the terrible heat of last July. He did venture outside, but only now and then. When he did go outside, Mr. Nelson went on foot since his horses had been moved to a farmer's barn at the edge of town. The farmer's son was paid to feed and exercise the horses; Mr. Nelson owned five horses, a costly stallion, two mares and two colts. He told his nearest neighbor, a Mr. Homer Adkins, he moved his horses to the farm to give them more exercise. However, Mr. Adkins said before that time, Nelson was known to ride a horse each day for at least an hour. He rode his big stallion at least every other day."

"I say that was odd." Richardson looked perplexed.

"What would be the cost of a stallion like Nelson's?" asked Morgan.

"I'm not an authority on horse flesh, Major, but I would think that stallion, a superb racing horse, is easily worth a thousand pounds or more. His high value is not simply because of his speed and the money that can be made from him at the races; it's also because of his splendid good looks. I myself have wagered on that big beast a time or two and made a tidy sum on each occasion. Is there anything in addition in the report, Conway?"

"One more thing, sir. When Mr. Nelson did leave his house during the day, he was seen wearing a jacket. Even in the midday sun! One of the neighbors thought he suffered from some illness that cooled his bones. Another thought he was hiding an ugly growth that protruded from his side. A third said the intense heat had made a madman of him…"

"That's quite enough, Conway. The next thing we will hear is that Nelson was blighted by a vengeful witch. You see what we put up with here in Charles Towne, Major." He sighed. "So what do you think of Nelson's odd behavior?"

"It appears Nelson was afraid of something or someone."

"That's my thinking, too. The bolts and locks make it look that way. I also think Nelson was armed when he went into the streets and he wore a jacket to hide his weapons."

"I agree." Morgan looked at Conway. "Is there anything in the report to suggest that the fire was not accidentally started?"

"N-no, sir. The captain of the fire brigade said the fire appeared to be 'set by accident by a known pipe s-smoker.'" Conway stammered as he spoke to Morgan. "Would you like the street location of his house, Major Morgan?"

"No. What I would like is a list of the names of those sentries who guarded the city gates on the night of July 21." Morgan turned to Richardson. "Would that be possible, sir?"

"Of course. Good thinking, Major Morgan. You want to know if someone suspicious or unknown to the sentries entered or left Charles Towne that night. It all does look odd, doesn't it? I'll write a letter to the captain of the guards and ask his permission for you to talk to the sentries. While Conway takes the letter to the captain, we can have a spot of tea and you can tell me more about William Lyman Nelson."

Morgan spoke to five sentries before he found one soldier who remembered that summer night in July. He met Colin Delaney at a dingy tavern called *Ye Ale House*. The tavern stood a street away from the gates that opened to the road leading south to Savannah. The major bought the short unshaven Irishman several glasses of ale and a lunch of rabbit stew.

"So, you're sure you remember the night of July 21?" Morgan had waited while Delaney devoured his stew and downed two glasses of ale. The man ate every morsel of the stew and then picked up the bowl and drank the remaining soup at the bottom. After wiping his greasy mouth and chin on his shirtsleeve, he finished the ale. The major ordered another as Delaney banged the empty glass down hard on the table.

"Ah, it was a fine meal, Major. Thanks be to you."

"I'm glad you liked it, Delaney." Morgan saw the sentry's eyes shift to the tavern owner, who was pouring his next glass of ale. "You said you remembered that night because of an odd man who passed through the gates. Is that correct?"

"Aye, I do recall that night. Aye, quite clearly indeed." Delaney nodded and reached for the glass on the table.

Morgan stopped his hand and gripped his wrist tightly. "You'll get the ale when you tell me all you know." He squeezed the man's wrist harder and cut off the circulation.

"That hurts," whined Delaney, trying to free his hand from the vice-like grip. He gave up when he saw Morgan's narrowed eyes and stony face.

"Now, it's time for you to tell me what you recall. Do you understand, Delaney?"

"Yes, sir." He grimaced, feeling his fingers becoming numb.

"Good. I need to know what you remember about the lone man who passed through the gate late that night." Morgan released his wrist. "You said there was something odd about him. What was it?"

"It was a long time ago, sir. Hard to recall." Delaney massaged his tingling fingers with his other hand. "But I do recall the fellow leaving town that night. I had the late duty. Starts at ten and goes to eight in the morning. I seen him coming from town about midnight. Could have been a bit earlier or later – I don't know for sure."

"Even though you're not sure of the time, you know it was late at night?" Morgan stared at him. "Is that right?"

"Yes, sir. It was a quiet night and no one else took the road that late. I recall now he come out of the dark on me all of a sudden." Delaney looked about to see if anyone he knew was in the tavern. "I must have dozed a moment or two I guess." He smiled, showing Morgan a mouth with more than half his yellowed teeth missing. "You'll not be telling them that I hope, Major."

Morgan shook his head. "I'm not interested in what you were doing before the man rode up to the gate. I want to know what happened when he arrived."

"Yes, sir. As I said, he come out of the dark – I smelled him before I seen him…"

"You smelled him before you saw him? What smell did he have?"

"He smelled smoky like he'd been eating over a fire."

"I see. What else happened?"

"He said not a word and pointed to the gate so I let him out – no reason not to. Then the lad was gone, he was."

"Why do you call him a lad? Was he that young?"

"I don't know. He wore a cloak with a hood and I never seen his face. Seemed odd to me. It was hot as Hades that night."

"So, if you never saw his face, what made you think he was young – a lad?"

"I don't know." Delaney shook his head. "Don't know – he just seemed a lad."

"Was he small like a boy?"

"No, he looked to be about my size."

Morgan frowned. "Do you recall what he was wearing besides the hooded cloak?"

"No, sir." Delaney gave Morgan a pleading look.

"Go ahead, drink the ale, but don't think you'll get away without telling me the rest of it."

"Yes, sir." Delaney downed half the ale in three swallows.

"What about his horse? Was there anything unusual about him?"

"No, sir, not that I recall. Could have been a small horse. Aye, he rode a small horse."

Morgan studied Delaney, who already had finished the ale. He doubted the description of the horse. He suspected the sly little man was simply trying to come up with something to keep the ale coming. "Is there anything else that you recall about the hooded man?"

"Let me think." Delaney's eyes looked bloodshot and bleary from all the ale he had drunk that day. He had finished off three pints before Morgan arrived. "There's a thing I can tell you, but you can't be telling a soul about it." He smiled crookedly. "Can I count on you, Major?"

"Yes. Whatever you tell me will not be repeated in Charles Towne."

Delaney belched loudly and smiled. "Aye, it was a good rabbit stew. I thank you."

Morgan said nothing and waited for Delaney to continue.

"Well then, Major, it's kind of a practice at the gates for them that pass through to give the sentry a coin or two. The officers know nothin' about it, but the sergeants take a portion. At night, we get to keep most of what we take in. They don't know how much we get from them few riders that come and go in the night." Delaney smiled again, showing his stained teeth. "Well, now, the lad passed though like all the others and put a coin in my palm and when I look at it in the guard house, I see it's silver. I can't read, but I knowed the crown of Spain when I see it. The moneychanger gave me six shillings for it and told me it was a King Charles coin."

"The king's name was Carlos."

"That's it – King Carlos. I seen one or two of them coins before."

"So, the lad gave you a silver coin." Morgan had used the coins in Havana and knew they had been minted in Mexico and Peru. He pictured one of the coins with Spain's shield of Castile and Leon imprinted on one side along with the king's name, Carlos II. "Tell me, Delaney, what was on the coin?"

Delaney scratched his chin. "Castles and lions and something else—aye, a cross."

"Castles and lions separated by a cross?"

"Yes, sir. The castles and lions was just that way – on each side of the cross."

Morgan nodded, knowing Delaney had been given a Spanish peseta. "The lad never said a word even when he gave you the coin?"

"No, sir. Not even when I said, 'May the wind be always at your back.'"

"You expected him to reply, 'Until we meet again.'"

"Yes, sir. I did expect that. But he says nothin' and just rides off, he does. Major, I'd be obliged if you would order me one more glass for the road."

Morgan sighed and signaled the tavern owner for another ale. "Before I leave, I want you to think what it was about the man that made you believe he was young and a lad?"

Delaney blinked his eyes and looked up at the ceiling. "There was something about him, but for the life of me, I can't recall what it was. He looked to be a lad. That's all I can tell you."

"One more question and you better tell me the truth." Morgan glared at him. "Were you drinking that night, the night you saw the hooded rider?"

Delaney shrugged. "I might have had one or two glasses at the time."

After Morgan left, Delaney remained in the tavern to drink the last of his ale. As he tilted the glass to his mouth, he recalled what had made him think the rider was a lad. "It was that small boot in the stirrup," he said aloud. "That's what it was, sure and begorra."

Morgan was exhausted when he walked into his office on Friday morning. He arrived at 9:30 after a poor night's sleep, awakening every time he shifted in bed. Morgan had ridden from dawn to dusk on his last day on the road and his entire body ached from the effort. Though he had stopped periodically to rest his horse as well as himself, he was exhausted when he finally reached Savannah. Every muscle seemed to hurt whenever he moved, especially those in his legs and thighs after riding his big horse so many hours. Worst of all, his bad shoulder throbbed even when he did nothing. On Friday morning, Morgan was still in pain and walked, rather than rode, to the courthouse. He winced as he eased himself down into his chair.

"A long ride, wasn't it? I know I couldn't do it no more." Stockwell shook his head.

"It seemed endless. I haven't ridden that far since we returned from Fort Frontenac. And that's seven years ago. I'm bone-tired as they say. I can hardly put my legs together and my arse feels like I've been spanked for an hour."

"That's the price you pay for getting old. You're forty now and it's a 'step by step walk to your grave' as my ol' dad would say."

"I suppose so. Any mail?"

"Nothing as yet. Thackery's waiting as well. I saw him in the hall a while ago. He looks quite the lil' lord. Got himself some new suits made. He's been strutting about these days in a lot of new clothes. He must of inherited some money."

"That must be it. I doubt Palmer would raise his salary."

"A tailor must have had remnants from a suit he made for a rich man's boy." Stockwell laughed loudly at his own joke. "But whatever Thackery wears, he's still a lil' weasel, afeared of his own shadow."

Morgan smiled. "Would you go see if there's any mail now? I should have heard from Claudia by now."

Stockwell paused and turned as he reached the door. "I haven't as yet found my way to talk to Moses. They had him doing something at their house these past few days."

"There's no hurry. Do it when you can."

"Nothin' from Claudia," Stockwell said, when he returned from the mail container in the assembly hall. "But here's a letter from Colonel Rodríguez in Havana." He handed Morgan the envelope and sat down at his desk.

Morgan saw the colonel's name on the envelope and his family's shield in the red sealing wax. He peeled the edges away from the seal and opened the envelope. A four-page letter was folded inside.

Major James Morgan
Justice of the Peace, Parish of Christ Church
Savannah, Province of Georgia

Esteemed Major Morgan,

I am writing to inform you of the contents of the report attached to the salvage records of the Nuestra Señora de la Soledad. The report is titled "The Attack on the Village of San Isidro" and was written April 26, 1763. Lieutenant José Valdez Herrera wrote the report two days after the attack. The contents of the report are summarized in my own words, herein.

San Isidro was a Yamassee Indian village founded by the Franciscans in the seventeenth century. The little village was located six miles northwest of San Agustín on a tributary of the Río San Juan. The settlement was established for those Indians who converted to Christianity. Under the helpful guidance of the Franciscans, the Indians of San Isidro lived in peace and raised their crops. Though attacked by English forces in 1702 and 1740, the pueblo survived until La Florida was transferred to England in the Treaty that ended the last war.

On April 24, 1763, in the late afternoon, a band of five or six armed horsemen rode into the village from the pine forest to the south; the number of brigands was disputed by those few observers who saw them come and go. During the attack at San Isidro, they set fire to three of the houses and killed one family, including all four of the children. The families of the other two nearby houses escaped into the woods. The villagers armed themselves with bows and arrows and gathered together behind wagons they hastily pulled together at the far side of the village. They rolled barrels and stacked boxes beside the wagons to make a barricade. The villagers expected to be attacked, but, to their relief, they were ignored. The asesinos never even approached the barricade or any of the other ten houses. Nor did they ride away with any of their animals or possessions. While the three houses burned, they rode away through the woods to the north.

During the attack, one villager rode to San Agustín for help and a squad of soldiers hurried north on foot to the settlement. The king's cavalry, at the time, was searching for the robbers of the bullion caravan. Lieutenant José Valdez Herrera and a squad of soldiers from the Castillo arrived at dusk, but, by then, the bandits had ridden away. A Franciscan by the name of Brother Jerome accompanied the squad and prayed over the remains of the family as they were buried. It was too late for the soldiers to pursue the raiders that night, but a detachment of thirty cavalry troops rode to the village the next day and followed their tracks to the Río San Juan. An officer, Captain José Jiménez de Mosquera, assigned to the salvage of the Nuestra Señora de la Soledad, accompanied the cavalrymen.

They found the place where the raiders spent the night before crossing the river. There were marks in the ground indicating that rafts had been used to carry the murderers and their horses across the river. The detachment searched the site and one of the soldiers found a silver coin in the shallows where the rafts had been tied up. Captain Jiménez de Mosquera recognized the coin as one salvaged from the Nuestra Señora de la Soledad.

The Indian tracker who guided the detachment said the shoe prints they followed showed six horses ahead of them. That number was confirmed by a boy who counted six riders entering the village. However, a hunter in the woods saw them riding north and said there were only five horsemen; the hunter did see a sixth horse, but he said it was laden with canvas bags. He noticed one man at the head of the line of horsemen because he wore a hat adorned with a white feather.

The murdered family included a Mestizo named José Vargas, his Indian wife, Isabella, a fifteen-year-old girl, María, a fourteen-year-old-boy, Fernando, a six-year-old boy, Carlos, and a ten-week-old baby boy named Felipe. Brother Jerome said the baby had been baptized only a week earlier. The raiders also killed the family's dog, their three hogs and a cow.

A boy from one of the neighbors, the Fuentes family, disappeared during the attack. The two families on either side of the Vargas family's house fled into the woods when the armed men arrived. It was believed that the missing boy, Francisco, had run into the woods and would soon return home. He was thirteen, but not yet confirmed. His father said the boy knew the way of the woods and would make his way back to the village in good time.

Lieutenant Valdez Herrera interviewed everyone who saw the raiders. He arrived in San Isidro the next day and spent the afternoon talking to the villagers. From what they told him, he concluded the asesinos were English, wore colonists' clothing and rode costly horses. Their fine boots were noticed by everyone. They covered their faces with blue bandannas. One man stood out because of a white feather in his hat. The raiders were well armed, each with a pistol and a sword. Three of the men also had muskets hung on their saddles. Poorly armed with bows and arrows, the cautious villagers did not dare attack the armed men during the day. They planned a night assault, but the pillagers were gone well before dark.

No one saw the family murdered, but everyone heard their screams of pain. One woman said the screams filled the air and they shivered listening to them. They assumed José Vargas was tortured and the woman and young girl were raped. When the screams finally ended, they knew the family was dead. Moments later, they saw smoke rise from the Vargas house followed by flames. They then saw the demonios set fire to the two nearby houses. The flames and thick smoke kept the villagers from seeing anything else. They waited with their weapons ready for a long while before anyone left the barricade to look at the devastated houses. Since no one had a timepiece, the Indians were unsure of how long they waited, fearing an attack.

The fire burned too fiercely for anyone to attempt a rescue inside the house even if one of the Vargas family was still alive. They could only stand a distance away and watch the last of the fire consume the building. Most of the villagers did not stand there long. The stench of burning flesh drove them away. They returned to the barricade and waited for the soldiers from San Agustín. By that time, the two families who fled into the woods had emerged from their hiding places and joined their neighbors at the barricade.

The report included nothing else that would interest you. Of course, it clearly indicates the robbers of the bullion caravan were the same men who murdered the Vargas family and set fire to the houses in San Isidro. The question is, what was the purpose of the raid? It seems unlikely there was anything of value in the house of the Vargas family. If the diablos were seeking other spoils, why did they ignore the other houses in the village? They surely had no fear of the poorly armed Indians.

I can understand why the raiders rode west around San Agustín rather than take the road directly north toward Savannah. It would have been foolish to ride anywhere near the presidio. But why did they pause at San Isidro, instead of riding as fast as possible away from the Spanish presidio and its troops? They must have known the cavalry would pursue them. So, why waste time tormenting the Vargas family or burning houses in the village? It defies all reason.

What does emerge from the vicious killings is the probable explanation for the murders in Savannah. It appears that someone who had affection for one or all of the Vargas family has set out to avenge the murders. What has befallen the three men in Savannah and, perhaps, Nelson as well, is therefore, quite understandable. I think the murderer either witnessed the slaughter of the Vargas family or somehow knew the men who committed the terrible killings. He then must have followed them to Savannah and exacted his vengeance. Why he waited three years to dispose of them is another question I cannot answer. But, by this time, I suspect he has killed them all or will very soon unless you can identify the other diablos and the murderer himself.

I trust this report helps you in your search for the murderer. I will look to that end and await notice of such results with eagerness.

The entire sentence of the robber's shout has come into my mind. It appeared to me one morning as I awoke from sleep. You may very well have translated it by this time, but if not I am including my version. "Hurry up Willington, Nelson says the patrol is on the way."

It may amuse you to know that a number of higher ranked and titled officers here studied the words and concluded they were incomprehensible. One said that Ramírez made up the words in an endeavor to obtain a promotion. The commander of the Castillo de San Marcos did indeed promote Ramírez to sergeant after hearing his testimony at the crown's inquiry in 1763. Quien sabe, perhaps, there are just rewards to be found in the king's service after all.

Atentamente,
Juan Rodríguez y Rivera, Colonel
Fourth Infantry Regiment of Havana
His Catholic Majesty's Colony of Cuba
September 7, 1766

"It is almost over now. One more obligation remains and it must be honored. That time will soon come and then all will be ended. These past three years here have passed so slowly and now everything seems to be moving so quickly; at times, I think too quickly. It will all be over within the month. He has told me so."

CHAPTER THIRTEEN

SAVANNAH:
TUESDAY, SEPTEMBER 17 –
WEDNESDAY, SEPTEMBER 18, 1766

Stockwell met Moses Thursday night at the office of Sterling Shipping Company. At five o'clock, the sergeant rode to River Street and watched the company office from a tavern across the road. The tavern, *The Seven Seas*, was little more than a drafty plank shack with a bar and four scarred tables. He sat drinking beer at a sticky table that faced the one dirty window in the shack. The window was streaked with grime, but Stockwell could see well enough through a small clear section in the glass.

As time passed, several seamen the sergeant knew sat and drank with him as he watched for activity at the office. At 6:15, he saw Luke and Mark Sterling emerge from their office and walk away. Stockwell assumed the brothers were on their way home, but he waited an hour to be sure they did not return. He left the tavern when it was dark and, then, crossed the road when no one appeared to be about. He walked his horse a few yards from *The Seven Seas* and crossed at a spot where the rotted beams of a dilapidated building littered that side of the street. At Sterling's building, Stockwell tied his horse on the north side beside the stable gates.

Entering the gates, he found Moses sitting in a small room at the back of the stable. The room had once been a horse's stall, but had been painted with what Stockwell assumed was left over whitewash from the company office. Its furniture included a dented sea chest, a rough handmade chair and table and an old door that served as a bed. The bed had a straw mattress covered with sacking and one stuffed pillow that looked like it had once been on a bed in the home of the Sterlings. To his surprise, Stockwell noticed that the bed had sheets and a pillowcase. There was also a stuffed pillow on the chair and a tarnished brass oil lamp on the table.

The lamp wick had been set at its lowest point, providing only enough light to illuminate the table. A worn logbook lay on the table along with a quill and pot of ink. Moses looked up guiltily from the logbook and stood as soon as Stockwell entered the room.

"Yassuh." Moses and bowed his head. The man's eyebrows and hair were totally white.

"Sit, Moses. I'm not here to bother you. You're not in any trouble. I only want to ask you a question or two. I'll be here and gone in less than a blink of your eye."

Moses nodded, but did not sit. He had been warned never to sit in front of a white man.

"Nobody knows I'm here and nobody will ever know. Do you understand?"

"Yassuh." Moses stood with his head bowed, averting his eyes away from Stockwell.

"Masters Mark and Luke will never know I was here. Do you take my meaning?"

"Yassuh." Moses looked away, a twitch prominent in the

side of his face.

"I want to know if you remember when old Mr. Sterling went away three or so years ago. Not Mark or Luke, but their father. He was gone for ten days or so. Do you remember?"

Stockwell spent almost an hour with Moses. It took him half that time to assure the slave that his masters would never know he had spoken to the sergeant. The rest of the time was spent struggling to get him to say more than, "Yassuh" or "nossuh." Stockwell left the stable at ten o'clock after pressing three shillings in his hand. Moses initially refused the money, stubbornly shaking his head, and only accepted it when the big man squeezed his arm and forced him to take it.

"The man has a head as hard as a paving stone," he told Morgan the next morning. "He never would hold out his hand for the money – I had to make him take it."

"Moses may be stubborn, but he gave you some useful information. We now know that Sterling returned from St. Augustine with bulging saddlebags and a heavy bundle. The bundle was tied with rope and wrapped in canvas exactly as the Spanish soldier reported."

"It was the bars in the bundle, I'd wager. They couldn't fit many bars in the saddlebags, so they filled them with coins. Sterling had both and he told Moses 'to leave them be, I'll take care of everything.'"

Morgan smiled. "Of course, Sterling didn't want anyone, even his slave, to know he had the bullion."

"That's right. Moses said it surprised him since Sterling never lifted or carried a thing if he could help it. In fact, he often said, 'A mind makes money, not a body.'"

Morgan nodded. "I don't doubt it. I've seen him after assembly meetings with someone carrying his papers and personal possessions."

"A fat man he was with big belly. You couldn't miss him

in that purple suit; he looked like an over-ripe pear."

Morgan smiled. "The old slave has a good memory. He also sketches, you said."

"That he does and they look good to me. Mrs. Sterling saw to it that he got paper, quills and ink to do his drawings. She also gave him old house things as well. Moses had an oil lamp and even sheets on his bed. He told me she asked him for a couple of his sketches of ships at sea and put them on the kitchen wall."

"I'll have to look at his work one of these days. Was there anything else Moses told you about Sterling's return that day?"

"I almost forgot. Moses said Sterling's horse was sweating hard from the heavy load he carried. He also limped in with a loose shoe. He said the stallion looked burned out, but did get better over time. It was the same horse that Sterling took to the lake the day he got killed."

"What about Sterling?" Morgan watched Stockwell pick at a hangnail. "Did Moses say anything about how he looked when he arrived?'

"He did. He said Sterling looked pale and scared, like he had seen a ghost. Moses said he had little to say for days. It was something unusual since he talked most of the time."

"It's no wonder. He had seen the slaughter of the Indian family in San Isidro. Though he and Chapman were both involved in the bullion robbery, I doubt they had anything to do with the murders. Willington would be the one I would most suspect was the murderer of that family."

Morgan also doubted his father had anything to do with those murders. His father would never have killed anyone unless his own family was threatened. He was a softhearted man who disliked killing of any kind. Matthew even had trouble ending the lives of his old and sick dogs.

He fished for food, but avoided hunting. He depended on his Indian neighbors to barter meat for his family's needs during the first years at Morgan's Creek and later encouraged his sons to hunt when they were old enough. In the last decade of his life, he avoided meat entirely and ate only fish or stews made with seafood. "No, my father had nothing to do with the murders," Morgan said to himself.

"I'm surprised Sterling was there at all – even with his need for money. I can't imagine him riding a horse so far, never mind robbing the bullion. It's a miracle he didn't have a heart attack on the road somewhere."

"It is. He must have been desperate for the money. So were they all. Sterling for a new bigger dock, Chapman for his own ship, Willington perhaps to buy himself a place in heaven and Nelson for who knows what? Maybe more race horses?" Morgan wondered what had made his father, one of the wealthiest planters in the province, join the band of robbers. He shook his head, bewildered that his father had been involved at all.

"I heard it said that greedy men never have enough, even if rich."

"That may be true."

Morgan left the courthouse and rode to the home of his father's lawyer, Clarence Blake. He had delayed the meeting long enough and knew it was time to settle his father's affairs and read his final will. Blake lived in St. James Square only a few houses away from the Sterling mansion, but in a much smaller and modest house. Morgan noted that the house needed a fresh coat of paint as well as the replacement of a number of rotted planks above the door.

The lawyer himself answered Morgan's knock and invited him inside his house. They sat in Blake's sparsely furnished office, which included a stained cylinder desk, an old desk chair and two straight-backed chairs for his clients. There was also a worn rug on the floor and a coat rack that tilted to one side. The room had whitewashed walls without decorations of any kind.

Morgan recalled his father telling him that Blake had plenty of land and money, but went about his law practice in faded and patched suits, showing far too many years of wear. "Blake," Matthew said, "looks like he's only one step from the poorhouse. Apparently, he rose to where he is now from poverty and spends little money fearing he might return to it."

Clarence Blake was a short thin man with stooped shoulders. He had small brown eyes, a long narrow nose, with unusually large nostrils and an almost lipless mouth. Blake wore no wig. His gray hair, tied at the back of his head, gave him the severe look of a scolding preacher. His grim expression added to that impression.

"I assume you are here to settle your father's affairs. It's about time, too," Blake began with undisguised irritation. He sat with his elbows on the arms of the chair, his hands clasped together. The cuffs of his brown suit jacket were threadbare and the elbows had leather patches.

Angered at Blake's manner, Morgan stared at him for a second without saying anything. "I've come to settle his affairs when it suited me and I don't care whether you like it or not." He glared at the man. "You, Mr. Blake, were my father's lawyer, not mine and I have no need to be concerned with your advice or summons. Is that understood?" Morgan did not like Blake and distrusted lawyers in general. He viewed them as corrupt and greedy.

"Yes, Major Morgan. Quite understood. I only want to see your father's affairs settled as soon as possible. It's what he wished." Blake regretted his remark to the scowling man and now wrung his hands in the uncomfortable silence that followed.

"Well then, let me hear what I am to know about my father's affairs." Morgan continued to stare at Blake, but no longer scowled.

The lawyer turned his back to Morgan and leaned down to the bottom drawer on the right side of his desk. He unlocked the drawer with a small key that hung from a leather string around his neck. The drawer was filled with a number of sealed parchments and Blake held up one with Matthew Morgan's elaborate signature on it.

"As you can plainly see, Major, it's your father's last testament. It was signed and sealed on June 3, 1765, two weeks after your mother's death. No alterations have been made to it since that time and your father never examined it again. Do you wish me to read it aloud or would you prefer to read it yourself?"

"I'll read it myself." Morgan took the parchment from the lawyer's hand. He broke the seal and opened the one page statement. At the bottom, he saw his father's signature along with those of Clarence Blake and his wife, Mary Anne Blake, who served as witnesses.

Morgan read the four paragraphs quickly and then looked up at the lawyer. "It's exactly as he said it would be. I am the heir to all his land and possessions. I have the original property deeds in our lock box and I assume you have the copies."

"I do and I will draw up new deeds in your name if that is your wish."

"Yes. That will do and I will pay you for that service as well as the same yearly payment my father paid for keeping the copies in your care." Morgan looked into the lawyer's eyes.

"That is quite agreeable." Blake averted his eyes. "Do you have any questions about the distributions he determined in the third paragraph?"

"No. He set aside the distributions for Abraham and

Beatriz and those, too, are in the lock box. I will see to it that those distributions are made this week. I have made my own arrangements with Catalina, who now is engaged as the housekeeper at Morgan's Creek."

"Are you also satisfied with the land settlements he made to the slave families?"

"I am. He and Abraham made a list of those to be given property and I understand from his will that you have already prepared the deeds."

"That is correct. I will now execute the deeds as your father stipulated in his testament."

"Well, then, that should conclude our business." Morgan rose from his chair.

"There is one more item to be presented to you." Blake remained seated.

"If that's a bill for your services, the will says you have been paid in full." Morgan again glared at the lawyer. "I assume that also includes your efforts preparing the land deeds as well as the costs of executing them."

Blake's face reddened. "That is correct. All costs have been fully paid and nothing is due. What I have for you is a sealed letter your father left with me."

Morgan walked his horse to the end of the street where three huge live oaks stood. He let his stallion loose and, while the horse nibbled on the grass in the undergrowth, he sat against the trunk of the oak nearest the road. He sighed with relief when a soft breeze blew through the trees. It was now time to read his father's letter and he withdrew it from his jacket pocket.

Morgan looked at the thick envelope and turned it over several times before breaking the seal. It was dated August 13, 1766 and he realized his father had written the letter a month to the day before he died. Morgan withdrew the letter from the envelope and counted the pages. There were six pages written in his father's small precise penmanship. Every page was covered with his writing except the last one, which ended in the middle. Morgan read the last two paragraphs and then put the letter in his lap. His eyes immediately filled with tears.

James, I want you to know that I regard you to be a much better man than I have been. I say that not because of the many foolish mistakes I have made in my life, but because of the high principles you hold and follow. I know you have always thought I favored your brother and, for a time, I did. He was more like me – a man who loved the sea, the cultivated lands, the success of our business venture at Morgan's Creek and the importance we enjoyed in the province. You had none of those interests and at times seemed like a stranger to me, especially when you stood up against me in the slavery dispute. It was not until the war, when I learned of your bravery not only in battle, but also in your struggle to surmount the loss of your arm, that I recognized and, then, admired the stalwart, resolute man you had become. I also came to appreciate your unwavering convictions that led you to condemn slavery and the Christian hypocrisy that has permitted it to exist. As you see from my will, I have been persuaded by your principles and now have begun to make changes to improve the circumstances of the slaves who serve at Morgan's Creek. I will leave it to you in the future to take further measures for them.

Now that my own end has come, I hope you will forgive me my failures and appreciate me for the successes I made for my family. Perhaps, you will also appreciate me for those parts of you that come from me. At my funeral, I trust you will be able at least to say of me, 'He was a man who loved his family and this productive land he carved out from the wilderness.

Morgan dropped the letter into his lap and sobbed. He wept for several minutes and then wiped his eyes on the sleeve of his jacket. Sighing, he leaned his head against the tree trunk and looked into the sky. As he looked up, instead of the billowing clouds that floated above him, he saw visions of his father at different times of his life. He saw him as the big robust man he was in Morgan's youth and, then, as the paunchy limping figure he became as the years passed. His last view of Matthew Morgan was the smiling man who waved to him from the porch as he rode away that steamy morning at the end of July. He saw his father with clarity and he hoped to hold that memory of him for the rest of his life.

Morgan sighed again and picked up the letter. Brushing a wandering ant off the top page, Morgan looked down at his father's writing. He read the letter slowly. After finishing it, he once again stared up into the sky. Much of the letter remained fixed in his mind.

James, My Son,

You are reading this letter because I have come to a bad end. Whatever the appearance or manner of my death, be assured it was neither natural nor accidental. It was murder. I have been slain by the same murderer who struck down the others one by one.

It appears I am to be the last to die. I therefore have the time to write this letter and leave it with Clarence Blake for safekeeping. Of course, I still hope to survive and so have hired Claus Bruckmann to protect me. But, even with his presence at Morgan's Creek, I know I am in mortal peril no matter the safeguards I take. The murderer is clever, much too clever and determined to be deterred by any one or many armed men. If I do survive, it will be because of his decision to spare me. But I have no such expectations and if I still lived you would not be reading this letter.

I am therefore writing this letter to inform you of the unfortunate events that resulted in my murder as well as the murder of the others.

What I tell you may well help you find the murderer, but that is not the principal purpose of my revelation. Rather, I am relating what has occurred to explain how my foolish pride led me to my ruin and ultimately my death.

Morgan paused before reading further. His hand trembled as he tightly held the letter and prepared to turn to the next page. He feared what he would read on the succeeding pages, though he desperately wanted to know why his father had participated in the robbery. He also wanted to know what part he had played in the robbery itself and the events that led to his murder. After a long moment of thought, Morgan sighed and looked at the next page.

As you know, during the war, in 1761, I bought ninety acres of land from my neighbors, forty acres from Arnold James and fifty acres from Jonathon Harris. At the time of the purchase, I gave them each half the price they required for the land with the promise that I would pay them the balance in two installments, one in 1762 and the other in 1763. The installments were to be paid on June first of each of the two years.

I paid the first installments easily following a good crop the preceding summer. But the next year, the crop as you know was washed away in August by the storm waters that flooded the entire plantation. It was a bad year for all the planters and I could not find anyone in the colony willing to loan me the money I needed, even with my offers of exorbitant rates of interest.

With the date of the final payments fast approaching, I did not know what to do. I found myself in desperate straits and feared I would lose Morgan's Creek and everything I had worked for all my life. As the months passed without the available funds to pay my debts, I became more and more desperate. It was at that time, in early February, that I received a letter from Thomas Sterling inquiring if I would meet him for a discussion "that might be mutually advantageous." As I told you in the past, I did not respect Sterling, but, in my wretched financial state, I met him as he requested a week later. I recall it was on the day after a rare snowstorm in Savannah.

We met here at Morgan's Creek and Sterling informed me of his own financial needs and told me he had heard of mine as well. He told me about the planned robbery, which I'm sure you now know about, and asked if I would be interested in joining the enterprise. I inquired why he would ask me to be involved and he replied in words I still recall, "It's well known, Mr. Morgan, that you are a man of determination who is willing to take risks for his advantage."

Sterling said since we were still at war, the robbery would be an act against our enemies, the Spaniards, and we would be no different than those pirates who fought for England in earlier times. He mentioned Francis Drake, John Hawkins and pointed to our ancestor, Henry Morgan, who captained English privateers against Spain and its colonies. There would be one important difference between us and those famous English pirates of the past. In the robbery, we would not engage in battle with the Spaniards. We would seize the bullion in stealth. It was essential not to kill any of the Spaniards and risk retaliation against our communities and lands in Georgia.

Sterling told me the robbery had been planned and would be led by a former army officer named Nelson – William Lyman Nelson. He was quite proud of his name and claimed to have a noble lineage. I later learned Nelson had been cashiered from the English army for drunkenness and insubordination. Sterling informed me that Willington was an associate of Nelson who knew the Spanish territory south of the Río San Juan. I soon learned that villain was an outlaw from New Hanover. Chapman, whom I knew only vaguely as a seaman who sailed for the shippers in town, would captain the vessels ferrying us and our horses to and from Spanish Florida. I found him to be the most likable of the men in the venture. Chapman admitted that he and Sterling had previously engaged in the smuggling of foreign goods in the company of Archibald Willington.

The costs of the enterprise were financed by Sterling and me and we were expected to pay for the construction of three rafts and refitting an old skiff to cross the Río San Juan. Willington knew a carpenter near the river, who was paid to build the rafts and make the skiff seaworthy. The skiff would be used to take us across the river and the horses would follow, two to a raft. A sixth man, a Mestizo named Juan Vargas, already lived in Florida and would guide us to and from the location of the robbery. We brought an additional horse across the river for him to ride as we went south on our mission. Vargas lived in the tiny Indian village of San Isidro and knew Willington from previous smuggling ventures. It was Vargas who informed Willington of the treasure the Spaniards were salvaging from the sunken ship south of St. Augustine.

While Sterling was optimistic about the plan, he confessed concerns. He had never taken such risks – risks that could cost him his life. He had engaged in smuggling over the years, but never on a grand scale. Sterling described himself as a petty smuggler. He said all the shippers smuggled goods into the colonies, especially in bad times, but this venture was beyond anything he had ever dared to consider. Sterling said he joined in the enterprise because he saw no other choice. "It's a new dock or my ruin," he said with an honesty I admired.

Needless to say, I agreed to take part in the scheme. I agreed immediately. I knew there would be risks, but I resolved to take them to be free of my debts. Unlike Sterling, I did not fear the loss of my life as much as the possibility of capture and imprisonment in a Spanish dungeon.

Looking back at my decision to take part in such a perilous plot, I realize how foolhardy I was to agree. I did not know the men who would be involved, I did not know the robbery scheme for the robbery and I did not know anything about the Spanish forces or the measures they had in place to guard the bullion. I only knew I would be relieved of my debts if the robbery succeeded. If not, and I was captured or killed, I knew you would make sure Morgan's Creek was preserved.

Not only was I foolish to join the robbers, I was too proud to satisfy my debts in a more sensible way. I never even asked James or Harris if I could delay their payment for another year. They are both reasonable men and undoubtedly would have accommodated me for the charge of additional interest on the remaining debt. I also could have approached Hugh Douglas for a one-year loan, which I'm sure he would have willingly given me. But I did neither because I was too proud to admit my mistake of purchasing both parcels of land at the same time without available assets to pay for them. Desperate to get the property, I gave up most of my savings for the down payment with the expectation of paying the remainder of the cost from plantation profits. It was my foolish assumption that I would have two good crop years to pay my debts. Therefore, when the flood of 1762 left me with losses and the inability to pay for the property, I was too proud to admit my needs and ask for assistance. So, my son, what has befallen me has been of my own doing and because of the imprudent pride that has marked my life.

The robbery was accomplished exactly as planned, as I expect you now know, after your trip to Cuba. When it was done, we rode north through the woods to San Isidro. Upon arriving at the village, we discovered that Sterling, who rode poorly and was the last in line, was missing. Chapman and I immediately retraced our route and found the man sprawled out senseless on the ground a mile or so south of the village. Sterling had fallen from his horse and so we set about to revive him. Once revived, it took all our strength to hoist him into his saddle. As you know, he was a fat man and very heavy, but we managed with his feeble help. My rheumatism at that time did not yet plague me to the extreme I now suffer.

When we reached San Isidro, we found Vargas' house in flames and Willington lying on the ground bleeding and begging for his life. The front of his breeches was soaked with blood and his left ankle was bloody as well. Nelson stood over him with his long sword poised above his neck. He had stabbed Willington in the groin and severed his Achilles' tendon as well. As we dismounted, we smelled the sickening stench of burning flesh and, since Vargas was not to be seen, we knew he must be inside the burning house. We were all appalled and Sterling vomited all over his horse's neck.

Nelson told us that Willington had killed Vargas, raped his wife and left the entire family tied up in the burning house. "Even the baby," he snarled, kicking the sobbing man. "I should have run him through and thrown the bastard into the fire as well."

While we searched for Sterling, Nelson had ridden north to the river to see if any Spanish cavalry was in the vicinity. He had a fast horse and rode there and back quickly. When Nelson returned to the village, he found Willington buttoning up his breeches and the house aflame. He could hear the children screaming from the inferno inside. Willington said he killed the family to prevent them from telling the Spaniards about us. "They're only Indians anyway," he said. It was at that moment that Nelson struck him with his sword and we arrived with Sterling in tow.

We urged Nelson to spare Willington, not because we had any sympathy for the man, but because we worried his dead body might lead the Spaniards to us in Savannah. Nelson agreed and he stepped away, kicking Willington as he went. Chapman bound up Willington's wounds and we lifted him into his saddle. He had to be tied to the horse since he was in no condition to ride. We knew if he survived the trip home, with his severed tendon, he would never ride again, never mind walk without pain. None of us, however, had any sympathy for him.

We left San Isidro soon afterward, setting fire to the two nearby houses. It was our hope the Spaniards would think we attacked the northern end of the village, not just the Vargas house. The families living nearby had fled when they saw us ride into view. The other villagers had run to the southern end of town where they barricaded themselves behind a line of barrels and wagons. We ignored them as we left and rode away on a route Nelson had found through the pine woods. There were still many miles to ride before we reached the Río San Juan.

We arrived at the river as night fell and stayed on the south side until first light the next morning. We had made a campsite upon our arrival and our boats were hidden among a thicket of cedar knees in shallow water. Nelson had hoped the skiff could tow all three rafts in a line, but the river was too choppy and we were forced to sail and row the skiff back and forth towing one raft at a time. We had not faced such troubling conditions on the way across, but the return trip took us three hours to ferry the horses and ourselves to the other side. We worried every minute that the pursuing Spanish cavalry would catch us before we could escape.

The rest of our return trip was uneventful, though exhausting, especially the crossing of the St. Mary's and Altamaha Rivers on punts (rafts propelled by poles). We left Willington in a place south of Savannah called Sunbury at the house of a woman of ill repute. Chapman told her to tell him to come see him when he recuperated. For punishment, Nelson took all but four silver bars from Willington's saddlebags and divided them along with his coins among us. His bars were consigned to Chapman to give him if and when he came for them. Although we searched for a while, Vargas' share was not found and we assumed Willington had concealed it somewhere nearby. Nelson wanted to force him to tell us where it was hidden, but, by that time, he was unconscious and we were all too tired to wait for him to awaken.

Willington, of course, did recover and, made his way to Savannah. Chapman gave him the four bars and never spoke to him again. He warned Willington he would shoot him on sight if he ever appeared at his house again. Chapman told me about him the only time we chanced to meet in town. From what I later heard about Willington's many donations to Christ Church, it appears the villain retrieved Vargas' bullion from San Isidro and brought it back to Savannah.

Sterling was the only one who had any contact with Willington. I have no notion why he met him so often as you learned from Bartholomew. Sterling no more liked the man than the rest of us and he was horrified by his cold-blooded murder of the Vargas family. He even suggested we leave Willington in the woods to die once we had safely crossed the St. Mary's River.

I myself never spoke with Willington again. I saw him only once about a year and a half ago, when Abraham and I went to town to buy supplies. When I stepped down from the carriage, I saw him limping along on the other side of the street. He looked grim and had good reason to look that way. He had lost more than his ability to ride a horse or walk without unremitting pain. As we rode away from Sunbury, Nelson told us he had made sure that Willington would never be intimate with a woman again. Although enraged at him for the murder of the Vargas family, he had the presence of mind to carefully aim his sword thrust at the man's groin. Nelson turned his wrist twice as he struck Willington to incapacitate him for life.

Nelson, of course, now is dead, too. I went to Charles Towne to warn him in July – it was after the murders of Sterling, Chapman and Willington. But he was murdered a few weeks after my visit. I inquired about him about a month later in a letter to a planter I know there in town. He told me Nelson died in a house fire. Both Nelson and Willington burned to death most likely in retribution for what the Vargas family suffered in San Isidro. I think the two other murders in town were devised similarly to be as long lasting and painful as possible. The use of fire ants and alligators, of course, assured the murderer of such an end. He wanted them all to suffer as much as possible and I fear my death will be full of suffering as well.

There is little else I can tell you about the men with whom I consorted in the robbery or the vengeance that has been visited upon them. I have no notion who the murderer might be. Despite endless hours thinking about his identity, I have no one to suggest as even a possibility. I assume he has some affiliation to the Vargas family, but surely you have come to that conclusion as well. I know no more about him except that he is probably planning my death as I write this letter.

Morgan reread the last two paragraphs and again wept. He wanted more from his father than this last letter and yet he knew there would be nothing else. He folded the letter into the envelope and put it in the buttoned pocket of his jacket.

Morgan spoke to Palmer the next morning in his office. He credited Colonel Rodríguez with everything he had learned from his father's letter. Oliver Palmer would not know the truth nor would anyone else. Whatever now happened, he would never reveal his father's part in the robbery and eventually burn his letter. With all the robbers dead, only the murderer knew their names and Morgan had begun to think the clever man would never be found.

"So, there were five robbers, not six. I assume Cuba is the source of everything we now know?" Oliver Palmer appeared preoccupied as Morgan made his report.

"Yes, Colonel Rodríguez has provided us with invaluable information about the bullion robbery. We owe him a debt of gratitude."

"Yes, do write a letter thanking him and I'll sign it. I must say the robbery was indeed a bold scheme for so few men. Of course, with the exception of Vargas, they all were of English blood." Palmer nodded knowingly. "Even if a robbery, it shows us the strength of our English character and conversely the obvious weakness of the Spanish soul. I'm not at all surprised they succeeded in the scheme with Nelson as their leader. Didn't you say he was a former officer in the king's army? If so, he was an English gentleman."

"Nelson was an English gentleman who was cashiered from the army for drunkenness and insubordination." Morgan also wanted to remind Palmer that Willington, with his English blood, had murdered Vargas and burned his wife and children alive. But he decided it would be a waste of time to contradict the pompous Englishman. Palmer would ignore what he said anyway.

"Be that as it may, Major," Palmer paused to smile smugly, "but let's not forget, while Nelson robbed the Spaniards for personal gain, he did it against our enemy in war. Nelson also severely punished Willington for his crimes – in much the same way an English officer would properly punish a soldier for malicious behavior."

"Willington was not properly punished! In the British army he would have been hung for the murder of the Vargas family. Also, at the time of the robbery, the war was over! It was over in March of 1763, a month or so before the robbery. That's when the peace treaty was signed."

"Yes, but they didn't know it was over here in these remote provinces." Palmer smiled, pleased to prove his point. "In addition, Major, as I recall, our soldiers didn't officially occupy Spanish Florida until later that summer. So, here in America the war was *not* over."

Morgan sighed. "Would there be any purpose," he thought, "to point out that the fighting had already ended since everyone knew the treaty had been written and soon would be signed?" He decided to say nothing more and only stared at the attorney general.

"I'm afraid I can't offer you any tea or biscuits, Major. Thackery is home sick with some stomach illness. He probably picked up something at one of those appalling taverns he frequents with those fops he calls his friends. He needs a good wife to prepare him decent meals."

Morgan smiled, thinking the obese man facing him had eaten too many decent meals.

Palmer saw his smile and assumed he agreed. "Well, Major, where are we headed in this tiresome investigation? The robbers are dead and we know why they were murdered. Someone obviously saw them kill the Vargas family and has now exacted his revenge. One was killed in Charles Towne and three others in Savannah. Is there any reason why we should now think the murderer has returned here after he killed Nelson in Charles Towne? Since he was the last one to die, the murderer might have remained there or gone elsewhere for that matter. Since he was never seen, except by that drunken lout Delaney, the man could be anywhere in the colonies. He also could even be in Florida."

"That's true, but I doubt it." Morgan looked at Palmer, unsure of how he could convince him the murderer was still in Savannah. He had been here to kill his father, but certainly could be gone by now. "I think he is in Savannah, though I have no knowledge of his presence here."

"Then, Major, how can you make such an assertion?" Palmer no longer appeared willing to flatter him. He also seemed much less interested in searching for the murderer.

"My belief comes from what we know about him. We know he lived in the Indian village of San Isidro at the time of the robbery. Therefore, he is either an Indian or a Mestizo. He also is a Catholic since all the people in the village were Catholics. The Franciscan monks Christianized the Indians and helped them establish San Isidro earlier this century. We also know the murderer speaks Spanish and probably English as well. Savannah thus would be a perfect refuge for him."

Palmer's jowls shook as he disagreed. "The Indians learned Spanish, not English from the Franciscans. How then did he learn enough of our language to move about this colony?"

"I don't know. But he did know enough English to write that letter luring Chapman to his death. Savannah is the only city in this colony with a large number of Spanish Catholics; it's the closest city to St. Augustine. The murderer could have been living here among the workmen and servants all along. He could have been here since the Vargas family was slaughtered."

"He also could have returned to San Isidro once he had satisfied his vengeance." Palmer leaned back his chair and laced his fingers over his stomach.

Morgan nodded. "That's true, but most people living in Spanish Florida left the colony before the British army arrived in 1763. The Spaniards transported almost everyone

– Spanish Floridians, Indians and Africans – to Cuba or Mexico. As a result, St. Augustine now is virtually empty except for English soldiers. All the other Spanish settlements, including Pensacola, and the Indian villages are also empty. While in St. Augustine, I saw one Indian village that looked to have been abandoned at least three years ago."

"I see. So you think the murderer is still here among us?" Palmer looked doubtful.

"Yes. And there's another reason why I think he's still here in Savannah. The murders of Sterling, Chapman and Willington took place in a period of a month – from the middle of May to the middle of June. The murderer had to be living here for that period or even longer to plan and execute the killings. In that time, he had to find food, a roof over his head and a way to survive. I doubt he's a man of means. So, I think the murderer has found a way to support whatever needs he requires in Savannah. That's why I suspect he has been in here since 1763."

"What you say has some merit." Palmer looked at the bracket clock on his desk. He was tired of talking to the argumentative man and impatient to end their conversation.

"I have one additional argument. It's something I have thought about for a long time. I think Sterling was lured out to the hidden lake by someone he knew. I can't imagine him riding all the way out there at the behest of some stranger. We know he rode poorly and, to make such an arduous trip, he must have had some acquaintance with the murderer. He would not have been enticed there by a note of the kind that snared Chapman."

Palmer sighed and again looked at the clock. "It's hard to imagine what drew Sterling to that distant wilderness. If it involved something secret, I would think he could have discussed it in his office if privacy was needed. I must say it's quite bewildering."

"Perhaps he was enticed there by a scoundrel with plans

for another illicit activity."

"I doubt that, Major! Even though Sterling was involved in the robbery – and do keep in mind he attacked our Spanish enemy at the time – he was a sound man whose life and good deeds reveal a Christian morality. He was a devout and generous Anglican, a devoted husband and father and a respected assemblyman who assisted the governor in managing the affairs of this colony. I see from the look of doubt on your face that you disagree with my assessment of him. Well, be that as it may, Major, I'm quite sure Thomas Sterling was a good man of, ah, sterling character." Palmer grinned at Morgan, who grimaced.

"A good man indeed! How then do you explain the good man's willingness to ride out to such an isolated spot? He was obviously going to a secret rendezvous."

"I don't have to explain anything to you, Major." Palmer spoke sharply. "But to indulge your suspicions of him, I can offer any number of plausible reasons for his trip. For example, he went there for the serenity of the place… or to ponder a difficult shipping problem and so on."

At that moment, Morgan wanted to strangle Palmer for his obvious ridicule. Instead, he stared at him and spoke calmly. "Sterling went to the lake for a rendezvous – a secret rendezvous because he was up to no good. The good man you describe was not only involved in a robbery; he was involved in an illegal plot that cost the lives of six people. Four of them children!"

"He had nothing to do with those murders. He was not even there when Willington killed that family. It's in the Spanish reports!" Palmer's face reddened, as he got angry.

"That's true, but according to English law, Sterling's participation in the crime made him as responsible as Willington for the murders. They all were responsible. If the robbers had been arrested and tried in an English court, they all would have been hung for the murders."

Palmer made a face, reluctant to admit Morgan had bested him in an argument. "I suppose you do have a point. Well, we still don't know who or what could have persuaded him to ride to a rendezvous in such a secluded spot." Palmer reached for his teacup and, seeing it was empty, frowned in irritation.

Morgan shook his head. "No, we don't know. But whatever convinced him to go to that secret rendezvous cost him his life."

Morgan rode to the Sterling Shipping Company after leaving Palmer's office. He found Luke writing an entry into a logbook with Mark looking over his shoulder. Luke closed the book when the justice entered the room. Morgan assumed the brothers had ended business for the day since the windows had been shut and only one oil lamp was lit.

"Major Morgan. I just made my last entry of the day and we are about to leave for home." He put the logbook in the top drawer of the desk and offered the justice his hand.

Morgan shook Luke's hand and nodded to Mark. "I'm here to ask a few more questions. It shouldn't take long."

"I trust your questions concern our father's murder." Mark frowned at Morgan. "We've wondered what progress has been made in the investigation. It's been five months now and no one has been arrested for the hideous killing."

Morgan gave Mark a hard look, but replied in a soft voice. "I understand your concern, Mr. Sterling. It has been a long time and I am still investigating his murder. The investigation will continue as long as the murderer is at large."

"We appreciate your efforts." Luke gave his brother a

disapproving look.

"I'm here to inquire if your father told you anything about the person he intended to meet the day he disappeared. I know it was a long time ago."

"Not that I recall." Luke looked at his brother.

Mark shook his head. "That's what was so odd. Father usually told us exactly where he was going, whether to the courthouse, the church or his lawyer's office. But he said nothing."

"He did say he would return well before we closed the office." Luke saw his bother nod in agreement. "I did ask where he was going, but he was already out the door when I spoke. We always wanted to know his whereabouts in the event some business here needed his attention. In that event, someone would be sent to fetch him, unless he was attending an assembly session."

"Did he say anything about why he was leaving that afternoon?"

"No," replied Mark quickly. "But that was not at all unusual. He rarely talked about his meetings, although he certainly told us about those things concerning the company."

"Was he often absent?" Morgan doubted he would learn anything new from the brothers. It appeared the interview would be a waste of time.

"More and more as business improved with the new dock and, even more so, when Father became an assemblyman. He became so busy he kept a list of his appointments and obligations. Father said it was a sign of his aging, but even a young man would've had trouble remembering so much," said Luke with a smile. His pride in his father was obvious.

"I don't suppose you still have any of his appointment lists?"

Mark nodded. "We have his appointment book. That's where he listed everything. We put the book away with some of his other things in that chest in the corner."

"May I look at it?" Morgan tried not to show his excitement.

"Yes, of course, but there's nothing in it about his meeting the afternoon he disappeared." Mark swallowed twice before continuing. "That was the first place we looked."

"I would like to see it, nevertheless."

Mark went over to the chest and squatted to open it. He quickly found the worn book and handed it to Morgan. "He began using it in January of this year… the last year of his life." Mark tried to look away, but Morgan saw the tears in his eyes.

Morgan opened the book and immediately turned to the page dated May 10. There were two appointments shown for the morning; one with a fellow assemblyman and the other with his tailor who had been scheduled at ten o'clock to measure him for a suit. The afternoon portion of the page showed no appointments, but Sterling had written one tiny item on the bottom. In his large bold lettering it said, "Three o'clock – finally!"

Morgan rode back to the courthouse with the appointment book in his buttoned pocket. Stockwell was gone when he returned to his office, but he left two letters from Claudia on his desk. Morgan smiled, recognizing her handwriting on the envelopes. He wanted to open them immediately, but decided to wait until after he examined the appointment book. He wanted his mind free of the murder investigation when he read her letters.

Morgan began his inspection of the appointment book from the first entry in September 1765. He saw nothing unusual until the last week in December. On the thirtieth of the month, he found an unexplained numerical formula: 125 x 1SB – 12.5AW = 112.50. It took Morgan only a few seconds to figure out its meaning and he laughed when he understood. "I see," he said aloud, "so, that's why Sterling met

Willington at the church." He used the outlaw to exchange his Spanish bars for English coins of the realm. Sterling exchanged one silver bar (SB) worth £125 for £112.50, giving Archibald Willington (AW) a ten percent commission of £12.50 when he later sold it.

Sterling could easily spend the stolen Spanish coins, whether silver pieces-of-eight or gold doubloons, but not the heavier ingots with their telltale markings. They were rarely, if ever, seen in Savannah and might have invited unwanted questions if he used them in his business or about town. Sterling therefore sold his bars to Willington and, though he lost ten percent of their value, he avoided any comment about having them in his possession.

Morgan assumed Sterling had used some of the Spanish bars to pay for the construction of his new dock and warehouse; his shipping facilities afterwards were among the three best on the river. He probably had paid the carpenters with bars, but, at that time, since the war had recently ended, no one would have been surprised he had them. Spanish bullion then was more conspicuous in Savannah and other English colonies close to the Caribbean. English attacks on Spanish shipping had often earned the raiders a variety of gold and silver items including ingots.

The carpenters who built Sterling's dock were undoubtedly delighted to get the ingots in payment, knowing what they would fetch from the moneychangers in town. The sale of their bars would amount to much more than they charged Sterling. Like the Parker brothers, whom Morgan also suspected had been paid with stolen bullion, the carpenters would tell no one about their good fortune. They would keep silent without Sterling even asking them.

Morgan guessed Sterling only met with Willington to exchange his remaining bars. The shipper did not need them once his business again prospered and he probably worried they might reveal his role in the robbery and murders in

San Isidro. Sterling certainly had more ingots than Chapman who had only one remaining after his house and ship were built. Whatever number of bars Sterling still held, he had been selling them in 1765, if not earlier as well.

Morgan found seven other transactions in the appointment book. Studying the ingot sales, he saw that Willington consistently took advantage of Sterling. The scoundrel not only charged him a costly fee for the exchanges, but also undervalued the bars he bought from him. In their initial transaction of 1766, Willington exchanged three gold bars for Sterling. In addition to his charge of ten percent, Willington gave him five percent less than the bars were actually worth. Morgan knew a Spanish gold ingot had a value of at least £450 in town and might have brought as much as £470 from the moneychangers. However, Sterling received £427.50 for each of the bars and he paid Willington a commission of £42.50. Thomas Sterling therefore lost £65 or more in every gold transaction he made with Willington.

Morgan was not surprised. It's what he would have expected from the villain. Stockwell had said, "Willington got what was coming to him," and as usual the shrewd sergeant was right. Morgan assumed Sterling knew about Willington's scheme; he was too experienced in business to be fooled by such a blatant swindle. The shipper probably paid the rogue what he required to remain anonymous in the sale of the stolen bullion. Wealthy from his business, he was satisfied with whatever Willington gave him for the bars.

The bullion transactions appeared in his book every few weeks beginning in December of 1765 until his death in May 1766. Altogether, Sterling disposed of thirteen ingots – eight silver and five gold. He concealed the sales with a simple code – SB for silver bars and GB for gold bars. The code was obvious to Morgan, but would puzzle anyone unfamiliar with the robbery.

Morgan spent two hours examining Sterling's appointment book. He found nothing else unusual. There were the typical dates and times of upcoming meetings, notes of payments due and expected, reminders of errands and tasks to be completed for the business as well as for his family. Sterling included the birthdays of his wife and children in large letters and put an asterisk a day ahead to alert him of the date.

The only repeated item in Sterling's appointment book that surprised him was a monthly visit to see Doctor Nunes Ribeiro. Beginning November 19, 1765, the assemblyman went to see him every four weeks at one o'clock on Tuesday afternoons. Morgan recalled the doctor telling him Sterling and his daughter had come see him a week before his death, but he had no memory of the assemblyman's scheduled visits months before his murder. He made a mental note to ask the doctor about the visits when he saw him in the morning.

María Adela had told him that mornings were the sick man's best times of day. He sighed. Morgan knew the doctor would soon be dead and he would lose the one man who meant as much to him as his father. The thought of his death made his stomach tighten. Every time Morgan saw him now he looked thinner and weaker. It was all too obvious his death was imminent. Morgan visited him every morning and always worried as he left his bedside that he might have seen him alive for the last time.

María Adela had promised to ride and find him, day or night, when he looked to be close to death. Claudia's friend Carolina was now helping María Adela, every day along with a group of Portuguese women who took turns caring for him. Two women were always in the house with him to make sure his every need was instantly met. Those women who were not needed to nurse him brought cooked meals and lingered outside to dispose of bedpans or go on needed errands.

"I'm in a heavenly sanctuary," the doctor told Morgan on his last visit. "If there is a heaven it can't be much better than the one I now have in my house." Morgan smiled recalling what his friend had said. Despite his physical deterioration, the doctor's mind remained as astute as ever and occasionally there was even a twinkle in his eyes.

Morgan tore open the top envelope on his desk and read the first of Claudia's two letters. It was dated August 30 and included three pages. Claudia told him her mother seemed better and had begun to resume her daily life. She still spent time alone staring out the upstairs window, but no longer stayed hours in bed during the day. Sofía María seemed more herself and ordered her daughters about as if they were children. They smiled at each other, happy to see her once again in charge of her household. A day earlier, Sofía María told Claudia the time had come for her to return to Savannah. "You have spent enough time here in Havana," she announced. "Your place is not here, hija (child), but with your new husband. Go make a home for him."

The second letter was written a day later and announced her plans to sail home. Claudia informed him she would sail as soon as the storm that was expected in the Caribbean had passed. Morgan smiled elated to know they soon would be together. They had been too long apart and he longed to hold her close and look down into her sparkling eyes. At times like this, he wanted to hold onto her as if for life itself.

Claudia told him that Colonel Rodríguez and his wife had come to pay their respects and offer their condolences. He invited the family to visit his finca when the weather cooled and the storm season finally ended. Claudia said the handsome colonel charmed everyone in the house. Sofía María insisted they stay for the midday meal and she seemed elated to have guests other than grieving family and friends.

The last paragraphs of both letters were full of her words of love. Morgan felt his face flush and a feeling of inner warmth wash over him. He perspired even though the afternoon had cooled and a chilling breeze blew in through the window. Morgan never imagined he could be so affected by the love of a woman. Nor did it ever occur to him that he could want a woman the way he wanted Claudia.

CHAPTER FOURTEEN

SAVANNAH:
WEDNESDAY, SEPTEMBER 18 –
MONDAY, SEPTEMBER 30, 1766

Lieutenant Gerald Jenkins had been expected and Conway ushered him immediately into the justice's office. A few steps into the room, he stopped, stood at attention and saluted Justice Richardson. The young lieutenant, who looked no more than sixteen to Richardson, entered the room hesitantly, expecting the justice's instructions. He saluted Richardson again before sitting in the chair offered him. Once seated, he took off his hat and laid it in his lap.

"It's not necessary to salute me, Lieutenant. I am not in the king's army." In spite of his best intentions, Richardson could not suppress a smile.

"Yes, sir." The lieutenant sat erect, his spine held ramrod straight against the back of the chair. He kept his right hand on the hilt of his sword and his left on the hat in his lap.

"You are new to Charles Towne, Lieutenant?" Richardson asked the rhetorical question in an attempt to relax the young officer, whose flushed face showed his tension.

"Yes, sir, I arrived here from London on the second of September, sir." The lieutenant had blond hair, blue eyes and a smooth pale face he had nicked several places shaving.

"Is this your first assignment abroad?" Richardson suspected the young officer had never been out of his English village before sailing to Carolina.

"Yes, sir. I received my commission in May of this year."

"I see." Richardson sighed, thinking the boy was barely out of nappies. "They're taking them younger and younger these days," he thought. "How do you like Charles Towne?"

"Fine, sir. But it takes one a bit of time getting used to the heat, sir. I'm from Maidstone near London and it never gets this hot there."

"I can imagine. Well, Lieutenant, the message you sent me yesterday certainly aroused my interest. You stated that you have some significant information about the death of William Lyman Nelson. So, now that you are here, do tell me the nature of it."

"Yes, sir. I have two items of information. One is from a boy of eleven… the other is from the sergeant at the south gate."

"A boy of eleven?" Richardson frowned.

"Yes, sir. I know it's… unlikely, but I spoke to the boy myself, sir." The lieutenant's face seemed to redden to the color of a fully bloomed rose.

"All right, tell me what he said." Richardson ran a hand through his hair. "Good God," he thought, "another useless piece of gossip."

"Yes, sir. The boy is the son of the landlord whose rooms I rent. His name is Adkins, the landlord that is; the boy's name is Charles. Adkins was one of Nelson's neighbors and his house was singed by the fire. It's located beside Nelson's house on the left. On the night of the fire, the boy could not sleep. He had been sick and vomiting earlier in the evening so he got out of bed to drink some water. While up and about, he looked out the window. At first, he looked at the stars and then something caught his eye on the first floor of Nelson's house. Startled, he looked down at the house again and, to his surprise, he saw a hooded figure climb out of the kitchen window. He saw the figure close the window and walk away into the dark. The boy lifted his own window to see the figure again, but it had disappeared from sight. It was then that he noticed the flames in the upstairs windows of Nelson's house and he ran to awaken his father. His father hurried into the street, but, by that time, the upper floor and roof of the house were burning out of control.

After the fire was finally put out, Adkins told the firemen what his son had seen and they queried the boy at length. They wanted to make certain the hooded figure the boy saw was not a nightmare's goblin. In the end, one of the firemen believed the boy's story, the others did not. The captain of the fire brigade later talked to the boy as well, but I don't know his conclusions."

"How did you hear about these events?' Richardson now was attentive.

"I heard about it when I went to pay my rent. Adkins had his son, Charles, tell me what he saw and I believed him, sir. The boy may be young, but he is quite quick and I don't think he was dreaming. He told me everything in detail as if he was describing how to play a game."

"What is the other item of information?" Richardson was not convinced of the accuracy of the boy's account and thought it might in fact be a game he was playing on the adults.

"Well, sir, the same night Nelson's house burned down, the night-shift sentry, a soldier by the name of Colin Delaney, also saw a hooded figure leave town through the south gate. He saw the man late at night as the fire was burning. As I understand it, the justice from Savannah talked to Delaney a week or so ago and was told that as well."

"Quite right. Major Morgan thought Nelson might have been murdered. What about the man Delaney? Do you know if he told Major Morgan what he wanted to know?"

"Only partially, sir. A bit of an explanation is needed here, sir." The young lieutenant, aware of Richardson's apparent interest, no longer seemed nervous. The color in his cheeks had faded and he relaxed a little in his chair. He even leaned forward now and then to make a point.

"That's fine. Let me hear everything."

"Well, sir, it seems the sentries usually get a coin or two from those who pass through the gates. According to custom, they surrender a percentage to their sergeants…"

"I am well aware of the practice as are your superiors." Richardson frowned.

"Yes, sir. Well, it seems Delaney's meeting with Major Morgan in *Ye Ale House* resulted in a row between the sentry and Sergeant Dawson, the south gate sergeant. The meeting with the major was overheard and, when it was reported to Dawson, he assumed his percentage had been denied him. A brawl ensued in which Delaney got a black eye and a bloody nose. Dawson also had a black eye. The brawl was brought to my attention and, following a hearing, I reprimanded and penalized them both."

"I trust this story is coming to a close with some significant information."

"Yes, it is, sir. Delaney told me Major Morgan had bought him a meal of rabbit stew and a number of ales, but he had not given him any money. I believed the man and eventually so did Sergeant Dawson…"

"What is the significant information, Lieutenant?" Richardson raised his voice.

"Sorry, sir, I am getting to it. Delaney told Major Morgan all he could recall at the time, but it was of little help. He said the hooded rider never spoke and only motioned for him to open the gates. He gave Delaney a Spanish coin and then rode away. What he didn't remember at the time he spoke to Major Morgan was that the hooded rider wore small boots. Delaney noticed the small boot in the stirrup as the rider handed the silver coin to him. It appeared to be a lad's boot rather than a boot worn by a grown man. Since his meeting with Major Morgan, Delaney has begun to think the rider might well have been a midget or a dwarf. "

"Is there anything else, Lieutenant?" Richardson sighed, his impatience evident.

"Yes, sir… though probably of little importance. Delaney smelled smoke on the rider."

"So that's the significant information you have for me, Lieutenant?"

Richardson sent a brief letter to Morgan the same day. He was doubtful the lieutenant's information would be helpful, but, mindful of the responsibilities of his office, he sent the letter that afternoon before leaving for home. Despite his doubts, the justice knew from his eight years in office how a tiny detail could unexpectedly further an investigation. If the two questionable pieces of information turned out to be beneficial, so much the better; if not, he could sleep well knowing he had done his duty. Thinking of the young lieutenant, he smiled as he dipped his quill into the ink well. The gullible officer was still in his thoughts as began his letter to Morgan.

Charles Towne, September 18th. 1766
Major James Morgan
Justice of the Peace

Savannah
His Majesty's Province of Georgia

Major Morgan,

We have come upon new information here in regard to your recent inquiry into the death of William Lyman Nelson. It appears that a hooded figure was seen climbing out of a window in the Nelson house shortly before the fire was observed. Alas, the observer who viewed the figure was an eleven-year-old boy, but I have been assured the boy is quite clever and is to be believed.

We also have an additional statement from Colin Delaney, the night sentry at the south gate. He has informed his superior of a small, but perhaps significant item of information he neglected to tell you during your interview. It seems Delaney noticed the boots of the hooded man at the gate and thought them smaller than an ordinary man would wear. He believed the small boots would be worn by a lad or a very small man, perhaps a midget or dwarf. Delaney also said the rider's clothes smelled of smoke and he rode by well before the bell on the fire wagon was rung.

I trust this information will be of help to you.

With due respect,
Nathaniel Richardson, Esquire
Justice of the Peace, Charles Towne
His Majesty's Province of Carolina

Richardson underlined "a very small man, perhaps a midget or dwarf" since he thought it ridiculous to think a mere boy could have murdered Nelson. After all, the horseman had been an officer in the British army. The justice could not imagine that a boy could kill such a man, under any circumstances. He folded the letter into an envelope, addressed it and then closed the envelope with the seal of his office.

As Richardson walked along to his carriage, it occurred to him that he had made no effort himself to inquire into the death of Nelson. "With good reason," he thought. There was now no need for such an inquiry unless Major Morgan's search for the murderer in Savannah turned up new information relevant to Nelson's death. Richardson would not consider beginning a murder investigation on the basis of the statements of two such dubious witnesses – an eleven-year-old boy and a drunken Irish sentry. He would look ludicrous if he approached the attorney general with such a proposal. Instead, Richardson intended to retain the report he already had prepared and deposited in his files. His report included the fire captain's explanation for Nelson's death, which stated concisely, "The victim, William Lyman Nelson, a well known pipe smoker, died in a late night fire set accidentally by himself."

Morgan found Doctor Ribeira sitting in his chair when he visited him the last day of the month. It was the first time in a fortnight that the sick man had been out of his bed. He greeted his friend with a broad smile and motioned him to the chair across from him. A teapot and two cups stood on the table between them.

"You are surprised to see me sitting up, aren't you? I can see it on your face."

"I'm glad you're feeling better." Morgan knew better than to deny his surprise.

"For now, at least, you need not get your clothes cleaned for my funeral."

Morgan grinned. "You are feeling better."

"Yes, I am. It may be that María Adela will have to put up with me a while longer." The doctor smiled at her as she bent over him with a washcloth in her hand. María Adela wiped away the soap lather from his face and neck and then used a hot towel to dry him. When his face was dried to her satisfaction, she tucked a napkin under his chin.

"See, I told you I was in a heavenly sanctuary. I do nothing now and receive the service of a rich man. I guess illness has its virtue. Of course, I'm under her thumb and have to obey any number of orders I don't appreciate." He sighed. "As my mother often would say, 'With the best fish, you get the worst bones.'"

"How amusing." María Adela stuck her tongue out at him.

"So this is what you have to suffer when he feels better." Morgan smiled at María Adela as she set a plate of toasted bread and a pot of honey on the table.

"I ignore him." María Adela poured steaming tea into the two cups and, stirring sugar into one, handed it to the doctor. "See if you can keep from spilling it again."

"Do you hear how she speaks to me? Not only does she ignore my profound statements, which you heard her admit, but she also orders me about as if I were a child. If this abuse continues, I will definitely have to rewrite my will."

"What a shame! I'll lose all those useless medical instruments and potions."

Morgan sat back and smiled as they bantered back and forth. He knew the bantering was their way of facing the fears they both felt with what was coming. There had always been shared humor as they worked together in the doctor's surgery, but the exchange of teasing had increased as the sick man's condition worsened. They had deep feelings for one another and Morgan knew they both dreaded the end of their time together. He suspected María Adela used humor to hide the sadness she felt and would not show, especially to the dying man. Like Morgan, María Adela had found a father in the doctor and the thought of losing him was almost too much for her to bear. He saw her wipe away a tear as she turned away toward the kitchen.

Unaware of her tears, the doctor smiled at Morgan. "You see, she's far too clever for her own good. Certainly clever enough to use those instruments and potions and carry on here when I'm gone. I wish I could will her the right to be a physician in my place."

"But you know that's not possible." Morgan looked at María Adela in the kitchen and saw her nod in agreement.

"I do. Speaking of my will, it is in the hands of Clarence Blake. I have instructed him to put you in charge of all arrangements."

"Blake? That greedy little man. I went to see him myself the other day. Did you know he was my father's lawyer?"

"I did. It was your father who recommended him to me. Despite his dreary appearance and dim view of the world, he is circumspect and honest. That's all to be expected of him, isn't it? Well, now, James, tell me your current progress in the investigation. I was not too coherent the last few times you spoke to me about it." The doctor spread honey on his toasted bread.

"Do you recall our discussion about the letter from Colonel Rodríguez?"

"I do and I also remember what you discovered in Charles Towne. That's the last I recall, though some of it is a little vague." The doctor sipped his tea.

"Then you remember everything I told you in the past. I know much more now. In fact, I know the names of all the men who robbed the bullion caravan and how much they carried away. I also know what happened at San Isidro and why they were killed one after the other." Morgan related most of what his father had written in his letter, but made it seem as if Colonel Rodríguez had found the information in the Building of Records.

"It seems you know everything now, but the identity of the murderer. And I expect you will soon know that as well."

"I certainly hope so. I've been looking for five months now."

"I think your patience will soon be rewarded…"

"Pardon me for interrupting you, but I do know a bit more about the murderer." Morgan reached into his pocket and withdrew Richardson's letter. "This is a letter I received yesterday afternoon. It's from the justice in Charles Towne – I told you how helpful he was when I spoke to him." He read the letter slowly and stressed the line that mentioned the hooded figure's boots.

"So, Delaney saw the rider wearing the boots of a young lad or a very small man. That is helpful. It's hard to imagine a lad as the murderer, but a small or short man is a good possibility. But not midgets or dwarfs." He shook his head. "The only dwarf I have seen here in Savannah is the one who repairs shoes in the cobbler's shop."

"Yes, and he has a crippled leg and can't ride a horse. I think his name is Horace."

"That's my memory, too." The doctor nodded. "He's not the one, though he has strong arms and hands. So, where does that leave us? Surely not with a lad."

"Let's not dismiss the notion of a lad so quickly. Colonel Rodríguez mentions such a boy in his last letter. He said a boy from the house beside the Vargas house went missing at the time of the murders and had not returned when the report of the raid was written the next day. He was a thirteen-year-old Indian or Mestizo boy named Francisco – Francisco Fuentes. He now would be sixteen or seventeen and certainly capable of the killings."

"True! He could be the one, especially if he had an affection for the Vargas family. At that age, he's now a man and, even if small in stature, he could have avenged them."

"Exactly. However, we don't know if the boy speaks

English."

"Without English, it would be extremely difficult, if not impossible, to stay here without bringing unwanted attention to himself."

"It would indeed, but I cannot dismiss the boy without additional information. I, therefore, have written the colonel and asked him to see if the name Francisco Fuentes appears in the lists of people who sailed from St. Augustine to Havana. The Spaniards have thorough records of the evacuation of Florida in 1763 when England acquired the colony."

"That's a good idea. From what I've heard about Colonel Rodríguez, that information should be soon forthcoming."

"I hope so.

"You know, there's something I know about the murders that would help me if I could only recall it. It seems to be just on the edge of my mind, but out of reach for now. I have the notion that when it appears to me, I'll be able to find and arrest the murderer."

"I expect it will come to you sooner than you think."

Morgan sipped his tea, which had become lukewarm. He finished the remainder and filled their cups with warmer tea from the pot. It was not as hot as he liked, but María Adela looked to be preoccupied in the kitchen and Morgan did not want to bother her for another pot.

"Oh, I almost forgot to tell you about Sterling's appointment book." Morgan described the book and told the doctor about the shipper's transactions with Willington.

"So that's why they met at the church. It makes sense, of course. I wonder why Sterling went to Willington to dispose of the bars? Surely, there are moneychangers in town who would have given him more for them. I understand his intention to keep his name from any connection to the robbery, but moneychangers are as closed-mouthed as lawyers. And why did he wait so long to dispose of them? It would have been easier and less noticeable after the war."

"I agree and that's when he should have spent them." Morgan wondered what his father had done with his bullion. He had more than enough to pay whatever debts remained on the two properties. Knowing his love of Morgan's Creek, he probably put whatever was left of his share into the plantation. Unlike Sterling, his father would not have waited to exchange the ingots.

"Surely, he exchanged some of them earlier for the dock and his grand new house."

"Sterling may have begun to dispose of them earlier, but, from the number he sold to Willington, I doubt it would have been many. Mrs. Chapman said her husband had twenty-four bars and we can assume Sterling had the same number. As you say, he spent a number of them on the new dock and storage building. I would guess at least six or seven. Then, his new house was built for another four or five. Of course, we don't know how many of the bars were gold."

"That seems reasonable even if most of them were silver. Those bars would pay for a lot of construction in Savannah. So it seems that Sterling had twelve or thirteen left last year when he approached Willington to dispose of them."

"Yes. It seems Sterling decided to rid himself of all his remaining bullion. The question is why." Morgan thanked María Adela who had returned with a fresh pot of tea.

"I can suggest two possible answers. One is that, as a cautious man of commerce, Sterling kept them as security in the event his shipping business faltered. The second is that he wanted to wash away the stain of the robbery and murders like Shakespeare's Lady Macbeth."

"That's a good comparison. Even though Willington alone slaughtered the Vargas family, Sterling knew his part in the robbery had led to their murders and, since he was a religious man, he must have suffered guilt for what befell the innocent family." Morgan smiled crookedly. "Of course,

Bartholomew speaks with certainty of Sterling's Christianity, but I think the shipper's generous contributions to Christ Church gives him that impression."

"You are much too hard on Bartholomew. He was unstinting in his efforts for your father. No one else spent as much time at his side or did as much for him before and after his death."

"From what Catalina told me, you did as much if not more for my father. But let's return to Sterling. How well did you know him? I meant to ask you about that earlier. His appointment book shows his scheduled visits to your surgery every three weeks from last November through April of this year. He was killed before his appointment on May 13."

"Ah, I forgot about those visits. Sterling didn't come to see me; he brought his daughter, Margaret, for treatment of a skin condition she suffers. It's a disease called called Psora Leprosa (psoriasis) and the symptoms include dry, cracked and sometimes bleeding skin. For centuries, it was thought to be a form of leprosy, which we now know was incorrect. I treated Margaret with a salve that moistens her skin and makes it less itchy. It's mostly on her forearms and back and she hides it with long-sleeved dresses. I thought I told you about her visits sometime ago."

"I don't recall it. So you only talked to Sterling about his daughter's skin condition."

"Yes, but only the first time he brought Margaret to see me. He waited out here, while I treated her in the surgery. He spoke more to María Adela than me." The doctor turned his eyes to the kitchen. "I don't suppose Sterling said anything that would interest Morgan?"

"No." María Adela shook her head. "He said little to me. Most of the time, he sat here twiddling his thumbs. He always seemed in a hurry to leave."

"That's my memory of him, too. He seemed more preoccupied with other matters than his daughter's treatment. I did not view him as a concerned father."

"I wonder if his preoccupation had anything to do with Willington?"

"Quien sabe? With what you now know, what approach do you have in mind to find the murderer? I assume you think he's still in Savannah?"

"I do. As I told Palmer, he has somehow managed to live here while pursuing his victims and I think he has stayed on, especially since San Isidro is deserted. Where else would he go?"

"Why would he not return to Florida now that the war is over?"

"There is nothing left in Florida for him now. The Spaniards are gone, so he would find no refuge there, nor employment since St. Augustine is all but empty. Its only sizable population is the English army. It looked like one of those forsaken towns I saw in the north after the war. I saw few residents and they appeared to be struggling from one day to the next simply to survive. Let's not forget that María Adela's family left for Pensacola because of the lack of opportunity." Morgan turned his head to speak to María Adela in the kitchen. "Am I correct?"

"Yes. My father could not feed the family in St. Augustine."

"That's why I think the murderer is still here. He has undoubtedly found some means to earn his keep in Savannah. Whatever he does for food and lodging, he is probably doing it while we sit here and talk about him." Morgan nodded, certain of his assumption.

"Probably so. That means he speaks enough English to exist in this colony. Do you know anything else about him?" He grimaced as María Adela made him drink a dark liquid she brought to him. She stood over him until he drank every drop.

"I think he arrived here sometime after the robbery in the spring of 1763. But obviously I don't know when. He could have come here anytime in the three years since that time. I asked Thackery if there were any Spanish immigrants who arrived here from Florida after the war and he knew of none. With the exception of the few Spaniards who stayed in Florida, everyone else left the colony with the governor and the army. Thackery looked through the census records in the courthouse and found several Spanish names, but not as many as I expected. He saw the many Portuguese names, but did not mistake them as Spanish. The little attorney is quite intelligent as well as thorough. He even was aware of the two Spanish women married to colonists." Morgan smiled. "One, of course, is the former Claudia Barclay."

"Indeed." The doctor also smiled and then tried to hide a yawn with his hand.

"I should leave. I can see you're getting tired."

"Not yet, my friend. I would like to continue for a few minutes more – that is, unless you have other obligations that require your attention."

"No, I have nothing I must do this morning. Stockwell has been handling most of the petty crimes, while I have been involved in the investigation. I'm fortunate to have his help in the office, although he terrifies Thackery."

"I can understand that. He is a good man, but quite imposing in appearance. A moment or so ago, you said Thackery found some Spanish names in the census records. Have you begun to interview any of those people?"

"Not yet. Thackery hasn't finished looking through the names. I'll begin when the list is complete. He told me most of the recorded names are people who serve as house servants or gardeners and such. Of course, most are women, especially those who care for children. Many families in Savannah prefer Portuguese or Spanish servants to slaves. Still, it's my hope he finds someone who looks to be worthy of an interview."

"I must disagree with you, James, on one of your assertions. The murderer may still be in Savannah as you surmise, but I doubt he must stay here to earn his keep. I think he has more than enough money to go anywhere he wishes."

"What leads you to that conclusion? Surely, you don't think he's wealthy, do you?"

"Not from family or commerce. But I think it likely he has money from either Nelson or Willington. Keep in mind, he had time to frighten or torture them before he killed them. Under such circumstances, they would have given him anything he wanted. We know Willington was wealthy and surely Nelson had bullion left as well. So, what happened to their bullion? To my knowledge, there has been no mention of any gold or silver found in the ruins of their houses. In fact, as I recall, Stockwell sifted through the debris of Willington's house and found nothing. I therefore think at least some of their bullion is now in the hands of the murderer."

Morgan nodded. "That's a reasonable assumption. It had not occurred to me."

"I also have been thinking about the robbery and how much each of the six men earned for their effort. As I recall, Colonel Rodríguez told you they took 136 ingots, 38 of which were gold, a chest of 3,000 gold coins and half a chest or 1,500 silver coins. Correct?"

"Yes. That was the total. I've always thought they shared the coins equally, with each of them getting 500 gold and 250 silver coins. But I was uncertain how they divided up the bars."

"I, too, think they shared the coins equally, but not the bars. I surmise Nelson, the leader, took or was given more of them than the others. The 38 gold bars could be divided up nicely if Nelson's share was 8 and the others got 6. Similarly, 98 silver bars divided among the robbers would give each man 16 and Nelson 18. That means Nelson received a total of 26 bars and each of the others 22. However, according to Mrs. Chapman, her husband had 24 in his bag…

that suggests the division of the treasure was not as tidy as I figured. But I think it would be close."

"Good thinking!" Morgan smiled. The sick man never ceased to amaze him. "Even near death," he thought, "his mind is as good as ever." Of course, the doctor did not know Nelson had reduced Willington's share to four silver bars. The rest of his ingots were then divided among the other five men, which gave Chapman the twenty-four bars he showed his wife.

"Whatever division of the treasure was made, all of them, as they say, were 'rich beyond the dreams of avarice.'" The doctor turned away to hide another yawn.

"They were indeed." Morgan knew he should say something about his father's part in the robbery, but he could not bring himself to do it, not even to the dying man who meant so much to him. Though often tempted, he had never told him about his father's letter and what it revealed. At times he felt guilty for not disclosing his father's role in the robbery, but, as if the doctor had joined him in a conspiracy of silence, he never mentioned his father's name in their discussions. Morgan knew it was because the sick man realized he did not want to talk about him.

"I therefore assume Nelson and Willington still possessed a large part of their share when they were killed. Keep in mind, it was only three years after the robbery."

"What you say makes sense. It's unlikely they spent all of it in those few years. In fact, Willington's ingot sales for Sterling increased his wealth." From his father's letter, Morgan also knew the outlaw had returned to San Isidro for Vargas' share of the bullion.

"Indeed. That's why I think the murderer has a portion of the bullion." He yawned again and, this time, Morgan caught him in the act.

Morgan stood. "I know you're tired and it's time for me to leave anyway."

The doctor nodded. "Before you leave, my friend, I must warn you that the murderer can abandon Savannah at any time, that is, if he has not done so already."

After leaving the doctor's house, Morgan stopped at his office and then rode to Claudia's house. At the courthouse, he could find not find Stockwell or Thackery. He learned Stockwell had gone out to free a drunk from punishment in the stocks and Thackery was busy mediating a property dispute. He did find a letter from Claudia, but it did not include good news.

Instead of a message telling him of her expected departure, the hastily written letter told him she was delayed by a blockage in the Havana channel. During a storm, three ships had been swept from their moorings and wrecked at one of the narrowest points of the channel. She said the extensive wreckage had to be cleared before any of the larger ships could sail in or out of the harbor. Only sloops were permitted to sail past the shipwrecks and they were much too small to carry passengers. Claudia told him she had gone to the docks with Uncle Rafael and paid a sloop captain bound for Charles Towne to stop briefly in Savannah to deliver her letter.

Morgan was angry when he read of Claudia's delay and, on the way to her house, shouted at an elderly man to move out of his way. The man rode his horse unhurriedly ahead of him and Morgan scowled at him as he passed by. At Claudia's house, Carolina embraced him and invited him inside for an early lunch.

"When does Claudia come home?" she asked as he sat

down at the kitchen table.

"As soon as possible." Morgan told her about the storm that struck Havana and the shipwrecks obstructing the Havana channel.

"How sad! I hope the channel opens soon." Carolina could see the disappointment in his face and she patted his hand. "Claudia comes prontamente."

"I hope so. It's been too long." He exhaled his breath in exasperation.

"Yes, it is too long," she said. Carolina walked to the fireplace where a pot of fish soup hung over the fire. "It is not good for husband and wife apart."

"True. Carolina, I need some information about those who are Catholics in Savannah. I know you and Claudia attend mass whenever the priest is here."

She turned to look at him from the fireplace. "There is problem?"

"No, no. Not at all. I only want to know who attends mass."

"There are many people, even the English." Carolina ladled soup into a bowl and placed it on a plate in front of Morgan. She then cut two pieces of bread from a loaf wrapped in a towel on the table. Carolina laid the bread on his plate and poured him a glass of wine. A half bottle of Spanish Rioja already stood on the table.

"Are you not eating?" Morgan paused with a spoonful of soup at his mouth.

"I eat later with my son. I drink vino with you." She touched her glass against his.

Morgan sipped his wine. "Carolina, what I want to know is who attends mass with you and Claudia. I especially want to know the names of those who speak Spanish."

"She gave me the names of everyone who attended the last mass held in town," said Morgan. "There were more than thirty people there." He sat facing Thackery in his office.

"The woman has an exceptional memory. When was the last mass?"

"She certainly does. A week ago. The Catholics have an itinerant priest, a Father Francis – an Irishman. He travels from town to town and serves Savannah every second week."

"The Catholics must meet in someone's home since there's no church in town. Given the privileged position of the Anglican Church in town, it's a wonder they are allowed to worship at all." Thackery wore a new blue suit trimmed with gold buttons, a white lace shirt and stockings. He had a freshly powdered wig on his head.

"I take it you're not a parishioner of Christ Church." Morgan found the little lawyer more and more likable, despite his deference to Palmer and effeminate appearance as an English fop.

"No. I was reared a Presbyterian, but I have not attended the church in a number of years. I now find myself attracted to the Deist thinking. After all, this is the Age of Reason, is it not?"

Morgan chuckled. "Yes, it is, though you would hardly know it in Savannah. But, let's return to the Catholics in town. Not surprising, most are Portuguese. There are very few English Catholics, mostly women. One is the wife of Canfield."

"The hunter – one of the hunters who found Assemblyman Sterling's remains?"

Morgan nodded. "Carolina's list is short like the one you made from the census records. As you suspected, most of the Spaniards she mentioned are women. Her list includes Claudia Barclay, the four women married to the English soldiers, Maxwell, Persons, Sawyer and Trask, five servant women, Ana María Aguilar, Elvira Córdova, Marta Luisa

Gómez, Beatriz Murillo and Cristina Rivera. Then, there's Doctor Nunes Rebeiro's assistant, María Adela Macías."

"What about the men?" Thackery looked at the list of names he had brought with him.

"There are only four. Three of them are too infirm to mount a horse, never mind ride one. Alberto Alfaro sits all day making wooden toys he sells at the town market, the hunchback Juan Flores supervises the slaves who tend the governor's gardens and Gustavo Ocampo is bedridden with consumption. Everyone of them a certain murderer!"

Thackery laughed. "I've seen Flores while carrying reports to the governor's house. He also sits most of the day under an umbrella in the summer."

"That leaves only José Jiménez, who is the army blacksmith's assistant. The man is large and certainly strong enough to have committed all the murders. The only problem is that Jiménez hasn't all his wits about him. His mind is that of an eight-year-old child. Do you know him?"

"I do. Carolina's list matches the one I made from the census." Thackery held up the list he had brought with him. "So, where does that leave you?"

"I don't know, Thackery. I just don't know."

Morgan left his office and rode out to the hidden lake where Sterling's remains had been found. He had no reason to ride to the lake, but he went there on a whim, his only purpose to sit by the serene lake and think. It was a cool fall day with a sunny, almost cloudless sky. Morgan gave the stallion his head and the big horse trotted along at a leisurely pace. No one else was on the west road that afternoon and Morgan rode along enjoying the fragrance of the pines and the first color changes he saw in the trees. An early and unexpected frost one night had accelerated the appearance of orange, red and yellow in the maples and sweet gums he passed. The sumac along the road also had begun to show its crimson color.

Morgan tied his horse to a tree above the lake and cautiously climbed down to the bottom of the hill. He walked over to the clearing where Sterling had been staked, but there was nothing left to see. The clearing actually no longer existed and Morgan almost missed the place when he walked to it from the lake. A score of seedling pines had sprung up where the body had been and weeds now stood a foot tall among the pine needles. The only remaining sign of the murder was the fire ant mound, which appeared to be even larger than he remembered from the summer.

He sat on the shore and looked out over the lake. It shimmered in the sunlight. The only sounds he heard were the squawks of crows in the trees and the buzzing of insects in the woods. An occasional fly had to be swatted away, but gratefully there were no mosquitoes to annoy him. After sitting awhile, he saw four deer, one a fawn, drinking water at the other end of the lake.

As the afternoon waned, Morgan leaned back against a pine tree trunk and thought about the murderer. His mind immediately went to San Isidro. That was where it all began – with the slaughter of the Vargas family. Morgan had no doubt their deaths had prompted the murders that followed three years later. He was certain the robbers had been tortured and killed to avenge the vicious murder of the Vargas family.

That meant the murderer must have had some relationship to the family. He could be a relative who lived in the village. He also could be a childhood friend of Fernando, the fourteen-year-old son of José Vargas. The missing neighbor's boy, Francisco Fuentes, might have been that friend and the one who stalked and killed the robbers one by one. It was also possible a vengeful suitor of the family's fifteen-year-old daughter, María, might be the murderer. There were so many possibilities; unfortunately, none of them could be investigated.

The more Morgan thought about the massacre of the Vargas family, the more he became convinced the murderer had witnessed the killings himself. It seemed likely the man lived in the village and had seen Willington's savagery with his own eyes. The agony his victims suffered as they died suggested he had observed everything the heartless outlaw had done to the family – the rape, the torture and their terrible deaths in the burning house.

The murderer had somehow discovered the identity of the robbers despite the bandanas they had worn to cover their faces. Their names alone would not have helped him find them, but the murderer must have seen or heard something that located one of the men in Savannah. Since Sterling had been his first victim, it was reasonable to suspect his name had been revealed in San Isidro. Perhaps, his name and shipping company were mentioned when his father and Chapman brought him to the village after his fall on the trail. That was one possible explanation.

It was also possible the murderer heard about Savannah as the robbers discussed what to do with Willington. He might have been hidden near enough to hear what was said as they stood around the wounded man deliberating his fate. Since the villagers were barricaded far away, the robbers were unaware their argument was overheard by someone who understood English. With the knowledge of at least one of their names and location in Savannah, the murderer had enough information to hunt them down. He could then, at his leisure, wreak his vengeance upon them.

Once one of the men was in his hands, the murderer would quickly learn the location of the others, including

Nelson in Charles Towne. In the time it took the fire ants to kill Sterling, he would have revealed everything he knew. Under such torment, no man would refuse what was demanded of him. Morgan once had been bitten by fire ants and he still recalled the pain from only a few bites. The thought of hundreds or, perhaps, thousands was too terrible to imagine.

The murderer, Morgan knew, was a man of many parts. He spoke English and Spanish, could read and write, rode a horse well enough to ride to and from Charles Towne and seemingly possessed unusual strength. He had been able to subdue four of the robbers, including Nelson, a former British army officer as well as Chapman, a sea-hardened ship's captain. If not a lad, the murderer had to be a man under forty years of age with a hardy constitution.

Even though a slight man, if Delaney could be believed, his strength had been revealed in three of the murders. He had driven the stakes that held Sterling deeply into the ground; he had managed to swim, pulling Chapman through the tidal current from the shore to the sunken ship; he had carried a heavy watersnake, some three or four feet long, from the woods to the outhouse at Morgan's Creek. He also had dragged Sterling, a heavy man of at least 250 pounds, from the bottom of the hill near the lake to the clearing in the woods. The murderer then had been able to shift Sterling's rotund body about on the ground so the heels of his feet rested on the rocks where the ants nested. Morgan knew he was much too strong a man to confront face to face in physical combat, especially by a one-armed man. If and when he found the murderer, it would definitely take a pistol or sword to bring him down.

What made the murderer even more dangerous was his clever mind. Every single one of his killings showed his shrewdness. He had lured Sterling, a poor horseman, to ride to the hidden lake, planned Chapman's death to coincide with the changing river tides, entered Nelson's house despite locks and bolts and found a way to kill his father even with Bruckmann and his huge dog guarding him. It also seemed likely he had used a crafty ruse to enter Willington's house as well. Cunning, strong and cruel, this man was a formidable adversary.

Morgan decided to leave when shadows appeared on the western side of the lake. He saw two otters swimming in the water as he stood and stretched. Several small fish broke the surface of the water as they fled from the otters.

Morgan grimaced, thinking there was a critical piece of information he had forgotten or ignored. He suspected it had something to do with San Isidro, but nothing came to mind when he reviewed what was known about the village. No matter how hard he searched his memory, it remained beyond his reach.

"Damn, why can't I think of it?" he said aloud. "It's a detail I've read or was told in the past. If I can only recall it, I somehow know the murderer will be identified."

Morgan started up the hill from the spot where he had been sitting. He assumed the climb would be the same as from the place several feet away, where a vague path could be seen going up through the woods. Unknown to him, he had chosen the steepest section of the hill. Morgan clambered slowly upward. It was a hard climb with only one arm, but he managed by grasping the lower trunk of one slender tree after another as he ascended a few feet at a time. His method was slow, but sure. He knew a fall could seriously hurt him and possibly strand him on the hill.

He rested against a large pine halfway up the hill and massaged his aching arm. Morgan was breathing heavily by that time. The next section of the hill looked even steeper and, and after struggling up another ten feet, he rested again. He was now soaked in sweat as well as winded. He leaned against a large oak and waited longer before resuming his climb to the crest of the hill. From where he now stood resting beside a rocky outcrop, Morgan could see the blue sky above and knew he was almost there.

Moments later, he reached another rock layer that formed a narrow ledge along the side of the hill. Only several feet from the top, Morgan decided to sit on the ledge and look down at the lake before finishing his climb. He no sooner had squatted down to sit, when he heard a shrill cry from somewhere to his right.

Morgan glanced along the ledge and saw two bear cubs hurriedly backing away from him. The cubs were no more than fifteen feet away. He then saw their mother, a full-grown black bear glaring at him from behind the cubs. The bear reared up and snarled. Standing on two legs, the huge beast looked to be eight feet tall and four feet wide. As he stared at her in astonishment, the bear abruptly dropped to the ground and charged at him. He barely had time to stand before the bear bore down on him. He scrambled up the last few feet of the hill as the animal reached him. She stretched her long front claws out to seize him and one struck the back of his right leg as he crawled upward. Once over the top, he ran for his life. Morgan had no idea of how long he had run, when he realized the bear was not following him.

Too tired to run any farther, he looked back relieved to see the empty woods behind him. Utterly exhausted, Morgan collapsed on the ground. The sun had dropped below the trees when he finally stood and limped to where he had tethered his stallion above the lake. Bleeding from the bear's claws, Morgan groaned as his put his weight on his wounded leg to mount the horse. He grunted in pain again when he pressed his legs into horse's flanks

On the long ride to town, Morgan recalled the bear's attack and knew he had been lucky to survive. If the big bear had not altered her course as she charged, he would have been mauled or bitten to death. The cubs had been cowering in front of her and she had to run around them to get to him. The slight change of pace probably saved his life. As it was, the bear had come close enough to rake the calf of his leg with her claws and tear open his boot. Morgan had smelled her stinking breath as he leaped the last few feet over the crest of the hill. The stench was still in his nostrils as he ran as fast as he could.

"At any second," he told Stockwell the next morning, "I expected her to pounce on me and tear me to pieces. She was enormous and must have weighed 500 pounds. She was so close I'll never know why she gave up the chase. With only a swipe of her paw, she could have knocked me to the ground and mauled me at will."

Blood still seeped from his wounds as Morgan neared the city gates. He had wrapped his leg with the shredded stocking, but it failed to stem the flow of blood. At home, he knew enough to cleanse the deep cuts with alcohol before bandaging them. After the many months Morgan had spent caring for his wounded shoulder, he still kept a bottle of alcohol and cotton bandages in his house. He found them in the kitchen seconds after he entered the door.

Morgan went to sleep within an hour of feeding his stallion. After wrapping his wounds, he washed up, thankful to find a pail of well water left from the morning. Morgan ate a leftover crust of bread, two pieces of dried-up cheese and an apple. He intended to open his last bottle of Spanish wine, but forgot it when he went to the outhouse. Exhausted, Morgan fell asleep as soon as he lay down on his bed.

Morgan had just finished shaving the next morning when Stockwell knocked on his door. He had decided to remain in his own house until Claudia returned from Havana. Morgan opened the door and invited the sergeant inside. In the kitchen, he poured Stockwell a cup of tea and left him briefly to wash the soap off his face.

"What brings you here so early?" asked Morgan when he

returned to the kitchen.

"A message from María Adela. She came to my house last night late – said to tell you to be sure to see the doctor this morning."

"That's strange. I see him every morning now. I hope he's not failing."

"I asked her that and she said he's no worse."

"I wonder why she told you rather than me?"

"She came by last night, but you didn't answer the door when she knocked."

"I was deep asleep; that's why I didn't hear her knock." Morgan told Stockwell how the black bear had almost killed him. "I was dead tired when I got home and fell asleep before eight o'clock. I wouldn't have heard a cannon if it opened fire beside the house."

"You're a lucky man – first the snake, then a bear. What's next?"

"Nothing, I hope." Morgan sighed loudly. "Well, I better be on my way to the doctor's house. He worries these days about all the arrangements he must make. Yesterday morning, he was worried about his will. He wanted me to assure him the lawyer had made me both executor and second beneficiary to his house and possessions. María Adela, of course, is first beneficiary. The day before, he worried about the Jewish services to be performed at his funeral. He insisted I ask Mordecai Shefall, who will conduct the services, to come speak to him once again. It's the third time in a week."

"I can understand. The man has nothin' else to do, but think all day about his death."

"That's it, exactly. He thinks of the last few things he has left to determine."

It was finished – they were all dead. The time had come at last and there was no need to wait any longer. All the necessary preparations had been made and the end was in sight. After three long years, it was finally done.

CHAPTER FIFTEEN

Savannah: Tuesday, October 1, 1766

The doctor was awake, but lying in bed when Morgan arrived. The bed now stood in the front room with the headboard facing the door. Since he no longer got up, Morgan and María Adela had moved the bed into the middle of the room. He told them he felt cramped in his small bedroom and wanted more contact with everyone in the house. In bed, whether sitting up or lying down, he now could greet everyone who came into the house. Though not a modest man, a sheet was placed over his body when María Adela bathed him or he used the bedpan. His head lay on a pillow that morning and, with a trembling finger, he motioned Morgan to the bedside chair.

"Please move closer." The doctor spoke in a low voice, almost a whisper. "I have much to tell you, my friend, and I haven't the strength to raise my voice."

Morgan moved his chair close to the headboard and saw how shrunken and weak the sick man looked. He seemed much worse than when he had visited him the day before. His condition surprised him since María Adela told Stockwell he had not worsened. "Is this close enough?"

The doctor nodded. "I'll begin as soon as I have a sip of tea."

As if she heard had him speak, a Portuguese woman whom Morgan had never met before brought two cups of tea to the bedside table. He thanked her and then lifted the doctor's head so he could drink his tea. The doctor smiled when he had drunk all he wanted.

The doctor pointed to the gray-haired woman, who had returned to the kitchen where she was making vegetable soup for his lunch. "Her name is Julia Cabral and she will be here the rest of the morning. Donata Da Costa replaces her this afternoon at one o'clock and then Felicia Silva will be here with me tonight. It seems every Portuguese woman in Savannah will be coming here to tend to me. María Adela made all the arrangements for the next two weeks – if needed, which I seriously doubt."

"Where is María Adela?"

"She's gone."

"Where?" Puzzled, Morgan scrutinized the sick man and frowned.

"She's gone, alas forever! She is the one – the murderer. Her last name isn't Macías, it's Vargas! María Adela Vargas."

"No!" Morgan shouted and stood abruptly. "María Adela! Impossible!"

The doctor held up his hand and waved Julia Cabral away. Alarmed, she had rushed out of the kitchen, but stopped when she saw his hand. "Tudo bem (I'm fine)," he said.

The stout woman nodded and walked back into the kitchen. She sat at the side of the table facing the bed. It was the best place to watch the doctor while cutting up vegetables for the soup. Every few minutes, she glanced up to see if he needed anything. María Adela had instructed the women to keep him under constant scrutiny since he rarely asked for much or complained.

The doctor waved again to Julia and then turned his eyes to Morgan. "She understands a little English, but not enough to follow closely what we say. For now, I think it's best if we keep this to ourselves. I'll tell you everything and then you can decide what to say or do. I hope that seems sensible to you."

Morgan was speechless for a few seconds. "Yes, of course. María Adela?" He shook his head as if to shake an annoying fly off his face. "I can't believe it. She's but a girl, no more than twenty years old. She killed all those men?"

"Yes, she did. It's hard to believe, isn't it? She told me last night before she left. I was no less surprised than you. Actually, María Adela is only eighteen years old."

"Why did she leave now? We had no idea she was the – one. It never occurred to us that a woman could be the murderer." Morgan spoke softly and looked at Julia Cabral to see if she was listening to their conversation. He saw her standing by the fireplace, stirring a pot of soup over the fire. She seemed to be intent on her task.

"She thought you would soon suspect her. María Adela expected you to realize sooner rather than later that one of the Vargas children might not have been killed in San Isidro. It was the neighbor's son, Francisco Fuentes, who died with her brothers and sister in the burning house. That's why the Spaniards found the remains of six rather than five people after the fire. The boy ran to help when he heard the screams of the children in the burning house. Willington thought he was one of the family's children and struck him down with his fist. The boy was bound and then cast into the burning house with the others. María Adela expected you would think of that possibility when Colonel Rodríguez wrote and told you Francisco was never found after the attack."

"Then, why did she leave last night? I don't know when the colonel will write again and, even if he did mention Francisco, I wouldn't have known he died in the fire." Morgan absently rubbed his chin; still astonished by what he had heard about the girl he had known for so long.

"María Adela worried you could come to that conclusion before you heard from him. So she decided to leave. It was always her intention to leave when she had avenged the murder of her family. María Adela came to Savannah with that sole concern in mind. Though she would not admit it, the only reason she remained here afterwards was to take care of me." The doctor wiped his eyes with the edge of the sheet. "Without the worry of your discovery, she would have waited until my time had come. I will miss her – so much!"

"I am truly sorry about that." Seeing tears trickle down his cheeks, Morgan gently patted the sick man's arm.

"Don't be. Though I will miss her terribly, I preferred her to go now rather than see me at the end. You know, I loved that girl like a daughter and I confess I'm glad she left before it was too late. I would never want to see María Adela arrested, even though she murdered your father. I hope you won't hold that against me, my friend." His eyes were full of tears.

"Never. I understand your sentiments and, Samuel, so would my father." Morgan spoke the doctor's given name for the first time since he had known him. He, too, had tears in his eyes. But his tears were from the sadness of knowing that all too soon he would lose the second of the two most meaningful men in his life. "And both in little more than a month," he thought.

"I would hope so." The doctor sighed, relieved his admission had not angered his friend.

"How did María Adela escape from Willington?" Morgan changed the subject, fearful he would begin to cry unless they talked of something else.

"She wasn't at home when her father and the other robbers arrived in San Isidro. María Adela was in the woods behind the house searching for mushrooms. The mushrooms were to be added to the stew her mother was making for the evening meal. She heard her father's screams and ran home just in time to see Willington cut his throat. María Adela saw her father's murder from the edge of the woods. Her naked mother already lay motionless in a pool of blood on the ground. María Adela said she collapsed against a tree, too stunned to do anything, but stare at the bodies of her mother and father. Can you imagine the child's horror?"

"What a sight for the girl to see!"

"That was not the whole of it. The young girl then saw that monster Willington drag their dead bodies into the house and set fire to it. She didn't know where her brothers and sister were until the flames rose up the walls and she heard their terrified cries from inside." The sick man paused to sip more tea with Morgan's help. "María Adela said she was rooted like a tree to the spot where she sat and could not move even a muscle. Fortunately for her, she could not be seen in the high grass around the house. If that fiend had found her, he would have killed her without a moment's hesitation. The man had the compassion of a venomous snake. He went about hiding Vargas' bullion as the house full of screaming children burned to the ground."

"So, María Adela saw it all. The poor girl!" Morgan exhaled his breath loudly. "She was fifteen then, wasn't she?"

The doctor nodded. "Yes. It was an unforgettable sight and she vowed, then and there, to avenge the murder of her family. María Adela told me she would never have pursued the others if they had killed Willington. It seems when Nelson arrived and discovered what Willington had done, he struck him to the ground with that in mind. She watched as he stood over the wounded man with his sword poised over his throat. María Adela said she was sure Nelson wanted to kill Willington at that very moment. But then the others rode up to the burning house and dissuaded Nelson from taking his life. When Willington was spared, María Adela blamed them all for the murders. She made up her mind, then and there, that each and every one of them would not only die, but also suffer unimaginable pain as they did so. It was a pledge she made to herself."

Morgan nodded. "María Adela carried out that pledge as she killed them. I suppose it's understandable after what she saw that day at San Isidro. After all, she has Indian blood."

"Do you think that explains it? I wonder what you or I would have done to the murderers of our family. Even if they were found and arrested, would we be content to see them brought to trial or hung? I wonder." The doctor licked his lips. He shook his head when Morgan pointed to the remaining tea in his cup.

"I wonder, too. If I had witnessed what she saw, I don't know what I would have done at the time. I do know that at her age, I wouldn't have had the foresight or patience to wait three years to avenge the murders." Morgan knew he had too much rage and too little mind then to do anything except kill him immediately. He pictured himself charging Willington and plunging his sword into the man's stomach. He could see the point of the sword protruding from his back.

"Nor would most of us. But María Adela had to wait since they escaped to English lands before she could even think of how to avenge her family. After what the she had seen, I'm sure it took her quite some time to regain her strength of mind. It's a wonder she didn't go mad."

"It is. The pledge to avenge her family might well have kept her from madness." Morgan saw the doctor nod his head. "But by the time María Adela regained her strength, the robbers had resumed their lives without any worry of pursuit from Florida. Even if charged with the murders, they would never have faced trial or punishment here for a crime committed in a Spanish colony. Especially at that time. The war was almost over and everyone knew the Spaniards were leaving Florida." Morgan knew Palmer would have ignored any charges made against such distinguished men as Assemblyman Sterling or his father. "No charges would have been brought against any of them, not even that devil Willington. After all, he was the junior warden of Christ Church!"

The doctor nodded. "I think most townspeople would have seen the robbers as heroes. As you well know, there is little concern here for Spaniards, Catholics or Indians. Whatever happened to them here in Savannah, María Adela would have been dissatisfied with the results. Seeking *eye for eye* vengeance, her only recourse was to punish them herself."

"You're not justifying her murders, are you?" Morgan stared at the doctor.

"No, no. I am looking at the situation from her point of view. But keep in mind, James, we cannot be self-righteous ourselves – especially if we admit that under similar circumstances we might have also acted rashly. Don't you agree?" The doctor withdrew a handkerchief from beneath his pillow and blew his nose.

"I suppose so." Morgan nodded reluctantly. "Tell me, did María Adela know any of the men at her house that day? I assume she had never seen them before."

"Oddly enough, María Adela had seen Willington once before with her father. However, she did not know his name. Willington was not mentioned by name in San Isidro, but one of the men called Sterling by name when he reached the village. María Adela heard his name and never forgot it. As you know, she learned English in the house of Jesse Fish and understood it as well as any of us. She also heard one of the robbers speak of Savannah as they talked about crossing the river into Georgia. María Adela told me the words, Sterling and Savannah, remained fixed in her memory. Then, surprisingly, she saw Thomas Sterling in the street her first week in town."

"With all his weight, he would have been easy to recognize even after three years."

"Yes, but she recognized all of them when she saw them later in town. In San Isidro, she stared intently at them, one by one, and stored each man's face in her memory. María Adela did not intend to ever forget their appearance. She said their faces appeared in her nightmares for months afterward."

"I'm not surprised. Poor child. Tell me, how did María Adela manage to reach Savannah from San Isidro?"

"I don't know. María Adela never told me, though I know she arrived in Savannah in the winter of 1764. She had been here almost a month when I interviewed her. It was the twentieth of December – I remember the date because it was Rebecca's birthday. I hired her that day."

"So, she reached Savannah about eighteen months after the murder of her family."

"Apparently." He paused to clear his throat and sip his tea. "After the killings, she stayed briefly with one of the Indian families in San Isidro. María Adela said one of the priests from St. Augustine gave graveside rites, even though a Franciscan had prayed over the bodies when they were buried. By then, everyone knew Francisco Fuentes was the sixth victim and the funeral rites included the young lad as well. María Adela left San Isidro at the same time the villagers abandoned the settlement and sailed to Havana with the Spaniards. She didn't tell me where she went before coming here and I didn't think to ask. Now, I wonder how she survived."

"If any girl could find a way to survive alone for so long, it was María Adela. She was very shrewd. Tell me, how did she become your assistant and housekeeper?"

"Once in Savannah, she heard I was looking for someone who would care for my wife. As I'm certain you recall, my Rebecca had only nine months left to live." He sighed. "I hadn't found anyone who could speak English fluently and the Portuguese women who were available spoke it poorly. I wanted someone who could talk to my patients while I tended to Rebecca at various times during the day. I knew at once María

Adela was the one I needed and she moved into the house the afternoon we met. Although a young girl, I could see she would be caring to Rebecca and helpful to me. Later, I recognized her intelligence and made her my assistant."

"Did she tell you anything about her life before she came to Savannah?"

"María Adela told me the same account she told you. She said her name was María Adela Macías and told me her family lived in St. Augustine. Last night, she explained why she did not use her family's name. She worried that Willington and the others might hear of it and wonder if one of the Vargas children still lived. Even if they only suspected it, María Adela was sure they would have killed her. She admitted everything last night, even the lies she had told me at first." He sighed and closed his eyes.

Morgan was silent as he waited for the doctor to continue.

The sick man spoke again after sipping his tea. "Her mention of her baby brother's name, Felipe, was why she thought you would suspect her. María Adela unintentionally told you his name the day she talked about her family. Afterward, she recalled Colonel Rodríguez also had mentioned a ten-week old baby boy named Felipe as one of the Vargas children. It was in his letter and she heard you repeat the name to me as you listed those killed in the fire."

"Ah, that's what it was! I knew there was some important fact I had forgotten about San Isidro. I knew if and when I could recall it, the identity of the murderer would be known to me."

"I do recall your mention of it. But, James, tell me how the name of María Adela's baby brother would have led you to that conclusion."

"Her brother's name would have brought to mind the murdered Vargas baby also named Felipe. I would then have recalled Felipe Vargas had a fifteen-year-old sister named María! It was obviously too coincidental to believe two families from St. Augustine each had two children, one a boy, the other a girl, with the same names and ages. Such a coincidence could only occur in a fairy tale."

"Yes, of course."

"I would also have recalled my futile search for María Adela's family. Remember the map she drew of the location of their house before I sailed to Florida?" Morgan saw the doctor nod his head. "I rode to that village, found the house she described, but discovered it was empty. In fact, the entire village was unoccupied and appeared to have been abandoned long ago. I also saw the ruins of three houses, but, at that time, I was unaware the tiny village María Adela had drawn on the map was San Isidro. Nor did I know it later when I received Colonel Rodríguez' letter informing me of the raid on the village. I did not know it until you told me moments ago. Of course, if I had known of it earlier as well as the similarity of names, María Adela's involvement in the murders would have been obvious to me. I would have assumed she knew the murderer, but I would not have thought she was the murderer herself."

"Well, it's too late now, I'm pleased to say." The sick man looked up at Morgan, but his friend made no reply. He had feared Morgan's disapproval.

"Did María Adela tell you how she lured Sterling out to the hidden lake?"

"Yes, she did." He gritted his teeth and pressed a hand on his stomach.

Morgan said nothing until the doctor sighed. "Should I leave now?"

"No, I want to continue our talk. The pain comes and goes."

"Are you certain you want me to stay?"

"I am. Our conversation helps me take my mind from it." He sighed again. "Sterling was enticed to the lake by his lust for María Adela." He smiled seeing a grin spread across Morgan's face. "Sterling made an approach to her the first time he brought his daughter here for treatment. He made his intentions clear to María Adela when he asked to meet her alone. He suggested his office for their rendezvous at night. Sterling continued his urgings on successive visits. At first, she didn't accept his blandishments, which included gifts of jewelry and gold coins. However, she did show him enough attention to keep his hopes alive. María Adela wanted him so eager for his intended seduction that he would go wherever she suggested. Then, when he appeared to be at the height of his passion for her, she agreed to meet him at the lake. María Adela told him she had gone there once on a picnic."

Morgan laughed. "By that time, he must have been beside himself with desire and would have met her on the moon. Ah yes, Thomas Sterling, Bartholomew's *good Christian*."

"María Adela made two trips to the lake. The first, by horse. Incidentally, she left here on the horse I gave her some months ago. On the first trip, she took those things she needed to stake Sterling to the ground. I didn't ask María Adela where she acquired everything, but she did tell me all the items fit in the woven bag we use for shopping. On the second trip…" He grimaced again, pressing a hand on his stomach. "James, I must ask you to leave me for a few minutes. Julia will call you when…"

Morgan sprang up from his chair and hurried out the front door. He saw the agony in his friend's face and knew he needed to use the bedpan. Afterward, he usually would be exhausted and go right to sleep. María Adela previously told Morgan that each time he used the bedpan; he passed a large amount of blood. She said the blood appeared thick and black as tar. The quantity of blood had increased over the month.

His pain also had worsened and María Adela said he took a potion to sleep at night. She saw him make up the potion in the surgery before he became bedridden. He kept the potion in a corked bottle beside his bed and took a soupspoon of it nightly with a glass of wine. The doctor made another potion, which he kept in a smaller bottle under the bedcovers beside him. He made that powder on one of the last days he could stand without assistance. The yellowish substance was a mixture of odd-looking mushrooms, dried flowers and seeds he crushed with a mortar and pestle. María Adela told Morgan she had never seen him take any of that powder while she was in the room.

Morgan leaned against the side of the log house while he waited. He thought about how devoted María Adela had been to the doctor. She tended to his every need and sat by his bed day and night during her last days in Savannah. Many were the mornings he arrived to see her eyes red-rimmed from lack of sleep. "The doctor was right," he thought. "It was better for them both that María Adela left before she saw him suffer the last moments of his life."

Sometime later, Julia waved to him from the door and Morgan returned to his chair beside the bed. The sick man had his eyes closed, but he was not sleeping. Morgan could see that Julia had washed his face and brushed his hair and beard. She also had straightened up the bedclothes and plumped up his goose-feather pillow. A pot of hot tea was on the bedside table as well as two filled cups.

"Do you want to sleep? I can come back another time."

"No. I'll soon be sleeping without end." The sick man opened his eyes. "This is the best time of my day and our discussions keep my mind occupied. I sleep much of the afternoon."

"Let me know when you want some tea."

"I've already had some, but I'll tell you when I want more." He sighed. "Where was I? Ah, yes, on María Adela's second trip to the lake; as you know, she did not ride a horse there. Instead, she walked to the southern gate and got a ride on the wagon of a fur and hides trader, who was headed to

Charles Towne. María Adela told him she was on her way to the woods to pick mushrooms for a stew her mother was making. The trader went out of his way to leave her less than a mile from the lake. I told you she was clever."

"She was, in every murder she planned." Morgan sighed, thinking of the cunning and cruel manner in which she had killed his father.

"She carried the honey pot in the woven bag. María Adela told the trader she hoped to fill the bag with mushrooms. They both laughed, knowing how hard the edible ones are to find. You know she rode Sterling's horse part of the way to town so I won't repeat what she said."

"What about the honey pot? Did you realize it was missing from the house?"

"No. María Adela told me the one in the kitchen had broken and it never occurred to me that the honey pot at the lake was ours. It was something I never would have imagined." He put a hand over his stomach as it gurgled loudly. "That concerto plays day and night."

"I've heard it often, but it's certainly not the music of Joseph Haydn." Morgan raised the doctor's head so he could sip his tea.

"It definitely isn't. One more interesting bit about the Sterling murder. Those knots, the surgical knots I saw on the bindings that held Sterling as well as Chapman – I'm sure you remember. I taught María Adela to tie those knots! She assisted in many of my surgeries and often tied up the wounds with the knots. Is that not irony?" The doctor's eyes glistened.

"It is indeed. Did she tell you how she gained entry into Willington's house? Thanks to the neighbor's boy, we know how she entered Nelson's house. But I would assume Willington was wary of anyone, even a girl, after the murders of Sterling and Chapman."

"As a ploy, she borrowed money from him. It seems Willington was a notorious usurer known for charging exorbitant interest. María Adela went to his house late one night in June to pay what she owed him. Of course, Willington wasn't paid the money he expected. No! But he got what he deserved." The doctor smiled and saw Morgan smiling with him.

"I trust she saw to it he got more than he deserved."

"I doubt it. María Adela, however, did get his remaining bullion – much of it her father's share that Willington had hidden in San Isidro. Even after all his contributions to Christ Church, he still had sixteen bars, most of them gold, and a chest full of coins. Since coming to Savannah, he had accumulated additional wealth from his many unsavory activities. María Adela took all his coins and two gold ingots when she left last night. The remainder of the bullion is under the floorboards beneath her bed. She said you will have no trouble finding it."

"What am I to do with the bullion?" Morgan made a face.

"María Adela said you will know what to do with it. She was very fond of you, you know. María Adela told me she regretted that your father was one of those who had to die."

"Is that so?" Morgan did not know what to say to his friend. He could understand María Adela's need for vengeance, but he could not condone the killing of his father who had no part in her family's murders. He had not even been in San Isidro when Willington killed the family. At the time, he had been on the road searching for Sterling.

"I'm sure her regrets mean little to you now, but I wanted to tell you what she said. You know, James, we both have lost someone we loved and it may be best for us not to dwell on the reasons for those losses. We probably will be better for it, if instead we think of their meaning to us and remember the pleasure they brought us." The doctor looked into Morgan's eyes.

Morgan frowned. "I don't think I can do that. She killed my father and he had nothing to do with the slaughter of her family. She not only killed him, but killed him horribly!"

"It's true. I should never have made such a foolish suggestion." The sick man closed his eyes and neither of them spoke for several minutes.

"Do you have any suggestions of what should be done with the bullion?" Morgan finally spoke up, knowing he should do all he could to make the last days of the doctor's life as pleasant as possible. For the time being, he decided to put aside his own feelings and concentrate on his friend's concerns.

"There's the Bethesda Orphanage, of course. I'm certain the orphanage can always use a contribution. I suspect other places of need will also occur to you in time."

Morgan nodded. "That seems sensible. So, now we know everything, at least everything that matters. María Adela – the vicious murderer! It's still hard to believe."

"It is for me, too. I was blinded by my feelings for her." He smiled sadly. "María Adela was too precious for me to even conceive of such a possibility." The doctor smiled sadly. "If she had not told me herself, I don't know if I would have believed it."

"We were both blinded by her presence and what she wanted us to see."

The doctor nodded. "That was particularly true of me, though I would prefer to deny it. I assumed I knew her well, but actually knew her little."

"We all make such assumptions, especially about those whose lives we share." Morgan thought of his father's foolish pride. Deeply in debt and desperate, he never shared his worries with his son. Instead, he took part in a robbery that cost the lives of an innocent family as well as all the robbers including himself.

"I suppose so." The doctor sighed. "It was all there in front of my eyes, but I apparently didn't want to see it."

"It was there in front of my eyes as well. María Adela was in this room day after day as we discussed the murders. I don't know how many times I asked for her opinion or observation on a matter in the investigation. Often I sat here talking to her as if I were talking to you; it was as if you and María Adela were one and the same."

"I assumed she was one of us as well. Thank you," said the sick man as Morgan lifted his head so he could drink his tea. "I know there's nothing to be gained by 'looking at yesterday's mistakes with today's regrets,' as my mother would tell me, but I still can't forget my oversight. I missed so many signs of her involvement. I never even noticed that María Adela was away at the time of each of the murders, including the days when she rode to and from Charles Towne to kill Nelson. In fact, I sympathized with her when she mentioned her fatigue after riding all night from St. Augustine." He sighed. "I was simply too close to her to doubt what she said."

"It's understandable. I assume she made up the name Macías."

"No, the Macías family did in fact exist and had a daughter her age. María Adela stayed with them after her family was killed and her home burned down. Miguel Macías had the finest house in the village and that was where María Adela sent you when she drew the map. I suppose that house was where she would have preferred her family to live in San Isidro. Of course, like the other Catholic Indians in the village, the Macías family left Florida with the Spaniards. She sent you to their home knowing it was unlikely you might encounter someone in St. Augustine who had knowledge of the family." The doctor again sipped his tea with Morgan's help.

"It was unlikely since only a couple of Spanish families remained in St. Augustine. Such a shrewd girl! She fooled us both, but we also fooled ourselves. We expected the murderer to be a man when finally found. It never occurred to us that a woman or girl could have committed the killings. We simply could not imagine it, even though María Adela was strong of arm and rode a horse as well as a man. She also spoke and wrote English and Spanish, which we knew was true of the murderer as well."

"She also wore small boots like those the murderer wore in Charles Towne."

"Indeed. Colin Delaney saw it rightly despite his drunkenness that night." Morgan smiled, picturing the little man.

"He did. Delaney saw the same small hooded figure her victims saw when it is was too late. María Adela told me she wore men's clothes when she went after them. In such a disguise, there was little chance she would be recognized by some unanticipated observer. María Adela tried to foresee every possible risk and prepared carefully to avoid them."

"She was very clever."

"Yes, exceptionally so." The doctor recalled María Adela's eagerness to learn and how quickly she learned everything he taught her. "María Adela was much too clever for those she hunted as well as those who hunted her."

Morgan and Stockwell rode to the doctor's house on the chilly morning of October 15. They wore coats and kept their collars up the entire way. An unusually cold wind had blown into town overnight and brought the first hard frost of the fall. A thin white layer of frost covered the roofs of the houses they passed and the last vegetable plants of the season lay shriveled on the ground. The sharp wind still blew as they dismounted in front of the house.

Morgan dropped the key to the house twice before opening the door. He had forgotten his glove and his hand trembled as he tried to insert the cold key into the lock. "Damn it," he swore, bending over a second time. Once inside, they kept their coats buttoned since it seemed as chilly inside the house as outside.

"How about a glass of wine?" asked Morgan, as he closed the door and pocketed the key.

"Don't mind if I do. It might warm my bones." Stockwell followed Morgan into the room and sat down at the kitchen table. He watched as Morgan took a wine bottle down from a shelf across from the fireplace and started to open it. "You're pretty good at that, now."

"I should be after so much practice." Morgan held the corked bottle tightly under his arm and twisted the corkscrew with his one hand. As he pulled the cork up, Morgan cocked his head to the side and smiled at Stockwell. "You saw me when I couldn't open my breeches to piss."

"That I did." He looked about the room and noticed a thin coating of dust on everything. "Seems odd being here without him or her."

"It does. I've only been here one other time after the funeral. Bartholomew came with me to collect his clothing and some of the household goods for the poor. It was one of the few things he asked me to do. While we were here, we carried his bed back into the bedroom."

"I wondered when it was moved." Stockwell watched Morgan take two wine glasses from the kitchen cabinet and fill them with wine.

"To our good friend, the best of men." They both had tears in their eyes as Morgan gave the toast. They touched glasses and drank down their wine.

Morgan glanced around the room and sighed when his tearful eyes reached the doctor's empty chair. It was where he always sat when they played chess or talked late into the night. In his mind's eye, Morgan could see him now, his fingers stroking his beard, as he planned his next move. Before the dying man became bedridden, he would await his friend in that chair and greet him with a smile as he entered the door. The chair originally had been standing on the other side of the table, but María Adela moved it so Morgan would sit on the right side where his good arm was easily accessible to the chessboard and pieces. The doctor, so typically considerate, wanted him to be comfortable and also able to pick up and set down a glass of wine or cup of tea.

"The doctor died all of a sudden, didn't he? I know you expected it, but not that quick."

"It was sudden. I saw him that night and he looked no different than he had for the three previous days." Morgan sat across the table from Stockwell. "The last night I saw him alive…" He paused to blow his nose. "Claudia was with me. She had finally arrived the day before."

"I recall the day. It was Saturday, the fifth. Delayed by all them storms, she was."

"That's right. We went to see him the next evening, on Sunday. I saw him each morning because that's when he felt the strongest of the day. But, on that Sunday morning, he asked me to return in the evening with Claudia so he could congratulate us together on our marriage. He also wanted to give us a gift – it was a longcase clock he had ordered from London and stored in Hugh Douglas' warehouse. We came here a little after seven o'clock and he seemed fine. We talked for an hour or so and he even laughed once or twice. He waved to us as we left."

"Guess it was his time, that's all." Stockwell nodded his thanks as Morgan refilled his glass. He rubbed his cold hands together before taking his next drink.

"Perhaps, but he said something that still lingers in my mind."

"What was that?"

"As we stood to leave, he smiled and said, 'James, don't bother to come here early in the morning. It won't matter.' At the time, I thought he meant after our visit it wouldn't matter if I came back later than usual the next morning. As we talked earlier that evening, he urged me to spend more time with

Claudia and less time with him. But the more I've thought about it since the funeral I don't think that's what he meant."

"What did he mean then? You don't think the man knew he was going to die, do you?"

"Yes, I think he knew with certainty he was going to die – that very night. María Adela told me he had made a potion, a month or so earlier, which he kept in a small bottle beneath the bedcovers. I suspect the potion was poisonous…"

"Ah, he made it to take when his pain would be too much to bear."

"Exactly. I think, when I saw him last, the pain had already become too much to bear and, on that Sunday night, he took the potion ending his life. I found the empty bottle on the floor when we moved the bed."

"With all his pain, I can't blame him. I saw what he suffered the times I came here and I would have done the same if it had been me."

"I agree. I saw him suffer more almost every day. He did what he had to do." Morgan twirled the stem of the half-full glass and stared into the red liquid.

"The doctor had a grand funeral, didn't he? There must have been more than three hundred at the graveyard. Course he deserved it. He was good to so many. There's many a man I heard in the taverns saying he did this or that for him without charge."

"I've heard much the same. He was truly esteemed in town. That's why so many townspeople went out to the Jewish burial grounds. They took that long trip in the pouring rain and stood there in the mud. It was a fitting tribute to the man. I'm certain every Portuguese man and woman in Savannah was there, never mind many of his countless other patients. As you know, Claudia stood with the other Spanish Catholics, since no one knew of our marriage at the time. I was glad to see the governor, lieutenant governor and even Palmer at the funeral. Thackery was also there.

You saw the Sterling family, didn't you?"

"I seen them all and Mrs. Chapman, too. Even the Parker brothers was there. The town shops and taverns was mostly closed yesterday, with everybody at the funeral. There's not many riding or walking about the streets even today. I never seen anything like it in all the time I been living here in Savannah.

Morgan filled their glasses again, emptying the wine bottle. "It seems everyone of meaning in town was at his funeral. The only one missing was María Adela and, once or twice, I thought I saw her face in the crowds of people. Of course, I know it was my imagination."

"I'd say so, though it would be my guess that María Adela knows the doctor's gone, no matter where she might be. Do you have any notion where she went?"

"No. She could be anywhere, though somehow I think she went westward to be far away from the settlements on the coast. If she thought we were still looking for her, that would be the sensible direction to take."

"She could have gone into Indian country."

"She could, but I doubt it. María Adela has lived too long a time in the colonies to fit in with the Indians. I wouldn't be surprised if she is living somewhere by herself. Wherever she went, I'm sure she planned it well before her escape from Savannah. I assume she selected her place of refuge with the same careful planning she did with everything else."

"As you said, there's no point looking for her."

"No. It would be futile trying to find her. It was even too late to start a search the day the doctor told me she was the one." Morgan shrugged. "There was nothing that could be done."

"She was too long gone, even if you knew exactly where she went."

"Exactly! It didn't matter anyway. By that time, Palmer no longer seemed interested in the murders of Sterling and

Chapman. Four months had passed and most colonists had all but forgotten them. Palmer wanted to forget them as well. I saw him lose interest last month. He spoke of the 'tiresome investigation' when we met and he often stared out the window during our discussions. Even earlier, I knew he was tiring of the investigation when he argued anew that Willington died accidentally in the fire. He knew better, I'm certain."

"A fool he's not. Palmer knows all about the robbery and those that got the bullion."

Morgan nodded. "Palmer knows all the robbers were killed, including Nelson. But now he shakes his head when I include Willington and Nelson among those murdered. Since none of the Englishmen in Savannah, including the governor, now seem concerned about the murders, he wants to forget them."

"Palmer's only interested in what can bring him notice to the governor. The harder it was to find the murderer, the less his chance to look good to the governor. It's much better for him if there's no more talk of the murderer."

Morgan nodded. "Of course, Palmer met with the Sterlings and Mrs. Chapman a few days before the funeral and assured them he wouldn't 'rest until the heinous murderer was apprehended.' Mrs. Chapman told me what he promised and said she didn't believe a word of it."

"That woman's no fool."

"No, she's not. She has a keen eye for a man's character. As it turned out, Palmer proved her right when I talked to him a day after he met with her and the Sterlings."

"What did he say?" Stockwell drank down the rest of his wine.

"It's what you would expect from him. He said, 'Keep in mind, Major, you are the Justice of the Peace. You have spent far too much time on the fruitless search for the murderer whom I expect is now in another colony or the western mountains. It has been a failed effort and not the kind of performance I would expect from a king's official.'"

"What did you say to that?"

"I told him I would resign the office forthwith."

"But he didn't want that, did he? Too much trouble looking for somebody who wants the office. You know what they say, Major, 'It's better to drink the middling ale than to order some other that could be much worse.'" Stockwell's face reddened and he held up a finger. "I'm not saying you're middling, Major."

Morgan guffawed. "I know what you meant. No, Palmer doesn't want me to resign. In fact, he urged me to accept an extension on the term of office. He wants to keep everything as it is now. Not only is it too much trouble to look for another justice, he knows it would be hard to find a man willing to wrestle drunks to jail and chase down petty thieves – that is, given what the crown pays its officials these days."

"You didn't tell Palmer that María Adela was the murderer, did you?"

"No. Palmer's not interested anyway." Morgan sipped his wine. "Besides, I didn't want Palmer or anyone else to know the murderer was the doctor's assistant. Since María Adela now is gone and unlikely ever to be arrested, there is no reason to stain his reputation in Savannah."

Morgan said nothing about María Adela to protect his father's reputation as well. It was improbable anyone would ever know his father had been a robber and an accomplice to murder, but he did not intend to take any chances. He never even told Stockwell or Claudia. His father's crimes would remain a secret he would keep to himself the rest of his life.

"I'm glad you didn't tell Palmer. Those robbers got what was coming to them and I'm glad María Adela got away. I would of done the same if it was me. If we can go to war and kill for the king, we can surely kill for our families."

Morgan stared at the big man, a smile on his lips. "Once again, Stockwell has seen into the heart of the matter," he thought. "Well, it's all over now anyway. The investigation is ended, María Adela has disappeared and I only have a few months left to my term of office."

"There's another thing, too. María Adela was more than a murderer; she showed herself the way she cared for the doctor until his death. She never stopped doing what was needed for him day after day for months even as she avenged the killing of her family. She did the same for his wife, Rebecca, before she died."

"Yes, she did. María Adela cared for Rebecca all through the last days of her life. María Adela was as devoted to the doctor and his wife as any daughter could possibly have been."

"That she was."

Morgan looked into Stockwell's eyes, knowing the man's feelings for the girl. "You can be sure wherever María Adela has gone, she will live the rest of her life in peace."

Stockwell nodded, a satisfied look on his face.

"By the way, I meant to tell you that your suspicions about Canfield were correct. He did find something on the clay path that day…"

"Ah, that lying little weasel!"

"He found María Adela's silver crucifix. She lost it as she rode away from the lake. The thong holding it around her neck must have broken somehow, perhaps as she mounted Sterling's horse. Anyway, Canfield found the crucifix and gave it to his wife, a Catholic, for her birthday. He told her he had saved money secretly to buy it."

Stockwell snickered. "That's a good one! How did you find out?"

"From Claudia's friend, Carolina. After the funeral, she inquired about María Adela and asked me where she had gone. I told her I didn't know and we spoke awhile about how close she had been to the doctor. Carolina then said something odd had happened involving María Adela that she didn't understand. I thought Carolina might say something about her sudden departure, but she said it concerned María Adela's silver crucifix. You recall it, don't you?"

"I do. She kept it polished and wore it all the time. It was given to her by her father. "

"That's right." Morgan drank the last of the wine in his glass. "Well, Carolina noticed the crucifix was gone over the summer and she asked her about it. María Adela said it was lost and changed the subject. Then, one Sunday near the end of August, Mary Canfield wore the crucifix to Mass. She told Carolina her husband had given it to her as a birthday gift. Carolina couldn't understand what had happened, though she eventually assumed María Adela had sold the cross to Canfield. I told Carolina I knew nothing about the silver crucifix, though her explanation as to what had happened to it seemed sensible to me."

Stockwell grinned. "So, the lil' weasel was more afeared of his wife than me. Can't blame him, of course. Once he gave it to her as a birthday gift, he couldn't take it back. Do you think it would have helped if Canfield told us about the crucifix?"

"Who knows? If asked about the crucifix, María Adela could have said she lost it while walking in the woods looking for mushrooms. We certainly would never have suspected her at the time and I think she would have continued to wreak vengeance on the robbers. She was much too determined to be stopped by such an easily explained incident."

"Yes and rightly so!" Stockwell curled his upper lip. "After what they done, she hunted them all down and did to them what they did to her family."

"Yes, she did. She got them dead to rights."

"What do you mean?" Puzzled, Stockwell frowned.

"It means the murders satisfied María Adela's resolve to avenge the killing of her family. The expression comes in part from the last century and implies her vengeance set things right."

"It did at that. Well, what's left for you now?'

"I'll spend my time as I did before the murders, although Palmer wants me to put 'all future efforts into the preservation of peace and order in the colony.' Those are his most recent words of wisdom as well as 'You must be aware of the mood of the populace in these perilous times.'"

"I'm not surprised. That's the king's officials for you. One day they want one thing from you, the next day, it's another thing they want. What do you think he meant by perilous times?"

"They're worried about the possibility of unrest in the colony. The rumors from England say parliament will levy new taxes in America. They are expected next year by summer. Charles Townshend is now the Chancellor of the Exchequer and he has vowed to raise revenue by taxing the American Colonies. That's why the governor and Palmer are worried."

"They should worry. Rumor in town says the colonists won't be paying no more taxes. I heared more than a few say they'll take up arms before they give the king anymore money."

"I've heard the same declarations and I doubt they're just words. The English apparently didn't learn their lesson from the Stamp Tax." Morgan stood and motioned to Stockwell. "Let's pack up the bars. We have a long ride ahead of us."

EPILOGUE

SAVANNAH: TUESDAY, OCTOBER 1, 1766

The public announcement of the marriage of Major James Morgan and Claudia Barclay appeared in the same issue of the *Georgia Gazette* as the obituary of Dr. Samuel Nunes Ribeiro. The birth of a son, Samuel, in February 1767, was followed in successive years by the births of Miguel and Matthew. Morgan left the justice's office when his term ended and became one of the vociferous critics of the new Townshend taxes. He joined the Liberty Boys and stood out as a bellicose spokesman in defiance of the English government in Georgia.

He and his family were in Cuba attending the funeral of Claudia's mother when the Revolutionary War began. Morgan returned to Savannah by himself and served as a colonel in the Georgia militia. He was among the troops of General 'Mad' Anthony Wayne, who eventually liberated Savannah from English occupation. After the war, he devoted himself to the restoration of Morgan's Creek, which had been devastated in the bloody battles between the colonists and the English army. In 1783, he ran for election to the General Assembly and lost.

Stockwell stayed in Savannah throughout the war and was badly wounded in one of the first major battles for the city. He lost a leg when a cannon shot exploded near him during an English assault. His hearing and eyesight were also critically weakened by the explosion. A moody invalid thereafter, Stockwell did little more than drink all day, seldom leaving his house. In the months after the war, Stockwell became more and more morose and, one night in March of 1782, he took his life. Morgan, who visited him daily, bringing his meals, arrived the next morning and found him lying dead on the floor. Stockwell had shot himself in the head.

Martha Chapman became a close family friend to the Morgans and helped Claudia raise their three rambunctious boys. Since her son and his wife never had any children, she became a grandmother to them as well as a welcome companion for Claudia. Especially during the boys' infancy, Mrs. Chapman spent more time in Morgan's house than her own. She also helped write his speeches and many of the anti-English broadsheets the Liberty Boys printed and distributed about town. When Morgan was away fighting in the war, she continued to write and distribute a variety of declarations accusing the English officials of injustice and tyranny even when the city was still under army occupation.

Carolina Braga Furtado and her son moved into the doctor's house. Claudia did not ask her to leave the house they shared, but Carolina knew the newly married couple needed to live by themselves. Morgan, as executor of the doctor's will, signed the house over to Carolina after disposing of the medical instruments and drugs. He gave them to a new physician who opened an office in town. Carolina visited Claudia weekly and along with Martha Chapman helped her when the children were young.

Colonel Rodríguez retired from the Spanish army during the Revolutionary War. He left the king's service when Spain entered the war allied with the colonies and his request for active duty was denied. Thereafter, Rodríguez spent most of his time at his ranch south of Havana. He purchased additional pastureland and, within two years of his retirement, he had become one of the wealthiest cattle ranchers in the area.

Morgan always visited the colonel on the trips he and Claudia made to her family home in Cuba. During his first trip, he met him in Havana and they talked at length about the murder investigation. Morgan disclosed everything he knew except his father's part in the robbery. In reply to Rodríguez' question about the identity of the sixth robber, Morgan said he never learned the man's name. He explained that María Adela had escaped from Savannah before she could be interrogated. The Spaniard looked closely at Morgan, raised an eyebrow, but made no comment.

Oliver Palmer left Savannah in 1771, never to return. He sailed off to England with the governor, who took a two-year leave of absence in frustration with the Georgia Assembly. The assembly refused to implement the Townshend Act in the colony and, instead, drew up a statute to boycott all imports from England. Governor Wright returned to Savannah in 1773, but was forced to flee the city three years later. Palmer, meanwhile, remained in London where he soon became an influential member of Prime Minister North's entourage. He served Lord North for a number of years and, then, finally retired without the title he had sought for so long in the king's service. Palmer purchased a large country manor a short distance from London where he lived until his death in 1794. Disappointed not to be a peer of the realm, Oliver Palmer had to be satisfied with the customary greeting of Lord the local villagers gave the owner of the manor.

Edward Thackery remained in Savannah and joined the colonists' cause. He was arrested after the English army seized the city in 1778 and jailed on the charge of treason. The long siege of Savannah delayed his trial and Thackery languished in jail until freed by the liberation forces of General Wayne. Morgan led the soldiers who emptied the jail and greeted him with a smile and a hearty handshake. After the war, Thackery was busily employed as a lawyer in the numerous property disputes that emerged in and around Savannah. He eventually became well known for his legal ability and became attorney general when Georgia approved the national constitution. Respected for his trusted service, he continued in office when the capital was moved to Augusta. He retired from office in his late sixties and returned to Savannah, residing in a large house in the middle of town.

After the war, Morgan returned to his father's ruined plantation and spent the last of the stolen bullion rebuilding it. Only four gold coins remained of the twenty-seven gold and silver bars once in his possession. He had taken seven gold and seven silver ingots from María Adela's bedroom and, then, increased his wealth with the discovery of thirteen more ingots at Morgan's Creek. His seven-year-old son, Samuel, found the Spanish bars while playing one morning near the family cemetery. A heavy rain the night before washed away a portion of Rachel Morgan's grave and exposed a termite-infested wooden chest buried at its foot. The heavy chest contained six gold and seven silver bars.

Morgan had previously given Stockwell all of Willington's gold and silver coins as well as two gold ingots when he took the hoard María Adela left in her bedroom. Morgan gave half the silver bars to the Bethesda Orphanage as the doctor had suggested. He spent the other seven as well as eight gold ingots in support of the fifty Savannah men who followed him into the war. Morgan not only armed and outfitted them for battle, but later gave those soldiers who survived a sizable severance payment. The widows of the sixteen men who died were given twice as much.

As Morgan spent the last gold bars on the reconstruction of the house where he had lived almost half his life, it occurred to him that his father would have been pleased and proud of him. He could almost hear him saying, "Well, James, it seems you are a Morgan after all."

María Adela disappeared, but Morgan never forgot her. Even years later, he would think of her as he rode past the doctor's house on his way elsewhere. During the war, he thought of her almost daily as his troops moved through unfamiliar places in Carolina and Georgia. No matter where he rode, Morgan would look for her among the hundreds of women he passed in the towns and villages along the roads. Many were the times he turned abruptly in his saddle to stare at a face he thought was hers. But he never saw María Adela again and, when he wondered what he would do or say to her if they ever met by chance, Morgan knew he would only smile and wish her well. There was nothing else to be done.

ABOUT THE AUTHOR

ROBERT L. GOLD

Robert L. Gold is a Professor Emeritus of History, an entertaining speaker and a prolific writer. He has contributed articles and reviews to many magazines and newspapers in the southeast and especially in Florida, where he has lived for more than thirty years. In St. Augustine, he has written the popular newspaper column, *Essays from El Dorado*, a script for sightseeing train guides, and *The Story of St. Augustine*, a brief history of the city given to millions of visiting tourists.

Extensive research in English, French and Spanish history and his book, *Borderland Empires in Transition*, have provided the historical basis for his current project, a trilogy of colonial murder mysteries. *Dead to Rights*, set in Savannah, is the first in the series and will be followed by *Cut of the Cross*, set in St. Augustine and *Gone for Good*, in New Orleans – both scheduled for future publication by Marcinson Press.

In addition to the suspenseful mysteries, the trilogy offers readers a penetrating look into the cultural and political life of colonial America in the eighteenth century. Each of the novels reveals the colonists' everyday struggle for survival, their search for meaning in the world and the simplicity and shortness of their lives. The series also offers a graphic view of the lush and virtually undisturbed landscape that once existed in what is now the southeastern United States.

The author has enjoyed a long professional career in Florida. He has served as state historian in St. Augustine, professor of Latin American history at the University of South Florida and executive director of the Historic St. Augustine Preservation Board. Dr. Gold also has been a speaker for the Florida Humanities Council, giving presentations entitled, "Characters and Crooks in Florida History." A bit of a character himself, he continues to offer those talks throughout North Florida.

Robert Gold lives in Jacksonville, Florida with his wife, LaDonna Morris, and Baxter, his four-year-old Airedale Terrier. A devoted dog servant, he confesses to being led by the nose of the furry-faced beast, walking him at least six miles a week and spoiling him rotten. With Baxter at his feet, he writes the quarterly column, *Tails from the Hood*, in *The American Airedale*, a magazine published by the American Airedale Club of America.

AUTHOR'S COMMENTS

DR. ROBERT L. GOLD

Although set in eighteenth-century Savannah, *Dead to Rights* is primarily a work of fiction. With the exception of the Portuguese physician, Nunes Ribeiro, the principal characters are all fictional. The plot is likewise invented. Yet, the murder mystery does depend on the history of colonial Savannah in its first fifty years of existence. As a result, several historical figures, including the founder of the Georgia colony, James Oglethorpe and the last English Governor, James Wright, appear in the mystery. Their appearances, activities and conversations, however, with few exceptions, are also fictional and used as needed to develop the plot. Finally, for the purposes of clarity and understanding, none of the characters speak eighteenth-century English, though occasional expressions, phrases and words may give that impression.

An effort has been made to describe colonial Savannah and its surroundings as accurately as possible. That effort includes the description of flora and especially fauna since animals play such an important part in the story. The use of them in the novel is based on the vast number of venomous and vicious animals known to have existed in colonial Florida and Georgia and my belief that hundreds of explorers and settlers must have been killed by them in the first centuries of colonization. Alligators and venomous snakes, of course, are still plentiful as well as red and black fire ants. But, unfortunately for the story, those ants were not in North America in the colonial period. Though I initially thought the black fire ants (Solenopsis richter) were extant at that time, Professor Lance Durden (Entomologist at Georgia Southern University) has advised me they entered Georgia in the early twentieth century, possibly from Argentina. Red fire ants (Solenopsis invicta) arrived later, probably also from South America.

The use of the title, medical examiner, for Doctor Nunes Ribeiro is anachronistic. In the eighteenth century, coroners examined the dead in the English colonies. They were appointed by the kings and lacked medical training. Trained doctors were not appointed medical examiners until more than a hundred years later.

No such archive named the Building of Records existed in eighteenth century Havana. Most of the colonial records concerning Spain's empire in the New World were kept in Spain. They are currently housed in the vast Archivo Nacional de Cuba in Havana, as well as in Spain.

The *Nuestra Señora de la Soledad* was not one of the eleven treasure ships lost in the hurricane of 1715, nor was it sunk anywhere in proximity to St. Augustine. The ship, a schooner much too small to carry a quantity of bullion, was built later in the eighteenth century. Readers are, therefore, warned not to purchase metal detectors and make plans to travel down to St. Augustine in search of Spanish treasure.

PREVIEW

BOOK TWO: CUT OF THE CROSS

CHAPTER ONE

SEPTEMBER 19-30, 1788

Fernando Núñez noticed the flies as he reached down to pick up his end of the fishing net. In the beginning dusk of that autumn day, Núñez and his son had dragged the heavy net to shore for the last time when he glimpsed the flies out of the corner of his eye. Núñez ignored them as he pulled his end out of the shallows and dropped it in the sand. The heavy net was full of seaweed and shells and his arms ached from pulling it into shore. He had already freed the numerous tiny fish brought up in the net. Núñez sighed wearily and straightened up. Hot and hungry, he pictured himself sitting in the shaded patio at the back of his house, a bowl of black beans and rice in his lap. He longed to be home now as the first breeze of the evening blew in from the river. The incessant buzzing of the flies interrupted his thoughts and Núñez turned to look at them.

The flies flew in a cloud around a leafy green palmetto, only ten steps from where he stood at the edge of the north river. Núñez followed the flies with his eyes and saw a leg and foot sticking out from beneath the palmetto's fronds. He stood stone still. A chill swept over him, cooling the sweat on his back and making him shiver.

"Dios mío!" Núñez crossed himself. "Oh, Mother of God!"

"Que pasó?" His son, Rafael, heard Núñez cry out and saw him cross himself. The boy kneeled in the shallows, gathering the other end of the net in his hands. He frowned when his father did not answer him.

Núñez continued to stare at the leg. It took him almost a minute before he responded to his son. "There's a body there beneath the fronds." Núñez pointed to the palmetto, where the bare leg, seemingly detached, lay on the ground.

"A dead body? Let me see it!" His brown eyes bright with excitement, the boy stood, trying to look under the palmetto fronds. But, from where he stood in the shallow water, even on tip-toes, he could not see it. "I want to see it," he announced, coming out of the water.

Núñez said nothing. His eyes were focused on the leg and the buzzing flies circling the palmetto. He waved the boy back without looking at him. The leg held him entranced; he could not take his eyes from it.

"No, you can't see it." Núñez slowly turned to look at his son. He raised his right hand in warning. "Stay where you are! Rafael!" Núñez' tanned face, darkened in the Florida sun, was stern as he stopped the boy with his shouted words. "Don't take another step!" Seeing the boy stop, Núñez lowered his voice. "Rafael, listen to me. Look at me! The presidio must be told what we've found here. You must run to the city gates and tell the sentries. Now!"

"What about our catch?" Rafael cautiously moved two short steps forward and squatted down, trying to see the body beneath the palmetto fronds.

"I'll take care of it. Now, go, Rafael! Hurry!" Núñez, a

lean man with long muscular arms, motioned the boy away with a sweep of his hand.

As Rafael set out for town, Núñez shouted after him, "Run, hijo, it's getting dark." He watched his son run down the sandy trail through the pine trees, the bottoms of his feet flashing white against the green foliage. Seeing Rafael run without looking down, Núñez worried the boy would step on one of the many sandspur vines lying along the overgrown path.

Núñez waited only until Rafael disappeared into the woods and then he walked slowly toward the palmetto. He unsheathed his knife and held it ready in his right hand. Núñez was curious, but wary of what he would find under the palmetto fronds. The noise of the buzzing flies increased as he carefully pushed the fronds aside and looked down at the body.

"Dios mío!" Núñez gasped, instantly recognizing the face of Gloria Márquez García, the governor's sixteen-year-old niece. The young girl was known to every one of the 2,010 residents of St. Augustine. Her beauty alone made her stand out even if she had not been the governor's niece. Men and women alike stared at her as she passed them in the streets. With big black eyes, lustrous hair and a mature woman's figure, young Gloria was the prettiest girl in the colony. Now, the beautiful girl lay dead on the ground, dirt and leaves on her body, her face bloated in death.

Looking down at the dead girl, Núñez smelled the stench of her body and got sick to his stomach. He retched, tasting his midday meal of fish and rice. Fighting the urge to faint, Núñez hurriedly backed away from the corpse. His heel caught on a protruding rock and he stumbled backward, abruptly sitting on his buttocks. He put his head down between his knees, hoping to end the dizziness. It was something he remembered his mother telling him to do, when a boy.

Núñez held his head in that position until the dizziness left him and then he stood up again. He returned his eyes to the dead girl, but remained several feet away to avoid the odor.

Núñez stood close enough to see her opened eyes and the tip of her tongue protruding from her mouth. She was nude except for her neck and the upper part of her chest. A wrinkled white bodice was bunched about her shoulders and breasts, but her brown nipples peeked out below the bottom edge of the bodice. Núñez stared at them for a moment and then moved his eyes above the bodice to her face which looked swollen. Her hair fell away in all directions and several strands fluttered in the breeze. Her slender arms extended outward and her hands were cupped as if they had held something round.

Núñez then looked at the beard of black hair below her stomach and he felt his cheeks flush with shame. He inhaled deeply and then let out his breath slowly. Núñez had avoided looking there for as long as he could, but now he intended to stare at her no matter the shame. It was where he had wanted to look as soon as he saw she was naked.

Maintaining his distance, Núñez walked a few steps to his left to look between her legs. He had never had seen a naked woman so closely before. He knew his wife, Margarita, only by touch since she hastily undressed at night well away from the bedside candle. Even in that faint light, she always made certain her back was turned to him while undressing. She would then blow out the candle before coming to bed.

Núñez had seen Margarita only once without clothing in daylight, a month before they were married. He recalled hiding in the bushes and watching her bathe in the brook beside her family's home in Santiago, Cuba. He saw her only in profile from the faraway woods. It was in 1775, the year when he had entered the king's army before coming to Florida. Núñez never saw Margarita naked again and, although it was something he wished, he was too shy to make such a request of her.

As he stared at the dead girl, a big brown cockroach emerged out of the high grass and scurried along her right leg. The two-inch long insect stood defiantly on her thigh, seemingly twitching its antennae at him. Núñez gagged, the bitter taste of bile in his mouth. He instantly pushed himself farther away from the girl's corpse and collapsed in the weeds.

"Dios, Pardóname por favor (Please pardon me, God)," Núñez prayed, certain he had been punished for staring at the girl's naked body.

Núñez got up slowly and lurched unsteadily to the river. He fell upon his knees, leaned forward and thrust his face into the water. The salt stung his eyes, but the nausea left him. He sat back on his haunches with water dripping down his face. Núñez stood a few minutes later and went to see if the net was still secure in the shallows.

BOOK TWO: CUT OF THE CROSS

Also from Marcinson Press:

Are You Ready to Adopt? An Adoption Insider's Look from the Other Side of the Desk

Geezer Dad: How I Survived Infertility Clinics, Fatherhood Jitters, Adoption Wait Limbo and Things that Go "Waa" in the Night

Dear Creator: An Anthology of Hope & Prayer in Word, Image, and Song

Jazzy's Quest: Adopted and Amazing!

The New Crunch-Time Guides to Parenting Language for Adoption

Ladybug Love: 100 Chinese Adoption Match Day Stories

COMING SOON

- Cut of the Cross
- Willie Walks: Southwest Ireland
- Awakening East: Moving our Adopted Children Back to China

Available through amazon.com, indiebound.com, barnesandnoble.com, and by request through most major and independent bookstores.

For bulk purchases or to
carry this book in your
library or bookstore,
please contact the publisher
at marcinsonpress.com.

Made in the USA
Charleston, SC
28 October 2015